The
Hangman's
Daughter

OLIVER PÖTZSCH

The Hangman's Daughter

**Translated by
LEE CHADEAYNE**

MARINER BOOKS
HOUGHTON MIFFLIN HARCOURT
BOSTON   NEW YORK

First Mariner Books edition 2011

First published in Germany in 2008 by Ullstein Buchverlage GmbH
as *Die Henkerstochter*
Translated from German by Lee Chadeayne
First published in the United States in 2010 by AmazonCrossing

Text copyright © 2008 Ullstein Buchverlage GmbH
English translation copyright © 2010 by Amazon Content Services LLC
Map illustration copyright © Peter Palm

For information about permission to reproduce selections from this book,
write to Permissions, Houghton Mifflin Harcourt Publishing Company,
215 Park Avenue South, New York, New York 10003.

www.hmhbooks.com

Library of Congress Cataloging-in-Publication data is available

ISBN 978-0-547-74501-5

Cover design by Ben Gibson
Interior design by Sabrina Bowers
Map illustration by Peter Palm, Berlin/Germany
Author photo © Dominik Parzinger

Printed in the United States of America

DOC 10 9 8 7 6

To the memory of Fritz Kuisl

For Niklas and Lily

at the other end of the line

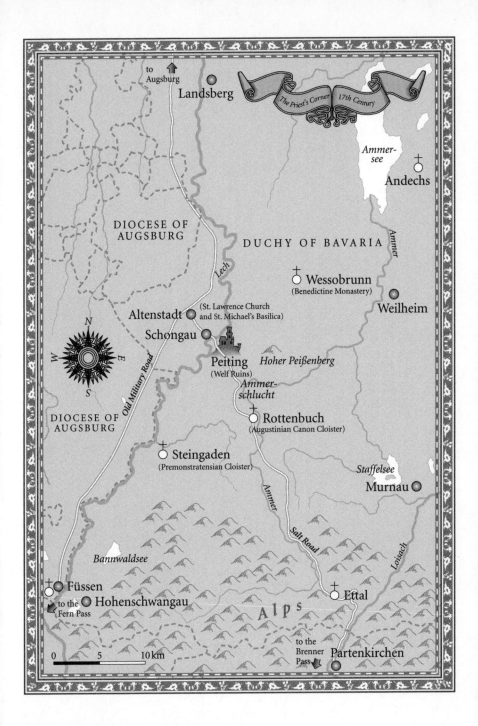

DRAMATIS PERSONAE

JAKOB KUISL, the hangman of Schongau
SIMON FRONWIESER, the town physician's son
MAGDALENA KUISL, the hangman's daughter

ANNA MARIA KUISL, the hangman's wife
THE KUISL TWINS, Georg and Barbara

BONIFAZ FRONWIESER, the town physician
MARTHA STECHLIN, midwife
JOSEF GRIMMER, wagon driver
GEORG RIEGG, wagon driver
KONRAD WEBER, parish priest
KATHARINA DAUBENBERGER, midwife from Peiting
RESL, serving maid at the Goldener Stern Inn
MARTIN HUEBER, wagon driver from Augsburg
FRANZ STRASSER, innkeeper in Altenstadt
CLEMENS KRATZ, grocer
AGATHE KRATZ, the grocer's wife
MARIA SCHREEVOGL, the alderman's wife
COUNT WOLF DIETRICH VON SANDIZELL, the secretary of the
   Duke-Elector of Bavaria

THE ALDERMEN

JOHANN LECHNER, court clerk
KARL SEMER, presiding burgomaster and landlord of the
   Goldener Stern Inn

MATTHIAS AUGUSTIN, member of the inner council
MATTHIAS HOLZHOFER, burgomaster
JOHANN PÜCHNER, burgomaster
WILHELM HARDENBERG, superintendent of the Holy Ghost
    almshouse
JAKOB SCHREEVOGL, stovemaker and trial witness
MICHAEL BERCHTHOLDT, baker and trial witness
GEORG AUGUSTIN, wagon driver and trial witness

THE CHILDREN

SOPHIE DANGLER, ward of linen weaver Andreas Dangler
ANTON KRATZ, ward of grocer Clemens Kratz
CLARA SCHREEVOGL, ward of alderman Jakob Schreevogl
JOHANNES STRASSER, ward of innkeeper Franz Strasser in
    Altenstadt
PETER GRIMMER, son of Josef Grimmer, mother deceased

THE SOLDIERS

CHRISTIAN BRAUNSCHWEIGER, ANDRÉ PIRKHOFER, HANS
    HOHENLEITNER, CHRISTOPH HOLZAPFEL

PROLOGUE

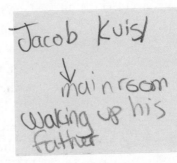

OCTOBER 12 WAS A GOOD DAY FOR A KILLING. IT had rained all week, but on this Friday, after the church fair, our good Lord was in a kindlier mood. Though autumn had already come, the sun was shining brightly on that part of Bavaria they call the Pfaffenwinkel—the priests' corner—and merry noise and laughter could be heard from the town. Drums rumbled, cymbals clanged, and somewhere a fiddle was playing. The aroma of deep-fried doughnuts and roasted meat drifted down to the foul-smelling tanners' quarter. Yes, it was going to be a lovely execution.

Jakob Kuisl was standing in the main room, which was bathed in light, trying to wake up his father. The bailiff had called on them twice already, and there was no way he'd be able to send him away a third time. The hangman of Schongau sat bent over, his head lying on a table and his long straggly hair floating in a puddle of beer and cheap brandy. He was snoring, and at times he made twitching movements in his sleep.

Jakob bent down to his father's ear. He smelled a mix of alcohol and sweat. The sweat of fear. His father always smelled like that before executions. A moderate drinker otherwise, he began to drink heavily as soon as the death sentence had been pronounced. He didn't eat; he hardly talked. At night he often woke up screaming and drenched in perspiration. The two days immediately before the execution there was no use talking to him. Katharina, his wife, knew that and would move to her sister-in-law's with the children. Jakob, however, had to stay behind, as he was his father's eldest son and apprentice.

"We've got to go! The bailiff's waiting."

Jakob whispered at first, then he talked louder, and by now he was screaming. Finally the snoring colossus stirred.

Johannes Kuisl stared at his son with bloodshot eyes. His skin was the color of old, crusty bread dough; his black, straggly beard was still sticky with last night's barley broth. He rubbed his face with his long, almost clawlike fingers. Then he rose to his full height of almost six feet. His huge body swayed, and it seemed for a moment that he'd fall over again. Then, however, Johannes Kuisl found his balance and stood up straight.

Jakob handed his father his stained overcoat, the leather cape for his shoulders, and his gloves. Slowly the huge man got dressed and wiped the hair from his forehead. Then, without a word, he walked to the far end of the room. There, between the battered kitchen bench and the house altar with its crucifix and dried roses, stood his hangman's sword. It measured over two arm's lengths and it had a short crossguard, and though it had no point, its edge was sharp enough to cut a hair in midair. No one could say how old it was. Father sharpened it regularly, and it sparkled in the sun as if it had been forged only yesterday. Before it was Johannes Kuisl's, it had belonged to his father-in-law Jörg Abriel, and to his father and his grandfather before that. Someday, it would be Jakob's.

Outside the door the bailiff was waiting, a small, slight man who kept turning his head toward the town walls. They were late as it was, and some in the crowd were probably getting impatient now.

"Get the wagon ready, Jakob."

His father's voice was calm and deep. The crying and sobbing of last night had disappeared as if by magic.

As Johannes Kuisl shoved his heavy frame through the low wooden doorway, the bailiff instinctively stepped back and crossed himself. Nobody in the town liked to meet the hangman. No wonder his house was outside the walls, in the tanners' quarter. When the huge man came to the inn for wine, he sat alone at the table in silence. People avoided his eyes in the street. They said it meant bad luck, especially on execution days. The leather gloves he was wearing today would be burned after the execution.

The hangman sat down on the bench in front of his house to enjoy the midday sun. Anyone seeing him now would hardly believe that he was the same man who had been deliriously babbling not an hour before. Johannes Kuisl had a good reputation as an executioner. Fast, strong, never hesitating. Nobody outside his family knew how much drink he used to down before executions. Now he had his eyes closed, as if he were listening to a distant tune. The noise from the town was still in the air. Music, laughter, a blackbird singing nearby. The sword was leaning against the bench, like a walking stick.

"Remember the ropes," the hangman called to his son without so much as opening his eyes.

In the stable, which was built onto the house, Jakob harnessed the thin, bony horse and hitched it to the wagon. Yesterday he had spent hours scrubbing the two-wheeled vehicle. Now he realized that it had all been in vain. Dirt and blood were eating into the wood. Jakob threw some straw on the filthiest spots, then the wagon was ready for the big day.

Though he was only twelve years old, the hangman's son had

seen a few executions up close: two hangings and the drowning of a woman three times sentenced for thieving. He was barely six when he saw his first hanging. Jakob remembered well how the highwayman wriggled and writhed at the end of the rope for almost a quarter of an hour. The crowd had cheered, and Father had come home with an extra large leg of mutton on that evening. After executions, the Kuisl family was always in for a feast.

Jakob grabbed a few ropes from the chest way back in the stable and stuffed them into a sack together with the chains, the rusty pincers, and the linen rags used for mopping up the blood. Then he tossed the sack onto the wagon and led the harnessed horse to the front of the house. His father scrambled onto the wagon and sat down cross-legged on its wooden bed, the sword resting on his powerful thighs. The bailiff walked ahead at a swift pace, glad to be out of the hangman's reach.

"Off we go," Johannes Kuisl called out.

Jakob pulled at the reins, and with much squeaking, the wagon started to move.

As the horse plodded along the wide lane that led to the upper part of the town, the son kept looking back at his father. Jakob had always respected his family's work. Even if people called it a dishonorable trade, he couldn't see anything shameful about it. Painted whores, yes, and itinerant street artists—those people were dishonest. But his father had a hard, serious trade that demanded a lot of experience. It was from him that Jakob learned the difficult craft of killing.

If he was lucky, and if the Elector permitted it, he would be able to become a master executioner in a few years. To qualify, he would have to perform a professional, technically perfect beheading. Jakob had never seen one take place, and so it was all the more important that he pay full attention today.

In the meantime the wagon had entered the town along a narrow, steep lane and came to a halt in the market square. There were rows of stalls and tents along the patrician housefronts.

Little girls with filthy faces sold roasted nuts and small, fragrant rolls. In one corner a group of traveling minstrels had gathered. They were juggling balls and singing crude ballads mocking the child murderess. The next town fair wasn't to take place till the end of October, but the news of the beheading had reached the nearby villages. People were gossiping, eating, buying sweets, and looking forward to the bloody drama as the high point of the day.

From his seat on the wagon, Jakob looked down at the people crowding around the hangman's wagon, some laughing and some just staring in amazement. There was not much more going on here. The market square had emptied out and most Schongauers had already moved to the execution site just outside the town walls, to get good seats. The execution was to take place after the noonday ringing of the bells, and that was less than half an hour away now.

As the hangman's wagon entered the paved square, the music broke off. Someone screamed, "Hey, hangman! Have you sharpened your sword? But perhaps you want to marry her?!" The crowd howled with delight. True, it was customary in Schongau that the hangman could spare the offender if he married her. But Johannes Kuisl had a wife already, and Katharina Kuisl wasn't exactly known to be kind and gentle. She was the daughter of the infamous executioner Jörg Abriel, and people called her the "Bloody Daughter" or "Satan's Wife."

The wagon rumbled across the market square, past the Ballenhaus, the building that doubled as warehouse and town hall, and toward the town wall. A tall, three-story tower stood there. Its outer walls were covered with soot and its tiny barred windows mere slits, like embrasures. The hangman shouldered his sword and descended from the wagon. Then father and son stepped through the stone gateway into the cool darkness of the tower. A narrow, worn flight of stairs led down into the dungeon. Here they found themselves in a gloomy corridor lined on both sides with heavy, iron-studded doors with tiny barred openings at eye level. Childlike whimpering and a priest's whisper emerged from a peephole on the right, and Jakob heard fragments of Latin words.

The bailiff opened the door and immediately the air was filled with the stench of urine, excrement, and sweat. The hangman's son involuntarily held his breath.

Inside, the woman's whimpering ceased momentarily, then turned into a hollow, high-pitched wailing. The child murderess knew that the end was at hand. The priest's litany, too, became louder, and prayer and screaming merged into one infernal din.

"Dominus pascit me, et nihil mihi deerit . . . The Lord is my shepherd; I shall not want . . . "

Other bailiffs approached to help drag the human bundle out into the daylight.

At one time Elisabeth Clement had been a beautiful woman with blonde shoulder-length hair, smiling eyes, and a puckered mouth that seemed to be pursed in a perpetual, slightly sardonic smile. Jakob had often seen her with other girls washing linen down at the Lech River. Now the bailiffs had shorn her hair; her face was pale and her cheeks hollow. She was wearing a sinner's shift, a simple gray shirt covered with stains. Her shoulder blades seemed to pierce the skin and the shirt. She was so gaunt that it seemed she had hardly touched the hangman's feast, the generous last meal that a condemned person was entitled to for three whole days and was traditionally provided by Semer's inn.

Elisabeth Clement had been a maid at Rösselbauer's farm. She was beautiful and therefore popular with the farmhands. They'd been attracted to her like moths to a flame; they'd given her small gifts and picked her up at the door. True, Rösselbauer did scold her for it, but it didn't do any good. They said that one lad or the other had taken a roll in the hay with her.

It was another maid who had found the dead baby behind the barn in a pit, the soil covering it still fresh. Elisabeth broke down under torture right away. She couldn't say, or didn't want to say, whose baby it was. Womenfolk in town gossiped. It was Elisabeth's beauty that had been her downfall, and that was enough to restore peace of mind to many an ugly burgher's wife. The world was no longer out of joint.

Now Elisabeth was screaming with fear, struggling and kicking as the three bailiffs tried to drag her from the hole. They tried to tie her up, but again and again she slid away like a slippery fish.

Then something remarkable happened. The hangman moved forward and placed both hands on her shoulders. Almost tenderly, the huge man bent down to the slight girl and whispered something in her ear. Jakob alone was close enough to understand his words.

"It won't hurt, Lisl. I promise. It won't hurt."

The girl stopped screaming. She was still trembling all over, but she allowed herself to be tied up now. The bailiffs eyed the hangman with a mix of awe and fear. It had seemed to them that Johannes Kuisl had whispered an incantation in the girl's ear.

Finally they stepped out into the open, where a throng of Schongauers was already waiting for the poor sinner. Whispers and murmurs filled the air; some crossed themselves, others mumbled a brief prayer. High up in the belfry a bell began to ring: a high-pitched shrill note that the wind picked up and carried across the town. Now the jeering stopped and the bell was the only sound that broke the silence. Elisabeth Clement had been one of them. Now the crowd gazed at her—a wild, captured beast.

Johannes Kuisl lifted the trembling girl onto the wagon. Again, he whispered something in her ear. Then he handed her a vial. When Elisabeth hesitated, he suddenly seized her head, pulled it back and dripped the liquid into her mouth. It all happened so quickly that only a few bystanders realized what was going on. Elisabeth's eyes glazed over. She crawled into a corner

of the wagon and curled up. She was now breathing more quietly and was no longer trembling. Schongauers knew about
Kuisl's potion. It was a kindness, however, that he didn't extend
to all those who were condemned. Peter Hausmeir, a murderer
who had also robbed the church offertory box, had felt every single blow when Kuisl smashed his bones ten years ago. He had
been broken on the wheel, and he screamed the whole time, until
the executioner finally shattered his cervical vertebrae.

Usually those condemned to death had to walk to the site of
their execution, or they were wrapped in an animal skin and
dragged behind a horse. But the hangman knew from experience that a condemned child murderess would not ordinarily be
able to walk there by herself. These women would receive three
liters of wine on their last day to calm them, and his potion did
the rest. Most of the time, the girls were half-conscious lambs
who had to be almost carried to the slaughter. That's why
Johannes Kuisl preferred using the wagon. Also, its tailboard
prevented certain folk from dealing the poor sinner an extra
blow on her way to eternity.

Now the hangman himself was holding the reins, and his son
Jakob was walking alongside. The gaping crowd thronged
around the vehicle so that they could barely move forward.
Meanwhile, a Franciscan friar had climbed up next to the condemned woman and said the rosary at her side. Slowly the wagon
passed the Ballenhaus and creaked to a halt north of the building. Jakob recognized the blacksmith from the Hennengasse
who was already waiting with his brazier. He pumped the bel-
lows with his sinewy, callused hands to blow air into the coals,
and the pincers glowed as red as fresh blood.

The two bailiffs pulled Elisabeth up. She was as limp as a
puppet, and her eyes stared into space. When the hangman
pinched the girl's right upper arm with the pincers, she screamed,
shrilly and sharply, then seemed to drop off into another world.
There was smoke and a hissing noise and Jakob smelled the odor

of burned flesh. His father had told him what the procedure was, yet he had to fight an urge to vomit.

Three more times, at each corner of the Ballenhaus, the wagon stopped and the procedure was repeated. Elisabeth's left arm was pinched, then her left breast, and then her right breast. Owing to the potion, however, the pain was bearable.

Elisabeth began to hum a nursery rhyme and smiled as she stroked her belly. "Sleep, baby, sleep . . . "

They left Schongau through the Hof Gate and followed the Altenstadt Road. Soon the execution site appeared in the distance. It was a grassy field with patches of bare soil situated between farmland and the edge of the forest. The whole of Schongau and the neighboring villages, it seemed, was assembled here with benches and chairs brought in for the aldermen. The commoners were standing in the back, passing the time gossiping and snacking. The execution site was in the middle of the field: a masonry structure seven feet tall with wooden stairs leading to the top.

As the wagon approached the site, the crowd parted and everyone tried to catch a glimpse of the child murderess curled up on the bed of the wagon.

"Make her get up! Up! Up with her! Hey, hangman, show her to us!"

The crowd was obviously annoyed. Many had been waiting since the morning, and now they didn't even get to see the criminal. Some of the onlookers began hurling rocks and rotten fruit. A Franciscan ducked to protect his brown habit, but several apples hit him in the back. The bailiffs tried to push back the people who were crowding in on the wagon from all sides, as if to swallow it up along with its passengers.

Calmly Johannes Kuisl steered the wagon to the platform. There the aldermen were waiting together with Michael Hirschmann, the Elector's secretary. He was the representative of the Prince-Elector, and as such he had pronounced the death sentence over the girl two weeks ago. Now he looked deep into her eyes once more. The old man had known Elisabeth since she was a child.

"My, my, Lisl, what *have* you done?"

"Nothin'. I've done nothin', Your Excellency." Elisabeth looked at the bailiff from eyes that were already dead and kept stroking her belly.

"Our good Lord alone knows that," murmured Hirschmann.

The bailiff nodded and then the executioner led the murderess up the eight steps to the scaffold. Jakob followed. Twice Elisabeth tripped, then she took her last step. Another Franciscan friar and the town crier were waiting on the platform. Jakob surveyed the meadow below and saw hundreds of curious faces; their mouths and eyes were wide open. The aldermen had taken their seats and in the town the bell was pealing the death knell. The air was filled with the tension of expectation.

Gently, the hangman pushed Elisabeth Clement down on her knees. Then he blindfolded her with one of the linen cloths he had brought. She shivered slightly and murmured a prayer.

"Hail Mary, full of grace, the Lord is with thee; blessed art thou among women . . ."

The town crier cleared his throat, then he proclaimed the death sentence one more time. Jakob perceived his voice only as a distant murmur.

" . . . that thou shalt turn to God with all thy heart and thus obtain a blessed and peaceful death . . . "

His father poked him in the side.

"You've got to hold her for me," he whispered as softly as possible so as not to interrupt the reading.

"What?"

"You've got to hold her shoulders and her head up, so that I hit the mark. Just take a look at Lisl—she's just going to tip over otherwise."

And in fact, the woman's body was slowly sagging forward.

Jakob was confused. It had been his understanding that he was merely to *watch* the execution. His father had never mentioned *helping*. But now there was no time for hesitation. Jakob grabbed Elisabeth Clement's stubbly hair and pulled her head upward. She whimpered. The hangman's son felt his fingers damp with sweat. He held his arm out to make room for his father's sword. The trick was to strike precisely between two of the cervical vertebrae with a single blow of the sword dealt with both hands. Just a twinkling of an eye, a breath of air, and the matter would be over and done with. Over and done with, that is, if the job was done properly.

"May God have mercy on your soul . . . "

The town crier was finished. He produced a thin, black wooden rod, held it over Elisabeth Clement, and snapped it in two. The sharp sound of the breaking wood was audible all over the meadow.

The Elector's secretary nodded to Johannes Kuisl. The hangman lifted his sword and took a swing.

At this very moment Jakob felt how the girl's hair slipped from his sweaty fingers. Just a moment before he had been holding up Elisabeth Clement's head, but now she fell forward like a sack of flour. He saw his father's sword whiz by, but instead of striking her neck it hit her head at about ear level. Elisabeth Clement writhed about on the platform, screaming like an animal impaled on a stake, and there was a deep gash in her temple. In a pool of blood Jakob glimpsed part of an ear.

Her blindfold had fallen off and, her eyes wide with fear, she looked up at the executioner, who stood over her with raised sword. The crowd groaned in unison and Jakob felt a gagging sensation in his throat.

His father pushed him aside and swung again with the sword, but Elisabeth Clement rolled to the side when she saw the sword coming down. This time the blade struck her shoulder and cut deep into the nape of her neck. Blood spurted from the wound and splattered the hangman, his helper, and the horrified Franciscan.

On all fours, Elisabeth Clement crawled to the edge of the platform. Most Schongauers gazed at the spectacle in horror, but others shouted their disapproval and began pelting the hangman with rocks. People didn't like to see the man bungling the job.

Johannes Kuisl wanted to put an end to that. He stepped up to the groaning woman and took yet another swing. This time he struck her right between the third and fourth vertebrae, and the groaning stopped at once. But her head wouldn't come off—it was still connected by tendons and flesh, and it took a fourth blow to sever it from the body.

It rolled over the wooden planks and came to rest right in front of Jakob. He started to faint; his stomach churned, then he dropped to his knees and threw up the watery beer and oatmeal he'd had for breakfast that morning. He retched and retched until nothing would come but green bile. As through a veil he heard the screaming of the people, the railing of the aldermen and his father's heavy panting next to him.

Sleep, baby, sleep . . .

Just before he mercifully blacked out, Jakob Kuisl made a decision. Never would he follow in his father's footsteps; never in his life would he become a hangman.

Then he dropped headlong into the pool of blood.

CHAPTER

I

SCHONGAU,
THE MORNING OF APRIL 24, A.D. 1659
THIRTY-FIVE YEARS LATER

𝕸AGDALENA KUISL WAS SITTING ON A WOODEN
bench in front of the small, squat hangman's house, pressing the
heavy bronze mortar tightly between her thighs. Pounding
steadily, she crushed the dried thyme, club moss, and mountain
lovage into a fine green powder, breathing in the heady fragrance
that offered a foretaste of the summer to come. The sun shone in
her deeply tanned face, causing her to blink as pearls of sweat
rolled down her brow. It was the first really warm day this year.

Her little brother and sister, the twins Georg and Barbara,
six years old, were playing in the yard, running between the elder
bushes that were just beginning to bud. Again and again, the
children squealed with delight when the long branches brushed
over their faces like fingers. Magdalena couldn't help smiling.
She remembered how, just a few years ago, her father had chased
her through the bushes. She pictured his massive frame as he ran
after her, raising his huge hands and with a big bear's threatening
growl. Her father had been a wonderful playmate. She had never

understood why people would cross to the other side of the street
when they met in town or murmur a prayer as he approached.
Only later, when she was seven or eight, had she seen how her
father didn't just play with his huge hands. They were on
Hangman's Hill, where Jakob Kuisl had drawn the hemp noose
around the neck of a thief and pulled tight.

Nevertheless, Magdalena was proud of her family. Her
great-grandfather Jörg Abriel and her grandfather Johannes
Kuisl had been hangmen. Magdalena's father Jakob had been
apprenticed to Granddad just as her little brother, Georg, would
someday be apprenticed to their own father. Once, when she was
still a child, her mother had told her at bedtime that Father had
not always been a hangman. He had marched off to the Great
War and only later felt the call to return to Schongau. When little Magdalena asked what he had done in the war and why he
would rather cut people's heads off than put on his armor and
take up his shining sword and march off to foreign lands, her
mother simply fell silent and put her finger to her lips.

After she had finished grinding the herbs, Magdalena emptied the green powder into an earthenware container, which she
carefully closed. After it had boiled down to a thick broth, the
fragrant mixture would help women resume their interrupted
menstruation—a well-known remedy used to prevent an
unwanted birth. Thyme and club moss grew in every other garden, but only her father knew where to find the much rarer
mountain lovage. Even the midwives from the surrounding villages came to get their powder from him. He called it "Our
Lady's Powder" and thus earned one or two extra pennies.

Magdalena pushed a lock from her face. It kept falling back.
She had her father's unruly hair. Thick eyebrows arched above
black, glowing eyes, which seemed continually to blink. At age
twenty, she was the hangman's oldest child. Her mother had
given birth to two stillborn babies after her, and then to three
infants that were so weak they didn't live to see their first

birthday. Then the twins had come, finally. They were two noisy rascals and her father's pride and joy. Sometimes Magdalena felt something like pangs of jealousy. Georg was his father's only son and would one day be apprenticed in the hangman's trade. Barbara was still a little girl, dreaming of all the things possible in this world. Magdalena, however, was the "Hangman's Wench," the "Bloody Maiden," whom nobody could touch and who was the object of gossip and laughter behind her back. She heaved a sigh. Her life seemed to be already prescribed. She'd marry a hangman from another town, as executioners' families always stuck together. And yet there were a few young men in town whom she fancied. Especially one . . .

"When you're done with Our Lady's Powder, go in and do the laundry. It won't wash itself, you know!"

Her mother's voice awakened Magdalena from her reveries. Anna Maria Kuisl looked at her daughter with disapproval. Her hands were covered with dirt from yard work and she mopped her brow before she continued.

"Dreaming of the boys again, I can tell by the looks of you," she said. "Get your mind off the boys. There's enough gossiping as is."

She smiled at Magdalena, but the hangman's daughter knew that her mother was being serious. She was a practical, strait-laced woman who cared little for her daughter's dreams. Also she thought it was a waste of time that her father had taught Magdalena to read. A woman who buried her nose in books was regarded with suspicion by the men. And if she was the hangman's daughter on top of that and liked to flirt with the lads, then she wasn't far from the pillory and the scold's bridle. More than once, the hangman's wife had prophesied in the darkest tones how her husband would have to clap his own daughter into the shrew's fiddle and lead her through town at the end of a rope.

"All right, Mother," said Magdalena and set the mortar down on the bench. "I'm taking the laundry down to the river."

She grabbed the basket of soiled bedsheets and walked through the garden and down to the Lech River. Her mother's eyes followed her pensively.

Right behind the house, a well-worn path led past herb and flower gardens, barns, and handsome houses down to the river, to a place where the water had shaped a shallow cove. Magdalena gazed at the whirling eddies that were forming in the middle of the river. It was springtime, and the water was high, reaching the roots of the birches and carrying along branches and entire trees. For a moment Magdalena believed she saw something that looked like a shred of linen in the earth-brown waters, but when she looked more closely, she saw just branches and leaves.

She bent down, took the laundry from her basket, and started scrubbing it on the damp gravel. She was thinking of the festival at St. Paul's Fair three weeks ago, especially how she had danced with *him* . . . It was only last Sunday that she'd seen him again, at Mass. She'd sat down in a pew way back in the church and bowed her head, but then he got up to fetch himself a prayer book. And he had winked at her. She'd giggled, quite involuntarily, and the other girls had glared at her.

Magdalena was humming a song now and rhythmically slapping the laundry on the gravel.

"Ladybird, fly, your father's gone to war . . . "

She was so absorbed in her thoughts that at first she believed the screaming was only in her imagination. It took her a while to realize that the cries were coming from somewhere upstream.

A woodcutter from Schongau up on the steep bank was first to see the boy. He'd grabbed hold of a tree trunk and was spinning around like a tiny leaf in the foaming water. Initially, the woodcutter was not sure that the tiny thing down there in the rushing water was really human. But when it started to kick and struggle wildly he called to the raftsmen who were getting ready for their first run to Augsburg in the early-morning fog and asked for help. Not until just before Kinsau, four miles north of Schongau, did the riverbank flatten out, with the Lech calm enough for the men to try to reach the boy. They tried to pull him from the water with their long poles, but each time he slid away like a slippery fish. At times he went under completely, remaining beneath the surface for a troubling length of time, then popped up again like a cork at a different spot.

Once more the boy gathered enough strength to pull himself up onto the slippery log and raise his head above the surface to breathe. He reached for the pole with his right hand, his fingers outstretched, but he missed. With a loud thud, the log bumped against the other logs that were clogging the raft landing. The impact caused the boy to lose his grip; he slipped down and sank among dozens of gigantic floating tree trunks.

Meanwhile the raftsmen had steered toward the small pier at Kinsau. Tying their rafts together with great haste, they carefully ventured onto the treacherous surface of the logs closest to shore. Balancing on the slippery logs was a challenge even for these well-seasoned raftsmen. It was easy to lose one's grip and be crushed to a pulp between the mighty beech and fir trunks. But the river was calm at this spot, and the trunks just bobbed up and down lazily.

Soon two men had reached the log with the boy. They prodded in the gaps with their poles in hopes of feeling a soft object. The logs underneath their feet began to wobble and roll. Again and again the men had to get their balance; their bare feet were slipping on the glistening bark.

"I've got him," the larger and stronger of the two suddenly called out. With his powerful arms he pulled both boy and pole from the water and tossed them to the safety of the shore like a fish on a hook.

The raftsmen's calls had made others aware of the emergency. Washerwomen from nearby Kinsau had come running to the river together with some wagon drivers. Now they were all standing on the rickety pier, gazing at the dripping clump at their feet.

The burly raftsman brushed the boy's hair from his face, and a murmur went up from the crowd.

The boy's face was blue and puffy, and the back of his head was crushed in as if he'd been struck hard with a heavy piece of wood. He was groaning. Blood was oozing through his wet coat, soaking the pier and dripping into the river. This boy had not just fallen into the water. Someone must have pushed him, and that someone had dealt him a fierce blow before that.

"Why, that's Josef Grimmer's boy, the son of the wagon driver in Schongau," a man exclaimed. He was standing close by with his wagon and team of oxen. "I know the kid. He used to come to the landing site with his father. Quick, put him on the wagon. I'll drive him to Schongau."

"And somebody run and tell Grimmer that his boy is a-dying," a washerwoman screamed. "Good Lord, and him having lost so many kids already!"

"It would be better to tell him right away," the stocky raftsman grumbled. "This one's not going to last long." He slapped at some nosy boys standing around. "Run along. And fetch the barber or the physician."

As the boys took off toward Schongau, the injured child's groans grew fainter. He was shaking all over and seemed to be muttering something. A last prayer? He was about twelve years old and looked skinny and pale like most children his age. He must have eaten his last square meal weeks ago, and the watery barley broth and watery beer he had consumed over the past few days had made his cheeks hollow.

The boy's right hand kept reaching out; his murmuring rose and ebbed like that of the Lech River beneath him. One of the raftsmen was on his knees, bending over the boy to hear what he was saying. But the murmuring gave way to gurgling, and bright red bubbles of blood and saliva trickled from the corners of his mouth.

They lifted the dying child onto the wagon, the driver cracked his whip, and they rumbled along Kinsau Road to Schongau. It was a journey of over two hours, and as they moved along, more and more people joined the silent procession. When they finally reached the landing site in the nearby town, more than two dozen onlookers followed the wagon: children, peasants, crying washerwomen. Dogs were yapping at the oxen, someone was mumbling a Hail Mary. The driver brought the vehicle to a halt at the jetty next to the storage shed. Two of the raftsmen lifted the boy off with great caution and gently placed him on some straw right by the shore of the rushing, gurgling Lech River that was flowing restlessly against the pillars.

The murmur of the crowd was suddenly interrupted by heavy footsteps on the pier. The boy's father had been waiting off to one side, as if he were afraid of the last and final moment. Now deathly pale, he pushed his way through the throng.

Josef Grimmer had had eight children, and they had all died, one after the other, from the plague, diarrhea, fever, or simply because the good Lord had willed it. Hans was six years old when he fell into the Lech and drowned while playing. Marie, aged three, had been run over by drunken mercenaries on their horses in a narrow lane. His wife, together with their youngest child, had perished in childbirth. Little Peter was all that was left to old Grimmer. And as he saw him lying before him, he knew that the Lord would be taking this last son away from him as well. He fell on his knees and tenderly brushed the boy's hair from his face. The child's eyes were closed already, his chest was heaving convulsively, and a few moments later a spasm shook the little body. Then there was silence.

Josef Grimmer raised his head and screamed his grief across the Lech. His voice was high and shrill like a woman's.

The scream reached the ears of Simon Fronwieser along with the sound of pounding downstairs at the front door. The physician's house in the Hennengasse was just a stone's throw from the river. Earlier, Simon had looked up from his books several times, distracted by the shouting of the raftsmen. Now that the screams were resounding through the narrow lanes of the town, he knew that something must have happened. The knock at the door grew more urgent. With a sigh he closed one of his hefty anatomy volumes. Like all the others, this book never went below the surface of the human body. The composition of the humors, bleeding as a universal remedy . . . Simon had read these same litanies far too many times, but they hadn't really taught him anything about the inside of the body. And nothing would change today, as along with the knocking there was now shouting downstairs.

"Doctor, doctor! Quick, come! Grimmer's boy is lying in his blood down at the landing site. It doesn't look good!"

Simon threw on his black overcoat with the shiny copper buttons, ran his fingers through his black hair, and straightened his beard in front of the small mirror in his study. The shoulder-length mane and the Vandyke beard, which was again fashionable, made him appear older than his actual age of twenty-five. Some Schongauers regarded Simon as a dandy, but he didn't care. He knew that girls saw the matter differently. The ladies of Schongau liked him on account of his dark and dreamy eyes, his well-shaped nose, and his slim figure. Moreover, he was well-groomed. He still had all his teeth; he took regular baths. And he had rose-scented perfume delivered specially from Augsburg, as expensive as his meager salary permitted it. It was only his height that bothered him. He didn't stand taller than five feet, so he had to look up to most men, and to some women as well. But of course that could be remedied by high-heeled boots.

The knocking had now become a regular hammering. Simon hastened downstairs and flung the door open. Outside was one of the tanners who worked down at the river. His name, Simon remembered, was Gabriel. The physician knew him from an earlier occasion. He had put his arm in splints last year, when he had gotten himself into a drunken fight at St. Jude's Fair. Simon put on an official mien. He knew what he owed to his profession.

"What's the matter?"

The tanner regarded him suspiciously. "Where is your father? There's been a bad accident down on the Lech."

"My father is over at the infirmary. If it's urgent, you'll have to make do with me or with the barber."

"The barber's sick himself . . ."

Simon furrowed his brow. He still was regarded only as the physician's son here in town, even though he had studied medicine in Ingolstadt and had been his father's assistant in treating all possible ailments for almost seven years now. In recent years he'd even cured people on his own. His last case had been a dangerous fever. For days and days he'd applied cold ankle wraps and poultices to the cooper's little daughter and administered a new medication to her: a powder of ground-up yellow bark that came from the West Indies and was known as "Jesuits' Powder." The fever had indeed subsided and the cooper had been grateful enough to pay two guilders more than his due. And still townspeople didn't trust him.

Simon gave the man in front of him a defiant stare. The tanner shrugged, then turned to walk away. Over his shoulder he cast a disparaging glance at the physician.

"All right, come along then, if it isn't too late already."

Hurriedly, Simon followed the man and entered Münzstrasse along with him. It was the day after Saint George's, and most tradesmen had already opened their first-floor shops hours ago. Saint George's Day was also when maids and farmhands entered service on the farms surrounding Schongau. Accordingly, a great number of people were already about in the streets. On the left, clanging noises emerged from the blacksmith's shop where an alderman's horse had just been shod. The butcher next door had just slaughtered a pig, and thin rivulets of blood were trickling between the cobblestones, so that the physician had to step over them with one long stride in order not to soil his new leather boots. A few yards farther, a baker was selling fresh bread. Simon knew that it must be full of husks and would crunch between the teeth when you chewed it. Only the aldermen could afford real white bread these days, and only on special holidays.

And yet, Schongauers had to be glad to have anything to eat at all in that eleventh year after the end of the Great War. In the last four years, crops had twice been practically annihilated by hailstorms. In May of last year, a terrible rainstorm had caused the Lech to flood, and the town mill had been washed away. Since then, Schongauers had to take their grain to Altenstadt or even more distant towns to be ground, which, of course, was more expensive. Many fields in the nearby villages were left fallow, and farms lay abandoned. A third of the population had died of the plague or hunger in the past decades. Those who could, kept livestock in their houses and lived on cabbage and turnips from their own kitchen gardens.

As they crossed the market square, Simon cast a glance at the Ballenhaus. It used to be a warehouse and now served as a town hall and council chamber. It had once been the pride of the town when Schongau was rich, on a par with towns like Augsburg, and the wealthiest and most powerful merchants in the Holy Roman Empire had come and gone there. The little town on the Lech, where ancient trade routes intersected, was once an important trading place for all sorts of goods. But the war had put an end to all that. The Ballenhaus was in a state of decay: plaster was crumbling off the walls, and the entry gate hung crooked on its hinges. This time of murder and robbery had made Schongau poor. What had once been a rich, handsome town in the Pfaffenwinkel part of Bavaria had become a camping ground for unemployed mercenaries and other vagrants. After the war came famine, disease, cattle plague, and hailstorms. The town was finished, and Simon didn't know if it could pull itself together one more time. And yet the burghers had not given up. On his way through the Lech Gate going down to the river, Simon looked at a colorful hustle and bustle. Wagon owners were driving their ox carts up the steep incline toward the market square. Over in the tanners' quarter, the chimneys were smoking, and down by the riverbank women were busy with their washing, emptying troughs of dirty water into the raging Lech. Schongau, high on its hill, was enthroned above the forests and the river, peering almost like a proud matron toward Augsburg, its older and more powerful sister. Simon had to smile. No, this city would not go under. Life went on, despite all the dying.

At the landing, a large crowd had assembled.

Simon heard murmuring voices and again and again the laments of a man. He crossed the bridge and turned to the right, toward the storage shed, which was built right against the pier. With some difficulty he pushed himself through the throng until he reached the center of the crowd.

The wagon driver Josef Grimmer was kneeling on the wet planks, bending over a blood-smeared mass. His broad back blocked Simon's view. Simon put his hand on Grimmer's shoulder and felt that the man was shaking. His face was stained with tears, and he was deathly pale. Only some time later did the man notice the physician behind him.

His voice cracked as he hurled his curse in Simon's face.

"Look what they've done to my son! They stuck him like a pig! I'll kill them! I'll kill them all!"

"Who?" Simon asked softly. But the wagon driver had turned to his child again, sobbing.

"He's talking about the Augsburg wagon men," a man near him murmured. Simon recognized him as a member of the wagon drivers' guild.

"There've been quarrels with them lately," the man continued, "because they had to hand over their loads to us. They say we'd put some of the cargo aside for ourselves. Josef has picked a fight with those up there at the Stern."

Simon nodded. He had had to bandage a few broken noses himself after the brawl at the inn. Many fines had been imposed, but that only increased the hatred between the wagon drivers of Augsburg and those of Schongau. There was an ancient ducal ordinance that the Augsburgers were permitted to transport cargo from Venice or Florence only as far as Schongau. From there, the Schongauers were to take over. This transportation monopoly had long been a thorn in the flesh of the Augsburgers.

Gently, Simon led the grieving father to the side. Some of his friends from the wagon drivers' guild joined him. Then he bent over the boy.

So far nobody had bothered even to remove the child's wet shirt. Simon ripped it open, revealing a ragged landscape of stabs. Someone must have slashed at the boy in an insane rage. Light-red blood was oozing from a fresh, sizable cut at the back of his head. Simon assumed that the boy had been trapped between the floating logs. His face was black-and-blue, but that, too, could have been done by the logs. The gigantic trunks developed a tremendous power in the stream and could crush a person like a piece of rotten fruit.

Simon put his ear to the boy's chest. Then he took a small mirror and held it under his broken, blood-smeared nose. No breath was to be seen. The boy's eyes were wide open. Peter Grimmer was dead.

Simon turned to the bystanders, who were watching him in silence. "A wet cloth," he demanded.

A woman handed him a linen rag. Simon dipped it in the Lech and wiped the boy's chest clean. When he had washed off all the blood, he could count seven stabs, all of them around the heart. But despite the deadly wounds, the boy hadn't died at once. Gabriel the tanner had told Simon on their way down to the landing that the child had been murmuring to himself until just a short while ago.

Simon turned the boy on his belly. With a vigorous tug he ripped open the shirt on the back as well. A groan went through the crowd.

Beneath one shoulder blade there was a palm-size sign of a kind that Simon had never seen before—a washed-out purple circle with a cross protruding from the bottom:

$$♀$$

For a moment, there was total silence on the pier. Then the first screams rose. "Witchcraft! There's witchcraft involved!" Somebody bawled: "The witches have come back to Schongau! They're getting our kids!"

Simon passed his fingers over the sign, but it couldn't be wiped off. It reminded him of something, but he couldn't tell what it was. Its dark color made it look like a demonic sign.

Josef Grimmer, who until then had been leaning on a few friends, staggered toward the corpse of his son. He regarded the sign briefly, as if he couldn't believe what he saw. Then he shouted to the crowd, "He has that from the Stechlin woman! The midwife, the witch! She painted that on him! She killed him!"

Simon remembered that lately he had indeed seen the boy at the midwife's place several times. Martha Stechlin lived up at the Küh Gate right next to the Grimmers. Ever since Agnes

Grimmer had died in childbirth, the boy had often turned to her for consolation. His father had never forgiven Stechlin for failing to stop his wife's hemorrhaging. He held her responsible for his wife's death.

"Quiet! We don't even know whether . . . "

The physician tried to shout down the furious howling of the mob, but in vain. The name Stechlin spread across the pier like wildfire. Already some people were rushing across the bridge and up to the town. "The Stechlin woman! The Stechlin woman did it! Run for the bailiff; let him get her!"

Soon nobody was left on the pier except Simon and the dead boy. Even Josef Grimmer, filled with hate, had followed the others, and only the rushing of the river could be heard.

Heaving a sigh, Simon wrapped the body in a dirty linen cloth that the washerwomen had left behind in their hurry and shouldered the bundle. Stooped over, puffing and panting, he wended his way toward the Lech Gate. He knew that only one man could help him now.

CHAPTER
2

MARTHA STECHLIN STOOD IN HER ROOM, DIPPING her bloodstained fingers in a bowl of warm water. Her hair was matted, deep rings appeared under her eyes, and she had not slept for nearly thirty hours. The birth at the Klingensteiners' had been one of the hardest this year. The child had been lying wrong. Martha Stechlin had smeared her hands with goose fat and felt deep into the mother's body to turn the unborn child round, but it had slipped away from her again and again.

Maria Josefa Klingensteiner was forty years old and had already survived a dozen confinements. Only nine children had been born alive; five of them had not seen their first spring. Four daughters remained to Maria Josefa, but her husband still hoped for an heir. The midwife, feeling inside the mother's body, had already established that this time it was a boy. It seemed to be alive, but with every hour that passed it became more likely that neither mother nor child would survive the struggle.

Maria Josefa screamed, raged, and wept. She cursed her

husband, who mounted her anew after every birth like a randy goat, she cursed the child, and she cursed the Almighty. As dawn broke, the midwife was sure that the boy was dead. For a case like this she kept an old poker handy with a hook on the end that she could use in an emergency to pull the child out of the mother's body like a chunk of meat, sometimes piece by piece. The other women in the stiflingly hot room, the aunts, nieces, and cousins, had already sent for the parish priest; the holy water for an emergency baptism was ready over the fireplace. But then, with a last scream from Mother Klingensteiner, the midwife succeeded in grasping the boy's feet. He slid out into the daylight like a newborn foal. He was alive.

It was a robust child. *And probably the murderer of his mother,* thought Martha Stechlin, as she looked at Maria Josefa's pale, panting body and severed the umbilical cord with her scissors. The smith's wife had lost a lot of blood, and the straw on the ground was red and slimy. Her eyes were sunken like those of a corpse. But at least her husband had his heir now.

The birth had taken all night. In the morning Martha Stechlin prepared another strengthening decoction of wine, garlic, and fennel and washed the mother; then she went home. Now she was sitting at the table in her room and trying to wipe the weariness out of her eyes. About noon the children would look in on her, as they so often did recently. She herself could not have children, although she had brought so many into the world. It made the midwife happy that Sophie, little Peter, and the others came to visit her frequently, though she sometimes wondered what the children found to like in a forty-year-old midwife with her salves, pots, and powders.

Martha Stechlin felt her stomach rumble. She suddenly realized that she had eaten nothing for two days. After a few spoonfuls of cold porridge from the pot above the hearth, she wanted to tidy up thoroughly. She was missing something. Something which at all costs must not fall into the wrong hands. Perhaps she had just put it down somewhere . . .

Shouting was coming from the market square. At first it was only indistinct, a murmur of voices, quiet but menacing, like the angry buzzing of a swarm of hornets.

Martha looked up from her bowl. Something had happened out there, but she was too tired to go to the window and find out.

Then the shouts came nearer. Steps could be heard, people running across the paved market square, past the Stern Inn and into the narrow alley, up to the Küh Gate. Now Martha Stechlin could hear a name emerging from the confusion of voices.

It was her name.

"Stechlin, you witch! To the stake with you! Burn her! Come out of there, Stechlin!"

The midwife leaned out the ground-floor window to find out exactly what was going on, and a fist-size rock hit her directly on the forehead. Everything went black and she sank to the ground. When she came to herself she saw, through a mist of blood, that the door to her house was being forced open. With great presence of mind, she jumped up and threw herself against it. Several legs were trying to force themselves through the opening. Then the door fell shut. From outside came angry shouts.

Martha searched in her dress for the key. Where could it be? Someone was pushing at the door again. There, on the table next to the apples, there was something shiny. While the midwife held the door shut with her strong body, she fumbled, almost blind with blood and sweat, for the key on the table. At last she had it in her hand and turned it in the keyhole. With a squeaking sound the bolt slid into place.

The pushing from outside suddenly stopped, only to change after a few seconds into a furious hammering. Obviously the men were swinging a heavy beam against the door. Already the thin wood was splintering. A hairy arm appeared in the opening and felt for her.

"Stechlin, you witch. Come out, or we'll set your house on fire!"

The midwife could see the men outside through the broken door. They were raftsmen and wagon drivers; she knew many of them by name. Most of them were the fathers of children she had brought into the world. Now their eyes had a bestial glare; they sweated and screamed and hammered on the door and the walls. Martha Stechlin looked around like a hunted animal.

A window shutter splintered, and the massive head of Josef Grimmer, her neighbor, appeared. Martha knew that he had never forgiven her for the death of his wife. Was that the reason for the uproar? Grimmer brandished a piece of the window frame studded with nails.

"I'm going to kill you, Stechlin! I'll kill you before they even burn you!"

Martha ran to the back door. This gave onto a small herbal garden that lay directly behind the city wall. In the garden she realized that she had trapped herself. The houses to the left and right reached right up to the city wall, which was itself a good ten feet up to the parapet walk, too high to reach the top.

Directly by the wall was a small apple tree. Martha Stechlin hurried to it and climbed into the branches. From its top, she might possibly escape onto the parapet.

Once more she could hear the sound of breaking glass in her house, and then the garden door was broken open. In the doorway stood Josef Grimmer, panting and still holding the nail-studded lath in his hand. Behind him other wagon drivers pushed their way into the garden.

Martha Stechlin scrambled up the apple tree like a cat, higher and higher, until the twigs were as thin as children's fingers. She grabbed the edge of the wall and tried to reach the safety of the battlements.

The branch broke.

With bleeding fingertips the midwife slid down the wall and into a wet vegetable patch. Josef Grimmer came up to her and raised the lath for a death-dealing blow.

"I wouldn't do that."

The wagon driver looked up to see where the voice had come from. On the battlements, directly above him, stood a massive form dressed in a long coat full of holes and a broad-brimmed, soft hat sporting a couple of ragged feathers. The man beneath this hat had black unkempt hair and a full beard that had not been touched by a barber for a long time. The battlements threw a shadow, so that there was little to see of his actual features except a huge hooked nose and a long clay pipe.

The man had spoken without taking the pipe out of his mouth. Now he held it in his hand and pointed to the midwife, who was crouched and panting by the wall underneath him.

"Killing Martha isn't going to bring your wife back. Don't make yourself miserable."

"Shut up, Kuisl! It's none of your business!"

Josef Grimmer had himself under control again. Like all the others, he was at first astounded that the man up there had been able to approach without anyone noticing. But the moment of surprise was over. Now he wanted to take his revenge and nobody was going to stop him. With the lath still in his hand, he slowly approached the midwife.

"That is murder, Grimmer," said Kuisl. "If you strike now, I'll be very happy to put the noose round your neck. And I promise you, you'll die slowly."

Josef Grimmer stopped. He turned hesitantly to his companions, who were obviously as uncertain as he was.

"She's responsible for my son's death, Kuisl," said Grimmer. "Go down to the Lech and see for yourself. She put a spell on him and then stabbed him. A Satan's mark she wrote on him."

"If that's true, why didn't you stay with your son and send the bailiff for Martha?"

All of a sudden Josef Grimmer realized that his dead son must still in fact be down by the river. In his hatred he had just left him lying there and had hurried after the others. Tears came to his eyes.

With an agility that nobody would have suspected of him, the man with the pipe in his mouth climbed over the balustrade of the parapet and leaped down into the garden. He was taller by at least a head than all others there. The giant bent down to Martha Stechlin. She could now see his face quite close above her, the hooked nose, the wrinkles like furrows, bushy eyebrows, and deep-set brown eyes. The eyes of the hangman.

"Now you will come with me," whispered Jakob Kuisl. "We'll go to the court clerk, and he will lock you up. That's the safest thing for you at the moment. Do you understand?"

Martha nodded. The hangman's voice was soft and melodious, and it calmed her.

The midwife knew Jakob Kuisl well. She had brought his children into the world, both the living and the dead . . . Most often the executioner himself had lent a hand. Occasionally she bought from him potions and poultices to cure interrupted menstruation or unwanted pregnancies. She knew him to be an affectionate father who adored his youngest children, the twins, above all else. She had also seen how he laid the noose round the necks of men and women and pulled away the ladder. *And now he's going to hang me,* she thought. *But first he saves my life.*

Jakob Kuisl helped her up, then looked around at the bystanders expectantly. "I'm taking Martha to the keep now," he said. "If she really has anything to do with the death of Grimmer's son, she will receive her just punishment, I can promise you that. But until then, leave her in peace."

Without another word the hangman seized Martha by the scruff of the neck and pushed her through the middle of the group of silent raftsmen and wagon drivers. The midwife was quite sure he would make good on his threat.

Simon Fronwieser panted and cursed. He felt his back slowly getting damp. It was not sweat that he felt there, but blood, which had soaked through the sheet. He would have to resew his coat; the stains were all too clear on the black fabric. And the bundle across his shoulders was getting heavier with every step.

Simon crossed the Lech Bridge with his awkward burden and turned to the right into the tanners' quarter. As the physician entered the narrow lanes, he at once smelled the acrid odor of urine and decay, which pervaded everything. He held his breath and trudged past frames as high as a man, between which sheets of leather had been hung out to dry. Half-tanned animal skins even hung from the balcony railings, giving off their penetrating stench. A few apprentices looked down inquisitively at Simon and his bloodstained bundle. It must have looked to them as if he was taking a slaughtered lamb to the hangman.

At last he left the narrow alleys behind him and turned left up the path to the duck pond to the executioner's house, which stood under two shady oak trees. With a stable, a big garden, and a shed for a wagon, it was quite an impressive property. The physician looked around, not without a feeling of envy. The executioner's profession might be dishonorable, but still one was able to make a decent living from it.

Simon opened the freshly painted gate and entered the garden. It was April, the first flowers had already appeared, and everywhere aromatic plants were springing up.

Mugwort, mint, lemon balm, stinkwort, wild thyme, sage . . . the executioner of Schongau was known for the herbal riches of his garden.

"Uncle Simon, Uncle Simon!"

The twins, Georg and Barbara, scrambled down from the

oak tree and ran with loud cries to Simon. The physician was their friend, and they knew that he was always ready for a game or a romp with them.

Anna Maria Kuisl, aroused by the noise, opened the front door. Simon looked at her, smiling a little stiffly, while the children tried to jump up on him to see what he had in the bundle over his shoulder. Although she was just about forty, the hangman's wife was still an attractive woman, who with her raven-black hair and bushy eyebrows looked almost like his sister. Simon had often asked himself if she was not a distant relative of Jakob Kuisl's. Since executioners were regarded as dishonorable and could only marry burghers' daughters in exceptional circumstances, their families were often closely related by marriage. In the course of centuries whole dynasties of executioners had formed, and that of the Kuisls was the largest in Bavaria.

Laughing, Anna Maria Kuisl came out to meet the physician, but when she noticed the bundle on his back, his warning glance, and his defensive gesture, she motioned to the children to leave.

"Georg, Barbara! Go and play behind the house. Uncle Simon and I have something to talk about."

The children, grumbling, disappeared, and Simon was at last able to enter the room and lay the corpse on the kitchen bench. The cloth in which it was wrapped fell to the side. When Anna Maria saw the boy, she uttered a cry.

"My God, that's Grimmer's boy! What in the world has happened?"

Simon took a seat next to the bench and told her the story. Meanwhile Anna Maria poured him some wine mixed with water from an earthenware jug, which he drank in great gulps.

"And so you need my husband now to tell you what happened?" Anna Maria asked, when he had finished. Shaking her head, she kept on glancing at the boy's body.

Simon wiped his lips. "Exactly. Where is he?"

Maria shrugged her shoulders. "I can't tell you. He went up

to the town to the blacksmith's to get some nails. We need a new closet, you know. Ours is full to the bursting point."

She glanced once more at the bloody bundle on the kitchen bench. As the wife of the hangman she was more than accustomed to the sight of corpses, but the death of a child always moved her. She shook her head. "The poor lad . . . "

Then she seemed to come to herself again. Life went on. Outside the twins romped about noisily, and little Barbara screeched at the top of her lungs. "It would be best if you wait for him here," she said, getting up from the bench. "You can read a bit while you're waiting."

The hangman's wife smiled. She knew that Simon often came just to leaf through her husband's dog-eared old books. Sometimes the physician made up some rather feeble excuse for going down to the hangman's house to look up something.

Anna Maria gave the dead boy one more compassionate glance. Then she took a woolen blanket from the closet and laid it carefully over the corpse, so that there was nothing more to see in case the twins came in suddenly. Finally she went to the door. "I must see what the children are doing outside. Help yourself to the wine, if you like."

The door closed and Simon was alone in the room. The hangman's living room was large and spacious and took up almost the entire ground floor of the house. In the corner there was a large stove, which was stoked from outside in the corridor. Next to it was the kitchen table, and above it the executioner's sword hung on the wall. A steep staircase led from the passage to the upper room, where the Kuisls and their three children slept. Next to the oven was a low, narrow door, which led to another room beyond. Simon ducked under the lintel and entered the holy of holies.

On the left stood two chests in which Jakob Kuisl kept everything needed for executions and torture—ropes, chains, gloves, but also thumbscrews and pincers. The rest of this threatening arsenal was owned by the town authorities and was kept in the tower, deep down in the dungeons. Next to the chests, the gallows ladder was leaning on the wall.

But Simon was looking for something else. Almost the whole of the opposite wall was taken up by an enormous closet that reached to the ceiling. The physician opened one of the many doors and looked into a confused mass of bottles, pots, leather bags, and vials. Inside the closet, herbs were hanging to dry; they smelled like summer. Simon recognized rosemary, goat's rue, and daphne. Behind a second door were countless drawers, labeled with alchemical signs and symbols. Simon turned to the third door. Behind this were piled old dusty volumes, crackling parchment rolls, and books both printed and handwritten—the hangman's library, collected over the course of many generations, ancient knowledge, completely different from what Simon had studied in the course of his many dry-as-dust lectures at the university in Ingolstadt.

Simon reached for a particularly heavy volume, which he often held in his hands. He ran his finger over the title. "*Exercitatio anatomica de motu cordis et sanguinis,*" he murmured. A disputed book that was based on the idea that all the blood in the body was part of a perpetual circulation powered by the heart. Simon's professors in Ingolstadt had laughed at this theory, and even his father had found it far-fetched.

Simon continued browsing. The *Buch der Medicie*, or *Book of Medicine,* was the name of a handwritten, poorly bound little book in which all kinds of remedies against illnesses were listed. Simon's gaze was arrested by a page on which dried toads were recommended as a remedy against the plague. Next to it on the shelf was a work that the hangman could have acquired only recently. *Das Wundarzneyische Zeughaus*, or *Surgical Armory,* by Johannes Scultetus, the city physician of Ulm, was so new that probably not even the University of Ingolstadt had acquired it yet. Reverently, Simon let his fingers glide over the binding of this masterpiece of surgery.

"Pity that you have eyes only for books."

Simon looked up. Magdalena was leaning in the doorway and looking at him brightly. The young physician couldn't help swallowing. Magdalena Kuisl, twenty years old, was aware of the effect she had on men. Whenever Simon saw her, his mouth became dry and his head seemed empty. In the past few weeks, it had become worse, he always kept thinking of her. Sometimes before he fell asleep, he imagined her full lips, the dimples in her cheeks, and her laughing eyes. If the physician had only been a little superstitious, he would have supposed that the hangman's daughter had cast a spell over him.

"I'm . . . waiting for your father . . . " he stammered, without taking his eyes off her. Smiling, she came up to him. She appeared not to have noticed the dead boy on the bench as she walked past, and Simon had no intention of bringing it to her attention. The few moments they had together were too precious to fill with death and suffering.

He shrugged and put the book back on the shelf.

"Your father has the best medical library for miles around. I'd be foolish not to use it," he murmured. His glance wandered over her plunging neckline in which two well-formed breasts were apparent. He quickly looked the other way.

"*Your* father sees that differently," said Magdalena and slowly came nearer.

Simon knew that his father considered the hangman's books to be works of the devil. And he had often warned him about Magdalena. Satan's woman, he had said.

And he who has dealings with the hangman's daughter will never be a respected medical man.

Simon knew that there could be no question of a marriage with Magdalena. She was "dishonorable," just like her father.

But he couldn't stop thinking of her. Only a few weeks before, they had danced together for a short time at St. Paul's Fair, and for days this had been the subject of gossip in the town.

His father had threatened to beat him if he was seen with Magdalena again. Hangmen's daughters married hangmen's sons—that was an unwritten law. Simon knew it very well.

Now Magdalena stood in front of him and ran her fingers across his cheek. She was smiling, but in her eyes there was an unspoken grief.

"Do you want to come to the meadows with me tomorrow?" she asked. "Father needs mistletoe and hellebore . . . "

Simon thought he heard a pleading note in her voice.

"Magdalena, I . . . " There was a rustle behind him.

"You can very well go alone. Simon and I have a great deal to talk about. Now off with you."

Simon looked round. Unnoticed by him, the executioner had entered the narrow room. Magdalena looked once more at the young physician and then ran out into the garden.

Jakob Kuisl gave Simon a piercing and severe look, and for a moment it seemed he might throw him out of the house. Then he took his pipe out of his mouth and smiled.

"I'm pleased that you like my daughter," he said. "Just don't let your father know about it."

Simon nodded. He had often had angry words with his father about his visits to the executioner's house. Bonifaz Fronwieser considered the hangman to be a quack. However, his son wasn't the only person he was unable to dissuade from making the pilgrimage to the hangman; half the people of Schongau went to him with their aches and pains. Jakob Kuisl earned only a part of his income from hanging and torturing. The major part of his business concerned the healing art.

He sold potions for gout and diarrhea, prescribed tobacco for toothaches, splinted broken legs, and set dislocated shoulders. His knowledge was legendary, even though he had never studied at a university. It was clear to Simon that his father just *had* to hate the executioner. After all, he was his toughest competitor and, in fact, the better physician . . .

Meanwhile Jakob Kuisl had gone into the living room again. Simon followed. The room immediately filled with great clouds of tobacco smoke—the hangman's lone vice, but one that he cultivated intensely.

Pipe in mouth he went purposefully to the bench, lifted the dead boy onto the table, and turned back the blanket and cloth. He whistled quietly through his teeth.

"Where did you find him?" he asked. At the same time he filled an earthenware bowl with water and began to wash the face and chest of the corpse. He looked quickly at the dead boy's fingernails. Red earth had collected under them, as if little Peter had been digging somewhere with his bare hands.

"Down by the raft landing," said Simon. He related all that had happened up to the point where everyone had run up into town to take revenge on the midwife. The hangman nodded.

"Martha is alive," he said, continuing to dab at the dead boy's face. "I took her to the keep myself. She is safe there for the time being. Everything else will have to be looked into."

As so often before, Simon was impressed by the executioner's composure. Like all the Kuisls, he seldom spoke, but what he said had authority.

The hangman had completed washing the corpse. Together they examined the boy's ravaged body. The nose was broken, the face beaten black-and-blue. In the chest they counted seven stab wounds.

Jakob Kuisl took a knife from his coat and tried inserting the blade into one of the wounds. On either side there was a gap at least half an inch wide.

"It must have been something wider," he murmured.

"A sword?" asked Simon.

Kuisl shrugged. "More likely a saber or a halberd."

"Who could have done something like that?" Simon shook his head.

The hangman turned the body over. On the shoulder was the sign, faded a bit more after being carried up from the river, but still quite visible. A purple circle with a cross under it.

♀

"What's that?" asked Simon.

Jakob Kuisl bent down over the boy's body. Then he licked his index finger, rubbed it gently over the sign, and put his finger into his mouth. He smacked his lips with relish.

"Elderberry juice," he said. "And not at all bad." He held his finger out to Simon.

"What? But I thought it was . . . "

"Blood?" The hangman shrugged. "Blood would have washed away a long time ago. Only elderberry juice keeps its color so long. Just ask my wife. She gets very angry when the little ones smear themselves with it. But anyway . . . " He began to rub the mark.

"What is it?"

"The color is partly under the skin. Someone must have injected it with a needle or a dagger."

Simon nodded. He had seen such works of "art" on soldiers from Castile and France. They had tattooed crosses or images of the Mother of God on their upper arms.

"But what does the sign mean?"

"A good question." Kuisl drew deeply on his pipe, puffed out the smoke, and remained silent a long time. Then he replied, "It's the Venus mark."

"The what mark?" Simon looked down at the sign. Suddenly he remembered where he had seen this sign before: in a book about astrology.

"The Venus mark." The hangman went back into the little

room and reappeared with a stained leather-bound tome. He turned the pages a little while until he found the one he wanted.

"There." He showed Simon the place. Here, too, the same sign could be seen. Next to it was a circle with an arrow pointing up and to the right.

"Venus, goddess of love, spring, and growth," read Jakob aloud. "Countersign to that of Mars, god of war."

"But what can this sign mean on the boy's body?" asked Simon, confused.

"This sign is old, very old," said the hangman, taking another puff on the long-stemmed pipe.

"And what does it mean?"

"It has many meanings. It stands for woman as counterpart to man, for life, and also for life after death."

Simon felt as if he could not breathe anymore. And this was only partly because of the clouds of smoke that enveloped him.

"But . . . that would be heresy," he whispered.

The hangman raised his bushy eyebrows and looked him straight in the eye.

"That's just the problem," he said. "The mark of Venus is a witches' mark."

Then he blew his tobacco smoke directly in Simon's face.

Schongau lay under the light of a pale moon. Again and again it was eclipsed by clouds, and the river and the town were plunged into darkness. Down by the Lech stood a figure looking into the murmuring waters, sunk in thought. The man put up the collar of his fur-lined coat and turned toward the lights of the town. The gates had long been closed, but for men like him there was always a way in. One only needed to know the right people and have the necessary small coins handy. For this man neither was a problem.

The man began to shiver. This was only partly due to the cold, which in April still was carried down from the mountains by the wind. Fear crept over his scalp. He looked carefully all round, but apart from the black band of the river and a few bushes on the bank there was nothing to be seen.

It was already too late when he heard a rustling behind him. The next thing he felt was the point of a sword in his back, boring through his fur coat, velvet cloak, and padded doublet.

"Are you alone?"

The voice was directly behind his right ear. He smelled brandy and rotten meat.

The man nodded, but that didn't seem to satisfy the person behind him.

"Are you alone goddamn it?"

"Yes, sure!"

The pain in his back diminished; the sword point was withdrawn.

"Turn around!" hissed the man.

He turned as ordered and nodded apprehensively at his partner. The stranger, wrapped in a black woolen coat, a wide-brimmed feathered hat pulled well down over his face, looked as if he had just risen from the underworld.

"Why have you called me here?" he asked, calmly returning the sword to its sheath.

The man in front of him swallowed. Then he regained his usually unshakeable self-confidence. He straightened up, before replying, "Why did I call you here? You have all failed. You know that very well!"

The stranger shrugged.

"The boy is dead," he said. "What more do you want?"

The man from the town was not content with this. Angrily he shook his head, the thin index finger of his right hand rising and falling. "And the others?" he hissed. "There were five! Three boys and two girls. What about the others?"

The stranger gestured dismissively.

"We'll get them too," he said and turned to go.

The other hurried after him.

"Damn! It wasn't supposed to end like that!" he cried and gripped the stranger hard by the shoulder, an action he regretted in the next moment. A muscular hand seized him by the throat in a viselike grip. In the stranger's face white teeth suddenly glistened and he smiled. A wicked smile.

"Are you afraid?" he asked quietly.

The man swallowed and noticed how difficult it was to breathe. Just before all went black the stranger let him go and flung him away like some annoying animal.

"You are afraid," he repeated. "You're all alike, you big, fat, rich people."

The man gasped and retreated a few steps. After straightening his clothes he felt in a position to speak once more.

"Finish the matter quickly," he whispered. "The children mustn't squeal."

Once again he saw the flash of his partner's teeth.

"That will cost you a bit more."

The man from Schongau shrugged. "I don't care. Just get it done with."

For a moment the stranger seemed to be thinking. Finally he nodded. "Give me the names," he said quietly. "You know them, so how about the names?"

The man swallowed. He had only seen the children briefly. Nevertheless, he thought he knew who they were. Suddenly he was overcome by the feeling that he was standing on the threshold of something. He could still draw back . . .

The names came tumbling out before he could think about it anymore.

The stranger nodded. Then he turned abruptly and in just a few seconds had vanished into the darkness.

CHAPTER
3

JAKOB KUISL WRAPPED HIS COAT TIGHTLY AROUND him and hurried along the Münzgasse, being careful not to step into the garbage and excrement piled up before the entryway of each house. It was early in the morning, the streets were enveloped in fog, and the air was damp and cold. Directly above him a window was opened, and somebody poured the contents of a chamber pot into the street. Kuisl cursed and ducked away as the urine splashed to the ground alongside him.

As Schongau's executioner, Jakob Kuisl was also responsible for the removal of refuse and sewage, a task that he performed on a weekly basis. Soon he'd be wandering through the lanes with his handcart and shovel again. But today there was no time for it.

Right after the ringing of the morning bells at six o'clock, the town jailer had shown up at Kuisl's house to tell him that Johann Lechner wanted to see him at once. Kuisl could guess what the court clerk might be wanting. The murder of the boy had been the talk of the town. Rumors of witchcraft and diabolical rites spread faster than the odor of excrement in a small town like Schongau.

Lechner was known as a man who made fast decisions, even on complicated matters. Moreover, the town council would meet today, and the notables would be eager to know the basis of the rumors.

The hangman had a powerful hangover. Last night Josef Grimmer had been at his place to collect his son's body. The man seemed almost a different person from the Josef Grimmer who had nearly clubbed the midwife to death a few hours before. He bawled like a baby, and only Kuisl's homemade herbal spirit was able to settle him somewhat. And the executioner shared a couple of glasses with him . . .

Jakob Kuisl turned to the right into a narrow lane and headed toward the ducal residence. In spite of his headache he had to grin, because the proud title of "residence" couldn't quite live up to what it promised. The building before him looked more like a hulking, run-down fortress. Not even the oldest Schongauers could remember a day when a duke had actually taken residence there.

And the Elector's secretary, who represented the interests of His Serene Highness in the town, hardly ever bothered to show himself there. He usually lived in a remote country house near Thierhaupten. Otherwise, the dilapidated building served as the barracks for two dozen soldiers and as the court clerk's office. In the secretary's absence, the former represented Ferdinand Maria, Elector of Bavaria, in Schongau.

Johann Lechner was a powerful man. While he was really only in charge of His Highness's affairs, he had expanded his position over the years, so that now he was able to influence town matters as well. In Schongau, no document, no ordinance, not even the smallest note, could bypass Johann Lechner. Jakob Kuisl was certain that the clerk had been brooding over town files for hours.

The executioner passed through the stone gate on which two rusty gates hung crooked on their hinges, and entered the courtyard. The sentry posts gave him a tired nod and let him pass.

Jakob Kuisl looked around the narrow, dirty courtyard. The Swedes had plundered it for the last time more than ten years ago, and since then the residence had fallen even deeper into decay. All that was left of the fortified tower on the right was a sooty ruin, and the roofs of the stables and the threshing floor were leaky and covered with moss. Broken wagons and all manner of bric-a-brac peered forth between the splintered planks of the walls.

Kuisl climbed the worn steps to the castle, crossed a gloomy corridor, and stopped at a low wooden gate. As he was about to knock, a voice called from within.

"Enter."

The clerk must have very keen hearing, he thought.

The executioner pushed the door open and stepped into the narrow chamber. Johann Lechner sat at his desk, all but concealed by piles of books and parchments. His right hand was scrawling notes into a register; his left hand directed Kuisl to a seat.

Despite the early morning sun outside the window, the room, lit only by a few sputtering tallow candles, was murky. The executioner took a seat on an uncomfortable wooden stool and waited patiently for the clerk to look up from his writing.

"You know why I've called you?"

Johann Lechner gazed at the executioner with piercing eyes. The clerk had the full black beard of his father, who had likewise officiated as Schongau's court clerk. The same pale face, the same penetrating black eyes. The Lechners were an influential family in this town, and Johann Lechner liked to remind others of it.

Kuisl nodded and began to fill his pipe.

"Stop that," said the clerk. "You know I don't like smoking."

The hangman pocketed his pipe and gave Lechner a provocative glance. It took a while before he spoke to him.

"On account of the Stechlin woman, I assume."

Johann Lechner nodded. "There's going to be trouble. In fact, there already is. And it happened only yesterday. People are talking . . ."

"And what business is that of mine?"

Lechner leaned across the desk and forced himself to smile. He was not quite successful.

"You know her. You have worked together. She brought your children into the world. I want you to talk to her."

"And what am I supposed to talk about?"

"Make her confess."

"Make her what?"

Lechner leaned even farther across the desk. Their faces were within inches of each other now.

"You heard me right. Make her confess."

"But nothing's been proved. A few women have gossiped. The boy was at her place a few times. That's all."

"The matter must be disposed of." Johann Lechner sat back in his chair, his fingers drumming on the armrests. "There has been too much talk as it is. If we let it drag on, then we'll have a situation like in your grandfather's days. Then you'll be one busy man."

The hangman nodded. He knew what Lechner was talking about. Nearly seventy years ago during the famous Schongau witch trial, dozens of women had been burned at the stake. What had started as an angry outburst and a few unexplained deaths had ended in mass hysteria, with everyone accusing everyone else.

Back then, his grandfather Jörg Abriel had beheaded more than sixty women, and afterward their bodies were burned. This had made Master Jörg rich and famous. On some of the suspects, they had found so-called witches' marks, or birthmarks, whose shape determined whether the wretched women lived or died. This time, an obviously heretical sign was involved. Not even Kuisl could say this didn't look like witchcraft.

The court clerk was right. The people would keep looking for signs. And even if there were no more deaths, there would be no end to the suspicion. A wildfire that could lay the whole of Schongau in ashes. Unless someone confessed and agreed to take the blame.

Martha Stechlin . . .

Jakob Kuisl shrugged. "I don't think the Stechlin woman has anything to do with the murder. Anyone could've done it. Perhaps strangers. The boy was floating in the river. The devil knows who stabbed him, perhaps marauding soldiers."

"And the sign? The boy's father described the sign to me. Didn't it look like *that*?" Johann Lechner handed him a drawing. It showed the circle with the inverted cross. "You know what that is," hissed the clerk. "Witchcraft."

The hangman nodded. "But that doesn't mean that the Stechlin woman . . . "

"Midwives are expert in such matters!" Lechner had raised his voice more than he usually did. "I have always warned against permitting such women in our town. They are keepers of secret lore, and they ruin our wives and children! There've always been children around her lately, haven't there? Peter among them. And now they find him in the river, dead."

Jakob Kuisl longed for his pipe. He would have loved to clear the room of evil thoughts with its smoke. He was fully aware of the aldermen's prejudice against midwives. Martha Stechlin was the first midwife whom the town had officially appointed. These women with their feminine wisdom had always been suspect to men. They knew potions and herbs; they touched women in indecent spots; and they knew how to get rid of the fruit of the womb, that gift of God. Many midwives had been burned as witches by men. Jakob Kuisl, too, knew all about potions and was suspected of sorcery. But he was a man. And he was the executioner.

"I want you to go to the Stechlin woman and make her

confess," Johann Lechner said. He turned to his notes again and was scribbling. The matter was finished for him.

"And if she won't confess?" asked Kuisl.

"Then you show her your instruments. Once she sees the thumbscrews she's bound to soften."

"You need the council's approval for that," whispered the hangman. "I can't do it alone, and neither can you."

Lechner smiled. "As you know, the council meets today. I'm certain that the burgomaster and the other notables will follow my suggestion."

Jakob Kuisl reflected. If the council agreed today to begin torture, the trial would proceed like clockwork, and the end would be torture and probably death at the stake. Both were the executioner's responsibility.

"Tell her that we'll begin the questioning tomorrow," said Lechner, as he continued scribbling in one of the files on his desk. "Then she has time to think it over. If she insists on being stubborn, however, well . . . well, we'll need your help."

His pen continued scratching across the paper. In the market square, the church bell struck eight. Johann Lechner looked up.

"That'll do. You may leave now."

The hangman rose and turned to the door. As he pushed the handle, he heard once more the clerk's voice behind him.

"Oh, Kuisl." He turned around. The clerk spoke without looking up. "I'm aware you know her well. Make her talk. That'll save her and you unnecessary suffering."

Jakob Kuisl shook his head. "She didn't do it. Believe me."

Now Johann Lechner looked at him again straight in the eye.

"I don't think that she did it, either, but it's what's best for our town, believe *me*."

The hangman didn't reply. He ducked under the low doorway and let the door fall shut behind him.

———

When the hangman's footsteps in the street had faded away, the clerk returned to his files. He tried to concentrate on the parchments before him, but that was difficult. Before him lay an official complaint from the city of Augsburg. Thomas Pfanzelt, a Schongau master raftsman, had transported a large pack of wool that belonged to Augsburg merchants together with a heavy grindstone. Owing to its weight the cargo had fallen into the Lech. Now the Augsburgers demanded compensation. Lechner sighed. The everlasting quarrels between the Augsburgers and the Schongauers were getting on his nerves. And especially today he couldn't be bothered with such petty grievances. His town was on fire! Johann Lechner could almost see how fear and hatred were eating their way from the outskirts to the very center of Schongau. There had been whispering in the inns last night already, both in the Stern and the Sonnenbräu. People were talking about devil worship, witches' sabbaths, and ritual murder. After all the plagues, wars, and storms, the situation was explosive. The city was a powder keg, and Martha Stechlin could be the fuse. Lechner twisted his quill nervously between his fingers. *We have to extinguish the fuse before disaster strikes . . .*

The clerk knew Jakob Kuisl as a clever and considerate man, but the question couldn't be whether or not the Stechlin woman was guilty. The town's welfare was a weightier matter. A short trial would help bring a long-sought-for peace back to the town.

Johann Lechner gathered his parchment scrolls, stashed them in the shelves along the wall, and set out for the Ballenhaus. The grand council meeting would begin in half an hour and there were still things to do. He had requested the town crier to summon all members of the council: the inner council and the outer council, as well as the six commoners. Lechner wanted to get everyone behind this.

After crossing the market square, which was busy at this hour, the clerk entered the Ballenhaus. The storage hall was more than twenty feet high, and inside it crates and sacks were piled high awaiting transport to distant cities and countries. Blocks of sandstone and trass were stacked in one corner and the fragrance of cinnamon and coriander filled the air.

Lechner climbed the wide, wooden stairway to the upper floor. As the official representative of the Elector he had no business in the town council, but since the Great War the patricians had become accustomed to having a strong arm in upholding law and order. So they gave the clerk full authority. It was almost natural that by now he chaired the council meetings. Johann Lechner was a man of power, and he had no intention of yielding it.

The door to the council chamber was open and the clerk was surprised to see that he was not as usual the first to arrive. Karl Semer, the presiding burgomaster, and the alderman Jakob Schreevogl had come before him and seemed engaged in lively conversation.

"And I am telling you that the Augsburgers are going to build a new road, and then we'll be sitting here like a fish on dry land," Semer shouted at Schreevogl, who kept shaking his head. The young man had joined the council just six months before, replacing his late father. Several times already this tall patrician had clashed with the burgomaster. Unlike his father, who had been close friends with Semer and the other council members, he had a will of his own. And he wasn't going to let himself be intimidated by Semer now.

"They can't do that, and you know it. They have tried already once, and the Elector stopped them."

But Semer would have none of that. "That was before the war! The Elector has other things on his mind now! Believe an old soldier, the Augsburgers are going to build their road and then we'll have these goddamn lepers to deal with, not to mention this terrible murder story . . . The merchants will avoid us like the plague!"

Johann Lechner cleared his throat as he entered and stepped

to the head of the U-shaped oak table that occupied the entire room. Semer, the burgomaster, hurried to greet him.

"Good that you are here, Lechner. I have tried to persuade young Schreevogl here to change his plans concerning the house for lepers. And right away! The Augsburg merchants are digging our graves, and if news should spread that we have at our very gates . . . "

Johann Lechner shrugged.

"The leper house is a church matter. You can speak with the priest, but I don't believe you'll have any luck. And now will you please excuse me?"

The clerk pushed past the stout burgomaster and unlocked the door that led to the back room. Here, an open cabinet with pigeonholes and drawers crammed with parchments towered to the ceiling. Johann Lechner climbed onto a stool and pulled out the papers that would be needed for the meeting.

As he was doing this, his eye fell on the file concerning the leper house. Last year the church had decided to build a new home for lepers outside of town on the road to Hohenfurch. The old one had collapsed decades ago, but the disease had not subsided. Lechner shuddered at the thought of the vicious epidemic. Next to the plague, leprosy was the most dreaded of afflictions. Those who contacted it rotted alive—nose, ears, and fingers would drop off like decayed fruit. At the end, the face would be nothing but a mass of flesh with no resemblance to anything human. As the disease was highly contagious, the poor souls were usually chased out of town or had to carry bells or clappers so that people could hear them from afar and avoid them. As an expression of mercy, but also to prevent further infection, many towns built so-called leprosaria, which were ghettos outside the city walls where the sick eked out their miserable existence. Schongau, too, was planning to build such a leper house. For the past six months there had been much activity at the construction site on the road to Hohenfurch, but the council was still arguing over that particular decision.

When Johann Lechner returned to the council chamber, most members of the council had already arrived. They were standing together in small groups talking and engaged in heated debates. Each one had heard his own version of the story about the boy's murder. Even after Johann Lechner had rung his chairman's bell, it took them a while until each had found his seat. According to custom, the presiding burgomaster and the clerk sat at the head of the table. At their right were the seats of the inner council, six men from the most respected families of Schongau. This council also supplied the four burgomasters, who took quarterly turns in office. The established families had shared in filling the mayoral office for centuries. Officially they were elected by the entire council, but it was the custom that the most influential families also supplied the burgomaster.

On the left sat the six members of the outer council, which likewise consisted of powerful patricians. And finally, the wall was lined with the commoners' seats. The clerk looked around. Town authority was centered here. Carters, merchants, brewers, gingerbread bakers, furriers, millers, tanners, stovemakers, and clothmakers . . . all these Semers, Schreevogls, Augustins, and Hardenbergs, who had for centuries decided on the town's welfare. Serious men in their dark garments with white ruffs and Vandykes, with fat faces and round bellies, tugging at their waistcoats decorated with golden chains. They looked as if they came from a different era. The war brought ruin to Germany, but it couldn't do any harm to these men. Lechner couldn't suppress a smile. *Fat will always float to the top.*

Everyone was greatly agitated. They knew the boy's death could harm their own businesses. The peace of their little town was at stake. The chattering in the wood-paneled council chamber reminded the clerk of the buzzing of angry bees.

"Silence please! Silence!"

Lechner swung his bell one more time. Then he slammed his hand down on the table and the room finally fell silent. The clerk picked up a quill to take minutes of the meeting. Karl Semer, the burgomaster, looked around with a worried face. Then he addressed the members of the council.

"You've all heard of yesterday's dreadful incident, a terrible crime that has to be solved as fast as possible. I have agreed with the clerk that this is the first item on today's agenda. Everything else can wait. I hope that's in our common interest."

The aldermen nodded gravely. The sooner the case was solved, the sooner they could return to real business.

Burgomaster Semer continued, "Fortunately it looks as if we've already found the culprit. The Stechlin midwife is already in prison. The executioner will pay her a visit soon, and then she'll have to talk."

"What makes her a suspect?"

With some irritation the aldermen turned to look at young Schreevogl. It was not customary to interrupt the presiding burgomaster that early. Especially when one had just been on the council for a short time. Ferdinand, Jakob Schreevogl's father, had been a powerful alderman—a little odd, perhaps, but influential. His son had yet to win his spurs. In contrast to the others, the young patrician wore no ruff but a wide lace collar. His hair, according to the latest fashion, fell on his shoulders in locks. His entire appearance was an insult to each and every long-serving alderman.

"What makes her a suspect? Well, that is simple, that is simple . . . " Burgomaster Semer was rattled. Picking up a handkerchief, he dabbed small beads of sweat from his balding forehead. His broad chest was heaving beneath his gold-braided vest. He was a brewer and the landlord of the largest inn in town, and he was not used to being contradicted. He turned to the clerk on his left for help. With relish, Johann Lechner came to his aid.

"She had been seen several times with the boy prior to the night of the murder. Furthermore, there are women who testify to having seen her perform witches' sabbaths in her house with Peter and other children."

"Who testifies to that?"

Young Schreevogl wouldn't give up. And in fact Johann Lechner wasn't able to name a single one of these women at that point. However, the night watchmen had informed him that such rumors were circulating in the taverns. And he knew the usual suspects. It would be easy to round up a few witnesses.

"Let's wait for the trial. I don't want to get ahead of the facts," he said.

"Maybe the Stechlin woman will kill these witnesses by witchcraft from her prison cell if she finds out who is accusing her," another alderman piped up. It was the baker Michael Berchtholdt, a member of the outer council. Lechner took him to be capable of spreading precisely this kind of rumor. Other men nodded—they had heard of such things.

"Oh, nonsense! That's absurd. The Stechlin woman is a midwife and nothing else." Jakob Schreevogl had jumped to his feet. "Remember what happened here seventy years ago. One half of the town accused the other half of witchcraft. Streams of blood flowed. Do you want to repeat that?"

Some of the commoners began to whisper. Back then it had hit the less affluent burghers most—the peasants, the milkmaids, the farmhands . . . But there had been some innkeepers' and even judges' wives among the accused. And under torture they had confessed that they had conjured up hailstorms and desecrated the host, indeed that they had even killed their own grandchildren. The fear was still deep-rooted. Johann Lechner remembered that his father had often talked of it. The shame of Schongau. It would be in the history books forever . . .

"I hardly believe that *you* remember these things. And now sit down, little Schreevogl," a soft but piercing voice said. It was clear that the owner of this voice was used to giving orders and not inclined to be toyed with by a young whippersnapper.

At eighty-one years, Matthias Augustin was the oldest member of the council. He had ruled the wagon drivers of Schongau for decades. Meanwhile he was nearly blind, but his word was still heeded in the town. Together with the Semers, the Püchners, the Holzhofers, and the Schreevogls, he belonged to the innermost circle of power.

The old man's eyes were focused on a point in the distance. He seemed to be looking right into the past.

"*I* can remember," he murmured. The room had fallen dead silent. "I was a small boy then. But I know how the fires burned. I can still smell the flesh. Dozens died at the stake in that nasty trial, innocent people too. No one trusted anyone anymore. Believe me, I don't want to see that again. And that's why the Stechlin woman must confess."

Young Schreevogl had resumed his seat. At Augustin's last words, he sucked the air noisily through his teeth.

"She has to confess," Augustin continued, "because a rumor is like smoke. It will spread, it will seep through closed doors and latched shutters, and in the end the whole town will smell of it. Let us put an end to the whole matter as soon as we can."

Burgomaster Semer nodded, and the other members of the inner council murmured in agreement.

"He's right." Johann Püchner leaned back in his chair. His mill had been razed to the ground when the Swedes ransacked the town, and only recently had it risen again in its old splendor. "We have to keep the people calm. I was at the raft landing last night. There is a lot of unrest there."

"That's right. I talked with my men yesterday as well." Matthias Holzhofer was another powerful merchant who had rafts that traveled all the way to the Black Sea. He played with the cuffs on his doublet as he was thinking aloud. "But they rather suspect the Augsburg raftsmen. After all, old Grimmer liked to pick a quarrel with them. They might want to harm us, to scare the people, so that they don't land at our rafting place anymore."

"Then the Stechlin woman has saved her head, and your whole nice plan is ruined," Jakob Schreevogl put in. He was sitting at the table with his arms crossed.

One of the commoners along the wall cleared his throat. It rarely happened that one of those men spoke in assembly. It was old Pogner, deputy of the grocers' guild, who murmured, "There has been a brawl between Grimmer and a few of the Augsburg carters. I was present in the Stern myself when it happened."

Burgomaster Semer felt that his honor as an innkeeper was at stake.

"There are no brawls in my inn," he said soothingly. "There may have been a small quarrel, that's all."

"A small quarrel?" Now Pogner came to life. "Ask your Resl, she was there. They pretty much smashed one another's noses, they did. The blood was streaming across the tables. And one of the Augsburgers got such a licking from Grimmer that he still can hardly walk. And he cursed him as he was getting away. I think they want to take revenge, that's what I think."

"Nonsense." Matthias Augustin, almost blind, shook his head. "You can say a lot about the Augsburgers, but murder . . . I don't think they'd go that far. Stick with the Stechlin woman, and act fast before hell breaks loose here."

"I have given the order to start with the questioning tomorrow," Lechner said. "The executioner will show the midwife the instruments of torture. In a week or less the matter will be taken care of." He looked up to the carved pinewood ceiling. Reliefs of scrolls indicated that laws were made in this hall.

"Mustn't we consult the Elector's secretary in a case like this?" asked Jakob Schreevogl. "After all, we are talking about murder. The town hasn't even got the authority to pronounce a sentence here on its own."

Johann Lechner smiled. True, a capital sentence was the responsibility of the Elector's representative. However, as was so often the case, Wolf Dietrich von Sandizell was sojourning at Pichl, his country house near Thierhaupten, far from Schongau. And until he showed up, Lechner was his sole proxy within the town walls.

"I have already dispatched a messenger to ask Sandizell to come here within the week and chair the trial," he explained. "I wrote him that we will have found a culprit by then. If not, the Elector's secretary will have to remain in town a little longer with his entourage . . . " the clerk added maliciously.

The aldermen groaned inwardly. The Elector's secretary with his entourage! With horses, servants, soldiers . . . That meant a lot of expenses. They were already mentally counting the guilders and pence that each of the visiting bigwigs was going to squander on food and drink every day until the sentence was pronounced. All the more important, then, to present a culprit to the secretary when he arrived. Then they'd get off relatively cheaply . . .

"We agree," said burgomaster Semer, mopping his balding forehead. "Start questioning her tomorrow."

"Very well." Johann Lechner opened the next register book. "Let's move on to other business. There's a lot to do today."

CHAPTER
4

JAKOB KUISL WALKED THROUGH THE NARROW ALLEY that led southward alongside the town wall. The houses here were freshly plastered; the tiled roofs shone red in the morning sun. The first narcissi and daffodils were blooming in the gardens. The area around the ducal castle, known as the Hof Gate quarter, was considered to be a better part of the town. It was here that the craftsmen who had been successful and had become wealthy settled. The hangman's path led him past quacking ducks and clucking chickens, which fluttered away in the alley before him. A joiner with a plane, a hammer, and a chisel sat on the bench outside his workshop smoothing the top of a table. As the executioner passed him, he turned his head away. One didn't greet the hangman; it was thought to be unlucky.

At last Jakob Kuisl reached the end of the alley. At its farthest end, directly at the city wall, lay the keep, a hulking three-story tower with a flat roof and battlements, built with massive blocks of stone. For centuries the building had served as a dungeon and torture chamber.

The city jailer was leaning against the iron-hinged door to catch the spring sun on his face. From his belt, next to the finger-long keys, dangled a cudgel. Other weapons were not needed. After all, the suspect was in irons. The jailer had protected himself against possible curses with a small wooden crucifix and an amulet of the Blessed Virgin, both hanging from a leather thong around his neck.

"I bid you a good morning, Andreas!" called Jakob Kuisl. "How are the children? Is little Anna well again?"

"They're all well, thank you, Master Jakob. The medicine helped a good deal."

The jailer looked around furtively in all directions to see if anybody had seen him talking to the hangman. The man with the big sword was shunned, but it was to him that people came if they were plagued with gout or a finger was broken. Or when one's little daughter, as was the case with jailer Andreas, was suffering badly from whooping cough. It was the simpler people who went to the executioner rather than to the barber or the physician. Mostly they came out better than when they went in. Anyway, it was cheaper.

"What do you think? Can you let me talk to the Stechlin woman alone?" Kuisl filled his pipe and offered the jailer some of his tobacco. Furtively Andreas stuffed the gift into the bag at his belt.

"I don't know about that. Lechner has forbidden it. I'm supposed to be present all the time."

"Say, didn't Stechlin bring your Anna into the world? And your Thomas?"

"Well, yes . . . "

"You see, she brought my children into the world too. D'you really believe that she's a witch?"

"No, not really. But the others . . . "

"The others, the others . . . Think for yourself, Andreas! And now let me in. And stop by at my house tomorrow; the cough mixture for your little girl is ready. If I'm not there, you can just take it. It's on the table in the kitchen."

With these words he stretched out his hand. The jailer gave him the key, and the hangman entered the keep.

There were two cells in the back part of the chamber. In the one on the left Martha Stechlin lay motionless on a bundle of dirty straw. It reeked powerfully of urine and rotten cabbage. Through a small barred window light fell into the front room, from which a stairway led down into the torture chamber. Jakob Kuisl knew it well. Down there were all the things the hangman needed for the painful questioning.

At first he would only show the instruments to the Stechlin woman—the red-hot pincers and the rusty thumbscrews with which the agony could be intensified one turn at a time. He would have to explain to her what it was like to be slowly stretched by hundredweights of stone until the bones cracked and finally sprang out of their sockets. Often it was sufficient just to show the instruments to break the victim's spirit. But with Martha Stechlin the hangman was not so sure.

The midwife seemed to be asleep. When Jakob Kuisl stepped up to the grill, she looked up, blinking. There was a clinking sound. Her hands were connected by rusty chains to rings in the walls. Martha Stechlin tried to smile.

"They've chained me up like a mad dog." She showed him the chains. "And the grub is just what you would give to one."

Kuisl grinned. "It can't be worse than in your house."

Martha Stechlin's expression darkened. "What's it look like there? They smashed everything up, didn't they?"

"I'll go there and have another look. But at the moment you have a much greater problem. They think you did it. Tomorrow I'll come with the court clerk and the burgomaster to show you the instruments."

"Tomorrow—so soon?"

He nodded. Then he regarded the midwife intensely.

"Martha, tell me honestly, did you do it?"

"In the name of the Holy Virgin Mary, no! I could never do anything like that to the boy!"

"But was he with you? In the night before his death too?"

The midwife was freezing. She was wearing only the thin linen shirt in which she had fled from Grimmer and his men. Her whole body was shivering. Jakob Kuisl handed her his long coat, full of holes, and without a word she took it through the grill and put it round her shoulders. Not until then did she begin to speak.

"It wasn't only Peter who was with me. There were some of the others as well. They miss their mothers, that's it."

"Which others?"

"Well, the orphans, you know—Sophie, Clara, Anton, Johannes . . . whatever they're all called. They visited me, sometimes several times a week. They played in my garden, and I made some porridge for them. They haven't anybody else anymore."

Jakob Kuisl remembered. He, too, had occasionally seen children in the midwife's garden, but he had never realized that they were almost all orphans.

The hangman knew the children from seeing them in the streets. They often stood together and were avoided by the others. Several times he had intervened when other children had banded together to attack the orphans and beat them. It seemed almost as if they had some sort of sign on their foreheads that led the others to choose them again and again as victims of aggression. For a moment, his mind went back to his own childhood. He was a dirty, dishonorable hangman's son, but at least he had parents—a blessing that meanwhile fewer and fewer children enjoyed. The Great War had taken the lives of many fathers and mothers. The city put such poor, orphaned souls under the care of a guardian. They were often citizens from the city administration, but they were sometimes master craftsmen, who also took over the possessions of the dead parents as part of the bargain. In these families, usually numerous, these children were the last link in a long chain. Barely tolerated, pushed about, rarely loved. One more mouth to feed because the money was needed. Jakob Kuisl could well understand why these children had seen something like a mother in the affectionate Martha Stechlin.

"When was the last time they were with you?" he asked the midwife.

"The day before yesterday."

"So then, the day before the night of the murder. Was Peter also with them?"

"Yes, of course. He was such a polite boy . . . "

Tears rolled down the midwife's blood-encrusted face. "He didn't have a mother anymore. I was with her in her last hours myself. They always wanted to know everything, Peter and Sophie. What I did as a midwife and what herbs I used. They watched closely when I pulverized them in the mortar. Sophie said she would like to become a midwife one day."

"How long did they stay?"

"Until shortly before dark. I sent them home then, because Klingensteiner's wife sent for me. I stayed with her until early yesterday morning. By God, there are witnesses to that!"

The hangman shook his head. "That won't help you. Yesterday evening I spoke with old Grimmer. Peter supposedly never returned home. Grimmer was at the inn until closing hour. When he went to wake his son the next morning, the bed was empty."

The midwife sighed. "So I was the last one to see him alive . . . "

"That's just it, Martha. It looks bad. Out there people are gossiping."

The midwife pulled the coat tighter around her. Her lips tightened.

"When will you begin with the pincers and the thumb-screws?" she asked.

"Soon, if Lechner has anything to say about it."

"Shall I confess?"

Jakob Kuisl hesitated. This woman had brought his children into the world. He owed her a favor. In any case, try as he might, he found it impossible to imagine that she could have inflicted wounds like that on Peter.

"No," he said finally. "Put it off. Deny it as long as you can. I'll treat you gently, I promise you."

"And if that doesn't help anymore?"

Kuisl drew on his cold pipe. Then he pointed the stem at Martha. "I'll get the swine who did it. I promise you. Hold on until I have the bastard."

Then he turned suddenly and made his way toward the outer door.

"Kuisl!"

The hangman stopped and looked round once more at the midwife. Her voice was a whisper, barely audible.

"There's just one thing more. You ought to know."

"What's that?"

"I had a mandrake in my closet."

"A man—! You know, the bigwigs hold that to be the devil's stuff."

"I know. In any case, it's gone."

"Gone?"

"Yes, disappeared. Since yesterday."

"Have any other things gone missing?"

"I don't know. I'd only just noticed it before Grimmer came with his people."

Jakob Kuisl remained standing by the door, pensively suck-ing at the pipe stem.

"Strange," he murmured. "Wasn't it the full moon last night?"

Without waiting for an answer, he walked out and the door

slammed shut with a great noise behind him. Martha Stechlin wrapped herself in the coat, lay down on the straw, and wept silently.

The hangman took the quickest way to the Stechlin house. His steps echoed through the alleys. A group of peasant women, loaded with baskets and sacks, looked up in astonishment at the huge man who hurried past them. They made the sign of the cross, then continued gossiping about the terrible death of the Grimmer child and about his father, the widower and drunkard.

As he walked along, Jakob Kuisl again thought about what the midwife had just said to him. The mandrake was the root of mandragora, a plant with yellow-green fruits, whose consumption had a numbing effect. The root itself resembled a tiny withered man, which is why it was often used for spells. Pulverized, it was an ingredient of the notorious flying salve, used by witches to anoint their broomsticks. It was supposed to flourish particularly well under the gallows and to thrive on the urine and sperm of those who had been hanged, but Jakob Kuisl had never seen one growing on the Schongau gallows hill. In fact the plant was excellent as an analgesic or for bringing about abortions. But if a mandrake was found in Martha Stechlin's possession, that would mean a certain death sentence.

Who could have stolen the plant from the midwife? Someone who wanted to harm her?

Someone who wanted her to be suspected of witchcraft?

Perhaps the midwife had simply misplaced the forbidden root. Jakob Kuisl strode on faster. Soon he would be able to form a picture for himself.

A short time later he stood in front of the midwife's house. When he saw the splintered window frame and the broken door, he was no longer sure that he would find anything significant there.

The hangman pushed at the door. With one final squeak it came off its hinges and fell inward.

In the room it looked as if Martha Stechlin had been experimenting with gunpowder and had blown herself up. The clay floor was strewn with broken earthenware pots, whose alchemical signs indicated their previous contents. There was a strong smell of peppermint and wormwood.

The table, chair, and bed had been smashed and their various parts scattered throughout the room. The kettle with the cold porridge had rolled into the corner, its contents making a small puddle, from which footprints led to the garden door at the back. Smeared footmarks were also to be seen in the herbal pastes and powders on the floor. It looked as if half of Schongau had paid a visit to Martha Stechlin's house. Jakob remembered that along with Grimmer a good dozen men had stormed the midwife's house.

When the hangman looked more closely at the footprints, he began to wonder. Between the big footprints were smaller ones, smeared but still clearly recognizable. Children's footprints.

He looked around the room. The kettle. The broken table. The footprints. The smashed pots. Somewhere in his brain a bell was ringing, but he couldn't say why. Something seemed familiar to him.

The hangman chewed the stem of his cold pipe. Then he went outside, deep in thought.

Simon Fronwieser sat downstairs in the living room near the fire and watched the coffee boiling. He inhaled the exotic and stimulating odor and shut his eyes. Simon loved the smell and taste of this strange powder; he was almost addicted to it. Just a year before, a merchant from Augsburg had brought a bag with the small hard beans to Schongau. He praised them as a wonderful

medicine from the Orient. The Turks would drink themselves
into a frenzy with coffee, and it would also lead to wonderful
performances in bed. Simon was not quite sure how many of the
rumors were true. He only knew that he loved coffee and after
drinking it he could browse for hours in his books without getting tired.

The brown liquid was now bubbling away in the kettle.
Simon took an earthenware beaker to fill it with the drink. Perhaps the effect would inspire him with more ideas about the
death of the Grimmer boy. Ever since he had left the hangman's
house the previous day, he could not stop thinking about that terrible story. Who could have done such a thing? And then that
sign . . .

The door flew open noisily, and his father entered the room.
Simon knew at once that there was going to be trouble.

"You went down to see the executioner again yesterday. You
showed little Grimmer's body to the quack. Go on, don't deny it!
Hannes the tanner told me. And you were flirting around with
that Magdalena too!"

Simon shut his eyes. He had indeed met Magdalena down by
the river yesterday. They had gone for a walk. He had behaved
like an idiot, unable to look her in the eyes, and kept throwing
pebbles into the Lech the whole time. He told her everything
that had come into his head since the death of Grimmer's boy:
that he didn't believe the Stechlin woman was guilty, and that he
was frightened of a new witch trial like the one seventy years
before . . .

He had babbled on like a six-year-old, and he had really only
wanted to say that he liked her. Someone must have seen them.
In this blasted town you were never alone.

"Maybe I was. Why does it bother you?" Simon poured out
his coffee. He avoided looking into his father's eyes.

"Why does it bother me? Have you gone crazy!" Bonifaz

Fronwieser was, like his son, of small stature, but as was the case with many small men, he could get very angry. His eyes almost popped out, the points of his already graying mustache trembled.

"I am still your father!" he screamed. "Can't you see what you are doing? It has taken me years to build this up for us here. You could have it so good! You could become the first proper doctor in this town! And then you ruin it all by meeting this hangman's wench and visiting her father's house. People are talking—don't you notice that?"

Simon looked up at the ceiling and let the sermon go over his head. By now he knew it by heart. In the war his father had made his way somehow as a minor army surgeon, where he had met Simon's mother, a simple camp follower. Simon was seven years old when his mother died of the plague. Father and son had followed the soldiers for a few years, cauterized gunshot wounds with boiling oil and amputated limbs with the bone saw. When the war ended they had traveled through the country in search of a place to settle. Finally they had been accepted in Schongau. In the past few years, with hard work and ambition, his father had advanced to barber and then to a kind of official town doctor. But he had not studied medicine. Nevertheless, the town council tolerated him because the local barbers were incompetent, and doctors from the distant towns of Munich or Augsburg were too expensive.

Bonifaz Fronwieser had sent his son to study in Ingolstadt. But the money had run out, and Simon had to return to Schongau. Since then his father had saved every penny and looked with suspicion upon his offspring, whom he thought was a careless dandy.

" . . . while others fall in love with decent girls. Take Joseph, for example: he's courting the Holzhofer girl. That'll be a rich alliance! He'll get on all right. But you . . . " His father ended the speech. Simon had not been listening for some time. He sipped his coffee and thought about Magdalena. Her black eyes, which always seemed to be smiling; the broad lips, which were moist yesterday with the red wine that she had brought to the river in a leather flask. Some drops had fallen on her bodice, so he gave her his kerchief.

"Look at me when I'm talking to you!" His father hit him with a ringing backhanded slap, so that the coffee, in a wide arc, flew through the room. With a rattle the cup fell to the floor and shattered. Simon rubbed his cheek. His father stood in front of him, slight and trembling. Coffee stains marked his doublet, which was spotted enough anyway. He knew that he had gone too far. His son was no longer twelve years old. But he was indeed his son. They had gone through so much together; he only wanted the best for him . . .

"I'm going to see the hangman," whispered Simon. "If you want to stop me, you can stick your scalpel in my stomach." Then he gathered up a few books from the table and slammed the door behind him.

"Go to Kuisl then!" shouted his father after him. "And a lot of good it may do you!"

Bonifaz Fronwieser stooped and picked up the fragments of the cup. With a loud curse he threw them through the open window out onto the street, behind his son.

Blind with anger Simon hastened through the alleys. His father was so . . . so . . . pigheaded. He could even understand the old man. It was after all about his son's future: study, a good wife, children. But even the university had not been the right thing for Simon. Dusty old knowledge, learned by heart, still partly drawn from Greek and Roman scholars. Actually his father had never gotten much further than purges, bandaging, and bleeding. In the executioner's house, on the other hand, a fresher wind blew, for Jakob Kuisl owned the *Opus Paramirum* of Paracelsus and also the *Paragranum,* treasures for bibliophiles, which Simon was occasionally allowed to borrow.

As he turned into the Lech Gate street, he bumped into a horde of children who were standing together in a group. From the middle of the group came a loud yammering. Simon stood on tiptoe and saw a tall, solidly built boy sitting above a girl. He was holding her down on the ground with his knees while he struck his victim again and again with his right fist. Blood flowed from the corners of the girl's mouth, and her right eye was swollen and shut. The cluster of children accompanied every blow with shouts of encouragement. Simon pushed the jeering pack aside, grabbed the boy by the hair, and pulled him off the girl.

"Pack of cowards!" he cried. "Attacking a girl, shame on you!"

The mob retreated a few yards, but only reluctantly.

The girl on the ground sat up and wiped her hair, sticky with filth, out of her face. Her eyes looked around warily as if seeking an opening in the crowd of children through which she could escape.

The big boy drew himself up in front of Simon. He was about fifteen and half a head taller than the physician. Simon recognized him. It was Hannes, the son of Berchtholdt, the baker in the Weinstrasse.

"Don't interfere, physician," he threatened. "This is our business."

"If you are knocking a little girl's teeth out, that's my business too," replied Simon. "After all, I am, as you say, a physician and I must reckon up what the fun will cost you."

"Cost me something?" Hannes scowled. He was not exactly the brightest of the group.

"I mean, if you cause the girl injury, you'll have to pay for it. And we have enough witnesses, haven't we?"

Hannes looked over at his comrades, puzzled. Some of them had already left the scene.

"That Sophie is a witch!" Another boy joined the discussion. "She has red hair, and moreover she was always with the Stechlin woman, just like Peter, and he's dead now!" The others murmured in agreement.

Simon shuddered internally. It was beginning. Now, already. Soon Schongau would consist entirely of witches and people pointing their fingers at them.

"Nonsense," he exclaimed. "If she were a witch, why would she let you beat her up? She would have flown away on her broomstick long before. Now be off with you!"

Reluctantly, the gang withdrew, but not without casting one or two threatening looks at Simon. When the boys were a stone's throw away, he heard them shout: "He goes to bed with the hangman's girl!"

"Perhaps she'll put a noose around his neck!"

"Difficult to make him a head shorter, he's short enough already!"

Simon sighed. His still fresh and tender relationship with Magdalena was no longer a secret. His father was right: people were talking.

He stooped down to help the girl up.

"Is it true that you were always at the Stechlin woman's house with Peter?" he asked.

Sophie wiped the blood from her lips. Her long red hair was full of dirt. Simon reckoned she was about twelve years old. Under a layer of filth an intelligent face looked at him. The physician thought he remembered that she came from a tanner's family in the Lech quarter down by the river. Her parents had died during the last outbreak of the plague, and another tanner's family had taken her in.

The girl remained silent. Simon grabbed her shoulder firmly.

"I want to know if you were with Peter at Goodwife Stechlin's. It's important!" he repeated.

"Could be," she murmured.

"Did you see Peter in the evening?"

"Goodwife Stechlin has nothing to do with it, so help me God."

"Who, then?"

"Peter went down to the river again afterward . . . alone."

"Why?"

Sophie pressed her lips together. She avoided his eyes.

"I want to know why!"

"He said it was a secret. He . . . was going to meet someone."

"Who, for God's sake?"

"Didn't say."

Simon shook Sophie. He felt that the girl was hiding something from him. Suddenly she broke from his grasp and ran into the next alley.

"Wait!" he cried and started to run after her.

Sophie was barefoot, and her little feet flitted lightly over the stamped earth. She had already reached the Zänkgasse and ducked between some servant maids coming from the market with fully laden baskets. As Simon rushed past them, his clothing caught on one of the baskets. The maid let go of the basket, and radishes, cabbages, and carrots flew in all directions on the street. Simon heard angry cries behind him, but he could not stop, as the girl was on the verge of making her escape. She had already disappeared around the next bend, where there were fewer people in the alleys. Simon held onto his hat with one hand and continued running. On the left stood two houses with their roofs almost touching and in between was a narrow alley, just about shoulder-width, leading to the town wall. The ground was covered with rubble and trash, and at the other end Simon could see a small form running away. Cursing, the physician bade farewell to his fine leather boots greased with beef tallow and sprang over the first mound of rubble.

He landed directly in a heap of refuse, slipped, and fell on the seat of his pants in a mass of rubble, rotten vegetables, and the fragments of a discarded chamber pot. He could hear the sound of distant footsteps. He groaned and rose to his feet as one story higher a window shutter was opened. Startled faces looked down on a rather shaken physician, who was carefully removing cabbage leaves from his coat.

"Mind your own business!" he shouted up at them. Then he limped off in the direction of the Lech Gate.

The hangman looked through the glass at a heap of yellow stars, which were glittering in the light of the tallow candle. Crystals like snow, each one perfect in its form and arrangement. Jakob Kuisl smiled. When he dipped into the mysteries of nature, he was sure that there must be a God. Who else could create such lovely works of art? Man's inventions could only ape those of his Creator. On the other hand, it was the same God who ensured that people died like flies, carried off by plague and war. It was difficult in such times to believe in God, but Jakob Kuisl discovered Him in the beauties of nature.

Just as he was carefully distributing the crystals on a piece of parchment with his tweezers, there was a knock at the door. Before he could say anything, the door of his study opened a crack. A current of air blew in and moved the parchment toward the end of the table. With a curse Jakob grabbed at it and prevented it from being blown down. Some of the crystals disappeared into a crack in the table.

"Who in the name of three devils?"

"It's Simon," said his wife, who had opened the door. "He wants to bring the books back. And he would like to talk to you.

He says it is very important. And don't swear so loud, the children are asleep."

"Let him come in," growled Kuisl.

When he turned toward Simon he saw a deformed face. Not until then did the hangman notice that he still had his monocle in his eye. The doctor's son, on the other hand, was looking into a pupil as large as a ducat.

"Just a toy," grumbled Kuisl, taking the brass-mounted lens out of his eye. "But sometimes fairly useful."

"Where did you get that?" asked Simon. "It must be worth a fortune!"

"Shall we say I did a favor for an alderman, and he repaid me in kind." Jakob Kuisl sniffed. "You stink."

"I've . . . I had an accident. On the way here."

The hangman, with a dismissive gesture, passed the lens to Simon and pointed to the little yellow heap on the parchment.

"Just take a look at that. What do you think it is?"

With the monocle, Simon bent over the little grains.

"That's . . . that is fascinating! I've never seen such a perfect lens . . ."

"What about the grains, that's what I want to know."

"Well, from the smell I would say it's sulfur."

"I found it together with a lot of clay in little Grimmer's pocket."

Simon abruptly took down the monocle and looked at the hangman.

"Peter? In his pocket? But how did the sulfur get there?"

"That's what I'd like to know too."

Jakob Kuisl reached for his pipe and began to fill it. Meanwhile Simon walked up and down in the little room and told about his encounter with the orphan girl. Occasionally Kuisl growled; otherwise he was fully occupied with filling and lighting his pipe. When Simon had finished his story, the hangman was already enveloped in a haze of tobacco smoke.

"I visited the Stechlin woman," he said finally. "The children had indeed been with her. And a mandrake is missing."

"A mandrake?"

"A magic herb."

Jakob Kuisl told briefly of his meeting with the midwife and of the chaos in her house. Again and again there were long pauses while he drew on his pipe. Meanwhile Simon seated himself on a wooden stool and fidgeted impatiently.

"I don't understand it at all," said the young physician at last. "We have a dead boy with a witches' mark on his shoulder and sulfur in his pocket. We have a midwife as a prime suspect, from whom a mandrake has been stolen. And we have a gang of orphans who know more than they will admit. None of this makes sense!"

"Above all we have very little time," mumbled the hangman. "The Elector's secretary is coming in a few days. Between now and then I have to make the Stechlin woman the culprit, otherwise the council will be on my back."

"And what if you simply refuse?" asked Simon. "Nobody can demand that you . . . "

Kuisl shook his head. "Then they'll send another, and I can look for a new job. No, it'll have to be like this. We must find the real murderer, and right soon."

"We?"

The hangman nodded. "I need your help. People don't like talking to me. The fine people turn up their noses as soon as they see me in the distance. Although . . ." he added with a smile, "they would turn up their noses at you now."

Simon looked down at his spotted, foul-smelling doublet. It was still covered with brown spots. A tear in his hose ran from the knee down the left leg. A faded lettuce leaf hung from his hat . . . to say nothing about the splotches of dried blood. He would need new clothes and had no idea where the money for them would come from. Perhaps if the murderer was caught the council might contribute a few guilders.

Simon thought over the hangman's proposition. What had he to lose? Not his reputation anymore; that was already ruined. And if he wanted to continue seeing Magdalena in the future, it would be an advantage to be on good terms with her father. And then there were the books. Just now there lay next to the monocle on the table a tattered work of the Jesuit Athanasius Kirchner, who wrote of tiny worms in the blood. That priest had worked with a so-called microscope, which could magnify things many more times presumably than Kuisl's monocle. The possibility of reading this book at home, alone in bed with a hot cup of coffee . . .

Simon nodded. "Good, you can count on me. By the way, the book on the . . . "

The doctor's son got no further in expressing his wish. The door flew open, and Andreas the jailer staggered into the room, panting for air.

"Forgive me for disturbing you so late," he gasped. "But it's urgent. They told me I would find Fronwieser's son here. Your father needs help!"

Andreas' face was as white as a sheet. He looked as if he had seen the devil incarnate.

"What in all the world can be so urgent?" asked Simon. Privately he wondered who could have seen him going into the executioner's house. It seemed that you could not take a step in this town without being observed.

"Grocer Kratz's son, he's dying!" exclaimed the jailer Andreas with his last bit of strength. He kept reaching for the little wooden crucifix that hung round his neck.

Jakob Kuisl, who up to that moment had listened in silence, became impatient. He slammed his hand down on the rickety table, so that the monocle and Athanasius' masterpiece jumped up a little. "An accident? Tell us, then!"

"Everything covered in blood! Oh, God, help us, he has the sign! Just like Grimmer . . . "

Simon sprang from his stool. He felt fear rising inside him.

Kuisl stared at the physician's son through clouds of tobacco smoke. "You go there. I'll have a look at the Stechlin woman. I don't know if she's really safe in the prison."

Simon grabbed his hat and ran out into the street. Out of the corner of his eye he caught a glimpse of Magdalena, who waved to him sleepily from the attic window. He had a feeling they would not have much time to see each other in the next few days.

The man stood at the window, his head only a hand's width away from the heavy red fabric of the curtain.

Outside night was falling, but what difference did that make? Here in this room it was always dusk, a depressing gray twilight, where even by day the sunlight was feeble. Through his inner eye the man saw the sun over the town. It would rise and set, again and again, nothing would stop it. The man would not let anything stop him either, even if delays occasionally occurred. These delays made him . . . irritable. He turned around quickly.

"What a useless ass you are! Good for nothing! Why can't you manage to finish anything properly?"

"I'll finish it all right."

In the half-light a second figure could be seen sitting at the table and stabbing about with a knife in a pie as if it were the stomach of a slaughtered pig.

The man at the window drew the curtains still closer together. His fingers clutched the fabric like claws. A wave of pain overcame him. He didn't have much more time left.

"That business with the children was totally unnecessary. The talk is just beginning now."

"Nobody will talk. You can count on me."

"Some people have already become suspicious. We can only hope that the midwife will confess. The hangman has already begun asking stupid questions."

The figure at the table continued to work the pie into a stew of meat and lumps of pastry. The knife rose and fell frantically.

"Bah, the hangman! Who's going to believe him?"

"Don't underestimate Kuisl. He's as sly as a fox."

"Then the little fox will run into the trap."

The man at the window quickly took the few steps to the table and struck him hard in the face with the back of his hand. The other held his cheek for a little, then looked up apprehensively into the face of his assailant. He noticed how his assailant put his hands on his stomach and was panting in pain.

A slight smile played on his lips. This problem would soon resolve itself.

"You will stop this nonsense now," murmured the older man, grimacing in pain. A steady ache throbbed from inside his abdomen. He leaned forward over the table.

"You leave it alone. I'll take care of it myself now."

"I can't."

"You can't?"

"I've handed it over to someone else. One who won't let us interfere with his work anymore."

"Call him off. It's enough. When the Stechlin woman confesses, we'll get our money."

The older man had to sit down for just a second. It was difficult for him to speak. Damn this body! He needed it still, just until they got hold of the money. Then he could die in peace. His life's work was in danger and this useless fool was ruining everything. But not as long as he himself could breathe. Not as long . . .

"This is an excellent pie. Would you like some?"

With his knife, the younger man had speared the pieces of meat spread out on the table and began to eat them with relish.

At the end of his strength, the old man shook his head. The younger man smiled.

"Keep calm, everything will be all right."

He wiped the gravy out of his beard, took his sword in hand, and hurried to the door.

Without waiting for the jailer, Simon headed to the Kratzes' house, which stood in a narrow side street in the Lech Gate quarter. Clemens and Agathe Kratz were regarded as hardworking grocers who had acquired a modest fortune over the years. Their five children all went to the local grammar school, and they did not treat their ward Anton, who after the death of his parents had been assigned to them by the town council, any differently than their own four children. Clemens Kratz, the father, sat huddled by the counter. With his right hand he mechanically caressed the shoulder of his wife, who was pressed against him, sobbing. In front of them on the counter lay the body of the boy. Simon did not need to look long at it to determine the cause of death. Someone had cut little Anton's throat clean through. Clotted blood had dyed his linen shirt red. The eyes of the ten-year-old boy were fixed on the ceiling.

When they found him an hour earlier he had still been breathing noisily, but in minutes the life had ebbed from his little body. The only thing that Bonifaz Fronwieser could do was confirm the death. When Simon came in, the work was already done. His father briefly looked him up and down, and after expressing his sympathy to the Kratzes packed up his instruments and went out without saying goodbye.

After Bonifaz Fronwieser had left the house, Simon sat for a few minutes by the dead child and looked at his white face. The second death in two days . . . Had the boy known his murderer?

Finally the physician turned to the boy's father.

"Where did you find him?" he asked.

No answer. The Kratzes were sunk in a world of grief and pain not easily penetrated by the human voice.

"I'm sorry, but where did you find him?" repeated Simon.

Only then did Clemens Kratz look up. The father's voice was hoarse from much weeping. "Outside on the doorstep. He just wanted to go over quickly to his . . . friends. When he didn't come back we opened the door to go and look for him. And there he was, lying in his blood . . . "

Mother Kratz began to whimper again. On a wooden bench in a back corner sat the four other Kratz children, their eyes wide open with fear. The youngest daughter pressed a doll made of scraps of cloth to her chest.

Simon turned to the children. "Do you know where your brother wanted to go?"

"He isn't our brother." The voice of the eldest Kratz boy sounded firm and defiant in spite of his fear. "He's an orphan."

And you certainly let him know that often enough, thought Simon. He sighed. "All right. Once more, then. Do you know where he wanted to go?"

"Just to the others." The boy looked him straight in the face.

"Which others?"

"The other orphans. They always met down by the Lech Gate. He wanted to go there again. I saw Sophie, the redhead, with him at the four o'clock bells. They were planning something. They had put their heads together like a herd of cattle."

Simon couldn't help thinking of the small girl he had only a few hours before rescued from a beating. The red hair, the defiant eyes. At the age of twelve it seemed that Sophie had already made a lot of enemies.

"That's right." The father chimed in. "They did in fact often meet at the Stechlin place. Sophie and the Stechlin woman, the same witches' brood. They are responsible! And they made this Satan's mark on him, for sure!"

Mother Kratz began to weep again, so that her husband had to comfort her.

Simon went over to the body and turned it carefully onto its stomach. On the right shoulder blade there was in fact the same symbol as had been found on the Grimmer boy. Not quite as clear, certainly. Someone had tried to wipe it off. But the color had already penetrated too deeply under the skin. Indelibly it still appeared on the child's shoulder.

Simon could sense that Clemens Kratz had come up behind him. Filled with hate, the father stared at the sign.

"The Stechlin woman did that to him. And that Sophie," he hissed. "For sure. They should burn them—burn them both!"

The physician tried to calm him. "Stechlin is in the keep, she couldn't have done it. And Sophie is still a child. Do you really believe that a child—"

"The devil has got into that child!" cried Mother Kratz from behind. Her eyes were bloodshot from weeping, her face pale and puffy. "The devil is here in Schongau! And he'll carry off other children!"

Simon looked once again at the faded mark on the boy's back. No doubt, someone had tried to remove it, without success.

"Did any of you try to wash this mark off?" he asked them.

Kratz crossed himself.

"We have not touched the devil's mark, so help me God!" The other members of the family shook their heads and signed the cross too.

Simon sighed inwardly. He wouldn't get any further here with logical arguments. He took his leave and went out into the darkness. Behind him he could still hear the sobbing of the mother and the murmured prayers of the old grocer.

At the sound of a whistle Simon turned around. His eyes searched the alley. At the corner a small form was leaning against the wall of a house and beckoning to him.

It was Sophie.

Simon looked around, then he entered the narrow alley and bent down to the girl.

"You got away from me last time," he whispered.

"And I'll get away from you again this time," replied Sophie, "but now just listen: a man asked for Anton, just before he was stabbed."

"A man? But how do you know …?"

Sophie shrugged. A slight smile passed over her lips. Simon wondered for a moment what she would look like in five years' time.

"We orphans have eyes everywhere. That saves us from beatings."

"And what did he look like, this man?"

"Tall. With a coat and a broad-brimmed hat. There was a feather in the hat. And across his face there was a long scar."

"And that's all?"

"His hand was all bones."

"Don't lie to me!"

"Down by the river he asked a few raftsmen where the Kratzes' house was. I was hiding behind the trees. He kept his left hand under his coat, but once it slipped out and I saw it shining white in the sun. A skeleton hand."

Simon bent farther down and put his arm around the girl.

"Sophie, I don't believe you. It would be best for you to come with me now … "

Sophie tore herself away. Tears of rage filled her eyes.

"Nobody believes me. But it's true! The man with the hand of bones cut Anton's throat. He wanted to meet us down at the Lech Gate, and now he's dead." The girl's voice became a whimper.

"Sophie, we can … "

With a quick turn the girl escaped from Simon's arm and raced away down the alley. After a short distance she had already disappeared into the darkness. As he started to chase after her, Simon realized that the purse with the money for new clothes was missing from his belt.

"You damned little—" He looked at the heap of dirt and rubbish in the alley. Then he decided to dispense with a pursuit this time. Instead he went home, so that he could finally get a good night's sleep.

CHAPTER
5

MAGDALENA WAS LOST IN THOUGHT AS SHE WALKED along the muddy road across the Lech Bridge and toward Peiting. In the bag she had slung across her shoulder she was carrying some dried herbs and the quantity of Our Lady's Powder she had ground yesterday. A few days ago she had promised to deliver the powder to midwife Daubenberger. The old woman was past her seventieth year and not very steady on her feet. Still, in Peiting and its surroundings she was the village midwife whom one called upon for help with difficult deliveries. Katharina Daubenberger had helped hundreds of children into this world. She was famous for her hands, with which she'd pull the most stubborn little imp into the light of day, and she was regarded as a wise woman, a healer, eyed suspiciously by priest and physician alike. But her diagnoses and her treatments were usually correct. Magdalena's father had often sought her counsel. His gift of Our Lady's Powder was a token of gratitude; and he was soon going to need one herb or another from her.

When Magdalena passed by the first houses in Peiting, she noticed that the peasants turned around to look at her and were whispering. Some crossed themselves. She was the hangman's daughter, and the villagers feared her. Many of them suspected she was having it off with Beelzebub. And they had heard that her beauty was based solely on a bargain with the prince of darkness. What he had received in return for it was nothing less than her immortal soul. She let people hold on to their illusions. At least it kept away obnoxious suitors . . .

Without a second thought for the peasants, she turned into a lane on the right and soon stood before the small, ramshackle house of the midwife.

At once she noticed that something was wrong. The shutters were closed despite the beautiful sunny morning, and some of the herbs and flowers in the little garden in front of the house were trampled. Magdalena approached the door and pushed the latch. The door was locked.

By now she had realized that something was fishy. Goodwife Daubenberger was known for her hospitality. Magdalena had never found her door locked. All of the women in the village could call upon the old midwife anytime.

She knocked vigorously on the heavy wooden door.

"Are you in, Goodwife Daubenberger?" she asked. "It's me, Magdalena from Schongau! I brought you Our Lady's Powder."

After quite a while, the gable window was opened. Katharina Daubenberger looked down at her with a suspicious eye. The old woman looked worried. There were more furrows on her face than ever. She looked pale and tired. When she recognized Magdalena, she forced herself to smile.

"Oh, Magdalena, it's you," she called. "That's kind of you to come. Are you alone?"

Magdalena nodded. Cautiously, the midwife looked in all directions, then she disappeared inside the house. Footsteps could be heard on the stairs and a bolt was pushed back. Finally the door opened. Hurriedly, Goodwife Daubenberger waved her in.

"What's the matter?" asked Magdalena as she entered. "Did you poison the burgomaster?"

"You ask what's the matter, you silly goose?" she snapped, stirring the fire in the hearth. "They waylaid me at night, the village lads did. They wanted to burn down my house. If it hadn't been for the farmer Michael Kössl, I'd be stone dead! He brought them back into line."

"It's because of Martha Stechlin, isn't it?" asked Magdalena as she sat down on a rickety chair near the fireplace. Her legs were weary from the walk. Katharina Daubenberger nodded.

"Now all midwives will be witches again," she murmured. "Like in my grandmother's day. Nothing ever changes."

She sat down beside Magdalena and poured her a cup of something dark and fragrant.

"Drink it," she said. "Honey water with beer and *aqua ephedrae*."

"Aqua what?" asked Magdalena.

"Essence of ephedra. That'll get you back on your feet again."

Magdalena sipped the hot liquid. It was sweet and invigorating. She felt the strength returning to her legs.

"Do you know what exactly happened in the town?" Katharina Daubenberger wanted to know.

Magdalena gave the midwife an outline of what she knew. The night before last, as they were walking along the Lech, Simon had told her of the dead boy with the witches' mark on his shoulder. She also had been able to overhear most of the conversation between her father and the physician through the thin wooden wall of his room on previous night.

"And now it seems another boy's been killed, and he had the same sign on his shoulder," she concluded. "Simon went to see him last night. I haven't heard from him since then."

"Elderberry juice scratched into the skin, you say?" asked Goodwife Daubenberger, deep in thought. "That's strange. You'd think the devil would've used blood, wouldn't you? On the other hand—"

"What?" Magdalena interrupted impatiently.

"Well, the sulfur in the boy's pocket, and then this sign . . . "

"Is it really a witches' sign?" asked Magdalena.

"Let's say it's a wise woman's sign. An ancient sign. As far as I know, it shows a hand mirror, the mirror of a very old and powerful goddess."

The old midwife rose to her feet and walked to the fireplace to put on another log.

"At any rate it's going to cause us a great deal of trouble. If matters go on like this, I'll move in with my daughter-in-law in Peissenberg until this nightmare's over."

Suddenly she stopped in her tracks. She had caught sight of a tattered calendar lying on the mantel.

"Of course," she murmured. "However could I forget that?"

"What is it?" asked Magdalena, moving closer to her. Meanwhile the midwife had picked up the calendar and was leafing through it frantically.

"Here," she said finally, pointing at a faded image of an abbess holding a pitcher and a book. "Saint Walburga. Patron of the sick and of women in childbed. Her day is next week."

"So?"

Magdalena had no idea what the midwife was trying to say. Puzzled, she looked at the stained print. The page was charred in one corner. The woman in the picture had a halo; her eyes were cast down modestly.

"Well," Goodwife Daubenberger began her lecture. "The day of Saint Walburga is May first. The night preceding it is therefore called Walpurgis Night . . . "

"Witches' night," Magdalena whispered.

The midwife nodded and continued.

"If we want to believe the peasants of Peiting, that's the night when the witches meet in the forest up at Hohenfurch to woo Satan. The sign right at this time may just be a coincidence, but it is strange in any case."

"You think?"

Katharina Daubenberger shrugged.

"I don't think anything. But it's just one week till Walpurgis Night. And didn't you find another dead boy with just the same mark only yesterday?"

She hurried to the room next door. When Magdalena followed her she saw how the midwife hurriedly shoved some garments and blankets into a knapsack.

"What're you doing?" she asked in surprise.

"What does it look like I'm doing?" the old woman wheezed. "I'm packing. I'm going to my daughter-in-law's in Peissenberg. If the killing continues, I don't want to be around. On Walpurgis Night at the very latest the lads will set my house on fire. If there's really a witch around here, I don't want anyone to think it's me. And if there isn't one, there'll always be the need for a culprit."

She looked at Magdalena and shrugged.

"And now get out of here. Better for you to be gone. You're the hangman's daughter, and in their eyes you're just as loathsome as a witch."

Without turning around, Magdalena hurried out. On her way down to the Lech, past the barns and farms, she felt that there was a pair of suspicious eyes staring at her from every window.

It was about ten o'clock in the morning. Simon was sitting at one of the tables in the back of the Stern Inn, lost in thought and stirring a stew of mutton and carrots. He didn't really have much of an appetite, although he hadn't eaten anything since last night. But the memories of that night—the sight of young Kratz, his parents' tears, and the turmoil in the neighborhood—had turned his stomach into a tight lump that wouldn't accept any food whatsoever. However, in the Stern he at least had some peace to think through everything that had happened yesterday.

The physician let his eyes roam through the lounge. There were over a dozen inns in Schongau, but the Stern was doubtlessly the best in town. The oaken tables were clean and smoothly planed, and chandeliers with fresh candles hung from the ceiling. Several maids watched over the few wealthy patrons, continually filling their goblets with wine from glass decanters.

At this time of day, the inn was frequented by only a few wagon drivers from Augsburg who had dropped off their cargo at the Ballenhaus early in the morning.

From Schongau, they would continue their journey to Steingaden and Füssen and across the Alps to Venice.

The drivers were smoking their pipes and had already drunk their fair fill of wine.

Simon could hear their loud laughter.

Seeing the drivers, Simon remembered the brawl the raftsmen on the Lech had told him about. Josef Grimmer had started an argument with some of his competitors from Augsburg. Was it because of this that his son had to die? But what about the other dead boy, then? And that man with the hand of bone whom Sophie had spoke of?

Simon sipped at his mug of weak beer, thinking. For a long time now, the Augsburgers had been planning a new trading route on the Swabian side of the Lech to avoid Schongau's transportation monopoly. So far, the Duke had always thwarted their plans. But there was no doubt that in the long run things were in their favor. If Schongau were avoided on account of diabolical activities, more and more merchants would be in favor of a new route. Furthermore, Schongau was currently planning a leper house. Not a few of the aldermen believed that it could frighten away merchants.

Was the man with the bony hand perhaps an emissary sent by Augsburg to spread fear and chaos?

"This one's on the house."

Awakened from his thoughts, Simon looked up. Burgomaster Karl Semer himself was standing before him. He plunked down a tankard of bock beer on the table so that the foam splattered. Simon eyed the landlord. It was not a regular occurrence that the presiding burgomaster of Schongau visited the lounge of his inn in person. Simon couldn't remember if he'd ever been addressed by Semer, except that one time when Semer's son had been in bed with a fever. But then the burgomaster had treated him condescendingly, like a vagrant barber, and had rather reluctantly handed him a couple of hellers. Now, however, he smiled in a friendly way and took a seat at his table. He beckoned to one of the maids with his chubby ringed fingers and ordered another beer. Then he raised his tankard to Simon.

"I've heard of the Kratz boy's death. Nasty business, that. Looks like the Stechlin woman has an accomplice here in town. But we'll find that out soon enough. Today we're going to show her the instruments."

"How can you be so sure it was really the Stechlin woman?" asked Simon without raising his tankard.

Semer took a hearty swig of the dark beer and wiped his beard.

"We have witnesses who've seen her celebrate satanic rites with the children. And on the rack at the very least she'll confess her sins, I'm sure of that."

"I hear there was a brawl with the Augsburgers in your inn," Simon replied. "Old man Grimmer supposedly gave a few of them a good beating . . ."

For a moment, Karl Semer looked irritated, then he snorted disdainfully.

"Nothing special. Happens every day. You can ask Resl here. She was waitressing that day."

He beckoned to the girl to come to the table. Resl was about twenty and not really a stunning beauty with her big round eyes and her crooked nose. She lowered her head bashfully. Simon knew that she had often looked at him dreamily. The maids still considered him one of the most desirable men in town. Besides, he was still a bachelor.

Karl Semer invited the maid to sit down at the table with them.

"Tell us about that brawl with the Augsburgers the other day, Resl."

The maid shrugged. Then she produced a shy smile, while she regarded Simon from the side.

"It was a couple of men from Augsburg. They were drinking too much and started criticizing our raftsmen. That they didn't tie down the goods properly and damaged them. That they drink liquor while they're working, and that Grimmer lost an entire cargo owing to that."

"Well, and what did Grimmer say to that?" asked Simon.

"He kicked up a fuss and whacked one of the Augsburgers right in the face. And then the dust started flying here. Our men threw them all outside. Then there was order again."

Karl Semer smirked at the physician and took another swig.

"As you see, nothing special."

Suddenly Simon had an idea. "Resl, on that day, did you happen to see a tall man with a feather in his hat and a scar on his face?"

To his astonishment the maid nodded.

"Yes, there was such a one. He was sitting back there in the corner with two others. Gloomy-looking men. I think they were soldiers. They had sabers, and the tall one, he had a long scar that went all across his face. And he limped a little. He looked like the devil had sent him here . . . "

"Were they involved in the brawl?"

The maid shook her head.

"No, they only watched, they did. But after the fight they left pretty quickly. They did—"

"That'll do, Resl. You may go back to work," the burgo-master intervened.

When the maid had left, he looked at Simon angrily.

"What sort of questions are those? Where does that get us? It was the Stechlin woman, and that's that. What we need is peace and quiet back in our town, and you and your questions will only cause further anxiety. Keep your hands off that business, Fronwieser. That'll only lead to more problems."

"But we can't even be certain—"

"I said, keep your nose out of it." Karl Semer tapped Simon's chest with a plump index finger. "You and the hangman, you are only causing unrest with your questions. Drop it, do you under-stand?"

With these words the burgomaster rose to his feet and, with-out a farewell, withdrew to the upstairs rooms. Simon finished his beer and made ready to leave.

As he was about to step outside, someone tugged at his over-coat. It was Resl, the maid. She looked around anxiously to see if they were being watched.

"I have to tell you one more thing. The three men . . . " she whispered.

"Well?"

"They didn't leave. They just went upstairs. They must've met someone up there."

Simon nodded. Anyone in Schongau who had business to discuss would go to the Stern. And anyone who wanted to do that unseen would rent a room on an upper floor. There were side doors that saved one from even having to set foot in the bar. But whom could the three men have met up there?

"Thank you, Resl."

"There's something else . . . " The maid looked around

furtively. Her voice was barely audible as she continued, her lips almost touching Simon's ear.

"Believe me or not, but when the tall one with the scar paid for his drinks, I saw his left hand. It was just bones. I swear to God, the devil is here in Schongau, and I've seen him."

The maid jumped when she heard her name called from the bar. With a last yearning glance at the young physician she turned away.

When the girl left, Simon's eyes wandered up the magnificent facade of the inn with its glass windows and painted stucco.

Who had the men met here?

Simon couldn't suppress a shudder. It looked as if Sophie had told the truth with her story after all. Maybe the devil really had come to Schongau.

"It's time now, Martha. You've got to get up."

Unnoticed, the hangman had stepped into the little cell. He was pulling at her coat, which she had thrown over herself as a blanket. Martha Stechlin had her eyes closed and was breathing quietly. A smile was on her lips. She seemed to be in a world that was free of fear and pain. Jakob Kuisl was sorry he had to call her back to this grim reality. Here, there was going to be a great deal of pain very soon. She had to remain strong.

"Martha, the aldermen will arrive soon."

This time he shook her. The midwife opened her eyes and looked around in bewilderment for a moment. Then she remembered where she was. She brushed her matted hair from her face, and looked around like a hunted beast.

"My God, it's going to start now . . ." She began to cry.

"You needn't be afraid, Martha. Today I'll only show you the tools. You've got to hold out. We'll find the murderer, and then—"

He was interrupted by a squeaking sound. The gate of the keep was opening and the light of a late afternoon sun came in. Four jailers entered and took their places along the walls. They were followed by the emissaries of the council and Johann Lechner, the court clerk. With consternation Kuisl saw the three aldermen. The prisoner was only to be shown the torture instruments today. The torture to follow needed approval from Munich, and the Elector's secretary had to be present. What if the court clerk really dared to commence the painful interrogation on his own?

Johann Lechner seemed to notice the hangman's hesitation. He nodded at him encouragingly.

"Everything's in order," he said. "The three aldermen will appear as witnesses. The faster we get this matter taken care of, the faster peace will return to our town. His Excellency, Count Sandizell, will be grateful for that."

"But . . . " Jakob Kuisl began. The court clerk's eyes made it quite clear that there was no point in protesting. What should he do? If nothing unexpected happened, he'd have to torture Martha Stechlin today. Unless . . .

Unless the witnesses arrived at a different verdict.

Kuisl knew from experience that aldermen, when they were invited to interrogations, often couldn't refrain from intervening themselves. Occasionally they cut short the interrogation if they had the feeling that there was no result to be expected in spite of the torture.

He glimpsed at the three aldermen. He knew the baker Michael Berchtholdt and young Schreevogl as well. But who was the third man?

Johann Lechner, the clerk, followed the hangman's eyes. "Alderman Matthias Augustin, the third witness, is sick," he remarked casually. "He's sending his son Georg."

Kuisl nodded as he eyed the three witnesses carefully.

Michael Berchtholdt was a great zealot before the Lord. He loved to see people tortured and was convinced that Martha Stechlin was a witch who should be burned at the stake. He was already looking her up and down with eyes full of hate and fear, as if the midwife could cast a spell over him even from a distance and turn him into a rat. The hangman grinned inwardly as he contemplated the small, wizened man, whose eyes were red-rimmed from all the brandy he drank. With his gray overcoat and rumpled fur cap he did resemble one of the mice that scurried through his bakery at night.

Young Schreevogl, who had entered the dungeon behind the baker, was considered a worthy successor to his father in the council, though he was somewhat rash at times.

Kuisl had heard from other members of the council that he did not believe Martha Stechlin was guilty.

One point for us . . .

Jakob Kuisl eyed this scion of Schongau's foremost family of stovemakers. With his slightly aquiline nose, domed forehead, and pale face, he looked just like the hangman's idea of a true patrician. Stovemakers produced earthenware as well as tiled stoves. The Schreevogls owned a small manufactory in town where seven journeymen made pitchers, plates, and tiles. Old Ferdinand Schreevogl had worked his way from rags to riches and always had a reputation for being a little odd. He was famous for the caricatures that adorned his tiles and that ridiculed the church, the town council, and the landowners.

After his death a year ago, his son seemed to purposefully invest his inheritance rather than wasting it. Only a week ago he had hired a new man. And only reluctantly had young Schreevogl accepted the fact that his father had bequeathed his property on Hohenfurch Road to the church. It was there that the leper house was to be built.

The young stovemaker was one of the few men in town who

occasionally exchanged a few words with the hangman. Now, too, he nodded at him briefly and gave him a tight-lipped but encouraging smile.

The third witness, Georg Augustin, was more difficult for Kuisl to judge. Young Augustin was known to be a rake and so far had spent most of his time in distant Augsburg and Munich, where, according to his father, he was doing business with the electoral court. The Augustins were an influential dynasty of wagon drivers in Schongau, and Georg certainly looked the part. He dressed as a dandy with a plumed hat, baggy breeches, and boots, and his gaze went right through the hangman. With obvious interest he looked at the midwife, who was huddled up in her overcoat, shivering and rubbing her toes, which were blue with frost. It was April, but the stone walls of the prison were as cold as ice.

"Let's start." The court clerk's voice cut through the silence. "Let's go to the cellar."

The bailiffs opened a trapdoor on the ground floor. From there, stairs led down to a sooty room with coarse stone walls. In the corner to the left there was a stained rack with a wooden wheel at the head. Next to that sat a brazier in which several pairs of pincers had been rusting away for years. Here and there, stone blocks with iron halter rings lay on the floor. A chain with a hook dangled from the ceiling. Yesterday a bailiff had brought thumbscrews and more pincers from the Ballenhaus and thrown them in a corner. In another corner there was a stack of rotting wooden chairs. The torture chamber looked neglected.

Johann Lechner looked around the room with the torch. Then he regarded the hangman reproachfully.

"Well, you could've tidied up a little in here."

Jakob Kuisl shrugged. "You were in such a great hurry." Stoically, he began to distribute the chairs. "And it's been a while since the last interrogation."

The hangman remembered it well. It had been four years

since he had tied the forger Peter Leitner's hands behind his back and fastened them to the hook in the ceiling. They had tied forty-pound boulders to his feet, and then his arms broke and he whimpered his confession. Previously, Kuisl had tortured him with thumbscrews and red-hot pincers. The hangman had been convinced from the start that Leitner was guilty, just as now he was convinced that Martha Stechlin was innocent.

"Goddamn you, get moving! We don't have all day!"

The clerk slouched down in one of the chairs and waited for Jakob Kuisl to find seats for everyone present. With his two enormous hands the hangman struggled to lift up a heavy oaken table and put it down hard in front of Lechner. The clerk gave him another look of disapproval, then he took out his inkwell and quills and spread a parchment scroll before him.

"Let's get started."

Meanwhile, the witnesses had taken their seats. Martha Stechlin cowered against the far wall, as though looking for a mouse hole through which to make her escape.

"Let her undress," said Johann Lechner.

Jakob Kuisl looked at him with surprise.

"But didn't you first—"

"I said, let her undress. We want to search her for witches' marks. If we find any, we'll have proof she's guilty and the interrogation can proceed all the more swiftly."

Two bailiffs approached the midwife, who was huddled in a corner, her arms crossed in front of her. The baker Michael Berchtholdt licked his thin lips. He was going to get his show today.

Jakob Kuisl swore silently. He hadn't expected that. Searching for witches' marks was a common way of hunting down witches. If there were strangely shaped birthmarks on a suspect's body, that was taken as a sign from the devil. Often the hangman would then perform the needle test and push a needle into the putative witch's suspicious birthmark. If no blood came out, she was certain to be a witch. Kuisl knew that his grandfather had ways to avoid bleeding during the needle test. That way, the trial was over sooner, and the hangman got his pay sooner.

The sound of ripping fabric interrupted his thought. One of the bailiffs had torn off Martha's stinking, soiled garment. Underneath, the midwife was pale and skinny. Bruises on her thighs and forearms bore witness to yesterday morning's fight with Josef Grimmer. She pressed back against the cellar wall, trying to cover her breasts and genitals with her hands.

The bailiff pulled her up by her hair. She screamed. Jakob Kuisl saw how Michael Berchtholdt's little red eyes groped the midwife's body like fingers.

"Is that really necessary? At least give her a chair!" Jakob Schreevogl had jumped to his feet and tried to restrain the bailiffs, but the clerk pulled him down again.

"We want to discover the truth. And for that we have to do it. And well, all right, let the Stechlin woman have a chair."

Reluctantly, the bailiff pushed a chair to the center of the room and sat the midwife down on it. Her frightened eyes darted back and forth between the clerk and the hangman.

"Cut off her hair," said Lechner. "We want to look for witches' marks there as well."

As the bailiff was stepping toward her with a knife, Kuisl quickly grabbed the weapon from his hand.

"I'll do that."

Cautiously he cut off the midwife's straggly hair. Tufts of it fell to the ground around the chair. Martha Stechlin wept softly.

"Don't be afraid, Martha," he whispered into her ear. "I won't hurt you. Not today."

Johann Lechner cleared his throat. "Hangman, I want you to search this woman for witches' marks. Everywhere."

The baker Berchtholdt leaned over toward the clerk.

"You don't really believe he's going to find anything," he muttered. "He's hand in glove with the Stechlin woman. I've seen it myself how she slips him herbs and goodness knows what else. And Keusslin's milkmaid told me that—"

"Master Berchtholdt, we really haven't got the time for your explanations." Johann Lechner turned away in disgust to avoid the baker's foul breath. He considered Berchtholdt a drunkard and a braggart, but at least he could trust him in this matter. He wasn't that certain, though, about his second witness . . . Therefore he turned to Berchtholdt again.

"If it helps us establish the truth, however, we will heed your counsel," he said encouragingly. "Master Augustin, will you kindly assist the hangman in his search?"

Contently, the baker leaned back in his chair as he kept eyeing the prisoner. Meanwhile the powerful wagon driver's son rose with a shrug and slowly strolled toward the midwife. His countenance was finely chiseled and pale, as if he had seen little sun. His eyes sparkled icy blue. He looked upon Martha Stechlin almost with disinterest. Then his index finger softly moved over her skinny body, circling each breast, and finally stopped above her navel.

"Turn around," he whispered.

Trembling, the midwife turned around. His finger glided across the nape of her neck and her shoulders. It paused on the right shoulder blade and tapped on a birthmark that actually seemed larger than the others.

"What do you think of this?"

The wagon driver looked straight in the eyes of the hangman, who had been standing alongside him the whole time.

Jakob Kuisl shrugged. "It's a birthmark. What am I supposed to think?"

Augustin wouldn't give up. Kuisl had the feeling that there was a slight smirk on his lips. "Didn't the two dead children bear this kind of mark on their shoulders as well?"

The clerk and the baker sprang to their feet, and even young Schreevogl came closer, curious to inspect the mark.

Jakob Kuisl blinked and looked more closely. The brown spot was indeed larger than the other birthmarks and tapered to a fine line at the bottom. A few black hairs grew out of it.

The men stood in a circle around Martha Stechlin. The midwife seemed to have given in to her fate and allowed herself to be inspected like a calf at the slaughterhouse. A few times she whimpered softly.

"So they did," whispered the clerk as he stooped over the mark. "It does resemble the devil's sign . . ." The baker Berchtholdt nodded eagerly and crossed himself. Only Jakob Schreevogl shook his head.

"If this is a witches' mark, you have to burn me along with her."

The young patrician had unbuttoned his shirt and pointed to a brown spot on his chest, which was covered with downy hair. Indeed this birthmark too was shaped rather strangely. "I've had this thing since the day I was born, and nobody has yet called me a sorcerer."

The clerk shook his head and turned away from the midwife. "This isn't getting us anywhere. Kuisl, show her the instruments. And explain what we're going to do if she doesn't tell us the truth."

Jakob Kuisl looked deep into Martha Stechlin's eyes. Then he took the pincers from the brazier and approached her. The miracle had not occurred, and he would have to begin the torturing.

At this very moment, the great bell in the tower started ringing the alarm.

CHAPTER
6

SIMON TOOK A DEEP BREATH OF SPRING AIR. FOR the first time in days, he felt fully free. At a distance he could hear the rushing of the river, and the fields were lovely in their rich green. Snowdrops shone between the birches and beeches, which had already started to blossom. Only in the shady patches between the trees could traces of snow still be seen.

He was strolling with Magdalena through the meadows above the Lech, on a footpath so narrow that he and Magdalena touched each other from time to time as if by chance. Twice she had nearly fallen, and each time she had held on to him for support. Longer than was in fact necessary.

After the conversation in the Stern, Simon had hurried down to the river. He needed a quiet moment to think things over and fresh air to breathe. He should have been mixing tinctures for his father, but that could very well wait until tomorrow. In any case Simon preferred to keep out of his father's way now. Even at the deathbed of the poor Kratz boy they had not spoken. The old man had still not forgiven him for leaving the house to visit the executioner. Sometime, as Simon knew, his anger would blow over, but until then it would be better not to get in his way too often. Simon sighed. His father came from a different world, a world in which the dissection of corpses was considered blasphemous and the treatment of the sick consisted exclusively of purges, cuppings, and the administration of evil-smelling pills. He remembered something his father had said at the burial of a plague victim: "God decides when we shall die. We should not meddle in His handiwork."

Simon wanted to do things quite differently. He wanted to meddle in the Lord God's handiwork.

Down by the Lech Gate he met Magdalena, whose mother had sent her to gather wild garlic in the wetlands. She smiled at him in that way again, and he simply followed her. A few washerwomen were standing on the Lech Bridge; he could feel how they were staring at him, but that didn't bother him.

All afternoon they rambled through the forest down by the river. When her hand brushed against his again, he suddenly felt hot. His scalp began to tingle. What was it about this girl that disturbed him so? Was it perhaps the charm of what was forbidden? He knew that he and Magdalena could never become a couple. Not in Schongau, not in this stuffy hole, where only a small suspicion was enough to send a woman to the stake. Simon frowned. Dark thoughts arose like thunderclouds.

"Is there something wrong?" Magdalena stopped and looked at him. She sensed that something was troubling him.

"It is . . . oh, nothing."

"Tell me, or we'll go back at once, and I'll never see you again."

Simon had to smile. "A terrible threat. Even if I believe you would never do it."

"You wait and see. Well, then, what is it?"

"It's . . . about the boys."

Magdalena sighed. "I thought as much." Near the footpath was a tree trunk, blown down in a spring storm. She pushed him toward it and sat down alongside. Her eyes looked into the distance. After a while she began to speak again.

"A terrible thing. I can't get the boys out of my head either, Peter and Anton. I used to see them in the market square, especially Anton. He didn't have anybody. As an orphan, you're worth about as much as a hangman's child. Nothing at all."

Magdalena pressed her full lips together until they only formed a thin red line. Simon put his hand on her shoulder, and for a long time they said nothing.

"Did you know that all the orphans used to meet at Stechlin's?" he finally asked.

Magdalena shook her head.

"Something happened there." Simon looked out across the forest. A long way away the town walls of Schongau were visible.

After a while he spoke again. "Sophie said that they were all at Stechlin's the evening before the murder. Then they all went home, except Peter. He went down to the river to meet someone else. Who could that have been? His murderer? Or is Sophie lying?"

"And what about Anton Kratz? Was he with the Stechlin woman too?" Magdalena was leaning against his shoulder now, her hand resting gently on his thigh. But Simon's thoughts were elsewhere.

"Yes, indeed, Anton too," he said. "And both of them had this strange sign on their shoulders, scratched into the skin with elderberry juice. On Anton it was a bit faded, as if someone had tried to wash it away."

"He himself?" Magdalena's head nestled against his.

Simon continued to gaze into the distance. "Your father

found sulfur in Peter's pocket," he murmured. "And a mandrake is missing from the midwife's house."

Magdalena, surprised, sat up suddenly. As the hangman's daughter she was well informed about magical ingredients.

"A mandrake? Are you sure?" she asked, obviously alarmed.

Simon jumped up from the tree trunk.

"Witches' marks, sulfur, a mandrake . . . It all fits together, don't you think? As if someone would like us to believe in all this spooky stuff."

"Or if all this spooky stuff is in fact true," whispered Magdalena. A cloud had passed over the warm spring sun. She pulled her woolen scarf over her shoulders.

"I visited Goodwife Daubenberger this morning," she began hesitantly. "She told me about Saint Walburga."

She told Simon about her conversation with the midwife and that she supposed the murders had some sort of connection with Walpurgis Night, which was just a week away. When she had finished, Simon shook his head.

"I don't believe in these superstitions," he said. "Witchcraft and such hocus-pocus. There must be some reason these children had to die."

Suddenly Simon remembered the man with the bone hand. Both Sophie and the maid from the Stern had spoken of him. Had he really inquired about the merchant's son? Or was that just one of Sophie's fantasies? With annoyance he recalled that the girl had stolen quite a large sum of money from him. You couldn't trust that child as far as you could throw her.

With a sigh he sat down again next to Magdalena on the tree trunk. He was feeling cold too. The hangman's daughter saw that he was shivering and spread her woolen scarf over his shoulders. She sought his hand, found it, and led it slowly to her bodice.

Simon could not stop thinking about the man with the hand of bone. If he really existed and was responsible for what happened to the children, why had he killed them? What connection was there between the two victims, apart from their having been at Martha Stechlin's on that night of the full moon?

And above all . . .

Who else had been with Goodwife Stechlin?

Magdalena looked at the young physician from one side. He had been so reserved all day. She had to know where she stood with him.

"Simon, I . . . " she began.

At this moment they heard in the distance the high-toned pealing of the alarm bell in the tower, carried to them by the wind. Here in the meadows, far away from the town, it sounded like the whimpering of a child. Something had happened! Simon felt a tightness in his chest. He jumped up and ran in the direction of Schongau. Not until he had run some distance did he notice that Magdalena was not following him.

"Come on, quick!" he cried. "And pray to God that there isn't another corpse in the river."

Magdalena sighed, then stood up and ran after Simon.

The hangman came running up the cellar steps of the dungeon, taking several of them at one stride. Behind him he heard the cries of the town clerk and the others, who were also hurrying to get out. The high-pitched tone of the alarm bell resounded through the town.

The bells in the watchtowers were rung only in extreme emergency, in case of an attack or a fire. Kuisl ruled out an invasion of hostile soldiers. There had been peace now for more than ten years. There were indeed still groups of marauding soldiers who concealed themselves in the woods and attacked isolated farmsteads, but Schongau was too big to be attacked by a handful of daring hooligans. There remained only a fire . . .

Most of the buildings in Schongau were still built of wood, and many roofs were thatched. If the wind was coming from the wrong direction, a smoldering fire could turn into a major conflagration and destroy the whole town. People were terrified of fire, and the hangman, too, was worried about his family.

When Jakob Kuisl reached the outer door of the keep he saw at once that the town was in no immediate danger. A thin column of smoke rose up from the other side of the town wall and spread out to form a cloud. The hangman supposed that the fire was down by the raft landing.

Without waiting for the others he hurried down the Münzstrasse to the Ballenhaus and turned left in the direction of the Lech Gate. Other burghers of Schongau, too, were hurrying to the gate to see what was happening. In the upper stories of the houses with a view over the river, curious people were again opening their shutters, which they had already closed for the night, and were looking down at the spectacle visible on the riverbank.

Jakob Kuisl ran through the Lech Gate and saw down at the raft landing that the Zimmerstadel had caught fire. The roof of the huge warehouse was ablaze. A small group of raftsmen had formed a bucket brigade and were pouring water on the flames. Others hurried to take crates and barrels out of the building. There was a rustling and cracking, and it did not seem to the hangman that the warehouse could be saved. Just the same, he ran toward the bridge to offer his help. He knew that a small fortune would be lost with every crate that went up in flames. Wool, silk, wine, spices . . . The Zimmerstadel held everything that was waiting to be shipped elsewhere in addition to serving as an overflow when there was no more room in the Ballenhaus.

When Kuisl got beyond the town gate, he stopped in his tracks. From up here he was able to see the entire landing area. Down by the dock a crowd of men could be seen engaged in a wild melee. Fists flew, some men already lay on the ground, and others were fighting with long boat poles. Kuisl recognized some of the wagon drivers and raftsmen, but there were strangers among them as well.

The evening sun was sinking behind the woods, and the men and the flames appeared in a surreal light. Jakob Kuisl couldn't believe his eyes: these men were fighting, while only a few yards away the Zimmerstadel was in flames!

"Have you gone mad!" he cried and ran down the last few steps to the bridge. "Stop it! The Stadel's on fire!"

The men did not seem to even notice him. They rolled on the ground. Some were bleeding from the forehead, and others had cuts and bruises on their faces. With his strong arms the hangman seized two of the men who were fighting and pulled them apart. Kuisl recognized one of the men, with a torn doublet, from various drunken brawls in the inns behind the market square. It was Georg Riegg of the Schongau wagon drivers. He was a noted ruffian but enjoyed a good reputation among his men. The other man seemed to be a stranger to the town. His lip was bleeding, and there was a deep cut over his right eyebrow.

"Stop it, I say!" Kuisl shook the pair until they took notice of him. "Go and help save the Stadel!"

"The Augsburgers started the fire. They can put it out!" Georg Riegg spat in the face of his adversary, who raised his fist for another blow.

Kuisl quickly grabbed them both by the hair and shook them before he spoke again. "What did you say?"

"He's talking nonsense!" said the stranger. His accent revealed him as an Augsburger. He waved his arms wildly toward the burning Stadel. "Your watchmen were careless, and now we have to take the blame. But count us out! You'll have to pay for the damage!"

Jakob Kuisl was aware of a movement behind him. He turned and saw from the corner of his eye a rafting pole poised to strike him. Instinctively he let the two ruffians drop and at the same time grabbed the shaft. With a jerk he pushed it away, so that the man at the other end fell screaming into the Lech. From his left side came another attacker, a solidly built raftsman, whom Kuisl recognized as one of the Augsburg guild. With a shout the raftsman charged at him. At the last moment Kuisl dodged and gave the man a strong blow from behind. Groaning, the Augsburger fell to the ground but got up a few seconds later to attack once more. He swung and missed. The next time he struck, the hangman caught his hand and squeezed until the man's fingers began to crack. Step by step he forced the Augsburger toward the end of the pier. Finally he pushed him into the water and let go. With a splash the man disappeared in the river and resurfaced farther down the landing, where he tried to hold on to a wooden pile.

"Stop! In the name of the law, stop it!"

Johann Lechner had arrived at the landing with the watchmen. The four bailiffs, with other Schongauers, pulled the combatants apart.

"You there, get over to the Stadel! Take the buckets with you!" With curt orders the court clerk brought the situation under control, although it was now too late. The roof had fallen in, and every entrance to the interior of the building was blocked by red-hot beams. Whatever remained of the goods in there would sooner or later be reduced to ashes—hundreds of guilders', worth. Charred chests and bales were piled up near the ruins of the Stadel, some of them still smoldering. A smell of scorched cinnamon hung in the air.

The bailiffs had herded the participants in the brawl into a corner of the landing and divided them into two groups, Schongauers and Augsburgers. Men on both sides glowered at each other, but seemed too exhausted to continue.

Jakob Kuisl could see Josef Berchtholdt, the brother of the master baker, among the Schongau fighters. His brother Michael was holding a damp cloth to Josef's swollen left eye and hurling wild curses in the direction of the Augsburgers. The other two witnesses to the examination in the dungeon had disappeared into the crowd.

Meanwhile Bonifaz Fronwieser, Simon's father, had also appeared, after being summoned by the court clerk. With water and linen bandages he began to treat the worst injuries. One of the Schongau wagon drivers had a stab wound to his upper arm. And among the Augsburgers, too, someone was bleeding from a wound in the thigh.

When Kuisl heard the voice of the court clerk he had quickly withdrawn from the fighters. Now he was sitting on one of the piles of the pier, sucking at his pipe, and observing the tumult on the landing.

It looked as if all Schongau had come down to the river to watch the spectacle. The line of people looking at the burned-out ruin went all the way back to the gate. Burning beams continued to crack and fall into the flames. The conflagration lit up the nearby forest like a midsummer bonfire as dusk slowly deepened.

In the meantime Lechner had found the watchman at the landing. He cowered before him, distraught, protesting his innocence.

"Believe me, master," he whimpered. "We don't know how such a fire could have broken out. I was just sitting here playing dice with Benedikt and Johannes, and when I turned around, there was the whole Stadel in flames! Someone must have set it deliberately, otherwise it wouldn't have burned so quickly."

"I know who started the fire," cried Georg Riegg from the Schongau group. "It was the Augsburgers! First they kill our children, and then they set fire to our Stadel so that nobody will want to tie up their rafts here, and everyone will be frightened and avoid our town. The dirty bastards!"

Some of the Schongau wagon drivers became restive again. Stones flew and curses were heard, and it was only with difficulty that the bailiffs were able to keep the two groups apart.

"You think we'd set fire to our own goods!" cried a voice from the Augsburger group. The Schongauers began to mutter and curse. "You didn't watch out properly, and now you want to put the blame on us! You'll pay us back every penny!"

"But what's that over there?" Georg Riegg pointed to the barrels and cases standing in front of the smoldering Stadel. "You had no trouble getting your own stuff out."

"Liar!" the Augsburgers replied. It was almost impossible to restrain them. "We carried them out when the fire started. You guys just stood around yammering."

"Silence, damn it!"

The voice of the court clerk was not particularly loud. Nevertheless there was something about it that compelled the others to silence. Johann Lechner's eyes wandered over the two hostile groups. Finally he pointed to the Augsburg wagon drivers.

"Who's the leader here?"

The huge man whom Jakob Kuisl had earlier pushed into the water stepped forward. Obviously he had succeeded in reaching the bank again. His wet hair hung down his face; his hose and doublet clung to his body. In spite of this he did not look as if he intended to be intimidated by a mere clerk from Schongau. The giant looked into Johann Lechner's face and growled.

"I am."

Lechner looked him up and down. "And what is your name?"

"Martin Hueber, head wagon driver for the house of Fugger."

A few isolated whistles were heard. The Fuggers were now not nearly as powerful as they had been before the Great War, but their name still meant something. Anyone who worked for this family could count on powerful advocates.

If Johann Lechner had taken this into consideration, he didn't let it show. He nodded briefly and said: "Martin Hueber, you will be our guest until this matter is cleared up. Until then you may not leave the town."

Hueber's face turned red. "You can't do that. I'm only subject to Augsburg law!"

"I certainly can do that." Lechner's voice was quiet and penetrating. "You've beaten up people here, and there are witnesses to that. So you can sit here in our jail and drink water."

Cheers and mocking laughter were heard from the Schongau raftsmen. The clerk turned to them.

"There's no cause for merriment at all. Georg Riegg, as leader of this riot you'll be held in the dungeon, and the lazy watchman at the bridge will keep you company. And then we'll see who laughs last."

Georg Riegg, the bridge watchman, and the Augsburger Martin Hueber, protesting loudly, were led away. On the bridge the wagon driver turned once more to the Schongau men.

"You'll be sorry for this!" he cried. "The Fuggers will know tomorrow what's happened here. And then God help you. You'll compensate us for every bale. Every single one!"

Lechner sighed. Then he turned to the burgomaster who stood beside him with a face white as chalk.

"There's a curse on this town. And all that since this witch killed the boy," he said.

Burgomaster Karl Semer looked at him, wondering.

"Do you think that the Stechlin woman set fire—?"

Lechner shrugged. Finally he smiled.

"It's possible. We must make sure that she confesses. That should clear the air, and everyone will be satisfied."

The burgomaster nodded, relieved. Then the two aldermen made their way back into the town.

———

The little girl pressed a wooden doll to her narrow chest, from which a rattling sound emerged with every breath. Her face was pale and sunken, and deep rings had formed under her eyes. Again she had to cough, hard and painfully. Her throat hurt. In the distance she heard the others down by the Lech. Something had happened. She struggled to sit up in bed and look through the window. But she could only see the sky, some clouds, and a column of smoke between them. Her father had told her that everything was all right, she should not get excited, and she needed to stay in bed. Later the physician would come and help her if the cold compresses didn't work. The girl smiled. She hoped the young doctor would come and not the old one. She liked the young doctor—once he had given her an apple in the market square and asked her how she was. Not many people asked her how she was, in fact nobody.

Clara was five years old when she lost her parents—first her mother, who after the birth of a little brother had not woken up again. Clara could still remember her mother's laughter and her big friendly eyes, and that before she went to sleep her mother had often sung to her. As she walked behind the wooden coffin she imagined that her mother was just asleep and she would soon wake up and come home. Her father had held her hand. When the funeral procession had come to the new cemetery at Saint Sebastian's Church and they were lowering the coffin down into the earth, he had grasped her hand so hard that she screamed. The women thought she was crying for her mother and patted her on the head.

After that her father steadily declined. It began with the same coughing that she herself now had, hard and dry. Soon he was spitting blood, and the neighbors looked down at her with pity and shook their heads. In the evening she often sat by her father's bed and sang the same songs her mother had always sung. He had only her, and she had only him. His brothers and sisters had moved away because there were enough basketmakers in Schongau, or they were dead, just like the little brother, who, without his mother's breast, had cried for three days and suddenly fell silent.

Her father died on a cold damp day in the fall, and they carried him to the same cemetery as his wife. The mother's grave was still quite new, and digging was easy.

Clara spent the next weeks with the neighbor woman, together with a half dozen other children. At the table they fought over the only bowl of barley porridge, but she wasn't hungry anyway. She crept under the bench near the stove and wept. She was all alone. If the neighbor sometimes gave her sweets, the others took it away from her. The only thing she had left was the wooden doll that her father had once carved for her. She never put it down, not during the day and not at night, for it was the last reminder of her parents.

A month later a friendly young man came. He stroked her head and told her that from now on she would be called Clara Schreevogl. He led her into a big two-story house directly by the market square. It had wide stairs and lots of rooms with heavy brocade curtains. The Schreevogls already had five children, and it was said that Maria Schreevogl could not have any more. They took her up like their own child. And when at first the other children gossiped behind her back and called her bad names, her foster father came and whipped them so hard with a hazel switch that they couldn't sit down for three days.

Clara ate the same fine food, she wore the same linen clothes, but even so she noticed that she was different. She was an orphan, living off charity. When there was a family celebration, at Easter or on the Eve of Saint Nicholas, she felt there was an invisible wall between herself and the Schreevogls. She saw the affectionate looks and embraces of the others, unsaid words, gestures, and caresses, and then she ran to her room and wept again. Silently, so that nobody would notice it.

Outside she could hear shouting and bawling in front of the

house. Clara couldn't bear to stay in bed any longer. She pulled herself up, pushed the heavy eiderdown comforter to one side, and slid down onto the cold wooden floor. Immediately a feeling of dizziness came over her. She had a fever, her legs felt like wet clay, but nevertheless she dragged herself the few steps to the window and looked out.

Down by the Lech, the Stadel was on fire. Tongues of fire licked up into the sky, and all of Schongau had come down to the raft landing. Clara's foster parents, the children, and the nurse-maid were also down there to witness the spectacle. They had left only her, the sick orphan, behind. In her wild escape three days before, she had fallen into the Lech. Before the current had carried her away she had managed, in the nick of time, to hold on to a bunch of rushes. She had crawled up the bank and run home through a swamp and thickets. She kept looking around for the men, but they had disappeared. The other children were gone too. Not until she had reached the oak tree near the Küh Gate did she meet Anton and Sophie again. Anton looked at her with eyes wide with terror and cried again and again that he had seen the devil. He didn't stop until Sophie gave him a box on the ear. And now he was dead, and Clara knew why. Although she was only ten years old, she could imagine what had happened. Clara was afraid.

At this moment she heard the squeaking of the front door. Her foster parents must have returned. Her first impulse was to call out to them, but something held her back. The Schreevogls' arrival home was always accompanied by noise, doors slamming, children laughing, noise on the stairs. Even when the nurse came back from the market you could hear the rattling of keys and baskets being put away. But now it was deathly quiet, as if some-body had tried to open the door carefully and had been betrayed by the squeaking. Clara heard a creak on the stairs. Instinctively she ran back to the bed and crept under it. Dust got into her nose, she had to repress a sneeze. From her hiding place she saw the door of her room slowly opening. Two mud-stained boots paused on the threshold. Clara held her breath. They were certainly not her foster father's boots; he paid great attention to his appearance. She didn't know whose boots they were, but she recognized the mud on them. Clara's shoes had looked just like that three days before. It was the mud from the swamp through which she had fled.

The men had come back, or at least one of them.

The dust made her nose itch again, she felt something tickling her right hand. As Clara glanced down, she saw a spider crawl over her finger and disappear in the darkness under the bed. She stifled a cry and stared at the boots still standing on the threshold. She heard the measured breathing of a man; then the boots disappeared. Steps tapped up the stairs to the rooms above. Clara listened carefully to the sound. It was different from the sound of normal steps. A dragging and scraping at regular intervals. She remembered the night of her flight. One of her pursuers had a strange gait. He had . . . limped! Clara was sure that the man up there on the stairs was the limper. Perhaps now he wouldn't be so quick?

Clara waited a moment, then crawled out from under the bed and hurried on tiptoe to the open door. She looked up the stairs but couldn't see anyone. The stranger must have gone into one of the upper rooms. Silently she crept downstairs.

When she had reached the entrance hall, she remembered that she had left her doll upstairs.

She bit her lip. In front of her the outside door stood wide open; she could hear the noise down by the river. The first people appeared to be making their way back to town.

Clara shut her eyes for a second, then hurried upstairs again and entered her room. There on the bed lay her doll. She picked it up and was just about to run downstairs again when she heard steps from above. Hurried steps.

The man had heard her.

The steps became quicker; the man was taking several stairs in one stride. Clara rushed out of the room, her doll pressed closely against her. On the threshold she glanced up the stairs. A black shadow seemed to fall over her, a bearded man in a cloak, his right hand stretched out toward her. It was the devil, and he had a white hand of bones.

Clara slammed the door of her room shut and bolted it. From outside something hit the door, and she could hear a voice cursing quietly. Then the man threw himself with his full force against the door, so that the frame shook. Once, twice . . . Clara ran to the window, which was still open. She wanted to call for help, but she was choked with fear. Only a hoarse croaking came out. Beneath her the street was still empty of people. A long way away she saw the crowds pressing through the Lech Gate back into town. She wanted to wave, but she realized that it would be useless. Probably the people would just wave back cheerfully.

Behind her, wood splintered. Clara turned and saw the point of a saber making its way through an ever-widening split in the middle of the door. She looked down again at the street in front of the house. Her room was on the second floor, about ten feet from the ground. Just next to the entrance of the house a peasant had left a cart with winter straw.

Without pausing to think Clara stuffed her doll down between her breast and nightgown and climbed over the sill. Then she slid down until she was hanging by both hands from the sill. Behind her the splintering was louder, a bolt was pushed aside. With a little cry Clara let go and fell straight into the hay wagon. She felt pain in her right shoulder as she scraped against the wooden frame. Without paying any attention to it, she scrambled over the side and slid to the ground. With straw in her hair and in her nightgown she fled along the street. She turned around once and saw the devil standing at the window, gesturing with his bone hand. He seemed to be calling something to her.

Farewell! We'll meet again soon . . .

Clara heard voices in her feverish head. Everything swam before her eyes; her legs kept running as if by themselves. The rattling in her chest continued to throb while she staggered through the empty alleys. The devil was at her heels, and there was nobody who could help her.

When Simon and Magdalena finally reached the raft landing, most of the Schongauers had already returned to town. Firefighters were busy pushing down the smoking beams and pouring water on the remaining embers. Otherwise only a few onlookers were watching. At least the danger of the fire reaching the watchmen's houses and the wooden pier had been averted.

Simon asked some of the men what had happened. Finally he noticed the hangman sitting on one of the wooden piles in the background smoking his pipe and thoughtfully contemplating the remains of the Stadel. As Simon and Magdalena approached him, he looked up.

"Well? Have you had a pleasant day?"

Simon felt the blood mounting to his face. Magdalena very sensibly looked in the other direction.

"I . . . we . . . I was helping Magdalena to gather wild garlic, and then we saw the smoke," the physician stammered. He looked at the ruins and shook his head. "This is terrible. It will cost the town a fortune!"

The hangman shrugged.

"If it was anyone from the town . . . Our raftsmen say the Augsburgers set fire to the Stadel after taking their own goods out."

Simon looked over his shoulder. There were indeed cases, bales, and sacks piled up at a safe distance from the smoking ruin. A few Augsburg raftsmen, casting black glances all around, stood near them and were obviously on guard.

"Well?" he asked the hangman. "What do you think?"

Jakob Kuisl took another drag on his pipe.

"Anyway, they put their goods in a safe place while we were fighting with them." He stood up and stretched his legs.

Finally he muttered: "One thing is clear. The fire was set deliberately by someone. I've lit a few fires myself, for executions. It takes a bit of work to get it to burn well. You can't just throw a torch on it."

"Arson?" inquired Simon.

"You can bet your life on that."

"But why?"

"Don't know. But we'll find out sooner or later."

The hangman started walking toward the bridge. As he passed them he shook his head.

"In any case, there's one good thing about the fire," he said.

Simon walked after him.

"What is it?"

"If they question the Augsburgers and Schongauers about it, then we get a reprieve for the Stechlin woman. At any rate, she's safe for today."

Jakob Kuisl trudged over the wooden bridge. Suddenly he turned around again.

"Oh, I almost forgot. You should just stop by at young Schreevogl's house. He asked me to tell you that his Clara is ill. And you send Magdalena home, understand?"

Simon turned to the hangman's daughter. She smiled.

"Father likes you."

Simon frowned. "You really think so?"

"Sure. Otherwise he'd have cut off your family jewels long ago and thrown you in the Lech. You can't imagine how fast."

The physician grinned. Then he considered what it must be like to have the hangman for an enemy. He hoped that Magdalena was right.

———

Jakob Kuisl headed back to the prison. In the meantime it was getting dark in the streets. A single bailiff was standing in front of the keep. They had left him there and ordered him to keep watch while all the others ran down to the raft landing. Since then a few of them had reappeared with Georg Riegg and the watchman at the bridge, had locked up the two of them without further comment, and had returned to the river again.

The young man looked worried. He seemed to be the only person in the town who didn't know what had happened. And now the hangman had come back alone. Where were the others? The court clerk? The witnesses?

"That's enough for today," growled Kuisl and pushed the bailiff aside. "Time to leave. Just have to put the things away. Did you lock up the Stechlin woman again?"

The bailiff nodded. He was barely eighteen years old, his face deeply marked with smallpox. Finally he could no longer restrain his curiosity. "What's been happening down there?" he asked.

"The Stadel burned down," said Kuisl. "Want to go and look?"

The bailiff looked uncertainly behind him into the entrance of the keep. The hangman clapped him on the shoulder.

"The witch won't run away, I'll take care of that. And now off you go."

The youth nodded thankfully, then handed the keys over to Kuisl. A few seconds later he disappeared behind the corner of the house next door.

Jakob Kuisl entered the interior of the keep. Immediately the chill of the stone walls enveloped him. A musty smell of urine and damp straw lay in the air. In the left-hand cell sat Georg Riegg and the bridge watchman. They had locked up the Augsburg wagon driver in the small but more comfortable room in the Ballenhaus, so as not to further provoke the powerful neighboring city.

The Schongauers seemed to have temporarily accepted their situation. Each had withdrawn into a corner of the cell and was dozing. When the raftsman saw the hangman, he jumped up and shook the bars of the grill.

"Kuisl, look here! They've locked us up with the witch. Do something, before she casts a spell on us," he shouted.

"Shut your mouth."

The hangman did not look at him and went on to the neighboring cell.

The bailiff had locked up Martha Stechlin again, but mercifully he returned her clothing to her. She had crept into a corner and covered her shorn head with both hands. As Kuisl approached the bars of the grille, a rat whisked between his feet.

"Martha, this is important," he said. "Look at me."

The midwife blinked at him.

"I need the names of the children," he whispered.

"Which names?"

The hangman put his finger to his lips and nodded toward the other cell. Then he continued whispering.

"The names of the children who were with you the night before the murder. Every single one. If we are going to get you out of here, I must know what happened."

Martha Stechlin told him the names. There were five. All except Peter Grimmer were orphans. Two of them were no longer alive.

Lost in thought, Jakob Kuisl drummed his fingers against the iron bars. These children must have some secret. He kicked out at another rat, slamming it into a corner, where it squealed and died.

"See you tomorrow, Martha," he said, this time aloud. "Tomorrow it may hurt a bit, but you must be strong."

"Ha, she'll scream, the witch! And we'll be right near, all right," Georg Riegg shouted at them. The wagon driver shook the iron bars again. At the same time he kicked the dozing watchman, who sat up suddenly and looked at him, shocked.

"You be quiet, Riegg," the watchman whispered. "Just be happy that they're not going to torture us."

The hangman went out into the night. But at the next corner he stopped and stood as if rooted to the ground.

From the market square a crowd with torches was coming toward him.

When Simon Fronwieser reached the Schreevogls' house to look at the sick child, he saw at once that something was not right. In front of the door a dozen people had assembled. A few had lit lanterns in the gathering darkness. The flickering light threw unnaturally big shadows on the walls of the houses, and the faces of the curious were bathed in a dull red light. People whispered, again and again fingers were pointed up at the second floor. Simon heard someone say: "He flew out of the window and took her with him. The devil incarnate, as true as I stand here!" Another uttered curses against Martha Stechlin and wanted to see her burn that very day.

Directly above the physician the shutters of a window stood wide open. The right shutter swung crookedly on its lower hinge, as if a heavy man had held fast to it. Splinters of glass were scattered on the street. From the upper rooms a woman could be heard sobbing. At that moment she uttered such a shrill cry of grief that Simon thought the other glass panes would be shattered as well.

The physician made his way through the crowd and began to climb the broad, thickly carpeted stairs up to the second floor. The crying came out of the room on the left. A maid and another servant, pale as death, were standing in front of the door. The maid was mumbling prayers and fingering a rosary. Simon examined the damaged door. The thin wood in the middle had been broken out and the splinters lay on the carpet. Through the chest-high hole Simon could see Maria Schreevogl lying on her stomach in the bed, her fingers clutching the comforter, her head buried in the pillows. Jakob Schreevogl sat alongside her on the edge of the bed and stroked his wife's hair, talking softly to her and trying to calm her. Two chairs in the room had been upset; a picture of the Holy Virgin lay on the floor, the frame shattered. Right across her peacefully smiling face was the impression of a boot.

When Jakob Schreevogl saw the physician standing at the splintered door, he nodded to him and asked him to come in.

"If you've come to see our sick Clara, you've come too late," whispered Schreevogl. Simon saw that he, too, had been weeping. The face of the young alderman was even paler than usual. The arched, rather oversize nose stuck out under eyes red with tears, his otherwise carefully arranged hair looked unkempt and fell over his forehead.

"What's happened?" Simon asked.

Maria Schreevogl began to scream again: "The devil has taken her! He flew into the room and took our little Clara . . . " The rest was drowned in sobs.

Jakob Schreevogl shook his head.

"We don't know exactly what happened," he said. "Someone must have . . . kidnapped her. He opened the street door, although it was locked, then he kicked down the upper door, seized our little Clara, and obviously jumped out of the window with her."

"Out of the window?" Simon frowned. He went over to the window and looked down. Directly beneath him stood a hay wagon.

The physician nodded. With a bold jump it would be possible to get down without breaking all one's bones.

"Someone down on the street said that he or it flew away with little Clara," Simon said, looking down at the crowd below.

He could hear angry sounds like the buzzing of bees coming from the crowd down below. "Are there any eyewitnesses?"

"Anton Stecher says he saw it with his own eyes," said Schreevogl and again took the hand of his wife, who was sobbing quietly to herself. He shook his head. "Until now I always believed that all this with the children and the murders had a natural explanation, but now . . . " Schreevogl's voice faltered. He turned to Simon. "What do you think, then?" he asked the physician.

Simon shrugged. "I don't believe anything that I haven't seen for myself. And I see that the house was broken into and that the child has disappeared."

"But the street door was locked."

"An experienced man with a skeleton key, nothing easier than that."

Schreevogl nodded. "I see," he said. "Then Anton Stecher was lying."

"Not necessarily," answered Simon. He pointed to the hay cart under the window. "I think it happened this way. A man got through the front door with a skeleton key. Clara heard him and bolted the door of her room. He broke down this door and there was a struggle. Finally he jumped out of the window with Clara right into the hay wagon. Then he made off with her."

Schreevogl frowned. "But why did he jump out of the window with the child? Couldn't he have just gone out again through the front door?"

Simon could think of no quick answer. Instead he asked: "Clara was an orphan, wasn't she?"

Schreevogl nodded. "Her parents died five years ago. The town assigned her to us as a ward. But we treated her exactly like one of our own children. My wife was particularly fond of her."

Tears came to his eyes. He wiped them away hastily. His wife had turned away from the men and was crying quietly into the pillows.

Meanwhile the crowd under the window had grown larger. A noisy disturbance could be heard. Simon looked out. Newcomers were arriving, bringing torches. Something big seemed to be happening down there.

The physician thought a bit. Anton Kratz had been an orphan too, and Peter Grimmmer had grown up without a mother—and all of them had been at Martha Stechlin's the night before the first murder . . .

"Did your Clara often visit the midwife Martha Stechlin?" he asked the alderman. Jakob Schreevogl shrugged.

"I don't always know where she went. It's possible . . . "

"She went to the midwife's quite often," his wife interrupted him. Maria Schreevogl's voice was now firmer. "She told me herself that they met at her house. I thought nothing of it . . . "

"Two days ago, in the morning, when little Grimmer died," Simon asked, "did you notice anything unusual about Clara?"

Jakob Schreevogl thought for a moment, then he nodded. "She was very pale and wouldn't eat her breakfast. We thought she was beginning to run a fever . . . Finally, later in the day, she did become ill. When she heard about little Peter, she went up to her room and didn't come down again until the evening. We thought it would be better to leave her alone for a bit. After all, Peter was her playmate."

"She had the mark on her."

"What!" Simon started up from his thoughts.

Maria Schreevogl had raised her head and gazed into the distance. Then she repeated: "She had the sign on her."

Jakob Schreevogl looked incredulously at his wife. "What are you saying?" he whispered.

Maria Schreevogl stared at the wall in front of her as she spoke: "In the evening I gave her a bath in the tub. I thought a hot bath with herbs would drive away the fever. She resisted, but finally I got her undressed. Then she tried to hold her shoulder underwater, but I saw it. It was the same sign they're all talking about, very faded, but still visible."

Simon could scarcely speak. "A circle with a cross under it?" he asked at last.

Maria Schreevogl nodded.

There was a long pause. Only the angry cries of the crowd outside could be heard. At last Jakob Schreevogl sprang up. His face was bright red.

"Why didn't you ever mention it to me, damn it?" he shouted.

His wife began to cry again. "I . . . I . . . didn't want to believe it. I thought, if I didn't think about it, it would go away . . . " She began to sob once more.

"You stupid woman! We might have saved her! We could have asked her what the sign means. Now it's too late!"

Jakob Schreevogl rushed out of the room and disappeared, slamming the door. Simon ran after him. Standing on the stairs, he heard loud cries from below. "Let's go!" someone cried. "We'll get her!"

Simon changed his mind and ran downstairs. Outside he encountered a mob armed with torches, scythes, and pikes heading off toward Münzstrasse. He could even recognize some of the bailiffs. There was nothing to be seen of the court clerk and the other aldermen.

"What are you doing?" Simon screamed after the mob.

One of the rioters, the tanner Gabriel, turned round. He had told Simon about the accident with little Grimmer. "We're going to get the witch before she takes any more of our children," he said.

His face was twisted into a strange grimace in the reflected light of the torches and his teeth shone bright white in the darkness.

"But the Stechlin woman is in prison," Simon said, trying to calm them down. "Anyway, they say it was a man who took little Clara."

"It was the devil!" roared another. Simon recognized him as Anton Stecher, the eyewitness who claimed to have seen the abductor.

"He had a white hand of bone, and he was flying! That Stechlin hag brought him here by witchcraft!" he cried, as he hurried after the others.

"But that's nonsense!" Simon shouted into the darkness, but nobody seemed to hear him anymore. Suddenly he was aware of noisy steps behind him. Jakob Schreevogl had hurried down-stairs, a lantern in his right hand, his sword in the left. He seemed to have recovered his composure again.

"We must go after them and stop them before there's a blood-bath," he said. "They are completely out of control." Simon watched as he headed into the Münzstrasse, then chased after him.

As he ran, he turned to the alderman and asked, "Then you don't believe in witchcraft anymore?" he asked.

"I don't believe in anything anymore," panted Schreevogl, as they turned into the Weinstrasse. "Neither in the devil nor the Heavenly Father. And now let's hurry, before they break open the door of the keep!"

The court clerk Johann Lechner was looking forward to a warm bath. He had instructed the servants to heat the boiler down in the court kitchen. In the meantime the wooden tub in his room had been lined with linen sheets and half-filled with hot water. Lechner opened his doublet and hose, laid his clothes neatly over the chair, and with a shudder of pleasure slid into the tub. It smelled of thyme and lavender. Brushwood and rushes were strewn on the floor. The clerk needed this bath urgently to think it all through.

Everything was happening so fast. There were now two dead children and a Stadel burnt to the ground. Lechner was still not quite sure there was any connection between the two events.

It was quite possible that the Augsburgers had set fire to the Stadel. The Schongauers' transport monopoly had long been a thorn in their side. And hadn't it happened once before, a long time ago? The clerk resolved to have a look at the records.

But it seemed too far-fetched to him that the Augsburg raftsmen would kill Schongau children. On the other hand . . . the Stadel fire, the horrible murders, and then the damned leper house being planned just outside town, only because the church had set its mind on it. There were certainly enough reasons to avoid Schongau at the present time and choose another route. So it was the Augsburgers who profited most from all the terrible events in the town. In his long years as clerk to the council Lechner had learned one thing above all else: if you want to know who is responsible for anything, ask who benefits from it.

Cui bono?

Lechner put his head under the water and enjoyed the warmth and silence that surrounded him. Peace at last, no boring discussions, no quarrelsome aldermen seeking only their own advantage, no intrigues. After a minute he ran out of air and had to surface, spluttering.

Whether or not there was a connection between the fire and the murders, there was one sure way to restore peace to the town. The Stechlin woman would have to confess. At the stake all the problems would go up in smoke. Tomorrow he would continue with the questioning, even if it was illegal without approval from Munich.

Perhaps, too, the questioning of the combative Schongauer Georg Riegg and that insolent Augsburger would somehow resolve itself. One of the Fuggers' raftsmen! As if anything like that would impress him, Lechner! And just for his arrogant behavior alone he would keep him under arrest for a few days in the Ballenhaus.

There was a knock at the door, and a servant entered with another steaming bucket. Lechner nodded his thanks, and a deluge of hot water poured over the court clerk's tense back. When the servant left, Lechner reached for the scrub brush. There was a second knock. Irritated, he let the brush sink.

"What is it?" he growled toward the door.

The servant's voice sounded nervous. "Sir, excuse the disturbance . . ."

"Just tell me what the matter is!"

"Something else has happened. They say that . . . the devil has flown away with little Clara Schreevogl, and now the people are running to the keep and want to see the Stechlin woman burned at the stake. They have pikes and lances and torches . . ."

Cursing, the clerk threw the brush into the water and reached for a dry towel. For a moment he considered letting things simply take their course. The sooner the Stechlin woman was put to the stake, the better. But then it occurred to him that he still represented the law in Schongau.

Hastily he pulled his shirt on. The Stechlin woman would burn all right. But only when he ordered it.

When the hangman saw the mob he knew at once where they wanted to go. He turned and ran the few yards back to the keep and stood resolutely at the front entrance. The huge tower had only one way in. Anyone wanting to get to the Stechlin woman would have to get past him. With a determined gaze and folded arms he waited for the group, which had now grown to two dozen men. In the light of the torches Kuisl recognized the usual troublemakers. The baker Michael Berchtholdt was marching at the head of the group. But some of the aldermen's sons were there also. He could recognize the youngest offspring of Semer, the burgomaster. Many in the mob were armed with pikes and scythe blades. When they saw the hangman, they stopped and started to murmur. Then Berchtholdt, eager to please the crowd, addressed him with a broad grin.

"We've come for the witch!" he shouted. "Hand over the key, Kuisl, or there'll be trouble."

Shouts of support were heard from the mob, and out of the darkness a stone was thrown at him, which bounced off his chest. The hangman didn't yield an inch but looked at Berchtholdt with a cold stare.

"Is this the elected witness to this morning's inquisition speaking, or a rabble-rouser whom I shall have to string up on the nearest tree this very night?"

The grin on the master baker's face disappeared. Then he regained his composure.

"You must not have heard what's happened, Kuisl," he said. "The Stechlin woman called upon the devil, and he's flown away with the little Schreevogl girl."

He looked around at a few of his companions. "If we don't hurry, he'll fly away with the witch too. Perhaps she's gone already."

The mob growled and pushed nearer to the heavy iron door, which the hangman defended with his broad shoulders.

"I know only this: that the law still applies here," said Jakob Kuisl, "and not a few stupid peasants running through the town with scythes and threshing flails to frighten peaceful burghers."

"You watch it, Kuisl," Stecher chimed in. "There are many of us, and you don't even have a cudgel. We'll kill you before you know it, and then we'll burn you and the witch together!"

The hangman smiled and raised his right arm. "This is my cudgel," he said. "Would anyone like to feel it on his back? Nobody?"

The crowd fell silent. Jakob Kuisl was famous for his

strength, and anyone who had ever seen how he hauled up a thief with the noose around his neck or raised the six-foot execution sword to strike a blow at his hapless victim certainly had no wish to start a quarrel with him. Fifteen years earlier he had taken over his father's office, and before that he had been in the Great War. They said that back then he had killed more people than would fit in the old Schongau cemetery.

The mob moved back several feet. There was silence. The hangman stood there rooted to the spot.

Suddenly Anton Stecher charged forward. He had a flail in his hand, which he brandished at Kuisl.

"Down with the witch!" he shouted.

The hangman turned away, avoiding the flail, seized it by the handle and pulled Stecher toward him. Then he punched him in the nose and tossed him effortlessly back into the crowd. The men withdrew, and Stecher fell to the ground, a stream of blood pouring onto the cobblestones.

The peasant, whimpering, crept back out of sight.

"Anyone else?" asked Kuisl.

The men looked at one another uncertainly, whispering nervously. Everything had happened so quickly. At the back of the group some started to put out their lanterns and scurry home.

Suddenly a rhythmic tread could be heard in the distance. Jakob Kuisl pricked up his ears. Marching feet were approaching from the castle. At last, followed by a squad of soldiers, Lechner and the presiding burgomaster appeared.

At the same moment Simon and Jakob Schreevogl arrived from the market square. When the young alderman saw the court clerk, he put his sword back in its sheath. "Thank God," he panted. "It isn't too late. They can say what they like about Lechner, but he has the town under control."

Simon watched the soldiers approach the mob with their lances poised. In just a few seconds the rioters had thrown down their weapons and were looking about fearfully.

"It's all over!" Lechner cried out. "Go home! Nothing will happen to anyone who goes now."

One after the other they disappeared into the narrow alleys of the town. Young Semer ran to his father, who gave him a rap on the head and sent him home. Simon shook his head. The boy had almost committed a murder, and the presiding burgomaster sent him home to have supper . . . Martha Stechlin's life was not worth a penny.

Only now did burgomaster Semer see the hangman, who was still on guard by the door of the keep. "You did well!" he called to him. "After all, the council rules here and not the man on the street." He turned to the court clerk and continued. "Although one can understand the people. Two dead children and a girl kidnapped . . . Most of us have families ourselves. It's time to put a stop to all this."

The clerk nodded. "Tomorrow," he said. "Tomorrow we shall know more."

The devil limped through the streets and held his nose into the wind, as if he could smell his victim. He paused at dark corners and listened carefully; he looked under every oxcart, he poked at every dung heap. She couldn't be far away. It was impossible that she had escaped him.

He heard a noise, and above him someone opened a window. The devil pressed against the wall of the house. In his black coat he was almost invisible in the night. A stream of urine poured into the street close by, then the window shut again. The devil pulled his coat closer around him and continued his search.

In the distance shouts could be heard, but they did not concern him. They were all about the woman they had put in prison. He heard they believed that the woman had summoned him. He couldn't help smiling. What a thing to imagine. What did the witch look like? Well, he'd get to see her soon, no doubt. First he had to make sure that he got his money. He was hoping that the others had been doing good work out there while he was tidying up here. He spat. Again they had left the dirty work to him. Or had he wished for it himself? Shadows appeared in his field of vision, bloody shapes, terrible images . . . Screaming women with gaping holes where breasts should have been, babies dashed to pieces like toys on the burnt remains of walls, headless priests in bloodstained cassocks.

He brushed away the images with his hand and put his cool bony fingers on his brow. That did him good. The images vanished. The devil marched on.

Up on top of the Küh Gate he saw the guard dozing. He was leaning on his lance and staring out into the night. He could hear a soft, snoring sound.

Then he saw the neglected garden near the Küh Gate. The fence had collapsed, the building behind was a ruin left over from the last days of the war. In the garden ivy and knotweed crept up the town wall. There, almost hidden by the leaves, a ladder was leaning. The devil jumped over the remains of the fence and looked at the ground beneath the wall. It was just past the full moon and there was sufficient light to see prints in the damp earth. Children's footprints. The devil bent down and inhaled the scent of the earth.

She had gotten away from him.

Though the ladder was not well attached, he was able to climb it nimbly, like a cat. At the top, a ledge, an arm's length wide, ran along the town wall. He looked to the left, from where the snoring of the night watchman could still be heard. He turned to the right and ran along the ledge, where battlements with arrow slits appeared at regular intervals. After about a hundred yards he suddenly stopped and then went back a few paces. He was not mistaken.

Next to one of the arrow slits some of the stones in the wall had been broken out, so that the hole was three times as big as before.

Big enough for a child.

On the other side, the branch of an oak tree stretched out to the wall. One or two of the twigs had been freshly broken off. The devil put his head through the hole, sniffing the cool April air.

He would seek her and find her. Perhaps then the pictures in his mind would go away.

CHAPTER

7

IT WAS A COLD MORNING, AND A THIN LAYER OF hoarfrost covered the meadows around the town. Dense fog was billowing from the river. The matins bell was sounding from the Church of the Assumption. Though it was still early, some peasants were already working the brown fields that lay above town in a checkerboard pattern. Bending low, they dragged their plows and harrows across the soil, which was still half frozen. Small clouds of white vapor were expelled from their mouths at every breath. Several of the peasants had hitched oxen to their carts and were prodding them along, swearing loudly. Some merchants had arrived early and were moving toward the Lech and Küh gates with their carts, which were piled with crates containing honking geese and squealing piglets. Tired wagon drivers were fastening a dozen barrels on a raft down near the bridge. It was five o'clock, the gates to the city were open again, and the town was slowly coming to life.

Jakob Kuisl was standing in front of his house outside the

town walls, watching the hustle and bustle of the morning. He was swaying slightly, and his throat was on fire. One more time he lifted the tankard to his parched lips, only to notice again that it was empty. Swearing softly, he hurled it onto the dung heap so that the chickens fluttered up in a panic, cackling despite the early hour.

With heavy feet the hangman plodded the thirty yards down to the pond. On the edge of the rushes, he stripped off his hose and doublet. Standing at the water's edge shivering, he took a short breath, then jumped off the wooden pier without further hesitation. The cold pricked him like needles. For a moment he was entirely numb. But at the same time it made him think clearly again. After a few vigorous strokes, the numb feeling in his head subsided, and the tiredness gave way to a refreshed and clear sensation. He knew that this sensation would be short-lived and soon followed by a leaden tiredness, but it could be counteracted with further drinking.

Jakob Kuisl had been drinking heavily all night. He had started off on wine and beer, then in the wee hours had moved on to brandy. Several times his head had dropped onto the table, but time and again he had straightened up and raised the mug to his lips. Occasionally, Anna Maria Kuisl had peeked into the smoke-filled kitchen, but she knew that she couldn't help her husband. These excesses occurred at regular intervals. Complaining was pointless: it would only have made him angrier and prodded him to drink even more heavily. So she let him have his way, as she knew that it too would pass. As the hangman always drank alone, most burghers weren't even aware of his periodic drunkenness. Anna Maria Kuisl, however, could predict with some accuracy when it would happen again. It was worst when an execution or a torturing was coming up. Then he sometimes screamed deliriously and his fingernails clawed the table, while his brain was swept by nightmares.

Jakob Kuisl was tall, and so he could hold his drink rather

well. Yet this time there seemed to be no way of getting rid of the alcohol. As he swam across the small duck pond once again, he realized how his fear was getting the better of him. He pulled himself up on the wooden pier, hurriedly put on his clothes, and headed for his house.

In the kitchen, he searched the cupboards for something to drink. When he found nothing there, he went to his apothecary cabinet in the room next door. On the top left shelf of the six-foot cupboard he discovered a vial that held a shining, bilious green liquid. Kuisl grinned. He knew that for the most part his cough syrup consisted of alcohol. The added herbs could only help him in his present state. The opium poppy in particular would have a soothing effect. The hangman tipped his head backward and let the liquid drip onto his tongue. He wanted to taste every drop of the potent brew.

When he heard the creaking of the kitchen door, he froze. His wife was standing there, sleepily rubbing her eyes.

"Drinking again?" she asked. "Wouldn't you rather stop now—"

"Leave me alone, woman. I'll need it."

He lifted the little bottle again and emptied it in one swig.

Then he wiped his mouth and stepped out into the kitchen. He reached for the heel of bread on the table. He hadn't eaten since yesterday noon.

"You have to go to see the Stechlin woman?" asked Anna Maria, who was well aware of the hard task that her husband faced.

The hangman shook his head. "Not yet," he said with his mouth full. "Not before noon. First the bigwigs have to discuss what to do on account of what happened to the Stadel. You see, there are others to be interrogated now too."

"And those you're also going to have to—"

He laughed dryly. "I don't really think they'll put the branding iron to one of the Fugger wagoners. And as for Georg Riegg—everyone knows him here, and he has his cronies."

Anna Maria sighed. "Yes, it's always the poor people who suffer."

Angrily, the hangman slammed his fist on the table, so that the beer tankards and the wineglasses tottered dangerously. "It's the wrong people that suffer, not the poor. The wrong ones!"

His wife stepped behind him and put her hands on his shoulders. "You can't change it, Jakob. Just let it be," she said.

He pushed Anna Maria's arms off and began to pace back and forth in the narrow room. He had been racking his brains all night about how he might avoid the inevitable. But nothing had occurred to him. The alcohol had made his thoughts slow and clumsy. There was no way out; after the twelve o'clock bell he'd have to start torturing Martha Stechlin. If he didn't go, he would be relieved of his office and banned from the town along with his family. He'd have to earn his living as an itinerant barber, or a beggar.

On the other hand . . . Martha Stechlin had brought his children into the world, and he was convinced that she was innocent. How could he torture this woman?

He finally stopped pacing in front of his apothecary's cupboard. The chest next to it, where he kept his most valuable books, was open. On the very top there lay a yellowed, worn copy of the book about herbs by the Greek physician Dioscorides, an ancient work, which, however, was still useful. On a sudden impulse, he reached for the book and began leafing through it. As so often, he felt admiration for the exact drawings and precise descriptions of many hundreds of plants. Each leaf and stem was perfectly described.

Suddenly, as his fingers scanned a few lines, he stopped, mumbled to himself, then finally a grin passed over his face. Grabbing his overcoat, hat, and knapsack, he hurried out.

"Where are you going?" his wife called as he left. "At least take a piece of bread with you!"

"I can't right now," he called back from the yard. "Time is pressing! Stoke the fire; I'll be back soon."

"But Jakob . . . "

Yet her husband didn't seem to hear her. At this very moment Magdalena was coming down the stairs with the twins. Barbara and Georg were yawning. Their father's shouting and banging about had awakened them and now they were hungry.

"Where is Father going?" Magdalena asked, rubbing the sleep from her eyes.

Anna Maria Kuisl shook her head. "I don't know. I really don't know," she said, pouring milk for the small children into a saucepan on the fire. "He was looking through his book on herbs, and then he ran off like he'd been stung by a bee. It's got to have something to do with the Stechlin woman."

"With the Stechlin woman?" Suddenly Magdalena was wide awake. She watched as her father disappeared behind the willows down by the pond, then snatched the last heel of bread from the table and ran after him.

"Magdalena, stay here!" her mother called. But when she saw her daughter running full speed toward the pond, she just shook her head and went back in, to the children.

"Just like her father," she mumbled. "I hope it won't all end in disaster . . . "

Simon was awakened by a knock at his bedroom door. Something had been bothering him all night and now, opening his eyes, he realized that it was no dream, but reality. He turned to the window and could see that outside dawn was breaking. Drowsily, he rubbed his eyes. Usually he slept at least until the eight o'clock bell and wasn't used to being awakened that early.

"What's the matter?" he grumbled, turning to the door.

"It's me, your father! Open the door; we've got to talk."

Simon sighed. Once his father had set his mind on something, it was difficult to stop him.

"Just a moment!" he shouted. He sat up on the edge of the bed, brushed the strands of hair from his face, and tried to gather his thoughts.

After yesterday's riot he had walked home with Jakob Schreevogl. The young alderman had needed someone to comfort him and listen to him. Well into the wee hours he'd been telling Simon about Clara, about her kind, affectionate nature, and how she was so attentive and eager to learn, much more so than her often lazy foster siblings. Simon had almost gotten the impression that Jakob Schreevogl was fonder of his ward Clara than of his own biological children.

Maria Schreevogl had been given a strong sleeping potion and a large dose of brandy by the young physician, and she had soon gone to bed. Simon had assured her that Clara was certain to return soon.

The rest of the brandy had found its way into the throats of Simon and Jakob Schreevogl. In the end, the alderman had told him everything about himself, about his worries over his wife, who was often silent and bitter, and about his fear that he wouldn't be able to profitably continue the business of his father, who had recently died. Old Schreevogl had been known as an odd bird but also as a thrifty and shrewd man who had had his men well in line. It was never easy to step into the shoes of such a father, especially when one was barely thirty years old. Old Schreevogl had worked his way up from rags to riches. The other members of the stovemakers' guild had always envied him for his rapid success. Now they were closely watching his son. One mistake, and they'd swoop down on him like vultures.

Just before the old man's sudden death—he had died of a fever—Jakob had had a falling-out with his father. It had been over a trifle, a cartload of tiles that had been burned, but the quarrel had been so intense that Ferdinand Schreevogl had changed his will and given his property on the Hohenfurch Road, where Schreevogl junior had already planned to build a second kiln, to the church. On his deathbed, the old man had wanted to whisper something into his ear. But the mumbling had turned into a final cough. A cough or a laugh.

Jakob Schreevogl still wasn't sure what his father's final words were to this world.

Memories of the previous night were circling in Simon's head, which was painfully throbbing from the alcohol. He was going to need a cup of coffee, and soon. The question was, would his father give him time for that?

Right now he was knocking again.

"Coming!" shouted Simon, slipping into his hose and buttoning his doublet. Hurrying to the door he stumbled over the full chamber pot, spilling its contents over the floorboards. Swearing and with soaked toes, he pulled back the latch. The door flew open and hit him on the head.

"At last! Why on earth did you lock the door?" his father said, rushing into Simon's room. His gaze fell on the books on the desk.

"Where did you get these?"

Simon held his aching head. Then he sat down on the bed to put on his boots. "You don't really want to know," he muttered.

He knew that in his father's eyes all those works that he borrowed from the hangman were considered to be the work of the devil. It didn't help at all that the author of the book lying open on top of the stack was a Jesuit. Athanasius Kirchner was as unknown to Bonifaz Fronwieser as were Sanctorius and Ambroise Paré. Even here in Schongau the old man remained a field surgeon whose knowledge was based only upon his experience with those injured in the war. Simon remembered how his father used to pour boiling oil into gunshot wounds and administered a bottle of brandy to relieve the pain. The screams of the soldiers had followed him through his entire child-hood—the screams and the rigid bodies that Simon Fronwieser dragged from the tent the next day and covered with lime for burial.

Without paying further attention to his father, Simon hastened downstairs to the kitchen. Hastily he reached for the pot by the fireplace, which still held some cold coffee from the previous day. The first sip revived him. Simon couldn't imagine how he used to cope without coffee. A glorious brew, a true devil's nectar, he thought. Bitter and invigorating. He had heard from travelers that across the Alps, in Venice and in elegant Paris, certain inns already served coffee. Simon sighed. It would take centuries for Schongau to get that far.

His father stomped down the stairs.

"We have to talk," he exclaimed. "Lechner was here yesterday."

"The clerk?"

Simon set down the clay beaker and looked at his father with interest. "Whatever did he want?"

"He has noticed that you're meeting with the young Schreevogl. And that you dig up things that are none of your business. He says stay away from that. It won't do any good."

"You don't say." Simon sipped his coffee.

His father wouldn't let up.

"It was the Stechlin woman, and that's that, Lechner says."

Old Fronwieser sat down beside him on the bench in front of the fireplace. The cinders were cold. Simon could smell his father's foul breath.

"Listen," said Bonifaz Fronwieser. "I'll be honest with you. You know that we are not respected burghers in this town. We aren't even really welcome here. We are tolerated, and that's only because the last physician died during the plague and the academic quacks prefer to stay far off in Munich and Augsburg. Lechner can kick us out on a whim. He can and he will, unless you shut up. You and the hangman. Don't put your livelihood at stake on account of a witch!"

His father placed a cold, stiff hand on his shoulder. Simon recoiled.

"Martha Stechlin isn't a witch," he whispered.

"Even so," said his father, "Lechner wants her to be one, and it's better for the town as well. Besides . . . "

Bonifaz Fronwieser grinned, giving his son a fatherly pat on the shoulder.

"Between the hangman, the midwife, and ourselves there are too many here in town who want to make a livelihood from curing the sick. Once the Stechlin woman is gone, there's more work for us to do. Then we'll be able to get by. You can help with the births; I'll leave that all to you."

Simon jumped to his feet. The beaker fell from the table into the glowing embers on the hearth; the coffee sizzled as it hit the cinders.

"That's all you ever think about—your livelihood!" he shouted. Then he hastened to the door. His father rose on the bench.

"Simon, I . . . "

"Have you all lost your senses, or what? Don't you realize there's a murderer at large? You're only thinking about your bellies, and out there someone's killing children!"

Simon slammed the door and rushed out into the street. The neighbors, startled by his shouts, peeked out of their windows.

Simon looked up angrily.

"Why don't you mind your own business!" he shouted. "You'll see! Once the Stechlin woman has been burned, the fun will start for real. And then one more will burn, and one more, and one more! And finally, it'll be your turn!"

He stomped off to the tanners' quarter, shaking his head. His neighbors watched as he left. Yes, it was true. Since Fronwieser's son had taken up with the hangman's daughter, he wasn't his old self anymore. She must have bewitched him, or at least turned his head, which amounted to the same thing, anyway. Perhaps more people had to burn in Schongau after all before order could finally be restored.

The neighbors closed their shutters and returned to their breakfast porridge.

With quick strides, Jakob Kuisl took the narrow path from his house down to the river. After a few minutes' walk upstream on the towpath, he reached the Lech Bridge.

Clouds of smoke were still rising from the ruins of the Stadel and there were occasional glowing embers. Sebastian, the second bridge sentry, was sitting on a bridge pile, leaning on his halberd. When he saw the hangman he saluted him with a tired nod. The short, squat sentry always carried a jug under his overcoat on cold days. This morning, Sebastian needed his drink more than ever. Since his comrade had been imprisoned, he had to do two men's sentry duty. It would be another hour until he was relieved, and he had been at his post the entire night. Also, he could swear that the devil himself had flitted right past him in the dead of night, a black stooped shadow, with a limp.

"And he waved at me; I saw it clearly," Sebastian whispered to the hangman, kissing the small silver crucifix he carried around his neck on a leather thong. "Have mercy on us, Holy Mary! Since the Stechlin woman has been practicing her foul sorcery here, the spirits of hell are walking about in town, I'm telling you."

Jakob Kuisl listened attentively. Then he took leave of the sentry and passed over the bridge, heading for Peiting.

The muddy country road meandered through the forest. Frequently he had to walk around puddles and potholes that seemed particularly deep after the severe winter. In some places the road was practically impassible. When he had walked half a mile he came upon an oxcart that was stuck in the muck. The peasant from Peiting who owned it was laboring to push it from behind but couldn't dislodge the stuck wheel. Without even waiting to be asked, Kuisl braced his massive body against the vehicle and with one push the cart was free.

Instead of thanking him, the peasant murmured a prayer, careful not to look into the hangman's eyes. Then he hurried around to the front of the cart, jumped into the driver's seat, and swung his whip. With a curse, Kuisl hurled a stone after him.

"Off with you, Peiting idiot!" he shouted. "Or else I'll hang you by your whip!"

It was nothing new to the hangman that many people avoided contact with him. But he still was hurt by it. He hadn't expected gratitude but at least a ride on the cart. As it was, he would have to plod along the muddy path. The oaks that lined it offered little shade. Again and again his thoughts returned to Martha Stechlin, who was brought closer to torturing and the stake with every peal of the bell.

It'll have to start this afternoon, he thought. *But I might be able to stall a bit . . .*

When a deer path opened to his left, he bent down and slipped beneath the branches into the forest. The trees surrounded him with a silence that once again comforted him. It was as though the good Lord was holding a protective hand over the world. Morning sunlight was breaking through the foliage, throwing specks of light on the soft moss. Late snow was still on the ground in some places. A cuckoo was calling from afar, and the buzzing of gnats, bees, and beetles hung in the air. As Kuisl was walking through the forest with determined steps, he kept getting entangled in cobwebs, which clung to his face like a mask. The moss muffled the sound of his steps. It was here in the forest that he truly felt at home. Whenever possible, he came here to gather herbs, roots, and mushrooms. It was said that nobody in Schongau knew as much about the plant kingdom as the hangman.

The cracking sound of a breaking branch caused him to stop short. It came from the right, from the direction of the road. Now another breaking sound could be heard. Somebody was approaching him, and this somebody was trying to sneak up on him. He wasn't doing it particularly skillfully.

Jakob Kuisl looked around and noticed a fir branch that reached down almost to his head. He pulled himself up on it until he disappeared among the branches. A few minutes later, the steps had come closer. He waited until the sound was directly underneath him, then he dropped.

Magdalena heard him at the last moment. She leapt forward and turned around to see how her father landed hard on the ground right behind her. Just before the impact Jakob Kuisl had realized who was underneath him and rolled to the side. Now he rose to his feet, angrily brushing snow and fir needles from his doublet.

"Are you crazy?" he hissed. "Why are you are you running through the forest like a highwayman? Shouldn't you be home with Mother, helping her grind herbs? Stubborn woman!"

Magdalena swallowed hard. Her father was known for his sudden outbreaks of rage. Nevertheless, she looked him straight in the eye as she answered.

"Mother told me you were here on account of the Stechlin woman. And so I thought I might be able to help you."

Jakob Kuisl laughed out loud.

"Help me? You? Help your mother; there's enough work to do there. And now shove off, before you're in for a spanking."

Magdalena crossed her arms.

"You can't just send me away like a little girl. At least tell me what you're intending to do. After all, Martha brought me into the world. As long as I can remember, I have carried herbs and ointments to her place every week. And now I shouldn't be concerned about her fate at all?"

The hangman sighed. "Magdalena, believe me, it's better

like this. The less you know, the less you can gossip. It's enough that you have a fling with the young physician. People are already talking."

Magdalena smiled her innocent little girl's smile, with which she had always been able to wangle candy from her father.

"You like Simon too, don't you?"

"Stop that," he grunted. "Who cares if I like him. He's the physician's son, and you're the hangman's daughter. So stay away from him. And now off you go to help your mother."

But Magdalena wasn't ready to give up yet. As she was searching for words, her eyes roamed the forest. Behind a hazelnut bush she suddenly noticed something bright and white.

What if that was ...?

She hurried over and dug up a white star-shaped flower that she handed her father with dirt-stained hands.

"It's a hellebore," he said, raising the flower to his nose and sniffing it. "It's been a long time since I saw one hereabouts. You know they say witches make an ointment from it that helps them fly on Walpurgis Night."

Magdalena nodded. "Goodwife Daubenberger from Peiting told me about it. And she believes that the murders of the children are somehow connected with Walpurgis Night."

Her father looked at her incredulously. "With Walpurgis Night?"

Magdalena nodded. "She thinks it can't be a coincidence. In three days it'll be the witches' sabbath, and then they'll fly and dance along the Hohenfurch Road, and—"

Jakob Kuisl interrupted her brusquely. "And you believe this rubbish? Go home and do the washing. I don't need you here."

Magdalena looked at him angrily. "But you just told me that there are witches and flying ointment!" she shouted, kicking against a fallen tree trunk. "Now what's the truth?"

"I said that's what people *say*. That's something different,"

Kuisl said. He sighed, and then he gave his daughter an earnest look. "I believe that there are evil people," he continued. "And I don't care if they are witches or priests. And, yes, I believe there are potions and salves that make you *believe* you're a witch. That make you wicked and like a cat in heat and, for all I care, that make you fly."

Magdalena nodded. "Goodwife Daubenberger knows the ingredients of this flying salve." In a hushed voice, she listed them. "Hellebore, mandrake, thorn apple, henbane, hemlock, belladonna . . . The old woman showed me a number of herbs in the forest. We even found a baneberry plant once."

Jakob Kuisl looked at her incredulously.

"A baneberry plant? Are you sure? I haven't seen one in my entire life."

"By the Holy Virgin, it's true! Believe me, Father, I know all the herbs around here. You've taught me a lot, and Goodwife Daubenberger showed me the rest."

Jakob Kuisl eyed her skeptically. Then he asked her the names of several herbs. She knew them all. When she had answered all of his questions satisfactorily, he asked for a certain plant and whether she knew where it could be found. Magdalena thought briefly, and then she nodded.

"Take me there," said the hangman. "If it's true I'll tell you what I'm planning."

After a good half hour's walk they had reached their destination: a shady clearing in the forest, surrounded by rushes. Before them lay a dried-up pond dotted with grassy islets. Behind that was a swampy meadow in which something purple was somewhat visible. There was the scent of a bog and peat in the air. Jakob Kuisl closed his eyes and breathed in the aroma of the forest. Among the resinous pine needles and the damp smell of moss he could distinguish the gentle fragrance of something else.

She was right.

———

Simon Fronwieser's anger had cooled a little. After the quarrel with his father he had hurried to the market square with a red face and eaten a small breakfast of dried apple rings and a piece of bread at one of the many stalls there. As he was chewing on the tough, sweet rings his anger subsided. There simply was no point in getting angry with his father. They were far too different. It was much more important to keep a cool head. Time was pressing. Simon frowned.

The patrician Jakob Schreevogl had told him that the Elector's secretary would arrive in Schongau in a few days' time to pronounce his sentence. Before then a culprit had to be found, as the aldermen had neither the inclination nor the means to feed the prince's representative and his entourage longer than necessary. Furthermore, court clerk Lechner needed peace and quiet in his town. Unless order was restored by the time His Excellency Wolf Dietrich von Sandizell appeared, the clerk's authority in Schongau would be seriously jeopardized. Therefore, they had three days left, perhaps four at the most. It would take the entourage of soldiers and servants that long to make their way to Schongau from the distant country residence at Thierhaupten. Once the secretary was in town, neither Simon nor the hangman nor the Almighty could save Martha Stechlin from the flames.

Simon stuffed the last apple ring into his mouth and crossed the crowded market square. Time and again he had to step out of the way of maids and farmers' wives at the farmstands quarreling over meat, eggs, and carrots. One or the other gave him a longing glance. Without paying any attention to it, he turned into the Hennengasse, where Sophie's foster parents lived.

The red-haired girl had been continually on his mind. He was certain she knew more than she let on. Somehow she was the key to the mystery, even if he wasn't sure what exactly her role in it was. Yet as he reached the small house wedged in between two larger half-timbered houses in need of a fresh coat of paint, a bitter disappointment awaited him. Sophie hadn't come home for two days. Her foster parents had no idea where she was.

"That brat will do whatever she likes," grumbled Andreas Dangler, the linen weaver, who had taken care of the child since her parents' death. "When she's here she eats us out of house and home, and when she's supposed to be working she'll just hang around in town. I just wish I'd never agreed to the whole business."

Simon wanted to remind him that the town paid him a handsome compensation for taking care of Sophie, but he contented himself with a nod.

Andreas Dangler continued to fume: "I wouldn't be surprised if she was hand in glove with that witch," he said, spitting on the ground. "Her mother, the wife of Hans Hörmann, the tanner, was just the same. She cast a spell on her husband, driving him to an early grave, and then she died of consumption herself. The girl was always stubborn, thought herself to be something superior to everyone else and wouldn't sit at a table with us weavers. Now she has what she deserves!"

He was leaning against the door frame, chewing on a chip of pinewood. "If I had my way, there'd be no need for her ever to return here. She has probably run off before the same thing happened to her as did to the Stechlin woman."

As the linen weaver continued his complaints, Simon sat down on a dung cart next to the house and took a deep breath. He had the feeling he wasn't going anywhere like this. He'd have loved to smack the nagging Dangler right in the face. Instead, he only interrupted his grumbling. "Did you notice anything about Sophie lately? Has she been acting differently?"

Andreas Dangler looked him up and down. Simon was fully aware that he must look like a perfect dandy to the linen weaver. With his high leather boots, his green velvet overcoat, and his fashionable Vandyke he would appear to the simple tradesman like an effeminate city dweller from Augsburg, the distant metropolis. His father was right. He wasn't a local, and there was no point in pretending he was.

"What's that got to do with you, you quack doctor?" asked Dangler.

"I'm the physician in charge of the Stechlin woman's torturing," Simon exaggerated. "Therefore, I should like to gain an impression of the woman, so that I know what powers of witchcraft she may possess. Now, has Sophie ever spoken of the Stechlin woman?" The linen weaver shrugged. "She did say once that she'd like to become a midwife herself. And when my wife was sick she had the necessary medicine right on hand. I suppose she got those from the Stechlin woman."

"Anything else?"

Andreas Dangler hesitated, then he seemed to recollect something. He grinned. "I saw her once as she was drawing that sign in the sand back there in the courtyard. When I saw her she wiped it away at once."

Simon pricked up his ears.

"What kind of a sign?"

The linen weaver thought for a moment, then he took the pinewood chip from his mouth, bent down, and drew something in the dust.

"It looked something like that," he finally said.

Simon tried to recognize anything in the blurry drawing. It resembled a triangle with a squiggle at the bottom.

It reminded him of something, but every time he thought something was coming back to him, the memory faded away. Again he looked at the drawing in the dirt, then he wiped it away with his foot and walked off toward the river. There was one other thing to do today.

"Hey!" Dangler called after him. "Now what does the sign mean? Is she a witch?"

Simon walked faster. The noise of the fully awake town had soon drowned out the shouts of the linen weaver. From afar, he could hear the blacksmith's hammer; children were driving a flock of cackling geese past him.

After a few minutes the physician had reached the Hof Gate, which was located right next to the Elector's residence. Here the houses looked sturdier and were built exclusively of stone. And there was less garbage lying around in the streets. The Hof Gate quarter was the neighborhood where the respected tradesmen and raftsmen lived. Those who had acquired some wealth moved to this part of town, away from the smelly tanners' quarter down by the river or the butchers' quarter, which lay a little to the east, with its common tailors and carpenters. Simon briefly greeted the sentry at the gate and walked on to Altenstadt, which was only about a mile away from Schongau to the northwest.

The sun shone rather gently, as it was still early on an April morning, but it nevertheless stung the physician's eyes. His head ached, as well, and his mouth felt dry. His hangover from the previous night's binge with Jakob Schreevogl was coming back. He knelt to have a drink from a brook near the side of the road. When a horse-drawn wagon piled high with wine barrels rumbled past him, he had enough presence of mind to jump on the back and crawl forward to the barrels that were lashed down. The wagon driver took no notice, and shortly afterward he arrived in Altenstadt.

Simon's destination was Strasser's inn, which was in the middle of the village. Before he had gone to the Schreevogls' last night, the hangman had given him five names—the names of the children who had routinely visited Martha Stechlin's house: Grimmer, Kratz, Schreevogl, Dangler, and Strasser. Two were dead, two were missing. There remained the last ward, that of Strasser, the innkeeper in Altenstadt.

Simon pushed open the low door that led into the lounge. A

smell of cabbage, smoke, stale beer, and urine hit him. Strasser's was the only inn in town. Anyone looking for something better went to Schongau. Here one came to drink and forget.

Simon sat down on a wooden stool at a table decorated with knife marks and ordered a beer. Two wagon drivers who were already sipping at their tankards at this early hour eyed him with suspicion. The landlord, a bald, potbellied man in a leather apron, shuffled to his table with a foaming mug and pushed the brew toward him.

"To your health," he mumbled and started to go back to the counter.

"Take a seat," said Simon, pointing at the empty stool next to his.

"Can't right now, I have customers, I'm sure you can see." He turned away, but Simon grabbed his arm and gently pulled him down.

"Please take a seat," he said again. "We have to talk. It's about your ward."

The innkeeper Strasser glanced cautiously at the wagon drivers, but they seemed to be absorbed in conversation. "About Johannes?" he whispered. "Have you found him?"

"Has he disappeared?"

Franz Strasser heaved a sigh and settled into a chair next to the physician. "He did, yesterday at noon. He was to look after the horses in the stable, but he didn't return. I guess he's run off, the little bastard."

Simon blinked. The inn was only dimly lit, and the drawn shutters allowed very little light to enter. On the windowsill, a pinewood chip was glowing faintly.

"How long has Johannes been your apprentice?" he asked the landlord.

Franz Strasser thought. "Over three years," he said after a while. "His parents were both from here, from Altenstadt. Good people, but weak chested. She died in childbirth, and the father followed her to the grave just three weeks later. Johannes was the youngest. I took him in, and he has always been well cared for here, so help me God."

Simon sipped at his mug. The beer was watery and flat.

"I hear he was over in Schongau a lot," he asked.

Strasser nodded. "Right. Every hour he could spare. The devil knows what he did over there."

"And you had no idea where he might have gone?"

The landlord shrugged. "His hideout, perhaps."

"Hideout?"

"He spent a few nights there," said Strasser. "Every time I gave him a whipping for doing mischief, he went off to his hideout. I tried to ask him about it once, but he said nobody would ever find it and he'd be safe there even from the devil."

Lost in thought, Simon sipped his beer. Suddenly, he didn't care about the taste anymore.

"Were there others who knew it too ... this hideout?" he asked cautiously.

Franz Strasser frowned. "Could be," he said. "He did play with other kids, he did. Once they smashed an entire shelf of beer mugs here. They went into the lounge, snatched a loaf of bread, and knocked over the mugs as they ran away, the little bastards."

"What did the children look like?"

Strasser had worked himself up into a rage.

"Nothing but bastards, the whole lot! Only mischief on their minds, all those orphans from the town. Ungrateful riffraff. They should be humble and glad that someone's taking care of them, and instead they just get fresh."

Simon took a deep breath. His headache was coming back.

"What they looked like is what interests me," he whispered.

The innkeeper stared, thinking it over. "There was a red-headed girl with them. Witches' hair ... I tell you, they're good for nothing."

"And you really have no idea where that hideout could be?"
Franz Strasser looked irritated.

"Why are you so interested in that boy?" he asked. "Has he
done anything to make you look for him so urgently?"

Simon shook his head.

"It's not important." He put down a copper penny for the
beer and left the gloomy room. Franz Strasser watched as he left,
shaking his head.

"Damned bastards!" he called after the physician. "If you see
him, give him a few behind the ears. He deserves it!"

CHAPTER
8

THE COURT CLERK SAT AT THE BIG COUNCIL TABLE
in the town hall drumming his fingers to the rhythm of some
military march whose melody kept going through his mind. His
gaze passed over the pudgy faces of the men sitting in front of
him. Red, sagging cheeks, watery eyes, thinning hair . . . Even
the modish cut of the coats and the carefully starched lace neck-
erchiefs could not disguise the fact that these men had passed
their prime. They clung to their power and their money because,
in Lechner's opinion, nothing else was left for them. In their eyes
was a helplessness that made him almost pity them. In their
small, beautiful town the devil was loose, and they could do nothing about it. The Stadel had burned down, some of them had lost
a lot of money, and something out there was taking their children from them. The servant girls and laborers, the peasants and
the simple people, expected that they, the masters of the town,
would do something about it. But they were all at a loss, and so
they looked at Lechner as if he could do away with the disaster

with a snap of his fingers or a scratch from his quill pen. Lechner despised them, even if he would never let it show.

Don't bite the hand that feeds you.

He rang his handbell and opened the meeting.

"Many thanks for having come on such short notice and interrupting your business, which is doubtlessly important, to attend this shortly convened meeting of the inner council," he began. "But I believe it is necessary."

The six aldermen nodded eagerly. Burgomaster Karl Semer passed his lace kerchief over his sweaty forehead. The deputy burgomaster Johann Püchner wrung his hands and muttered agreement. Otherwise there was silence. Only Wilhelm Hardenberg, the old superintendent of the almshouse, pursed his lips and uttered a curse toward the ceiling. He had just been calculating how much the fire at the Stadel would cost him. Cinnamon, sweetmeats, bales of high-quality cloth, all reduced to ashes.

"God in heaven, someone will have to pay for it!" he whined. "Someone must pay!"

The blind Matthias Augustin struck his stick impatiently on the oaken floor. "Cursing won't get us anywhere," he said. "Let Master Lechner tell us what the questioning of the wagon drivers has revealed."

The court clerk looked at him thankfully. At least there was one beside himself who was keeping a clear head. Then he continued. "As you all know, yesterday evening little Clara Schreevogl was abducted by an unknown person. Like the other two dead children, she used to visit the Stechlin woman. People maintain they've seen the devil on the street."

A whispering and murmuring went through the council chamber, and many crossed themselves. Johann Lechner held up his hands to calm them. "People see a lot, even things which don't exist," he said. "I hope that we will be able to say more after the examination of the Stechlin woman this afternoon."

"Why didn't you put the witch on the rack long ago?" grumbled old Augustin. "There was time enough all night."

Lechner nodded. "If it were up to me, we would be further along," he said. "But the witness Schreevogl asked for a postponement. His wife is not well. Anyway, first we wanted to ask the wagon drivers about the fire."

"Well then?" Almshouse superintendent Hardenberg looked up, his eyes flashing with anger. "Who was it? Who is the swine? He should be dancing at a rope's end by the end of the day!"

The court clerk shrugged. "We don't know yet. The watchman from the bridge and Georg Riegg both said the fire spread very quickly. Someone did more than just set the fire, but nobody saw any of the Augsburgers. They came later to rescue their goods."

"They came very quickly," said third burgomaster Matthias Holzhofer, a corpulent bald-headed man, who had made a fortune with gingerbread and sweets. "They got all their bales out and lost hardly anything. They did it all right."

Burgomaster Semer tugged at his thinning hair. "Would it have been possible for the Augsburgers to start the fire and then rush all their goods to safety?" he asked. "If they really want to set up a new trade route, they have to make sure that people can no longer store their goods here with us. And they have succeeded."

Püchner, the second burgomaster, shook his head. "I don't believe it," he said. "All it would have taken would be the wind coming from the wrong direction, or a burning beam, and they'd have lost their goods just as we did."

"What if they did?" said Karl Semer. "What are a few bales and barrels for the Augsburgers? If they get their trade road, then those are worth their weight in gold. First it's the leper house in front of the town wall, now it's the burning of the Stadel. They're cutting the ground from under our feet!"

"Speaking of the leper house," the court clerk broke in. "It wasn't just the Stadel that was destroyed yesterday, but someone also vandalized the site where they are building the leper house. The priest told me that the scaffolding was torn down and parts of the foundation were destroyed. Mortar has been stolen, building wood splintered . . . and weeks of work gone down the drain."

Burgomaster Semer nodded thoughtfully. "I have always said that the building of such an establishment for lepers is not welcome here. Quite simply, people here are afraid that traders will stay away if we set up an asylum directly in front of the gates. And who can guarantee that the disease will stop outside the town? Such diseases can spread!"

Wilhelm Hardenberg, the gray-headed almshouse superintendent, agreed with him. "This destruction is certainly reprehensible, but on the other hand . . . you can understand that people want to protect themselves. Nobody wants this institution, but in spite of that it's being built. And all because of a mistaken concept of compassion!"

Burgomaster Semer took a big gulp from his lead-crystal glass before speaking. "Compassion has to stop when the interests of the town are endangered, that's what I think."

Blind Augustin pounded the table with his stick, so that the expensive port wine in the carafes swished dangerously back and forth.

"Absolute rubbish! Who cares about the leper house at a time like this! We have bigger problems. When the Augsburgers find out we have locked up one of their head wagon drivers, and one of the Fuggers to boot . . . I tell you, let the wagon drivers go and burn the witch, and then we'll have peace again in Schongau!"

The second burgomaster Johann Püchner shook his head again. "None of this makes any sense," he said. "The fire, the murders, the kidnapping, the damage to the leper house . . . The Stechlin woman has been locked up for quite a time, and it still goes on nevertheless!"

The others, too, began to speak up, talking loudly all at the same time.

Court clerk Johann Lechner had been listening calmly to the dispute, occasionally taking notes. Now he cleared his throat. Immediately the aldermen fell silent and looked at him expectantly. He took his time before answering.

"I am not quite persuaded that the Augsburgers are innocent," he said finally. "I therefore propose that we have the Stechlin woman tortured today. If she confesses to causing the fire as well as to the murder of the children, we can still release the Augsburger wagon driver. If not, I shall not hesitate to question him as well."

"And the Fuggers?" asked burgomaster Semer.

Lechner smiled. "The Fuggers were a powerful clan before the war. But now nobody really pays them much attention. If the Augsburg wagon driver really confesses to arson under torture, then that'll be trouble for the Fuggers."

He rose and rolled up the handwritten parchment. "And then we have a good case against the Augsburgers, don't we?"

The aldermen nodded. It was good to have a court clerk. One like Lechner. He gave you the feeling that there was a solution for everything.

The devil's white bony hand grabbed at the girl's throat and closed its grasp slowly. Clara felt how he was cutting off her air, her tongue swelled to a fleshy lump, her eyes bulged out of her head, and she looked into a face that she could only see unclearly, as if in a fog. The devil was as hairy as a goat, and out of his forehead grew two twisted horns. His eyes burned like glowing coals and now the appearance of the face started to morph into a distorted mask of the midwife clutching her hands round the girl's neck, with a gaze that seemed to beg for forgiveness. It seemed that she whispered something, but Clara could not catch the meaning of the words.

White as snow, red as blood . . .

Once more the face changed. Her foster father Jakob Schreevogl knelt over her, his mouth twisted into a crooked grin, still pressing harder and harder. Clara felt her life ebbing away; from a distance she heard children's voices, the voices of boys. With horror she realized that they were the voices of her dead playmates, Peter and Anton, crying for help. The face changed again. It was Sophie, who was shaking her wildly and trying to speak to her. Now she raised her hand and gave Clara a resounding slap.

The slap brought her back to reality.

"Wake up, Clara! Wake up!" Clara shook herself. The world around her came into focus. She saw Sophie bending over her, stroking her burning cheek. The damp rock wall that surrounded them, smeared with ash-colored signs, crosses, and formulas, lent her a feeling of security. It was quiet and cool, and from a distance the rustling of the trees could be heard. Near her lay her wooden doll, dirty and torn but still a reminder of home. Clara leaned back, relieved. Down here the devil would never find her.

"What . . . what happened?" she whispered.

"What happened?" Sophie could laugh again. "You were dreaming, and you frightened me with your shouting. I was outside and suddenly I heard you scream. I thought they had found us."

Clara tried to sit up. When she put weight on her right foot, a stab of pain went up her leg to the hip.

Panting, she had to lie down again. The pain went away only slowly. Sophie, worried, looked down.

When Clara looked also, she could see that her right ankle was as big as an apple. The foot was covered with blue spots, and the shin above also seemed swollen. Her shoulder hurt when she turned her body. She was shivering. Her fever had returned.

Suddenly she remembered how she had run from the devil: the jump from the window, the panic-stricken rush through the streets of the town, the second jump from the oak by the city wall into the bushes below. She knew she had landed badly, but fear had driven her on, through the fields and into the woods. Branches slapped like hands across her face, once or twice she fell, but she forced herself to get up again and kept running. At last she reached the hiding place. Like a sack of grain she collapsed on the ground and fell asleep at once. It was not until the next morning that Sophie awakened her.

The red-haired girl had slipped out of the town just as Clara had. Clara was so happy that her friend was with her. Sophie was thirteen years old and seemed almost grown-up. She was like a mother to Clara when they played together out here in their hiding place. In fact, without Sophie their group would not even exist, and she would still be a lonely orphan, teased by her foster brothers and sisters, hit, pinched, and kicked, and the whole time her foster parents noticing nothing.

"Just keep still now."

Sophie took some oak bark and linden leaves, smeared with an ointment she had brought with her, and began to wrap Clara's ankle with them. Then she tied it up firmly with bark fibers. Clara felt a pleasant coolness on her foot, and the ankle did not seem quite so painful. While she was admiring the neatly applied bandage her blood sister had made, Sophie reached behind her.

"Here, drink. I brought it for you." Her friend held out an earthenware bowl containing a grayish liquid.

"What is it?"

Sophie grinned. "Don't ask, just drink. A . . . an elixir. I learned it from Mother Stechlin. It'll make you sleep again, and when you wake up your foot will be much better."

Clara looked rather skeptically at the brew, which smelled strongly of nettles and mint. Sophie had always been very attentive when she was with the midwife; nothing had escaped her sharp notice when Martha Stechlin had told them about women's mysteries. She had told them about poisons and potions and warned that only a few drops could sometimes make all the difference between the two.

Finally Clara made up her mind and drank the bowl in one gulp. It tasted hot and horrible, like liquid snot, as it went down her throat. But a short time later she felt warmth pulsing in her stomach, waves of pleasant feelings spreading through her body. She leaned back against the rocky wall behind her and suddenly nothing seemed so hard anymore. It seemed that nothing was out of reach.

"What . . . what do you think will happen? Will they find us?" she asked Sophie, who was suddenly surrounded by a halo of warm light.

The older girl shook her head. "I don't think so. We were already too far away from our hiding place. But maybe they will search nearby. In any case you should stay inside here."

Clara's eyes filled with tears. "People think we are witches!" she sobbed. "They found this accursed sign, and now they think we are witches! They'll burn us alive when we come back. And if we stay here the men will find us! The . . . the devil was close behind me, he grabbed me . . . " Her words were lost in sobs. Sophie took Clara's head and laid it in her lap to comfort her.

All at once Clara felt an infinite weariness. She felt that feathers were growing on her arms, wings that would carry her away from this vale of tears to a distant, warm land . . .

With her last bit of strength she asked, "Did they really kill Peter and Anton?"

Sophie nodded. Suddenly she seemed to be a long way away.

"And Johannes?" asked Clara again.

"Don't know," said Sophie. "I'll have a look for him while you sleep." She stroked Clara's hair. "Don't think about it. You are quite safe."

With her newly grown wings Clara soared upward toward heaven.

"I . . . I can never go back home again. They'll burn us," she muttered, almost asleep.

"Nobody will be burned," said a voice from far away. "There's somebody who will help us. He'll catch the devil, and then everything will be as it was, I promise . . . "

"An angel?"

"Yes, an angel. An angel with a huge sword. An avenging angel."

Clara smiled. "Good," she whispered. Then the wings carried her away.

About eleven o'clock in the morning Jakob Kuisl knocked at the door of the keep. From inside he heard a key turn in the lock, the heavy door opened, and the surprised bailiff Andreas looked him directly in the eye.

"You, here already?" he asked. "I thought the questioning wouldn't begin until midday—"

Kuisl nodded. "You're right, but I have to do some things to get ready. You know . . . " He gestured as if pulling at his own arm. "Today we begin with the pinching and pulling. I need a hot fire. And the ropes are worn out."

He held a coil of new rope under the chalk-white nose of the bailiff and pointed to the interior.

"I suppose it will be all right," Andreas muttered and stepped aside for the hangman to enter. Then he seized him by the shoulder.

"Kuisl?"

"Yes?"

"Don't hurt her, will you? No more than you must. She brought my children into the world."

The hangman looked down at the young man, who was a good head shorter. A smile came to his lips.

"What do you think I'm here for?" he asked. "To cure somebody? To set limbs? No. I unset them. You folks want me to do that, so that's what I do."

He pushed the bailiff aside and entered the dungeon.

"I . . . I didn't want that to happen, no, I didn't!" Andreas called after him.

Awakened by the shouting, Georg Riegg scrambled to his feet. As an instigator of the fight down at the Stadel he was still keeping the watchman company in the cell on the left.

"Ah, now we have important visitors!" he cried. "Now it's going to start! Hey, Kuisl, you'll do it nice and slowly, won't you, so that we can have some fun when we hear the witch whimper!"

The hangman walked up to the cell and looked thoughtfully at the bridge watchman. Then suddenly he reached through the bars and grabbed him firmly by the crotch. He squeezed hard, so that the eyes of the man on the other side stood out of his head and he gasped for breath.

"You just watch it, Riegg," whispered Jakob Kuisl. "I know your dirty secrets. I know all of you. How often have you come to me for some herb to give you a hard-on or a bottle of angel's bane, so that the wife can abort another kid? How often have you fetched the midwife to your house? Five times? Six times? And now she's the witch, and you're doing just fine. Bah, you make me sick!"

The hangman let his prisoner go and hurled him backward. He slid slowly down the wall of the cell, whimpering. Then Kuisl went across to the other cell, where Martha Stechlin was already awaiting him with frightened eyes, her fingers clutching the iron bars of the cell.

"Give me back my coat, I've brought you a blanket," said

Jakob Kuisl loudly. He passed a woolen blanket in, while the midwife, shivering, took off his coat. As she reached for the rolled-up blanket, he whispered to her, almost inaudibly.

"Unroll the blanket in the dark at the back. There's a little bottle there. Drink it."

Martha Stechlin looked at him questioningly. "What is—?"

"Don't talk, drink," he whispered again. The bailiff Andreas had meanwhile taken a seat again on a stool near the door. Leaning on his pike, he watched them with interest.

"The important gentlemen are coming when the bell rings at midday," Jakob Kuisl continued loudly. "You had best begin saying your prayers."

And quietly he added, "Don't be afraid. It's all the best for you. Trust me. But you must drink that bottle now."

Then he turned and descended the damp stairs down to the torture chamber to get things ready.

The two men sat together over a glass of port wine, but for one of them drinking was difficult. His pain caused him to tremble, so that drops of the precious liquid fell on his gold-brocaded coat. Spots like bloodstains spread over the garment. Since yesterday it had become worse, even though he had still been able to conceal it from the others.

"They got away from you," he said. "I knew that you'd just make things worse. You can't do anything by yourself, absolutely nothing!"

The other man sipped absently at his wine. "They'll get them all right," he said. "They can't be far away. They're children."

Once again a wave of pain flooded the body of the older man. Only with difficulty could he regain the mastery of his voice.

"This is getting out of control!" he groaned. His right hand clutched the cut-glass crystal goblet. He must not give up now, not relax, so near to the goal . . .

"This can be our ruin, not only yours or mine but the whole family, don't you understand? Our name will be disgraced forever after!"

"Oh, nonsense," said the other as he leaned back in his chair. "They are children. Who's going to believe them? It's good that the matter of the witch is dragging on. First the children must go, then the witch can be burned. Then no suspicion will fall on us."

He stood up and went to the door. Business was waiting; things had been neglected for too long. Someone like himself had been lacking, someone who would take the reins in his hand. They had all misjudged him.

"And what about the actual job you have to do?" the older man asked, as he tried to rise, holding on to the table.

"We paid them well to pull that off!"

"Don't you worry, that'll be taken care of. Perhaps even today." He pushed down the door handle and turned to go out.

"I'll give you another five days," the older man shouted after him. "Five days! If the matter isn't taken care of by then, I'll send our men to take care of the murderers. And don't think that you'll get one single penny!"

While he was still speaking, the other man left, shutting the heavy oaken door behind him, which made the shouted threats hardly audible anymore.

"In five days you'll be dead," he mumbled, knowing well that the older man inside couldn't hear him. "And if the devil doesn't take you, I'll send you to hell myself."

As he walked across the balcony with its elaborately decorated balustrade, his gaze wandered over the roofs toward the black, silent forest that stood just beyond the gates of the town. He felt a short thrill of fear. The man out there was unpredictable. What would happen when the children were out of the way?

Would he ever stop? Would he himself be next?

———

They came punctually with the midday pealing of the bells. An escort of four town bailiffs led the way, with the court clerk and the three witnesses following. Jakob Schreevogl's face was pale; he had slept badly. His wife kept waking up with nightmares and calling for Clara. Furthermore, he was still suffering from a hangover from drinking with the physician. He could no longer remember exactly what he had said to young Fronwieser. But he had the feeling he had been a better talker than listener.

In front of him walked Michael Berchtholdt. The baker had a bunch of herbs with mugwort hanging at his belt, which was supposed to protect him from witchcraft. He was softly reciting his prayers and fingering a rosary. When he entered the prison, he crossed himself. Jakob Schreevogl shook his head. No doubt the baker had blamed Martha Stechlin for all the times he had burned the bread and for the hordes of mice in his bakery. After the Stechlin woman was reduced to ashes and the bread was still burned, he would presumably seek a new witch, thought Schreevogl, and he wrinkled his nose in disdain. The sharp smell of mugwort wafted over to him.

Immediately behind him, Georg Augustin entered the prison. The son of the powerful wagon drivers' family reminded Schreevogl a bit of the young physician. Like him, the young patrician liked to dress in the latest French fashions. His beard was freshly trimmed, his long black hair carefully combed, the calf-long trunk hose perfectly tailored. His ice-blue eyes took in the prison with disgust. The son of a powerful wagon drivers' family was not used to such surroundings.

When the two Schongau prisoners noticed the arrival of the distinguished visitors, they began to rattle the bars of their cell. Georg Riegg still looked pale; he no longer felt like scolding.

"Your Excellency," cried the wagon driver as he turned toward the court clerk. "May I just have a word with you . . . "

"What's up, Riegg? Have you a declaration to make?"

"Let us out, please. My wife has to look after the cattle by herself, and the children—"

"You'll stay in here until your case comes up," Lechner interrupted him without looking at him. "And that goes for your comrade here, too, and the Augsburg wagon driver over there in the Ballenhaus. One law for everyone."

"But, Your Excellency . . ."

Johann Lechner was already descending the stairs. In the torture chamber it was warm, almost hot. In the corner, red-hot charcoal glowed in a brazier standing on a tripod. In contrast to the last time, the chamber had been tidied up. Everything was ready: a new rope dangled from the ceiling, and the thumbscrews and pincers lay, sorted and oiled, on the chest. On a stool in the middle of the room sat Goodwife Stechlin, shaved bald, in a torn dress, her head bowed. The hangman positioned himself behind her, his arms crossed.

"Ah, I see, Kuisl, all is prepared. Good, very good," said Lechner, rubbing his hands together as he sat down at the writing desk. The witnesses took their places on his right. "Then we can begin." He turned to the midwife, who up to now had taken no notice of her visitors. "Can you hear me, Stechlin?"

The midwife's head remained bowed.

"Can you hear me? I want to know."

There was still no reaction from Martha Stechlin. Lechner went over to her, raised her face with two fingers under her chin, and gave her a box on the ear. Now at last she opened her eyes.

"Martha Stechlin, do you know why you are here?"

She nodded.

"Good. I'll explain it to you again anyway. You are suspected of having caused the death of the children Peter Grimmer and Anton Kratz in a most disgraceful way. In addition, of having abducted, with the assistance of the devil, Clara Schreevogl and at the same time of having set fire to the Stadel."

"And the dead sow in my sty? What about my dead sow?"

Michael Berchtholdt had jumped up from his seat. "Just yesterday she was rolling about in the mud, and now—"

"Witness Berchtholdt," Lechner snapped at him. "You will only speak when you are required to do so. We are now concerned with more than a dead sow; this concerns our dear children!"

"But . . ."

One glance from the court clerk silenced Berchtholdt.

"Well then, Stechlin," continued Lechner. "Do you admit having committed the crimes of which you are accused?"

The midwife shook her head. Her lips were narrowed, tears flowed down her face, and she wept silently.

Lechner shrugged his shoulders. "Then we must proceed to the interrogation. Executioner, begin with the thumbscrews."

Now it was Jakob Schreevogl who couldn't keep his seat any longer. "But all this is nonsense!" he cried. "Goodwife Stechlin had already been in prison a long time when the little Kratz boy was killed. And it would have been equally impossible for her to have had anything to do with kidnapping my Clara and the fire at the Stadel!"

"Didn't people say that the devil himself abducted your Clara?" asked young Augustin, who was seated alongside Schreevogl. His blue eyes looked the merchant's son up and down, and he almost seemed to be smiling. "Couldn't it be that the Stechlin woman asked the devil to do all this, after she was locked up here?"

"Why, then, didn't she ask him to fetch her out of the prison? That doesn't make sense!" cried Jakob Schreevogl.

"The torture will lead us to the truth," the court clerk resumed. "Executioner, continue."

The executioner reached out and took a thumbscrew from the chest. It consisted of an iron clamp, which could be closed with a screw at the front. He took the midwife's left thumb and introduced it into the clamp. Jakob Schreevogl was surprised at the hangman's apparent indifference. Only yesterday Jakob Kuisl had spoken out forcefully against the torture, and also the young physician had told him, over a few glasses of schnapps, that the hangman was not at all in agreement with the imprisonment of Martha Stechlin. And now he was applying thumbscrews to her.

But the midwife, too, seemed to have accepted her fate. She gave her hand to the hangman almost with indifference. Jakob Kuisl turned the screw. Once, twice, three times . . . A brief shudder ran through her body, nothing more.

"Martha Stechlin, do you now confess the crimes with which you are charged?" the clerk inquired in a monotone singsong.

She still shook her head. The hangman turned the screw still tighter. No movement, only her lips became narrower, a pale red streak like a closed door.

"Damn it, are you screwing it up properly?" Michael Berchtholdt asked the hangman. Jakob Kuisl nodded. As proof, he opened the screw and held the tortured woman's arm up. Her thumb was one blue bruise, and blood seeped out from under the thumbnail.

"The devil is helping her," whispered the baker. "Lord God, protect us . . . "

"We shan't get any further like this." Johann Lechner shook his head and put the quill, with which he intended to make notes, back on the table. "Bailiffs, bring me the chest."

Two of the town watchmen handed the clerk a small chest, which he lifted to the table and opened.

"Look here, witch," he said. "All these are things we found in your house. What have you to say about them?"

To the astonishment of Jakob Schreevogl and the others he produced a small bag out of the chest, poured some dark brown seeds into his hand and showed them to the witnesses. The stove-maker's son took a few between his fingers. They smelled slightly of rotting flesh and their shape somewhat resembled caraway seeds.

"Henbane seeds," said the court clerk, as if he was delivering a lecture. "An important ingredient of the flying salve that witches spread on their broomsticks."

Jakob Schreevogl shrugged. "My father also used it to flavor his beer, and you aren't going to describe him, God rest his soul, as a sorcerer."

"Are you blind?" hissed Lechner. "The proof is clear. Here!" He held up a spiny capsule that looked something like a chestnut. "A thorn apple! Also an ingredient for the witches' salve, and also found at Stechlin's house. And here!" He showed them a bunch of small white flowers. "Hellebores! What they call Christmas roses! Freshly gathered. Also a witches' herb!"

"Excuse me for interrupting you," Jakob Schreevogl broke in again. "But isn't the Christmas rose a plant that is supposed to protect us from evil? Even our reverend parish priest recently praised it in his homily as a sign of new life and resurrection. Not for nothing does it bear the name of our Savior . . . "

"What are you, Schreevogl?" Georg Augustin interjected. "A witness or her advocate? This woman was with the children, and the children are dead or have disappeared. In her house we find the most devilish herbs and mixtures. She is scarcely imprisoned when the Stadel burns down and the devil stalks through our town. It all began with her, and with her it will come to an end."

"Exactly, you'll see in a minute," Berchtholdt scolded. "Turn the screw tighter, then she'll confess. The devil himself is holding his protecting hand over her. I have an elixir made from Saint-John's-wort here . . . " He produced a small bottle containing a bright, blood-red liquid and held it up triumphantly. "This'll drive the devil out. Just let me pour it down her gullet, the witch!"

"God Almighty! I don't know who is the biggest witch here," cried Jakob Schreevogl. "The midwife or the baker!"

"Quiet!" thundered the clerk. "It can't go on like this. Executioner, pull her up on the rope. Let's see if the devil will help here there too."

Martha Stechlin appeared increasingly apathetic. Her head nodded again and again to the front and her eyeballs seemed to be turned strangely inward. Jakob Schreevogl asked himself if she was actually aware of what was happening around her. Without attempting any resistance, she let herself be pulled to her feet by the hangman and dragged to the rope that was dangling from an iron ring in the ceiling further in the rear of the cell. At the end of the rope there was a hook. The hangman attached this to the manacles with which the midwife's arms were tied behind her back.

"Shall I tie a stone to her underneath?" Kuisl asked the court clerk. His face was remarkably pale, but otherwise he appeared calm and collected.

Johann Lechner shook his head. "No, no, we'll try it as it is at first, then we'll see later."

The hangman pulled on one end of the rope, so that the ground slipped from under the midwife's feet. Her body bent forward a little and began to bob up and down. Something cracked. She moaned quietly. The court clerk recommenced his questions.

"Martha Stechlin, I ask you once more. Do you confess to having taken the poor lad Peter Grimmer and . . . "

At this moment a shudder went through the midwife's body. She began to twitch and to shake her head wildly back and forward. Saliva flowed from her mouth; her face was turning blue.

"My God, look," cried baker Berchtholdt. "The devil's in her! He wants to get out!"

All the witnesses, even the clerk, had jumped up to see the spectacle close up. The hangman had lowered the woman to the ground again, where she writhed in cramps. She reared up one more time, then she collapsed completely, her head turned to one side at an odd angle.

For a moment nobody said anything.

At last young Augustin spoke. "Is she dead?" he asked, intrigued.

Jakob Kuisl bent over her and put his ear to her breast. He shook his head.

"Her heart's still beating."

"Then wake her up again, so that we can continue," said Johannn Lechner.

Jakob Schreevogl was very near to hitting him in the face.

"How dare you!" he cried. "This woman is ill, can't you see that? She needs help!"

"Nonsense! The devil has gone out of her, that's all!" said baker Berchtholdt and fell to his knees. "He's surely still here in this room somewhere. Hail Mary, full of grace, the Lord is with thee . . ."

"Executioner! You will wake this woman up again! Do you understand?" The clerk's voice had taken on a rather shrill tone. "And you . . . " He turned to the frightened bailiffs behind him. "You fetch me a physician, and quickly!" The bailiffs ran upstairs, relieved to be able to escape from this hellish place.

Jakob Kuisl took a bucket of water that was standing in the corner and dashed it in the midwife's face. There was no movement. Then he began to massage her chest and pat her cheeks. When all this proved of no avail, he reached into the chest behind him and brought out a bottle of brandy, some of which he forced her to swallow. The rest he poured on her chest and began to knead it.

Only minutes later steps were heard on the stairs. The bailiffs were returning with Simon Fronwieser, whom they had met outside on the street.

Standing alongside the hangman, he bent down to the

midwife and pinched her on the upper arm. Then he took out a needle and thrust it deep into her flesh. When she still didn't move, he held a small mirror to her nose. The glass clouded over.

"She's alive," he told Johann Lechner. "But she's in a deep swoon, and heaven alone knows when she'll wake up from it."

The court clerk let himself fall back in his chair and rubbed his graying temples. Finally he shrugged. "Then we can't examine her further. We'll have to wait."

Georg Augustin looked at him in amazement. "But the Elector's secretary . . . He'll be here in a couple of days and we have to present him with a culprit!"

Michael Berchtholdt, too, was pleading with the clerk: "Don't you know what's going on out there? The devil is about. We've seen it for ourselves. People want us to finish . . . "

"Damn it!" Johann Lechner pounded the table with his hand. "I know that myself! But at the moment we just can't continue with the questioning. Not even the devil will get a word out of her! Do you expect an unconscious woman to confess? We'll have to wait. And now everybody, up and out, all of you!"

Simon and Jakob Kuisl carried the unconscious midwife back to her cell and covered her up. Her face was no longer blue but chalk-white, her eyelids fluttered, and her breath came steadily. Simon looked at the hangman from one side.

"That was you, wasn't it?" he asked. "You gave her something to stop the torture and to give us more time. And then you told your wife to ask me to wait outside after midday so that the bailiffs would fetch *me* and not my father, who perhaps might have noticed something . . . "

The hangman smiled. "A few plants, a few berries . . . She knew them all, she knew what she was letting herself in for. It could have gone wrong."

Simon looked at the pallid face of the midwife. "You mean?"

Jakob Kuisl nodded. "Mandrake roots, there's nothing better.

I . . . we found some, luckily. They are very rare. You don't feel pain, the body relaxes, and the sufferings of this world are only shadowy figures on a distant shore. My father used to give this drink to poor sinners. However . . . "

He rubbed his dark beard thoughtfully.

"I put in perhaps almost too much monkshood this time. I wanted it to look real, right to the end. Just a bit more of it and the Lord God would have taken her. Now, good. We have at least gained a little time."

"How long?"

The hangman shrugged. "After one or two days, the paralysis will disappear and she can open her eyes again. And then . . . " He stroked the face of the sleeping Martha Stechlin once more before leaving the keep.

"And then, I fear, I shall have to hurt her very much," he said. His broad back filled the entire door frame.

CHAPTER
9

THE NEXT MORNING, THE PHYSICIAN AND THE hangman were sitting together in the Kuisl house over two mugs of weak beer, thinking about everything that had happened in the past few days. Simon had thought all night long about the unconscious midwife, realizing how little time they had left. He silently sipped his beer while next to him Jakob Kuisl chewed on his pipe. Magdalena's constant comings and goings in the room to fetch water or to feed the chickens under the bench didn't make thinking any easier. At one point she came and knelt down right in front of Simon and her hand brushed over his thigh as if by chance, causing a shiver to run through his body.

Jakob Kuisl had told him that his daughter was the one who found the mandrake root in the forest. Ever since then Simon had become even more attracted to her. This girl was not only gorgeous, she was also clever. What a pity that women were barred from entering the university. Simon was sure that Magdalena would have had no trouble holding her own in her studies against all those learned quacks.

"Would you like another beer?" asked the hangman's daughter, winking and filling up his tankard without waiting for an answer. Her smile reminded Simon that there was more to this world than missing children and self-appointed inquisitors. He smiled back at her. Then his thoughts returned to gloomier things.

The night before he had to accompany his father on a house call. Haltenberger's farmhand had come down with a bad fever. They'd given him cold compresses, and Simon's father had bled him. Simon was at least able to convince his father to use some of that ominous powder that had previously helped several times with fever and supposedly came from the bark of a rare tree. The patient's symptoms reminded him of another case in which a wagon driver from Venice had collapsed on the street in their town. A foul odor had come from the man's mouth, and his entire body was covered with pustules. People spoke of the French disease, and that the devil used it to punish those who indulged in unchaste love.

Simon would gladly have indulged in unchaste love last night, but during his rendezvous with Magdalena later on in a secret corner by the town wall, she had only wanted to talk about Goodwife Stechlin. She, too, was convinced of the midwife's innocence. Once he had tried to touch her bodice, but she had turned away. At his next attempt the night watchman had discovered them and sent them home. It was way past eight o'clock in the evening, and at that time young girls were no longer allowed out on the streets. Simon had the feeling of having missed a crucial moment, and he was not sure if luck would soon bring him another. Perhaps his father was right and he should keep his hands off the hangman's daughter. Simon was not sure if she was only toying with him or whether she really cared for him.

Jakob Kuisl couldn't fully concentrate on his work that morning either. While Simon sat there sipping weak beer and staring out the window, he mixed a salve of dried herbs and goose fat. He kept putting the pestle aside to fill his pipe. Anna Maria, his wife, was out in the field, and the twins were rollicking under the kitchen table, a few times almost knocking over the mortar. He scolded them and sent them outside into the yard. Georg and Barbara trotted off, pouting, but knowing full well that their father could not stay angry at them for long.

Simon leafed through the well-thumbed book the hangman had lying open on the table. Simon had returned two of his books and was eager to learn new things. The tome before him was not necessarily going to provide that. Dioscorides's *De materia medica* was still the standard text of the healing arts even though its author, a Greek physician, had lived in the days of our Savior. Also at the university in Ingolstadt they were still teaching his methods. Simon sighed. He had the feeling that humanity was running in place. So many centuries and they had not learned anything new.

He was still surprised that Kuisl owned this book as well. In the hangman's wooden chest and medicine cabinet there were over a dozen books and innumerable parchments, among these the writings of the Benedictine nun Hildegard of Bingen and newer texts on the circulation of blood or on the location of organs in the body. Even such a recent text as Ambroise Paré's *Writings on Anatomy and Surgery* in a German translation was among them. Simon did not believe that any Schongau citizen owned more books than the hangman, not even the court clerk, who had a reputation as a great scholar in town.

As Simon leafed through the Greek's text he wondered why he and the hangman could not simply leave the case of the midwife alone. Probably it was precisely this rejection of the obvious, this continuous probing prompted by curiosity, that created a bond between them. That, and a good portion of obstinacy, he thought with a smile.

All of a sudden his finger stopped on a page. Next to a drawing of the human body there were drawings of a few symbols for alchemistic ingredients. One of them showed a triangle with a squiggle below.

It was the old symbol for sulfur.

Simon knew it from his university days, but now he remembered where he had last seen this symbol. It was the symbol that the linen weaver Andreas Dangler had shown him, the same symbol that his foster child Sophie had drawn in the dirt in their backyard.

Simon pushed the book across the table to Jakob Kuisl, who was still crushing herbs in the mortar.

"This is the old symbol I told you about! The symbol Sophie drew! Now I recognize it again!"

The hangman looked at the page and nodded.

"Sulfur . . . the stink of the devil and of his playmates."

"I wonder if they really . . . ?" Simon asked.

Jakob Kuisl chewed on his pipe. "First the Venus symbol, and now the symbol for sulfur . . . well, it is strange."

"Where did Sophie learn such symbols?" Simon asked. "Only from the midwife. She must have told her and the other children about them. Perhaps she did teach them witchcraft after all." He sighed. "Unfortunately we can no longer ask her about it, in any case not now."

"Nonsense," the hangman growled. "The Stechlin woman is no more witch than I am. The children probably discovered the symbols in her room, in a book, on vials, bottles, who knows where."

Simon shook his head. "The symbol for sulfur maybe," he said. "But the Venus symbol, the witches' symbol? You said yourself that you've never seen such a symbol in her house. And if you had, then she would be a witch after all, wouldn't she?"

The hangman continued crushing the herbs in the mortar even though they had long been ground into a green paste.

"The Stechlin woman is no witch, and that's that," he growled. "Let's forget about her, and instead find the devil who is going through our town and kidnapping the children. Sophie, Clara, and Johannes, they've all disappeared. Where are they? I'm sure that when we find them we'll also find the solution to the puzzle."

"That is, if the children are still alive," mumbled Simon. Then he became lost again in his reveries.

"Sophie did see the devil. It was down by the river," he said finally, "and he asked about the Kratz boy. Not long after that, the boy was dead. The man was tall, he had a coat and a hat with a feather in it and a scar across his face. Also he is said to have had a hand made of bone, at least that's what the girl thinks she saw . . ."

Jakob Kuisl interrupted him. "The serving girl at Semer's inn also saw a man with a skeleton hand in the lounge."

"True," said Simon. "That was a few days earlier, together with a few other men. The maid said they looked like soldiers. Then they went upstairs to meet someone there. But who was that?"

The hangman scraped the paste from the mortar into a jar, which he sealed with a piece of leather.

"I don't like it when soldiers hang around our town," he growled. "Soldiers only bring trouble. They drink, they rob, they destroy."

"Speaking of destruction . . ." said Simon. "Schreevogl told me the night before last that not only is the Stadel destroyed, but on the same evening someone was at the building site for the leper house. Everything was razed to the ground there. Could that too have been the work of the Augsburgers?"

Jakob Kuisl dismissed this with a wave of the hand. "Hardly," he said. "They'll only welcome a leper house here. Then they hope that fewer travelers will stop in our town."

"Well, then perhaps it's wagon drivers from somewhere else who are afraid of catching leprosy in passing by," remarked Simon. "After all, the trade route runs not far from the Hohenfurch Road."

Jakob Kuisl spat. "Well, I know plenty of Schongauers who are just as afraid of that. The church wants the leper house, but the patricians are against it because they fear that business travelers will stay well clear of our little town . . . "

Simon shook his head. "And yet there are leper houses in many large cities, even in Regensburg and Augsburg . . . "

The hangman walked over to the apothecary's closet to put away the jar. "Our moneybags are cowardly dogs," he told Simon over his shoulder. "Some of them come and go regularly here at my house, and they tremble when the plague is still in Venice!"

When he returned he was carrying a larchwood truncheon about the length of his arm over his shoulder and grinning. "We need to take a closer look at that leper house in any case. I get the feeling that too many things are happening all at once for it to be a coincidence."

"Right away?" Simon asked.

"Right away," Jakob Kuisl said, swinging his truncheon. "Perhaps the devil is making his rounds out there. I've always wanted to give him a good thrashing."

He squeezed his massive body through the narrow door opening to the outside, into the April morning. Simon shivered with cold. It wouldn't be surprising if even the devil were afraid of the Schongau hangman.

The building site for the leper house was located in a clearing right next to the Hohenfurch Road less than half an hour's travel from the town. Simon had watched the workmen more than once as he passed the site. They had already set the foundations and raised brick walls. The doctor remembered having seen wooden scaffolding and a roof truss the last time. The ground walls of the little chapel next to it had also been completed.

Simon recalled how the priest had often mentioned with pride in his sermons during recent months the progress being made on the construction. In building the leper house, the church was fulfilling a long-held wish: it had always been its basic mission to care for the poor and the sick. Besides, the highly contagious lepers were a danger to the entire town. So far they had always been shunted off to the leper house in Augsburg. But the Augsburgers had enough lepers of their own, and lately they had only reluctantly accepted more. Schongau didn't want to plead for their help in the future. The new leper house would be a symbol of municipal independence, even if many in the council were opposed to its construction.

Not much was to be seen now of that once-busy building site. Many of the walls had collapsed as if someone had rammed them as hard as they could. The truss was now a sooty skeleton reaching up to the sky, and most of the wooden scaffolds were smashed or burnt. A smell of wet ashes hung in the air. An abandoned cart loaded with wood and barrels was stuck in a ditch at the side of the road.

In one corner of the clearing there was an old well made of natural stone. A group of craftsmen were sitting on the edge, staring in complete bewilderment at the destruction. The work of weeks, if not months, was destroyed. The construction had been a living for these men, and their future was now uncertain. As of yet, the church had not said what was going to be done.

Simon waved at the workmen and walked a few steps toward them. They eyed the physician with suspicion while continuing to chew on their bread. The doctor was obviously interrupting their meal, and they had no intention of wasting their short break on a chat.

"It looks pretty bad," Simon called out as he walked toward

them and pointed toward the building site. The hangman followed a few steps behind him.

"Do you know who did it?"

"And what business would that be of yours?" replied one worker, spitting on the ground in front of them. Simon recognized him as one of those who had tried a few days earlier to crash the keep to get at the midwife. The man looked over Simon's shoulder in the direction of Jakob Kuisl. The hangman smiled and rolled the truncheon back and forth on his shoulder.

"Greetings, Josef," said Kuisl. "How's the wife? In good health? Did my concoction work?"

Surprised, the others looked at the carpenter who had been hired by the town as site manager.

"Your wife is sick?" one of them asked. "You didn't say anything about that."

"It's . . . nothing serious," he growled and looked at the hangman as if seeking his help. "Only a little cough. Isn't that right, Master Kuisl?"

"That's right, Josef. Would you be so kind as to show us around?"

Josef Bichler shrugged and walked off in the direction of the collapsed walls. "There isn't much to see. Follow me."

The hangman and the physician followed while the other workmen remained at the well, talking to one another in hushed voices.

"What's wrong with his wife?" asked Simon in a whisper.

"She no longer wants to go to bed with him," said Jakob Kuisl as he surveyed the site. "He asked the midwife for a love potion, but she wouldn't give him one. She thought that was witchcraft. So he came to me."

"And you gave him?"

"Sometimes belief is the best potion. Belief and clay dissolved in water. There have been no complaints since then."

Simon grinned. At the same time he could not help shaking

his head over a man who wanted to see the midwife burned as a witch and at the same time ordered magic potions from her.

In the meantime they had reached the foundation of the leper house. Parts of the once six-foot-high walls had collapsed completely, and stones were scattered everywhere on the ground. A stack of planks had been thrown over and set on fire, and in some places smoke was still rising.

Josef Bichler crossed himself as he looked down on the destruction. "It must have been some kind of devil," he whispered. "The same one that murdered the little ones. Who else knocks down entire walls?"

"A devil or a couple of strong men using a tree trunk," Jakob Kuisl said. "This one there, for instance." He pointed to a thick pine trunk with its branches removed lying in the clearing not far from the north wall. Tracks in the dirt revealed how it had been dragged from the edge of the wood to the spot and from there on to the wall. The hangman nodded. "They probably used it like a battering ram." They climbed over part of the destroyed wall into the interior of the structure. The foundation had been smashed at several points as if someone had gone wild with a pickax. Slabs of stones had been pushed to the side and clumps of clay and pieces of brick were scattered around. In places the debris reached as high as their knees, so that they sometimes had to climb over heaps of rubble. It looked worse than after an attack by the Swedish forces.

"Why would someone do anything like that?" whispered Simon. "That's no longer vandalism, that's blind destructiveness."

"Strange," remarked Kuisl, chewing on his cold pipe. "Tearing down the walls would really have been enough to halt the building. But here . . . "

The carpenter looked at him anxiously. "I'm telling you . . . the devil," he hissed. "Only the devil has such power. Look at the chapel next to it—he crushed it with his fist as if it were a piece of paper."

Simon shivered. Now at noon the sun was trying to dissolve the morning mist but it couldn't quite do that. The mist still hung in thick clouds over the clearing. The forest, which began only a few yards behind the building site, could be seen only dimly.

In the meantime Jakob Kuisl had stepped out again through the masonry archway. He kept searching around in front of the western wall fragment and finally stopped. "Here!" he called out. "Clear tracks. Must have been four or five men."

All of a sudden he stooped down and picked something up. It was a small black leather pouch, no larger than a child's fist. He opened it, looked inside, and then sniffed it. A blissful smile brightened his face. "First-rate tobacco," he told Simon and the carpenter, who had both come closer. He rubbed the brown fibers into crumbs and deeply inhaled the aroma once more. "But not from around here. This is good stuff. I've smelled something like this up in Magdeburg once. For this stuff, traders got themselves slaughtered like pigs."

"You've been to Magdeburg?" asked Simon softly. "You never told me about that."

The hangman quickly stuffed the pouch into his coat pocket. Without answering Simon's question he walked toward the foundation walls of the chapel. Here, too, there was nothing but destruction. What had been walls were toppled over, forming small stone mounds. He climbed one of them and gazed all about. His mind seemed to be still on the pouch he had found. "Nobody smokes that kind of tobacco around here," he called down to the other two.

"How would you know?" asked the carpenter sourly. "All of this devil's weed smells the same!"

The hangman was torn from his thoughts and looked down angrily at Josef Bichler. As he stood there on the mound of stones surrounded by clouds of mist, he reminded Simon of some legendary giant. The hangman pointed his finger at the carpenter.

"You stink," he shouted. "Your teeth stink, and your mouth stinks, but this . . . weed, as you call it, is fragrant! It invigorates the senses and tears you from your dreams! It covers the entire world and lifts you into heaven; let me tell you that! In any case, it's much too good for a peasant numskull like you. It comes from the New World, and it is not meant for any old nitwit."

Before the carpenter could answer, Simon interrupted, pointing to a mound of wet, brown earth just next to the chapel. "Look, there are tracks here too!" he shouted. The mound was indeed covered with shoe prints. With a last angry look the hangman climbed down from the mound and examined the tracks. "Boot tracks," he said finally. "These are soldiers' boots, that's for sure. I've seen too many of them to make a mistake here." He whistled loudly. "This is getting interesting . . . " He pointed to a particular impression, somewhat blurred at the end of the sole. "This man limps. He's dragging one foot a little and cannot put much weight on it."

"The devil's clubfoot," hissed Josef Bichler.

"Nonsense," growled Kuisl. "If it were a clubfoot, then even you would be able to see it. No, the man is limping. He probably got a bullet in his leg during the war. They took out the bullet, but the leg has remained stiff."

Simon nodded. He could still remember such operations from his days as an army surgeon's son. Using long, thin grasping pincers, his father had burrowed into the wounded man's flesh until he finally found the bullet. Pus and gangrene had often developed afterward, and the soldier would die within a short time. But sometimes all went well, and the man could go back into combat, only to come back to them with a stomach wound the next time.

The hangman pointed at the mound of moist earth. "What is the clay doing here?" he asked.

"We use it to plaster the walls and the floor," the carpenter said. "The clay is from the pit by the brick hut behind the tanners' quarter."

"This property here belongs to the church, doesn't it?" Simon asked the carpenter.

Josef Bichler nodded. "Schreevogl, the old codger, willed it to the church shortly before he died last year, and the young heir wound up with nothing."

Simon remembered his conversation the day before yesterday with Jakob Schreevogl. That was more or less what the patrician's son had told him. Bichler grinned at him and poked at something that was stuck between his teeth.

"It sure bothered the young Schreevogl," he said.

"How do you know that?" asked Simon.

"I used to work for the old man, over at his kiln. They sure got in each other's hair, and then the old man told him that he was giving the land to the church for the leper house, and that heaven would reward him for it, and then he told his son to go to hell."

"And young Schreevogl?"

"He cursed mightily, mainly because he'd already planned a second kiln here. Now the church got it all."

Simon wanted to ask more questions, but a crashing noise caused him to whirl around. It was the hangman who had jumped over a stack of boards and was now running across the road toward the forest. There, almost swallowed up in the fog, Simon was able to make out another form, crouched down and running through the trees toward the high bank of the Lech.

Simon broke away from the surprised carpenter and ran diagonally across the clearing, hoping to cut off the other person. When he reached the edge of the woods, he was only a few yards behind him. From the right he could hear branches breaking as the hangman drew nearer, panting and swinging his cudgel.

"Run after him! I'll stay on the right so he won't escape over the fields," he panted. "We'll get him up on the steep bank at the latest."

Simon was now in the middle of a dense pine forest.

He couldn't see the fleeing person anymore, but he could hear him. In front of him twigs kept snapping, and muffled steps were moving away rapidly on the needle-covered ground. At times he thought he could distinguish a vague shape between the branches. The man, or whoever it was in front of him, was running in a crouch and somehow . . . strangely. Simon noticed that he was breathing harder, and there was a metallic taste in his mouth. It had been a long time since he had run so long and so fast. Come to think of it, it had been since his childhood. He was accustomed to sitting in his room reading books and drinking coffee, and he hadn't done much running in recent years, except for those few times when he had to flee from angry fathers of pretty burghers' daughters. But that, too, had been a while back.

Simon was losing ground to the runner in front of him and the snapping of twigs became less audible. From far off to the right he could hear the splintering of wood. That had to be the hangman, bounding like a wild boar over the fallen trees.

A few moments later Simon had reached the bottom of a small depression. The slope on the other side rose steeply before him. Somewhere beyond it began the bank of the Lech. Instead of pine trees, low intertwined bushes grew there, making it almost impossible to break through. Simon pulled himself up on one of the bushes and, with a curse, let go of it immediately. He had reached right into a blackberry bush and his right hand was now covered with small thorns. He listened, but all he could hear was splintering wood behind him. Now he saw the hangman coming from that direction. Kuisl leaped over a moldy tree trunk and finally came to a stop in front of him.

"So?" asked Jakob Kuisl. He too was breathless from the

chase, even if not nearly as much as the physician. Simon shook his head while bending over with a stitch in his side. "I think we've lost him," he panted.

"Damn," the hangman cursed. "I am sure it was one of the men who destroyed the building site."

"Then why did he come back?" asked Simon, still out of breath.

Jakob Kuisl shrugged. "Don't know. Maybe he wanted to see first if the site had been abandoned. Perhaps he wanted to see it once more, and perhaps he just wanted to look for his good tobacco." He hit his truncheon against a stunted fir tree. "Whatever. We've lost him in any case." He looked up the steep slope. "He must be pretty strong if he can climb this. Not everybody could."

In the meantime the physician had sat down on a moss-covered stump and was hard at work pulling the blackberry thorns out of his hand. A multitude of tiny mosquitoes swarmed around his head, looking for a good place to find blood.

"Let's get out of here," he said, waving his arms to ward off the mosquitoes.

The hangman nodded and walked ahead a few steps. Suddenly he stopped and pointed to the ground. In front of him lay an uprooted tree. At the spot where it had been rooted in the ground there was now a patch of moist, loamy soil. Two boot imprints were plainly visible in the center. The left one was less clear and ended in a sliding footprint.

"The limping man," whispered Jakob Kuisl. "It really was one of the soldiers."

"But why did they destroy the leper house? And what does that have to do with the dead children?" Simon asked.

"That's something we shall soon find out. Very soon," muttered the hangman. His eyes wandered once more over the crest of the hill. For an instant he thought he saw a human form up

there, but then clouds of mist drifted by once more. He pulled
the small tobacco pouch from his coat pocket and started to fill
his pipe as he walked along.

"At least the devil has good taste," he said. "You have to grant
the bastard that much."

As for the devil, he was standing at the top of the slope and, hidden behind a beech tree, looking down at the two small figures
directly below him. Next to him lay a large boulder. For a
moment he was tempted to get the rock rolling. It would loosen
other rocks as it fell, setting off an avalanche of gravel, rock, and
dead branches that would descend on those two down there and
possibly bury them. His pale skeletal hand reached for the boulder, but then the taller of the two figures suddenly turned his
head in his direction. For a brief moment he looked into the
man's eyes. Had the hangman seen him? He pressed himself
back against the beech tree and dismissed his idea. This man was
too strong and agile. He would hear the rockslide coming and
would jump to the side. The little quack was no problem, a snoop
whose throat he would cut the next time they met in some dark
corner of town. But the hangman . . .

He should not have come back here. Not in broad daylight.
Of course they would examine the building site at one time or
another. But he had lost his tobacco pouch, and that was something they might be able to trace to him. Besides, he had a nagging suspicion. Therefore he had decided to look into things
himself. Only the others mustn't know anything about it. They
were waiting for the devil to come and pay them off. If the workmen were to start building again, they would simply return and
pull everything down once more. That was their order. But the
devil was shrewd and had figured out right off that there was
more than that to this business. And so he had returned. That the
little snoop and the hangman had shown up at the same moment

was annoying. But they didn't catch him and he would simply give it another try at night.

He had told the others to look for the girl, but they had only reluctantly followed his order. They still obeyed him because they were afraid of him and had already accepted him earlier as their leader. But they were contradicting him more often now. They couldn't understand how important it was to eliminate the children. They had caught the little boy at the very start, and now they figured that the others would be terrified. They did not understand that the business had to be finished. The mission was in danger, and the payment was at risk. These dirty little brats who thought they could get away from him! A filthy little gang, squealing piglets whose throats had to be slit to make the shrill sounds in his head stop.

Shrill tolling of bells, crying of women, high-pitched wailing of infants that makes one's eyeballs burst . . .

Again, mist clouded his vision and he had to cling to the beech trunk so as not to topple down the slope. He bit his lips until he could taste blood, and only then did his mind clear. First he would have to eliminate the girl, then the snoop, and then the hangman. The hangman would be the most difficult. A worthy opponent. And then he would straighten things out down there at the building site. He was certain that the moneybags had kept something from him. But you can't fool the devil. And if anyone tried to, the devil bathed in his blood.

He breathed in the scent of fresh earth and delicate flowers. Everything was all right now. With a smile on his lips he walked along the edge of the hill until he was swallowed up in the forest.

When Simon and Jakob Kuisl returned to Schongau, the appearance of the ghostly figure had already become the talk of the town. Josef Bichler and the other workmen had run straight to the market square and told everyone of the devil's imminent arrival. The market stalls all around the Ballenhaus were abuzz with whispering and gossiping. Many of the local craftsmen had laid down their work and were now standing around in groups. The whole town was gripped with tension. Simon had the feeling that it wouldn't take much for the fuse to blow. One wrong word, one shrill cry, and the mob would force their way into the keep and burn Martha Stechlin themselves.

Under the suspicious looks of the market women and craftsmen, the physician and the hangman walked through the entrance gate of the town's parish church. A cool silence received them as they stepped into the town's largest house of worship. Simon's gaze wandered over the tall pillars with their peeling plaster, the darkened windowpanes, and the rotting choir seats. A few solitary candles were burning in dark side aisles and cast their flickering light upon yellowed frescoes.

Much like Schongau, the Church of the Assumption had seen better days. Quite a few Schongauers felt it would have made more sense to put money into the renovation of the church than into the construction of the leper house. The belfry more than anything else looked really dilapidated. In the inns across the street, people already painted dark pictures of what would happen if that tower were to collapse during Mass some day.

Now it was Saturday noon, and only a few old women were sitting in the pews. Once in a while one of them would get up and walk over to the confessional on the right side and emerge after some time, murmuring and running a rosary through her bony fingers. Jakob Kuisl sat in the rear pew observing the old women. When they noticed him they murmured their prayer with ever greater fervor and pressed close against the wall of the main aisle as they scurried past him.

The hangman was not welcome in church. His assigned seat was all the way in the back to the left, and he was always the last to receive communion. Still, Jakob Kuisl made it a point even today to give the old women his friendliest smile. They acknowledged it by crossing themselves and quickly leaving the church.

Simon Fronwieser waited until the last of them had exited the confessional and then stepped inside it himself. The warm voice of the parish priest, Konrad Weber, could be heard through the tight grate of the wooden window.

"*Misereatur tui omnipotens Deus, et dimissis peccatis tuis, perducat te ad vitam . . .* May almighty God have mercy on thee, and having forgiven thee thy sins, bring thee to life . . . "

"Father, I don't come to confess," whispered Simon. "I only need some information."

The Latin whispering stopped. "Who are you?" asked the priest.

"It's me, Simon Fronwieser, the surgeon's son."

"I don't see you often at confession, even when I am told that you have every reason for it."

"Well, I . . . I shall improve, Father. In fact I'll be confessing right now. But first I must find out something concerning the leper house. Is it true that old Schreevogl left you the land on the Hohenfurch Road, even though he had actually promised it to his son?"

"Why do you want to know?"

"The destruction at the leper house. I would like to find out what's behind it."

For a long time the priest said nothing. Finally he cleared his throat.

"People say that it was the devil," he whispered.

"And you believe that?"

"Well, the devil can appear in many ways, also in human form. It'll be Walpurgis Night in a few days, then the Evil One will mate once more with certain godless women. It is said that long ago witches' sabbaths were held on that piece of land."

Simon flinched.

"Who says so?"

The priest hesitated before continuing.

"People say so. The spot on which the little church is being built is where sorcerers and witches are said to have caroused in the past. A long time ago there used to be a chapel there, but it fell into ruin just like the former leper house. It's as if some evil spell lies over the area . . . " The priest's voice became a whisper. "They have found an old pagan stone altar there, which fortunately we were able to destroy. This was one more reason for the church to build a new leper house and chapel there. Evil must yield when it is touched by God's light. We sprinkled holy water over the entire site."

"Apparently without success," murmured Simon. Then he continued his questioning: "Had old Schreevogl already left this piece of land to his son? That is, was he already recorded as an heir?"

The priest cleared his throat.

"You knew old Schreevogl? He was a . . . well, yes, a stubborn old codger. One day he came to see me at the parish house, all upset, and told me that his son did not understand the least thing about business and that he would now like to leave the land down there at the Hohenfurch Road to the church. We changed his will, and the provost witnessed it."

"And not long after that he died . . . "

"Yes, from a fever. I gave him last rites myself. Still on his deathbed, he spoke of the piece of land, saying that he hoped we would have much joy from it and would be able to do much good. He never forgave his son. The last person he wanted to see was not Jakob Schreevogl but old Matthias Augustin. Those two had been friends ever since they served together on the town council. They had known each other ever since childhood."

"And even on his deathbed he did not take back the donation?"

The priest's face was now close to the wooden lattice.

"What should I have done?" he asked. "Tell the old man to

change his mind? I was glad that I could finally get that piece of land without spending a single guilder. The way it is situated makes it ideal for a leper house. Far enough from the town and yet close to the road . . . "

"Who do you think destroyed the building site?"

Father Konrad Weber fell silent once more. Just when Simon thought that he would say nothing more, he spoke up once again, in a very low voice.

"If the destruction goes on like this I won't be able to defend my decision to build the leper house before the council much longer. Too many are opposed. Even the provost feels that we cannot afford such a building. We shall have to resell the land again."

"To whom?"

Again, silence.

"To whom, Father?"

"Until now, nobody has shown any interest. But I could well imagine that young Schreevogl might soon show up at the parish house . . . "

Simon stood up in the narrow confessional and turned away.

"Thank you very much, Father."

"Simon?"

"Yes, Father?"

"The confession."

With a sigh Simon sat down once more and listened to the priest's monotonous words.

"*Indulgentiam, absolutionem et remissionem peccatorum tuorum tribuat tibi omnipotens et misericors Dominus* . . . May the almighty and merciful Lord grant thee pardon, absolution, and remission of thy sins . . . "

It was going to be a long day.

When Simon finally left the confessional, Father Konrad Weber paused for a moment. He felt as if he had forgotten something. Something that was on his tongue just before and he couldn't remember it now. After thinking about it for a short while, he returned to his prayers. Perhaps it would come to him later.

Simon sighed as he stepped from the dark church out into the open air. The sun had moved over the rooftops by now. Jakob Kuisl had gone to sit on a bench near the cemetery and was sucking on his pipe. With eyes closed, he was enjoying the first warm day of spring and the excellent tobacco he had found at the building site. He had left the cool church a while ago, and when he saw Simon approaching, he blinked.

"Well?"

Simon sat down next to him on the bench. "I believe we have a clue," he said. Then he told him of his conversation with the priest.

Lost in thought, the hangman chewed on his pipe. "All this talk about witches and sorcerers is pure nonsense as far as I am concerned. But the fact that old Schreevogl practically disinherited his son, that's worth thinking about. So you think young Schreevogl could have messed up the building site in order to get his land back?"

Simon nodded. "It's possible. After all, he had wanted to build a second kiln there, as he told me himself. And he's ambitious."

Suddenly Simon remembered something.

"Resl, the waitress at Semer's inn, told me about the soldiers meeting someone upstairs at the inn," he exclaimed. "One of them was limping, she said. That must have been the devil we saw today. Perhaps it was Jakob Schreevogl who met with the devil and the other soldiers up there at the inn."

"And what does all of that have to do with the fire at the Stadel, with the symbols and with the dead children?" Jakob Kuisl asked while he continued sucking on his pipe.

"Perhaps nothing at all. Perhaps the Stadel mess and the children are really the work of the Augsburgers. And young Schreevogl only took advantage of all the excitement in order to destroy the building site without being noticed."

"While his ward was being abducted?" The hangman rose, shaking his head. "That makes no sense! If you ask me, there are just too many coincidences all at once. Somehow it ought to fit together: the fire, the children, the symbols, the ruined leper house. Yet we don't know how . . . "

Simon rubbed his temples. The incense and the priest's Latin babbling had given him a headache.

"I don't know what to do anymore," he said. "And time's short. How much longer will Goodwife Stechlin remain unconscious?"

The hangman looked up to the belfry, where the sun had already passed the crest of the roof.

"Two days at the most. And then Count Sandizell will arrive, the representative of the Elector. If we don't have the true culprit by then, they won't screw around for long, and the midwife will be done for. They'll want to get rid of the count and his entourage as quickly as possible. He only costs them money."

Simon rose from the bench.

"I shall go and see Jakob Schreevogl now," he said. "That is the only lead we've got. I am sure something's fishy with that leper house."

"Go ahead and see him," grunted Kuisl. "As for me, I'm going to smoke a little more of the devil's tobacco for a while. There's nothing better to help a person concentrate."

The hangman closed his eyes again, breathing in the fragrance of the New World.

Johann Lechner, the court clerk, was on the way from his office to the Ballenhaus. On his way he noticed with some discomfort the whispering women and the grumbling workmen in the square. As he passed them, he dealt them light shoves and slaps here and there. "Go back to work," he called out. "There's a proper way to do everything. It will all be cleared up. Now return to your work, burghers! Or I shall have to have some of you arrested!"

The burghers slinked off to their workrooms, and the market women resumed sorting out their merchandise. But Johann Lechner knew that they would start gossiping again as soon as his back was turned. He would have to send a few bailiffs to the square to prevent a disturbance. It was high time for this tiresome business to be concluded. And just now it was impossible to talk to the damn midwife! The aldermen were breathing down his neck, wanting to see results. Well, perhaps he would soon be able to show them some. After all, he still had a second trump in his hand.

The court clerk rushed up the steps of the Ballenhaus to the second floor, where a small room with a locked door was provided for the more prominent burghers, those one did not want to throw into the rat-infested hole in the Faulturm tower or in the dungeon in the keep. A bailiff was posted in front of the door. He greeted Johann Lechner with a nod before opening the massive lock and pushing back the bolt.

Martin Hueber, the wagon driver from Augsburg, was sprawled over a small table in an alcove, peering through the window at the square below. When he heard the court clerk enter he turned around and greeted him with a smirk.

"Ah, the court clerk! So have you finally come to your senses? Let me go, and we won't say another word about this matter."

He rose and walked to the door, but Lechner let it slam shut.

"I believe there must be some kind of misunderstanding here. Martin Hueber, you and your team are suspected of having started the fire at the Stadel."

Martin Hueber's face turned red. He slapped his broad hand on the table.

"You know that's not true!"

"No need to deny it. A few Schongau rafters saw you and your men."

Johann Lechner lied without blinking an eye. With great curiosity he awaited the Augsburger's reaction.

Martin Hueber took a deep breath, then sat down again, crossing his arms over his wide chest in silence.

The clerk kept insisting. "Why else would you have been down there at nightfall? You had already unloaded your freight in the afternoon. When the Stadel went up in flames you were suddenly there, so you must have been hanging around beforehand."

The wagon driver remained silent. Lechner went back to the door and reached for the handle.

"All right then. We'll see if you maintain your silence under torture," he said as he pushed down the handle. "I shall have you taken to the keep this very day. You've already met the hangman down by the raft landing. He'll be glad to break a few of your bones."

Johann Lechner could see the turmoil behind the wagon driver's brow. He bit his lip, and finally the words burst forth.

"It's true, we were there," he cried, "but not in order to burn down the Stadel! After all, our own merchandise was in there too!"

Johann Lechner returned to the table.

"And what was it you wanted there?"

"We wanted to give the Schongau rafters a thrashing, that's what we wanted! Up at the Stern that wagon driver of yours, Josef Grimmer, gave one of our men such a beating that he'll probably never be able to work again! We wanted to make sure that such a thing would never happen again, but by God, we didn't set fire to the Stadel! I swear it!"

Fear gleamed in the wagon driver's eyes. Johann Lechner experienced a warm feeling of satisfaction. He had suspected something, but he had not believed that the Augsburger would cave in so quickly.

"Hueber, it doesn't look good for you," he continued. "Is there anything to support your case?"

The wagon driver thought briefly, then nodded.

"Yes, there is something. When we were down by the landing we saw a few men run away, about four or five of them. We thought they were yours. Just a little while later the Stadel was burning."

The court clerk shook his head sadly, like a father who is immensely disappointed with his son.

"Why didn't you tell us this earlier? It would have saved you a lot of suffering."

"But then you'd have known that we had been there before," sighed Martin Hueber. "Also, until just now I really did think these men were yours. They looked like town bailiffs."

"Like town bailiffs?"

The Augsburg carter was struggling for the right words.

"More or less. After all, it was already getting dark, and they were quite a ways off. I didn't see much. Now that I think about it, they may have been soldiers."

Johann Lechner gave him a puzzled look.

"Soldiers . . . "

"Yes, the colorful clothes, the high boots, the hats. I believe one or two of them were also carrying sabers. I . . . I'm no longer sure."

"Well, you really should be sure, Hueber."

Johann Lechner walked back to the door. "You should be sure, or else we'll have to help you remember. I'll give you one more night to think it over. Tomorrow I shall return with quill and parchment, and we'll set it all down in writing. If some uncertainties still remain, we'll quickly clear them up. It just so happens that the hangman is not busy right now."

With those words he closed the door behind him and left the wagon driver alone. Johann Lechner smiled. They would see what the Augsburger would come up with overnight. Even if he was not responsible for the fire, his confession would still be worth its weight in gold. A Fugger wagon driver as the ringleader of a conspiracy against the wagon drivers of Schongau! The Augsburgers would have to eat humble pie in future negotiations. It might even be possible, under such circumstances, to increase the rates for warehousing Augsburg goods. After all, the Stadel would have to be rebuilt at great cost. It was wonderful how everything was working out. Once the midwife confessed, all would be well again. Fronwieser, that quack, had said that she would be ready for interrogation tomorrow, or the day after tomorrow at the latest.

It would just take time and patience.

The Schreevogl house was in the Bauerngasse, in the Hof Gate quarter, not far from the castle. In this neighborhood stood the houses of the patricians, three-story showpieces with carved balconies and paintings on their facades. The air smelled much better here, mainly because it was far away from the malodorous tanneries down by the Lech. Servant girls were shaking out bedding on the balustrades, while merchants came to the door to supply the cooks with spices, smoked meat, and plucked geese. Simon knocked on the tall door with the brass knob. After a few seconds he could hear steps inside. A maid opened and led him into the entrance hall. A short time later Jakob Schreevogl appeared at the top of the wide spiral staircase. With concern he looked down on Simon.

"Any news about our Clara?" he asked. "My wife is still

sick in bed. Under no circumstances do I wish to upset her unnecessarily."

Simon shook his head. "We were down at the Hohenfurch Road. The building site of the leper house is completely ruined."

Jakob Schreevogl sighed. "I already know that," he said and with a gesture invited Simon to have a seat while he himself settled into a cushioned chair in the antechamber. He reached into a bowl of gingerbread cookies and started chewing slowly. "Who would do such a thing? I mean, of course there was opposition to the construction in the council, but from there to go and destroy the entire leper house . . ."

Simon decided to speak openly with the patrician.

"Is it true that you had already made firm plans for a second kiln on that land before your father left it to the church?" he asked.

Jakob Schreevogl frowned and put the gingerbread back into the bowl. "But I've already told you. After the argument with my father he quickly changed his will, and I could bury my plans."

"And your father, too, shortly thereafter."

The patrician raised his eyebrows. "What are you implying, Fronwieser?"

"With your father's death you no longer had any chance of having the will changed again. Now the land belongs to the church. If you want it back, you'd have to buy it back from the church."

Jakob Schreevogl smiled. "I understand," he said. "You suspect me of interfering with the construction until the church would give me back the land voluntarily. But you forget that before the council, I had always spoken for the building of the leper house."

"Yes, but not necessarily on a piece of land that is so important to you," interrupted Simon.

The patrician shrugged. "I am already conducting negotiations regarding another piece of land. The second kiln will be built but at another location. This particular spot on the Hohenfurch Road wasn't important enough for me to put my good name at risk for it."

Simon looked Jakob Schreevogl straight in the eye. He could detect no trace of deception.

"Who, if not you, could be interested in destroying the leper house?" he asked finally.

Schreevogl laughed. "Half the council was against building it: Holzhofer, Püchner, Augustin, and, leading them all in opposition, the presiding burgomaster Karl Semer." He quickly became serious again. "Which doesn't mean that I would suspect any one of them of such a thing."

The young patrician rose and started to pace back and forth across the room. "I don't understand you, Fronwieser," he said. "My Clara has disappeared, two children are dead, the Zimmerstadel has been destroyed, and you are questioning me here about a burned-out building site? What is that supposed to mean?"

"We saw someone at the leper house this morning," Simon interjected.

"Who?"

"The devil."

The patrician caught his breath as Simon continued.

"In any case, the one they call the devil now," he said. "It may be a soldier with a limp. The one who abducted your Clara and who was hanging out with other soldiers at Semer's inn a few days ago. And who met an apparently important person from the town upstairs in the inn's conference room."

Jakob Schreevogl sat down again.

"How do you know that he met someone at Semer's inn?" he asked.

"A servant girl told me," Simon replied sharply. "Burgomaster Semer himself claimed to know nothing about it."

Schreevogl nodded. "And what makes you think that this person was someone important?"

Simon shrugged. "Soldiers are hired for money; that's their profession. And in order to be able to pay four men, much money is needed. The question is, what were they hired to do?"

He leaned forward.

"Where were you on Friday of last week?" he asked softly.

Jakob Schreevogl remained calm and returned the physician's gaze.

"You're barking up the wrong tree if you think I had anything to do with this," he said sharply. "Don't forget that it was my daughter who was abducted."

"Where were you?"

The patrician leaned back and appeared to be reflecting. "I had gone down to the kiln," he said finally. "The chimney was clogged up, and we worked late into the night cleaning it. You're welcome to ask my workers."

"And in the evening, when the Stadel was burning? Where were you then?"

Jakob Schreevogl slammed his hand down on the table so that the gingerbread bowl jumped. "I've had enough of your suspicions! My daughter has disappeared, and that's all that counts for me. I don't give a damn about your ruined building site. And now get out of my home. Right now!"

Simon tried to calm him. "I'm only following every lead I can find. I have no idea either how all this fits together. But somehow it does, and the devil is the link."

There was a knock at the door.

Jakob Schreevogl walked the few steps to the door and opened it abruptly.

"What is it?" he asked angrily.

A small boy, about eight years old, was standing outside. Simon had seen him before. He was one of the children of Ganghofer, the baker in the Hennengasse. He stared up fearfully at the patrician.

"Are you the alderman Jakob Schreevogl?" he asked timidly.

"That's who I am. What's the matter? Speak quickly!" Schreevogl was about to close the door again.

"The father of Clara Schreevogl?" the boy asked.

The patrician paused. "Yes," he whispered.

"I'm supposed to tell you that your daughter is all right."

Schreevogl tore the door open and pulled the boy toward him.

"How do you know that?"

"I . . . I . . . am not supposed to tell you. I promised!"

The patrician grabbed the little boy by his soiled shirt collar and pulled him up to look right in his eyes.

"Did you see her? Where is she?" he screamed into his face. The boy struggled and tried to free himself from the man's grasp.

Simon stepped closer. He held up a shining coin and rolled it back and forth between his fingers. The boy stiffened, and his eyes followed the coin as if he were hypnotized.

"Your promise should not bind you. After all, it was not a Christian oath, was it?" he asked the child in a soothing voice.

The boy shook his head. Jakob Schreevogl carefully set him down and looked expectantly between Simon and the boy.

"Well," continued Simon. "Who told you that Clara was well?"

"It . . . it was Sophie," the boy whispered without taking his eyes off the coin. "The red-haired girl. She told me down by the raft landing, just before I came. I got an apple for bringing you the message."

Simon brushed his hand across the boy's head trying to calm

him down. "You did very well. And did Sophie also tell you where Clara is now?"

The boy shook his head fearfully. "That's all she told me. I swear by the Holy Mother of God!"

"And Sophie? Where is she now?" Jakob Schreevogl interrupted.

"She . . . she left again right away, over the bridge and into the woods. When I looked at her she threw a stone at me. Then I came here right away."

Simon looked at Jakob Schreevogl from the side. "I believe he's telling the truth," he said. Schreevogl nodded.

When Simon tried to give the child his coin, the patrician intervened and reached into his own purse. He pulled out a shiny silver penny and gave it to the boy.

"This one is for you," he said. "And another one just like it if you find out where Sophie or my Clara are. We're not out to harm Sophie, you understand?"

The boy reached for the coin and closed his small fist around it.

"The . . . the other children say that Sophie is a witch and will soon be burned, together with the Stechlin woman," he whispered.

"You need not believe everything the other children are saying." Jakob Schreevogl gave him a little nudge. "Run along now. And remember, this is our secret, right?"

The boy nodded. Seconds later he disappeared around the corner with his treasure.

Jakob Schreevogl closed the door and looked at Simon. "She's alive," he whispered. "My Clara is alive! I must immediately tell my wife. Please excuse me."

He rushed upstairs. Halfway up the stairs he stopped once more and looked down at Simon.

"I have much esteem for you, Fronwieser," he said. "Now as

always. Find the devil, and I shall reward you generously." He smiled as he continued. "You're welcome to look around my little private library. I think it contains a few books that may interest you."

Then he quickly went upstairs into his wife's bedroom.

CHAPTER
10

FOR A GOOD HALF MINUTE SIMON STOOD TRANSFIXED in the hall of the patrician's house. Thoughts raced through his mind. Finally he came to a decision and ran out into the street, down the Bauerngasse and into the market square. He bumped into a few market women and almost upset a stall with loaves of bread before running down behind the Ballenhaus to the Lech Gate, ignoring the cries and curses behind him. In a few minutes he was on the bridge over the river. He hurried across, leaving the burned-out Stadel on his right, and ran out onto the country road that led from the raft landing to Peiting.

After a short time he reached the edge of the forest. Now, at midday, the road was almost deserted, most of the wagons having already gone down to the river in the early hours of the morning. Birds were quietly chirping and sometimes a twig snapped in the depth of the forest, but otherwise it was peaceful.

"Sophie!"

In the silence Simon's voice sounded hollow and weak, as if the forest was about to swallow it up after only a few yards.

"Sophie, can you hear me?"

He cursed himself for this idea. Perhaps the girl might have run into the forest from here just half an hour before, but it was not likely that she was still within earshot. She could be far, far away by now. Anyway, why in the world would she *want* to listen to him? It was very possible she was at this moment sitting on a branch somewhere and watching him. Sophie had fled. She was suspected of engaging in witchcraft along with the midwife. As an orphan, without a good reputation or witnesses to speak for her, she was extremely likely to end up being burned at the stake along with the Stechlin woman even though she was only twelve years old. The physician had heard of cases where even much younger children had been put to the stake as witches. Why, then, should Sophie come forward now?

Simon sighed and turned on his heels.

"Stop right there!"

The voice had come from somewhere out in the depths of the forest. Simon stopped and looked back over his shoulder. A stone hit him in the side.

"Ouch! Damn it, Sophie . . . "

"Don't turn round," came Sophie's voice again. "You needn't see where I am."

Simon obeyed, shrugging his shoulders. The place where the pebble had struck him was terribly painful. He had no desire to be injured by another stone.

"The boy tattled, is that right?" asked Sophie. "He told you that I sent him."

Simon nodded. "Don't be angry with him," he said. "I would have guessed it anyway."

He focused his eyes on a point somewhere in the dense

undergrowth in front of him. This helped him to speak to the invisible girl.

"Where is Clara, Sophie?"

"She's safe. I can't tell you anymore."

"Why not?"

"Because they're looking for us. Clara and I are in danger, even in the town. They already got Peter and Anton. You must keep an eye on Johannes Strasser, at the innkeeper's in Altenstadt—"

"He's gone missing," Simon interrupted the girl.

She was silent for a long time. Simon thought he heard her sob quietly.

"Sophie, what happened that night? You were all together, weren't you? Peter, you, Clara, the other orphans . . . what happened?"

"I . . . I can't tell you." Sophie's voice trembled. "It will all come out. We'll be burned—all of us!"

"Sophie, I swear I will stand up for you," he said, trying to calm her down. "Nobody's going to get hurt. Nobody . . . "

He heard a branch break. The sound came not from behind, where he supposed Sophie was standing or sitting, but from the front. On the left, twenty paces in front of Simon, there was a stack of sticks.

Something was moving behind the pile.

Simon heard a thump behind him and steps hurrying away. Sophie was escaping.

Just a moment later a figure dashed out from behind the pile. The person was wearing a coat and a broad-brimmed hat. At first Simon thought it was the hangman, but then the figure drew a saber from under his coat. For one short moment the sun shone through the thick branches of the forest, and the saber glittered in the light. As the figure rushed toward him, Simon noticed something clutching the saber, something white.

It was the hand of the devil, a hand of bone.

Simon suddenly felt as if time had arrested. Every gesture and detail burned itself into his brain. His feet seemed glued to the earth, as if stuck in a swamp. Not until the devil was ten strides from him could he move again. Terrified, he turned and ran to the edge of the forest. Behind him he heard the steps of the devil, a rhythmic crunching of gravel and earth. Soon he could hear the breath of his pursuer drawing closer.

Simon dared not turn around for fear this would slow him down. He ran and ran, the metallic taste of blood in his mouth, and he knew that he would not be able to maintain this pace much longer. The man behind him was used to running, his breath was regular and even, very soon he would catch up. And the edge of the forest was still not in sight. All he could see was dense woods and shadows.

The sound of breathing came even closer. Simon cursed himself for his idea of going into the forest alone. The devil had seen him and the hangman at the building site. They had pursued him, and they had provoked him, and now the devil was at his heels. Simon had no illusions. When the man caught up with him he would kill him, as quickly and casually as one would kill a bothersome fly.

At last the forest seemed to brighten in front of him. Simon's heart raced. That must be the edge of the forest! The path went down into a hollow before it finally left the forest and led down to the river. Light broke through the treetops, the shadows retreated. Simon staggered on a few yards, then dazzling sunlight surrounded him. He had reached the end of the forest. He staggered over a bank and saw the raft landing beneath him. People were standing on the riverbank, and oxen were drawing a wagon up the hill toward the forest. Only now did he dare to look around. The figure behind him had vanished. The edge of the forest appeared to be nothing more than a black ribbon in the midday sun.

But he still felt he was in danger. After taking a few deep

breaths, he ran on unsteadily toward the raft landing, looking behind him all the way. As he turned his head once again toward the forest, he collided with someone in front of him.

"Simon?"

It was Magdalena. She had a basket in her hand filled with wild herbs. She looked at him, in astonishment.

"What's happened? You look like you've seen a ghost."

Simon pushed her down the few remaining yards to the raft landing and collapsed onto a stack of beams. Not until he was here amid the busy activity of the raftsmen and wagon drivers did he really feel safe.

"He . . . was after me," he stammered at last, when his breathing was more or less regular again.

"Who was?" Magdalena asked anxiously and sat down beside him.

"The devil."

Magdalena laughed, but her laughter did not sound genuine. "Simon, don't talk nonsense," she said finally. "You've been tippling, in the midday sun!"

Simon shook his head. Then he told her everything that had happened since the morning: the destruction at the building site, the pursuit with her father in the woods, the conversations with the parish priest, Schreevogl, and Sophie, and finally his flight down to the raft landing. When he had finished, Magdalena looked at him with worried eyes.

"But why did the devil pick on you?" she asked. "You don't have anything to do with it, do you?"

Simon shrugged. "Probably because we are on his heels and because we almost got him." He looked at Magdalena very earnestly. "Your father is in danger too."

Magdalena grinned. "I'd like to see the devil try to punch my father. My father's the hangman, don't forget that."

Simon got up from the pile of wood. "Magdalena, this is no joke," he cried. "This man, or whatever he is, has presumably murdered a few children! He wanted to kill me, and perhaps he's observing us at this very minute."

Magdalena looked around. Right in front of them, wagon drivers were loading two rafts with cases and barrels and lashing them into place. Further on, a few men were clearing away the charred remains of the Zimmerstadel, and elsewhere new beams were already being put up. One of the men occasionally turned to look at them and then whispered to his neighbor.

Simon could well imagine what they were whispering: the hangman's whore and her lover boy . . . the physician's son, who goes to bed with the hangman's wench and doesn't believe that the devil is making his rounds in Schongau, or that the midwife must be burned.

Simon sighed. Magdalena's reputation was ruined anyway, and by now, his as well. He put his hand against her cheek and looked deep into her eyes.

"Your father told me that you found a mandrake in the forest," he said. "You probably saved Martha Stechlin's life with it."

Magdalena grinned.

"That's a fair exchange. After all, she gave me my life. I was a real pain when I was born, my mother says. I was the wrong way around and didn't want to come out. If it hadn't been for Martha Stechlin, I wouldn't be here. Now I can pay her back."

Then she became serious again.

"We must go to my father and warn him," she whispered. "Perhaps he'll think of some way that we can catch the devil."

Simon shook his head. "Above all we must find out who took part in the meeting with this so-called devil and the other soldiers at Semer's inn. I'm sure this person is the key to everything else."

Both fell silent in thought.

"Why did the devil come back?"

"What?" Simon was startled out of his thoughts.

"Why did he come back to the building site?" Magdalena asked once more. "If he and his men were really responsible for the destruction there, why did he go there once again? They had already done everything they wanted to."

Simon frowned. "Perhaps because he'd lost something, perhaps the tobacco pouch that your father found. He didn't want people to discover that and draw conclusions."

Magdalena shook her head.

"I don't believe that. There was no monogram on the pouch, nothing that might have given him away. It must have been something else . . . "

"Perhaps he was looking for something," Simon suggested. "Something that he didn't find the first time."

Magdalena was deep in thought.

"Something draws him to the building site," she said. "Goodwife Daubenberger told me that witches used to dance there, and soon it will be Walpurgis Night again . . . Perhaps he really is the devil."

Both fell silent again. The sun was almost too hot for April. It warmed the stack of beams they were sitting on. From a distance they heard the voices of the raftsmen as they drifted down the river toward Augsburg. The water glittered like liquid gold. Suddenly it was all too much for Simon—the flight, all the questions, the brooding, the fear . . .

He jumped up, took Magdalena's basket, and ran upriver.

"Where are you going?" she called.

"To look for herbs, with you. Come on, the sun is shining, and I know a nice cozy place."

"And what about my father?"

He swung her basket and smiled at her.

"He can wait a bit. You said yourself that he fears neither death nor the devil."

Under the disapproving looks of the wagon drivers she ran after him.

Dusk stretched out its fingers from the west and settled on the woods around Schongau. The Hohenfurch Road lay in complete darkness, and so the man who now approached from the west could scarcely be discerned among the bushes at the edge of the clearing. He had decided against taking the road and had gone through the high thickets parallel to it. It took almost twice as long that way, but he could be sure that nobody would see him. The gates of the town had been closed half an hour ago and the probability that he would meet anyone out here was extremely small. But the man did not want to run any risk.

His shoulders ached from carrying the shovel. Sweat streamed over his forehead; thorns and thistles clung to his coat and left small tears in many places. The man cursed. What drove him on was the certainty that all this would soon be over. Then he could come and go as he pleased and there would be nobody to tell him what to do. Sometime in a distant future he would tell his grandchildren about it, and they would understand. They would realize that it was for their sake that he had done all this, for the survival of their family, their *dynasty*. That it was he who had saved the family. But then it occurred to him that he had already gone too far. He couldn't tell anyone about it anymore. Too much had already happened, too much that was dirty and bloody. He would have to take the secret with him to the grave.

A twig cracked in the darkness, a flapping noise could be heard. The man stopped and held his breath. Carefully he pulled out the small lantern that he had concealed under his coat until then and pointed it in the direction of the sound. Not far from him, an owl flew up into the air and across the clearing. He smiled. Fear had almost made a fool of him.

He looked around on all sides for the last time, then he entered the building site and hurried to the construction in the middle.

Where should he begin? He walked round the foundation walls that had been destroyed and looked for a clue. When he found nothing, he climbed over a heap of stones into the interior and struck a flagstone on the ground with his shovel. The metallic noise seemed to go right through him. He had a feeling they could hear it all the way to Schongau, and he stopped at once.

Finally he climbed a small wall adjacent to the main building and gazed over the clearing. The leper house, the chapel, heaps of beams, a well, sacks of lime, a few upset buckets . . .

His eye fell on an old linden tree in the middle of the clearing. Its branches reached almost down to the ground. For some reason the builders had left it standing. Perhaps the church did not want to chop it down, thinking of a future use as shade for the invalids.

Or perhaps because the old man had willed it so?

With hasty steps he ran to the linden, ducked under the branches, and began to dig. The earth was as firm as clay. A tough network of roots spread from the linden in all directions. The man cursed as he dug until streams of sweat began to soak through his coat. He gripped the shovel with both hands and drove the blade through roots as thick as arms, until they splintered, only to reveal other roots beneath them. He tried it in another place nearer to the tree, with the same result. He panted and spluttered. He hacked faster and faster on earth and wood, then he stopped, struggling for breath, and leaned on the shovel. It must be the wrong place. Nothing had been buried here.

With his lantern he examined the linden for possible knotholes. Beneath the first branch, just high enough to be out of his reach, there was a hole about as big as a man's fist. He put the lantern down and pulled himself up by the branch. The first time he slipped down because his hands were so wet with perspiration, but at last he managed to hoist his heavy body up. Slowly he moved toward the trunk until he could manage to put his right hand into the knothole. He felt wet straw and then something cold, hard. Obviously metal.

His heart jumped.

Suddenly a sharp pain shot through his hand. He pulled it out, and at the same moment he saw something large and black flying away protesting furiously. On the back of his hand there was a cut as long as a finger that began to bleed profusely. Cursing, he threw away the rusty spoon which he had continued to clutch in his hand, and let himself slide to the ground. He licked the blood from the wound, while tears of pain and despair flowed down his cheeks. The scolding of the magpies seemed to be mocking him.

Everything was in vain.

He would never find it. The old man had taken his secret to the grave with him. Once more he glanced over the building site. The walls, the foundations of the chapel, the well, stacks of wood, the linden, a few stunted pines at the edge of the clearing. There had to be something that had been there before—something noticeable, something that could be found again. But perhaps the builders, unknowingly, had already removed this landmark.

He shook his head. The site was too big. He could dig here night after night without finding the slightest thing. But then a defiant spirit welled up within him. He could not give up so easily. Not so soon. Too much depended on it. A new plan, then . . . He must proceed systematically, divide the site up into smaller parcels and then search it section by section. One thing at least was sure—the thing he was looking for was here. It would take patience, but in the end it would be worth it.

Not far away, leaning against a tree trunk near the clearing, the devil stood and watched the man digging. He blew a smoke ring into the night sky and watched it climb up toward the moon. He had known that there was something else interesting about the building site. He wouldn't be lied to. That made him angry. Actually, he would have liked immediately to cut the throat of the man down there between the walls and sprinkle his blood around the clearing. But then he would spoil things in two ways: he would not be paid for further mischief, and he would never find out what the man was so desperately seeking. He would therefore have to be patient. Later, when the man had found it, there would be time enough to punish him for his lies. Just as he would punish the physician and the hangman for pursuing him. This time the quack had managed to get away from him. That would not happen again.

The devil puffed another cloud into the night sky. Then he made himself comfortable on the soft moss at the foot of a fir tree and carefully observed the man digging. Perhaps, after all, he would find something.

CHAPTER

II

SUNDAY
APRIL 29, A.D. 1659
SIX O'CLOCK IN THE MORNING

SIMON WAS AWAKENED BY A CREAKING NOISE, A soft sound that had insinuated itself into his dreams. In a second, he was wide awake. Next to him, Magdalena was still in deep sleep. Her breath was even, and the smile on her lips suggested she was in the midst of a beautiful dream. Simon hoped that she was dreaming of last night.

He had walked with Magdalena along the river to gather herbs. He had tried not to say a word about the recent events in Schongau. At least for a brief moment he wanted to forget. He didn't want to think of the man they called the devil, who was intent on murdering him. He didn't want to think of the midwife in the town jail, who was still unconscious, nor the dead children. Springtime was here, the sun was shining warmly, and the waters of the Lech burbled along softly.

After a good mile through the meadowland along the riverbank they reached Simon's favorite spot, a small gravelly cove that could not be seen from the path. A large willow spread its branches over the cove, so that the river behind it sparkled through the leaves. In recent years he had often come to this spot when he wanted to sit and think. Now he was looking out over the river with Magdalena. They talked about the last market day, when they had danced together and people's tongues were wagging at the tables all around. They told each other about their childhood. Simon spoke of his time as an army surgeon, and Magdalena of the fever that had laid her low for many weeks when she was seven years old. During that time she had also been taught to read by her father, who remained at her bedside day and night. Ever since then she helped him mix his potions and grind his herbs, and she always learned something new when she rummaged through her father's books.

To Simon it seemed like a miracle. Magdalena was the first woman he could discuss books with. The first woman to have read Johann Scultetus's *Wundarzneyisches Zeughaus* or *Surgical Armory*, and to know the works of Paracelsus. Only now and then did he feel something like pangs of regret when he remembered that this girl could never become his wife. As the hangman's daughter she was dishonorable, and the town would never permit their union. They would have to go to some foreign country, a hangman's wench and a traveling field surgeon, and they would have to live by begging in the streets. But then, why not? His love for this girl was so strong now, at this moment, that he would readily give up everything for her.

All afternoon and evening they had talked, and all of a sudden they could hear the ringing of the six o'clock bell from the parish church. In another half hour the gates of Schongau would be closed. They knew that they would never get back in time. And so they went to an abandoned barn nearby, where Simon had already slept on previous occasions, and there they remained for the night. They talked on, laughing over the pranks they played as children long ago. Schongau, its gossiping burghers and both of their fathers were far, far away. From time to time

Simon ran his hand across Magdalena's cheek or stroked her hair, but every time his fingers approached her bodice she smiled and pushed him away. She did not yet want to give herself to him, and Simon accepted it. At some time in the night they had fallen asleep next to each other like two children.

At the break of dawn, the creaking of the barn door woke Simon out of a light sleep.

They had settled down high up under the roof, from where a ladder descended to the barn floor. Carefully, the physician peered around a bale of straw and far down to the barn floor. He saw that the door was open a crack and the first light of dawn was shining through. He was sure that he had closed the door the evening before, if only to keep out the cold. Silently he slipped on his trousers and cast a last glance at Magdalena, who was still asleep. Directly below him, hidden by the wooden floor of the loft, he could hear shuffling steps approaching the ladder. Simon felt around in the straw for his knife, a perfectly honed stiletto he had already used for dissecting corpses and amputating the limbs of wounded men. With his right hand, he firmly gripped the handle, and with his left hand he pushed an especially large bale of straw directly to the edge of the loft.

Below him a figure appeared. He waited for a moment, then gave the bale a last shove so that it fell directly onto the figure. With a piercing cry Simon jumped after it with the intention of pulling the stranger to the floor and, if necessary, stabbing him in the back.

The man ducked to the side without even looking up and the bale hit the floor next to him, bursting into a cloud of dust and straw. At the same time the man raised his arms and warded off Simon's attack. The physician felt strong fingers grabbing his wrists in a viselike grip. Groaning with pain, he released the stiletto. Then the figure rammed a knee into his abdomen so that he sank forward to the floor. All went dark before his eyes.

Blind with pain he crawled around on the floor, desperately

feeling for his knife. A boot came down on his right hand, softly at first, then harder and harder. Simon gasped for air as something started to crack inside his wrist. Suddenly the pain eased. The figure, which he was able to see only as through a fog, had removed the foot from his hand.

"If you seduce my daughter again I'll break both your hands and lay you out on the rack, understand?"

Simon held his abdomen and crawled some distance away.

"I didn't . . . didn't touch her," he groaned. "Not like you think. But we . . . we love each other."

The response was a dry, suppressed laugh.

"I don't give a damn! She's a hangman's daughter, have you forgotten that? She is dishonorable! Do you want to expose her to even more ridicule, just because you can't control yourself?" Jakob Kuisl was now standing directly over Simon and rolled him over on his back with his foot so that he was able to look directly into his eyes.

"Be glad I didn't castrate you on the spot," he said. "It would've saved you and some girls in town a whole lot of trouble!"

"Leave him alone, Father." Magdalena's voice came from the loft above. She had been awakened by the noise of the fight and was looking down, still sleepy-eyed and with straw in her hair. "If anything, I seduced Simon and not the other way around. And besides, if I am dishonorable anyway, then what does a little more matter?"

The hangman shook his fist at her. "I didn't teach you reading and curing the sick so that you could get yourself knocked up and shamed and chased out of town. Can you imagine me having to place the mask of shame on my own daughter!"

"I . . . I can provide for Magdalena." Simon, still rubbing his groin, replied again. "We could go to another town, and there we could . . . "

Another blow hit him on his unprotected side, in his kidneys, so that he doubled up again, gasping.

"What could you do? Nothing. Do you want to go begging or what? Magdalena is going to marry my cousin in Steingaden, that's been agreed. And now come down here!"

Jakob Kuisl shook the ladder. Magdalena's face had become white.

"*Who* is it I'm supposed to marry?" she asked, her voice flat.

"Hans Kuisl of Steingaden, an excellent match," growled the hangman. "I talked to him about it just a few weeks ago."

"And this is the way you're telling me, here to my face?"

"One way or the other, I would have told you sooner or later."

Another bale of straw hit the hangman's head, nearly knocking him down. This time he hadn't expected it. Simon couldn't help grinning in spite of his pain. Magdalena had inherited her father's quick reactions.

"I'm not going to marry anybody," she screamed down. "Especially not fat Hans from Steingaden. His breath stinks, and he no longer has any teeth! I'm staying with Simon, just so you know!"

"Stubborn wench," growled the hangman. But at least he seemed to have given up the idea of dragging his daughter home. He headed for the exit, opened the door, and the morning sun flooded the barn. Briefly he stopped in the light.

"By the way," he muttered as he walked, "they found Johannes Strasser dead in a barn, in Altenstadt. He, too, had the mark on him. I heard it from the servant girl at Strasser's inn. I'm going to have a look at that boy. If you want to, you can come along, Simon."

Then he stepped out into the cool morning. Simon hesitated briefly. He glanced up at Magdalena, but she had buried herself in the straw and was sobbing.

He looked up at her and whispered, "We . . . we'll talk later." Then he followed the hangman out, limping.

———

For a long time they walked along in silence. They passed the raft landing, where the first rafts were already tying up at this early hour, then turned to the left on the Natternsteig to reach the road to Altenstadt. They deliberately avoided going straight through town, as they wanted to be alone. Here on the narrow footpath winding its way below the town wall, not a soul could be seen.

Finally, Simon spoke up. He had been thinking it over for a long time and was choosing his words carefully.

"I . . . I'm sorry," he began haltingly. "But it is true, I love your daughter. And I can provide for her. I have attended the university, even though I didn't finish. I ran out of money. But I have enough to hold my head above water as an itinerant surgeon. That, together with all that your daughter knows . . . "

The hangman stopped and looked down from the rise into the valley below, where the forest extended all the way to the horizon.

He interrupted Simon without turning his eyes from the scene in front of him. "Do you have any idea what it means to earn your daily bread out there?"

"I've already traveled around with my father," replied Simon.

"He cared for you, and for that you should be forever thankful," said the hangman. "But this time you would be alone. You would have to take care of your wife and your children. You would have to go from one country fair to another, a quack advertising his cheap tinctures like sour beer, getting rotten cabbage thrown at him and being mocked by peasants who know nothing about your healing arts. The learned physicians would make sure that you get thrown out as soon as you set foot in their town. Your children would die of hunger. Is that what you want?"

"But my father and I, we always had an income . . . "

The hangman spat on the ground. "That was during the

war," he continued. "When there is war, there's always something one can do. Sawing off limbs, cleaning out wounds with oil, dragging off the dead, and covering them with lime. Now the war is over. There are no more armies to follow. And I thank God for that!"

The hangman started walking again and Simon followed a few steps behind him.

After a few minutes of silence, he asked, "Master, may I ask you a question?" Jakob Kuisl continued walking and spoke without turning around.

"What do you want?"

"I heard you haven't always been in Schongau. You left this town when you were about my age. Why? And why did you return?"

The hangman stopped again. They had almost circled the entire town. Before them, on the right, the road to Altenstadt appeared. An oxcart trundled slowly along the road. Beyond, the forest stretched all the way to the horizon. Jakob Kuisl remained silent for such a long time that Simon began to think he would never receive an answer. Finally the hangman spoke.

"I didn't want a trade that forced me to kill," he said.

"And what did you do instead?"

Jakob Kuisl laughed softly.

"I killed all the more. Indiscriminately. Aimlessly. In a frenzy. Men, women, children."

"You were a . . . soldier?" asked Simon carefully.

The hangman was again silent for quite some time before answering.

"I joined Tilly's army. Scoundrels, highwaymen, but also honest men and adventurers, like myself . . . "

"You told me once that you were in Magdeburg . . . " Simon asked again.

A brief shudder went through the hangman's body. Even here in Schongau, people had heard the horror stories about the fall of the town in the far north. The Catholic troops under General Tilly had practically leveled the place, and only very few inhabitants had survived the massacre. Simon had heard that the soldiers had slaughtered children like lambs, had raped women, and after that had nailed them to the doors of their homes like our crucified Savior. Even if only half the stories were true, it was enough to make Schongauers utter prayers of thanks for having been spared such a bloodbath.

Jakob Kuisl marched on. Walking briskly, Simon caught up with him on the road to Altenstadt. He sensed that he had said too much.

"Why did you come back?" he asked after a while.

"Because a hangman is necessary," mumbled Jakob Kuisl. "Otherwise everything goes to the dogs. If there has to be killing, then at least it should be the right kind, according to the law. And so I came home to Schongau so that things would be in order. And now be quiet. I have to think."

Simon tried one last time: "Will you think it over again, about Magdalena?"

The hangman gave him an angry look from the side. Then he walked on at such speed that Simon had trouble keeping up with him.

They had been walking side by side for a good half hour when the first houses of Altenstadt appeared. From the few sentences Kuisl had uttered during that time, Simon was able to gather that Johannes Strasser had been found dead very early that morning in his foster father's stable. Josepha, one of the servant girls at the inn, had discovered him among the bales of straw. After telling the innkeeper, she ran over to the hangman's house in Schongau to get some Saint-John's-wort. When woven into a wreath it was supposed to help ward off evil powers. The servant girl was convinced that the devil had taken the boy. The hangman gave

Josepha the herb and listened to her story. He left shortly thereafter, stopping only to give his daughter's lover a good thrashing before continuing on his way. In the gray morning light he had simply followed their tracks and had easily found the barn.

Now they were both standing in front of the inn at Altenstadt, which Simon had visited only a few days earlier. They were not alone. Local peasants and wagon drivers were crowded in the square around a makeshift bier nailed together from a few boards. They were whispering—some of the women held rosaries in their hands and two servant girls knelt at the head of the bier and prayed, their bodies swaying back and forth. Simon also recognized the village priest of Altenstadt in the crowd and heard mumbled verses in Latin. When the people in Altenstadt noticed that the hangman was approaching, some of them made the sign of the cross. The priest interrupted his litany and stared at the two, his eyes flashing with hostility.

"What is the Schongau hangman doing here?" he asked suspiciously. "There's no work for you here! The devil has already done his work!"

Jakob Kuisl wouldn't be put off. "I heard there was an accident. Perhaps I can help?"

The priest shook his head. "I told you already, there's nothing to be done. The boy is dead. The devil surely got him and branded him with his mark."

"Just let the hangman come!" It was the voice of Strasser, the innkeeper. Simon recognized him among the peasants standing around the bier. "Let him see what that witch did to my boy, so that he may give her an especially slow death!" The face of the innkeeper was white as chalk and his eyes glowed with hatred as he looked back and forth between the hangman and his dead foster son.

Inquisitively, Jakob Kuisl stepped closer to the bier. Simon followed him. It was nailed together from planks and covered with fresh pine twigs. The scent of their sap could not entirely cover the stench coming from the corpse. Johannes Strasser's body was already showing black spots on the limbs, and flies were buzzing around his face. Someone had mercifully put two coins on the open eyes that were wide with horror as they stared up at the sky. There was a deep cut below the chin which extended nearly from one ear to the other. Dried blood stuck to the boy's shirt, which was crawling with flies as well.

Simon couldn't help wincing. Who would do such a thing? The boy was twelve years old at the most and his greatest sin so far had probably consisted of swiping a loaf of bread or a pitcher of milk from his foster father. Now he lay here, pale and cold, having met a bloody death at the end of a much too short, unhappy life. Tolerated but never loved, an outcast even in death. Even now there was no one who would shed sincere tears for him. Strasser stood at the bier with his lips pressed together, furious and full of hatred for the murderer but not actually grieving.

The hangman turned the Strasser boy's body gently on its side. Below the shoulder blade was the purple mark, blurred but still quite visible, a circle with a cross extending beneath it.

"The devil's mark," whispered the priest, crossing himself. Then he intoned the Lord's Prayer.

"*Pater noster, qui es in caelis, sanctificetur nomen tuum . . .*"

"Where did you find him?" asked Jakob Kuisl without taking his eyes from the corpse.

"In the stable, all the way in back, hidden under some bales of straw."

Simon looked around. It was Franz Strasser who had spoken. Full of hatred, the innkeeper looked down on what had once been his ward.

"He must have been lying there all the time. Josepha went to look this morning because of the smell. She thought it was some dead animal. But then it turned out to be Johannes," he mumbled.

Simon shivered. It was the same kind of cut that little Anton Kratz had a few days ago. *Peter Grimmer, Anton Kratz, Johannes Strasser . . .* What about Sophie and Clara? Had the devil caught them too by now?

The hangman stooped down and began to examine the corpse. He brushed his fingers across the wound, looking for other injuries. When he did not find anything he sniffed at the body.

"Three days, no more," he said. "Whoever killed him knew his business. A clean cut through the throat."

The priest eyed him angrily from the side. "That's enough now, Kuisl," he barked. "You can go. This is the church's business. You look after that witch in your own town, that Stechlin woman! She's responsible for everything here, after all!"

Strasser, standing next to him, nodded. "Johannes was often at her place. Together with the other wards and with that red-head Sophie. She bewitched him, and now the devil is coming for the souls of the little children!"

Many people could be heard murmuring and praying in the crowd. Strasser felt encouraged.

"Tell those big shots in town," he shouted at the hangman, his face red with wrath, "that if they don't clean up that brood of witches soon, we'll come and get them ourselves!"

Some of the peasants agreed loudly as he continued his harangue. "We'll hang them on the highest gable and light a fire underneath. Then we'll see who else is in bed with them!"

The priest nodded deliberately. "There's truth to that," he said. "We cannot just look on as our children fall victim to the devil, one by one, without stopping him. The witches must burn."

"The witches?" asked Simon.

The priest shrugged. "It is obvious that this cannot be the work of one single witch. The devil is in league with many of them. And furthermore . . ." He lifted his index finger as if to provide the final proof in a logical chain of arguments. "The Stechlin woman is in jail, isn't she? Then it must be someone else! Walpurgis Night is coming very soon! Most likely Satan's lovers are already dancing with the Evil One in the forest at night and kissing his anus. Then they swarm into town, naked and besotted, to drink the blood of innocent little children."

"Come on, you don't believe that, do you?" interjected Simon, his voice somewhat uncertain. "These are just horror stories, nothing more!"

"The Stechlin woman had flying salves and witch hazel in her house," cried one of the peasants farther back in the crowd. "Berchtholdt told me so. He was there during the torture. Now she cast a spell to make herself unconscious so as not to betray her playmates! And on Walpurgis Night they'll come and get more children!"

Franz Strasser nodded in agreement. "Johannes was in the forest a lot. They probably lured him there. He always babbled something about some kind of a hiding place."

"A hiding place?" asked Jakob Kuisl.

For the past few minutes the hangman had been examining the corpse in silence, even taking a close look at the blood-smeared hair and fingernails. He had also inspected the sign once more. Only now did he seem to take an interest in the conversation again.

"What kind of hiding place?"

Franz Strasser shrugged.

"I already told the physician," he mumbled. "Somewhere in the forest. Must be some kind of cave. He was always covered with dirt when he returned."

One more time the hangman contemplated the boy's fingers, now rigid in death.

"What do you mean by 'covered with dirt'?" he asked.

"Well, full of clay, you see. It looked as if he had been crawling around somewhere."

Jakob Kuisl closed his eyes. "Damn it all! I'm a complete idiot," he mumbled. "It's so clear, and I didn't see it!"

"What . . . what is it?" whispered Simon, who was standing next to him and had been the only one to hear the hangman's words. "What didn't you see?"

Jakob Kuisl grabbed the physician by the arm and pulled him away from the crowd. "I . . . I'm not entirely sure yet," he said. "But I believe I know now where the children's hiding place is."

"Where?" Simon's heartbeat quickened.

"There is something else we must check out first," the hangman whispered, swiftly taking off down the road in the direction of Schongau. "But for that we'll have to wait until it's dark."

"Tell the highborn gentlemen we are not going to just stand by and wait much longer! The witch must burn!" Franz Strasser called after them. "And that redheaded Sophie, we're going to look for her ourselves in the forest. With God's help we shall find that hiding place, and then we shall smoke out that witches' nest!"

Hooting and cheering broke out, and through it all the priest's high voice could be heard intoning a Latin hymn, though they could make out only a few words.

"*Dies irae, dies illa. Solvet saeclum in favilla* . . . Day of wrath, that day of burning! Earth shall end, to ashes turning . . . "

Simon bit his lip. The day of wrath was indeed close at hand.

Court clerk Johann Lechner blew sand over what he had just written and then rolled up the parchment. With a nod he enjoined the bailiff to open the door to the small chamber. As he rose, he turned once more toward the Augsburg wagon driver.

"If you told the truth, you have nothing to fear. The brawl is of no interest to us . . . at least not yet," he added. "We only wish to know who set fire to the Stadel."

Martin Hueber nodded without looking up. His head was hanging over the table, and his skin was pale and sallow. Just one night in the detention room and the anticipation of possible torture had been sufficient to transform the formerly arrogant wagon driver into a bundle of misery.

Johann Lechner smiled. If the Fuggers' delegates were really going to come in the next few days and insist indignantly that their wagon driver be handed over to them, they would find a repentant sinner. Lechner would then generously order his release. It was quite possible that Martin Hueber would still have to sit in jail in distant Augsburg, if only to atone for his superiors' embarrassment . . . Lechner felt certain that next time the Augsburg merchants would be much more deferential.

On the whole, Martin Hueber had confessed to what he had already hinted yesterday. Less than two weeks ago, some of his men were involved in a brawl at the Stern, on which occasion Josef Grimmer had thrashed one of them so soundly that he had to be taken to the infirmary. Together with a gang of cronies they had then sneaked down to the raft landing on Tuesday night in order to teach the Schongau guards a lesson they wouldn't forget. But by the time they reached the Stadel, it was already burning. Martin Hueber did see a few figures looking like soldiers running away from there, but he had been too far away to make out more than that. A brawl occurred afterward nevertheless, but only because the Schongau men had suspected them of arson.

"And who do you think set fire to the Stadel?" Lechner asked just before leaving, as he was already standing in the door.

Martin Hueber shrugged. "Those were foreign soldiers, not from around here. That much is certain."

"It's just strange that no Schongau guard had noticed them, only you fellows from Augsburg," Lechner added.

The wagon driver resumed his lament. "By the Holy Virgin

Mary, I told you already! Because the Schongauers were so busy putting out the fire! And besides, it was difficult to make out anything with all that smoke!"

Johann Lechner gave him a piercing look. "May our Savior keep you from lying," he murmured. "Otherwise you'll hang, and I won't give a hoot that you are a wagon driver for the Fuggers or, for all I care, the emperor himself." He turned to leave.

"Give the prisoner some warm soup and a piece of bread, by God!" he called back to the bailiff as he went down the stairs to the Ballenhaus. "After all, we are no monsters!" Behind him the door of the cell fell shut with a squeak.

Johann Lechner stopped once more on the worn steps and from this high vantage point surveyed the town's warehouse. In spite of worm-eaten beams and peeling paint, the hall was still Schongau's pride. Bales of wool, cloth, and the finest spices were stacked up to the ceiling in places. A scent of cloves hung in the air. Who could be interested in seeing this wealth go up in flames? If they really were soldiers, they must have been under someone's orders. But whose? Someone in Schongau? An outsider? Maybe in fact the Augsburgers? Or could it have been the devil himself, after all? The court clerk furrowed his brow. He must have missed something, and he could not forgive himself such a thing. He was a man of perfection.

"Sir! I have been sent by Andreas, the bailiff at the jail." Johann Lechner looked down, where a young lad in wooden clogs and a threadbare linen shirt had just come through the door. He was out of breath and his eyes sparkled.

"The bailiff Andreas?" Johann Lechner asked inquisitively. "What does he want?"

"He says the Stechlin woman is awake again, and she's howling and whining like ten furies!" The boy was standing on the lowest step. He was not yet fourteen years old. Expectantly he looked at the court clerk. "Are you going to burn her soon, sir?"

Johann Lechner looked at him with satisfaction. "Well, we shall see," he said as he placed a few small coins in the boy's hand. "Just go look for the physician now, so that he may confirm the good health of the Stechlin woman."

The boy had already run off when he called him back once more.

"But get the old physician, not the young one! Do you understand?" The boy nodded.

"The young one is a little too . . . " Johann Lechner hesitated, then he smiled. "Well, we all want to see the witch burning soon, don't we?"

The boy nodded. The ardor in his eyes almost frightened Lechner.

Rhythmic knocking, as if a heavy hammer was being pounded again and again against a door, had awakened Martha Stechlin. When she opened her eyes, she noticed that the hammer was raging inside her body. A pain such as she had never experienced before ran through her right hand at regular intervals. She looked down and saw a shapeless black and blue pig's bladder. It took her a while to realize that this bladder was in fact her hand. The hangman had done a good job with the thumbscrews. Her fingers and the back of her hand were now swollen to more than twice their normal size.

She vaguely remembered having drunk the potion Jakob Kuisl gave her. It had tasted bitter, and she could imagine what it contained. She was a midwife, after all, and familiar with drugs made of thorn apple, monkshood, or mandrake. In small doses, Martha Stechlin had often used those as painkillers during childbirth. Of course no one was supposed to know this, as those plants were widely reputed to be witches' herbs.

The drink the hangman had given her was so strong that she could only vaguely remember the events that had followed. She had been tortured, but the court clerk, the witnesses, and also the hangman had been strangely far off, their voices sounding like fading echoes. She had not felt any pain, only a pleasant warmth in her hand. Then the blackness had come, and now finally the rhythmic pounding that had brutally fetched her back from the land beyond fear and suffering. The pain flowed into her like water into an empty vessel, filling her completely. She began to scream and to shake the bars of her cell with her undamaged hand.

"Well, you witch, can you feel the fire yet?" shouted Georg Riegg, the raftsman, from the adjoining cell. He and the guardsman from the raft landing were still imprisoned with her. Martha Stechlin's screams were a welcome diversion.

"Why don't you witch yourself out of here, if you can, or did the devil abandon you?" sneered Georg Riegg.

The guardsman who was locked up together with him grabbed his shoulder. "Stop, Georg," he admonished him. "The woman is in pain. We should call the bailiff."

But that was no longer necessary. Just as the raftsman was about to launch himself into yet another hateful tirade, Andreas the jailkeeper opened the door to the keep. The screaming had awakened him from his nap. When he saw that Martha Stechlin was rattling the bars he left in a hurry. Her sobbing and crying followed him out into the street.

Just half an hour later, the witnesses, Berchtholdt, Augustin, and Schreevogl, were informed and summoned to the jailhouse. There Johann Lechner was already waiting for them with the doctor.

Old Fronwieser was the town's most compliant henchman, meekly assenting to anything they asked him to do. Just now he was stooping down over the midwife, winding a damp cloth around her swollen hand. The cloth was spotted and stank as if it had been used in the past to cover other bodies.

"Well?" asked the court clerk as he contemplated the sobbing midwife with as much interest as he would some rare, mutilated insect. Her cries had now become a constant wailing, like that of a child.

"A simple blood swelling, nothing more," said Bonifaz Fronwieser, tying the cloth into a tight knot. "Of course the thumb and the middle finger are probably broken. I gave her a compress of arnica and oak bark. It'll make the swelling go down."

"What I want to know is whether she is ready to be interrogated," Johann Lechner insisted.

The doctor nodded obsequiously as he packed up his bag of ointments, rusty knives, and a crucifix. "However, I'd use her other hand for continuing the torture. Otherwise there is a risk she may again lose consciousness."

"I thank you for your pains," said Lechner, placing a whole guilder in Bonifaz Fronwieser's hand. "You may withdraw now. But stay within reach and we shall call you if we need you again."

Bowing and scraping, the physician took his leave and rushed out into the street. Once outside, he shook his head. He could never understand the necessity of healing someone who had already been tortured. Once the painful interrogation had started, the poor sinners almost inevitably ended at the stake or, like shattered dolls, on the wheel. The midwife would have to die one way or the other, even if his son Simon was convinced of her innocence. At any rate, Fronwieser had at least earned some money because of her. And who knows? It was quite possible that he would be called back once more.

Contently he played with the guilder in his pocket as he headed for the market square to buy himself a hot meat pie. The treatment had whetted his appetite.

Inside the torture cellar, the witnesses and the court clerk had already taken their places on their chairs. They were waiting for the hangman to bring down the midwife and render her compliant. Johann Lechner had ordered wine, bread, and slices of cold meat prepared for all of them, because today the interrogation might last a little longer. Lechner considered Martha Stechlin to be hardheaded. Never mind, however. They had at least another two days until the Elector's lieutenant and his entourage would make their appearance and start living at the town's expense. By then the midwife would have confessed. Lechner was certain of that.

But the hangman had not yet arrived, and without him they couldn't get started. Impatiently, the court clerk drummed his fingers on the tabletop.

"Kuisl has been told, hasn't he?" he asked one of the bailiffs. The bailiff nodded in reply.

"Probably drunk again," witness Berchtholdt piped up. But he also looked as if they had dragged him not from his bakery, but from one of the inns behind the market square. His clothing was spotted with flour and beer, his hair was ruffled up in tufts, and he smelled like an empty beer keg. He guzzled down his wine and refilled the goblet.

"Easy does it," Jakob Schreevogl admonished him. "This isn't a beer hall get-together but a painful interrogation." Secretly he hoped the hangman had run away and that they therefore couldn't proceed with the torture. Yet he knew that this was unlikely. Jakob Kuisl would lose his job, and in only a few days an executioner from Augsburg or perhaps from Steingaden would take his place here. But even a delay of a few days could be enough to find the real murderer or murderers. By now, Jakob Schreevogl was quite convinced that Martha Stechlin had been unjustly imprisoned.

The witness Georg Augustin sipped at his wine goblet and straightened out his white lace collar.

"Perhaps the hangman doesn't realize that we don't have unlimited time on our hands. These interrogations cost me a whole bunch of guilders each time." He cast a bored glance at the instruments of torture as he continued to speak. "Our wagon drivers will just sit around forever in the Stern unless we keep after them. And the paperwork doesn't get done all by itself either. So for heaven's sake, let's get started!"

"I am sure the witch will confess today, or tomorrow at the latest," Lechner said, trying to calm him down. "Then everything will be back to normal again."

Jakob Schreevogl laughed to himself. "Back to normal? You seem to forget that there is a devil on the prowl out there, a devil who has killed three children by now. And my beloved Clara is God knows where!" His voice broke and he wiped a tear from the corner of his eye.

"Don't make such a fuss," snapped Georg Augustin. "Once the witch is dead, the devil will come out of her and will disappear to wherever he came from. And your Clara will surely show up again."

"Amen," mumbled the witness Berchtholdt, belching audibly. In the meantime he had started his third goblet. His eyes were glassy as he stared into space.

"And anyway," Georg Augustin continued, "if it had gone the way my father wanted, we would have started this interrogation much earlier. Then Martha Stechlin would already be burning at the stake, and the matter would be settled."

Jakob Schreevogl clearly remembered last Monday's council meeting, when blind Augustin had reminded the gentlemen of the great Schongau witch trial seventy years ago and had urged a quick resolution. Five days had gone by since then, and to Schreevogl it seemed like an eternity.

"Be quiet!" Johann Lechner shouted at the son of the blind

alderman. "You know very well that we couldn't continue any sooner. If your father were here in your place, we would not have to listen to such gibberish!"

Georg Augustin winced at this rebuke. For a moment it seemed he wanted to say something, but then he reached for the goblet and looked again at the torture instruments.

While the gentlemen were arguing among themselves downstairs, the hangman silently sneaked into the midwife's cell. Under the watchful eyes of two bailiffs he removed the chains from the sobbing midwife and helped her sit up.

"Listen to me, Martha," he whispered. "You must be strong now. I am very close to finding the real culprit, and then you will get out of here, as God is my witness. But today I shall have to hurt you once more. And this time I cannot give you any potion. They would notice it. Do you understand me?"

He shook her gently. The midwife stopped sobbing and nodded. Jakob Kuisl's face was now very close to hers, so that the bailiffs could not hear him.

"Just make sure you don't confess anything, Martha. If you confess, everything is lost." He took her delicate, ashen face between his huge paws.

"Do you hear me?" he asked once more. "No confession . . . "

The midwife nodded again. He hugged her closely, then they climbed down the stairs to the torture cellar.

Hearing Martha Stechlin's bare feet on the stairs, the witnesses immediately turned their heads in her direction. Conversation stopped; the show could begin.

Two bailiffs set the accused woman down on a chair in the center of the room and bound her with heavy rope. Her eyes darted fearfully back and forth between the aldermen and finally settled on Jakob Schreevogl. Even from his place behind the table he could see how her rib cage was frantically moving up and down, much too rapidly, just like a young bird in mortal fear.

Johann Lechner began the interrogation. "We were interrupted last time," he said. "I would therefore like to start over from the beginning." He unrolled a parchment scroll in front of him and dipped his quill into the inkwell.

"Point one," he intoned. "Does the delinquent have witches' marks to show that could serve as evidence?"

Berchtholdt the baker licked his lips as the bailiffs pulled the brown penitent's garment over Martha's head.

"In order to avoid any disputes like last time, I shall conduct the examination myself," said Johann Lechner.

He scrutinized the midwife's body inch by inch, checking under her armpits, on her behind and between her thighs. Martha Stechlin kept her eyes closed. Even when the clerk poked his fingers into her genitals she did not weep. Finally, Lechner stopped. "The mark on the shoulder blade seems to be the most suspicious of them. We shall do the test. Hangman, the needle!"

Jakob Kuisl handed him a finger-long needle. Without hesitating the clerk pushed the needle deep into the shoulder blade. Martha Stechlin's scream was so shrill that Jakob Kuisl winced. They were starting and there was nothing he could do about it.

Johann Lechner observed the point of entry with great interest. Finally he smiled, satisfied. "Just as I thought," he said, returning to the desk and sitting down behind his writing implements. He started to write, speaking aloud as he did so: "Defendant's clothes removed. I stuck her with a needle myself and discovered a point from which no blood flowed—"

"But this is no evidence," Jakob Schreevogl objected. "Any child knows that hardly any blood flows across the shoulder bone! And furthermore—"

"Juryman Schreevogl," replied Lechner, interrupting him. "Did you notice that this mark is at the exact same spot where the children had their marks? And that this mark, if not exactly identical, nevertheless looks very similar?"

Jakob Schreevogl shook his head. "A birthmark, nothing more. Never in a lifetime will the Elector's secretary let you call this evidence!"

"Well, we're not done yet after all," said Lechner. "Hangman, the thumbscrews. This time we'll take the other hand."

Martha Stechlin's screams rose from the torture cellar through the narrow windows of the keep into the town. Anyone in the vicinity briefly interrupted their work and crossed themselves or prayed a Hail Mary. Then they continued whatever they had been doing.

The burghers were sure that the witch was receiving her just punishment. She was still obstinate, but soon enough she would spit out her nefarious doings to the honorable aldermen, and then it would finally be over. She would confess her whoring with the devil, and the wild nights with him when together they drank the blood of the innocent little children and branded them with the mark of the devil. She would tell of the orgiastic dances, and how she had kissed the devil on his backside and had done everything the devil asked. She would tell of the other witches who had ridden with her through the air on their brooms, excited by pungent witches' salve that they had smeared on their genitals. Wanton wenches, all of them! And many a good Schongauer was salivating at the mere thought of it. And many a Schongau housewife could well imagine who these other witches were: the neighbor with the evil eye, the beggar woman over in the Münzgasse, the maid who was pursuing the good, unsuspecting husband . . .

At a stand in the market square, Bonifaz Fronwieser was just biting into his warm pastry when Martha Stechlin's screams could be heard coming from the dungeon. Suddenly the meat tasted old and rotten. He threw the rest to a pack of dogs running about and then headed home.

The devil had entered Clara and wouldn't let go of her. The girl threw herself from one side to the other on her bed of brush-wood. Cold sweat stood on her brow; her face was waxen like a doll's. Again and again Clara mumbled in her sleep and at times cried out with such force that Sophie had to hold her mouth closed. At that moment the devil seemed to be very close to her again.

"He . . . he's gotten hold of me. No! Go away! Go away! Hellish claws . . . the heart from the body . . . it hurts so . . . so much . . . "

Gently Sophie kept pushing her little friend back on her bed and wiped her hot brow with a wet rag. The fever had not let up. On the contrary, it had become stronger and stronger. Clara was glowing like a little oven. The drink Sophie had given her pro-vided only temporary relief.

Sophie had now watched over her for three nights and four days. Only rarely did she go outside to gather berries and herbs or to pilfer something edible from one of the surrounding farms. Yesterday she had caught a chicken, killed it, and at night made hot soup for Clara. But she was afraid that someone would see the fire and soon went back inside. Her fears were not unfounded. She had heard footsteps in the night. They had passed very close to her hiding place and then had left again.

One time she had gone to the raft landing and had asked a boy to tell the alderman Schreevogl that his foster daughter was well. She had considered that a pretty good idea at first. But when that physician showed up in the forest, she cursed herself for it. And all the more when the devil himself appeared, coming as if from nowhere. She dropped quickly into a ditch covered with shrubs, and the man with the bony hand ran past her, toward the physician. Since then she did not know whether the young physician had been killed or had gotten away. She only knew that her pursuers were very close.

Last night she had considered several times whether to go into town and tell the whole story. Perhaps she could tell it to the physician, providing he was still alive, or to the hangman. They both seemed to be on her side. She could tell them everything, and Clara would be rescued. Perhaps they would only clap the midwife in the stocks, or her foster parents would have to pay a fine because their ward had gotten involved with things that were none of her business. Perhaps she would get away with a good spanking and nothing more. Perhaps everything would still be all right.

But that certain premonition of things that she'd always had, and which had made her the leader of the other children, told her that she wouldn't be believed, that things had gone too far already, and there was no way back now.

Next to her, Clara cried out again in her sleep. Sophie bit her lip and tears ran down her face, which was smeared with dirt. She no longer knew where to turn.

Suddenly, she heard shouts from far away, laughter and shouting that could be heard way down here in her hiding place. Sophie kissed Clara on her forehead and moved to a spot with a good view over the forest.

Shadows were flitting among the trees. Dusk had fallen, and at first she could not distinguish the individual figures. Soon, however, she heard dogs barking. Carefully Sophie pushed herself up a few inches higher. Now she recognized the men. They were peasants from Altenstadt, Franz Strasser, Johannes's foster father, among them. The big dog he was holding on a leash was pulling him toward the hiding place. Quickly Sophie crouched down and crawled to where she could no longer be seen. The voices of the men had a strange echo, as if coming from the far end of a long tunnel.

"Let's stop now, Franz!" one of the men called out. "We have been looking all day, and it will be dark soon. The men are tired and hungry and want to go home. Let's continue looking for this hiding place tomorrow."

"Just wait a moment! Just look here!" shouted Franz Strasser in reply. "The dog smells something!"

"What do you think he smells?" the other one said, laughing. "The witch? He's smelling Sepp Spanner's bitch. She's in heat. Can't you see how it pulls him off?"

"You dumb ass! This is something else. Look, he's going completely crazy . . . "

The voices had come closer. Sophie held her breath. Now they were directly above her. The dog started to bark.

"There must be something around here," murmured Strasser. "Let's search the area around here, and then we'll let it be."

"All right then, just around here. The dog is really acting crazy . . . "

Sophie heard shouting and hooting. The other peasants were becoming impatient. She heard steps above her, pacing back and forth on the gravel. The dog's panting sounded as if he were about to choke as he obviously was straining on the leash so hard that he was almost strangling himself.

At this moment Clara began to scream again. It was a long scream of fear, as once again she was overcome by the shadows of darkness that were scratching her soft young skin with long fingernails. As soon as Sophie heard the scream she threw herself down quickly next to Clara and closed her mouth with her hand. But it was too late.

"Did you hear that?" asked Strasser excitedly.

"Hear what? Your dog is panting and barking. I can't hear anything else."

"Damn cur, be quiet, will you!"

Sophie could hear a kick and then the dog's whimpering. The dog was finally silent.

"Somebody did scream. It was a child."

"Nonsense, the dog was howling. The devil must have taken a shit in your ears."

There was laughter. The shouts of the others became fainter.

"Hogwash. I am sure it was a child . . . "

Under Sophie's strong hands, Clara was tossing back and forth. Sophie was still holding her mouth closed even though she was afraid of suffocating the girl. But Clara could not be allowed to scream. Not now!

Suddenly she could hear a frightened panting above her. "Look, the dog!" called Franz Strasser. "He's starting to dig! There is something here!"

"True, he's digging . . . what in the world is he . . . "

The other man's voice turned to loud laughter.

"A bone, a stupid bone, that's what he's dug up! Ha-ha, that's sure a devil's bone!"

Franz Strasser began cursing. "You stupid cur, what are you doing? Leave it alone or I'll beat you to death!"

More kicks and whimpering. Then the steps retreated. After a while, nothing could be heard anymore. Nevertheless Sophie's hand remained clamped over Clara's mouth. She held her delicate head as in a vise. The sick girl's face had turned blue by now. Finally Sophie released her, and Clara sucked air into her lungs, gasping, as if she were about to drown. Then her breathing became more regular. The shadows had withdrawn. She drifted into a quiet sleep.

Sophie sat next to her and wept without making a sound.

She had almost killed her friend. She was a witch; people were right. God would punish her for what she had done.

While Martha Stechlin was being tortured, Simon Fronwieser was sitting in the hangman's house making coffee. He was still carrying a handful of the foreign beans in a small pouch on his belt. Now he had ground them up in the executioner's mortar and had set a pot with water on the fire. When the water was at a boil he used a pewter spoon to put a little of the black powder in the pot and stirred. Immediately, a sharp aromatic fragrance spread through the house. Simon held his nose directly over the pot and breathed it in. The scent cleared his head. Finally he poured some of the brew into a mug. As he waited for the grounds to settle he thought about everything that had happened in the past few hours.

After their brief detour to Altenstadt he had walked Jakob Kuisl home, but the hangman did not want to disclose the meaning of his enigmatic words at the end of their visit to Strasser's. Even when Simon had insisted, he only told him to be available during the night, and that they had come quite a bit closer to the solution. Then the otherwise grim hangman smiled quietly. For the first time in days, Simon had the feeling that Jakob Kuisl was highly pleased with himself.

This bliss was instantly disrupted when they arrived at the hangman's house in the Lech quarter. Two bailiffs were already waiting at the door to tell Jakob Kuisl that the Stechlin woman was again ready to be interrogated.

The hangman's face suddenly turned white.

"So soon?" he murmured, stepping inside and reappearing a short time later with the necessary tools. Then he took Simon briefly aside and whispered in his ear, "Now we can only hope that Martha remains strong. In any case, be at my house tonight at the stroke of midnight."

Then he had trudged off behind the bailiffs, up to the town, with a sack slung over his shoulders filled with thumb- and leg screws, ropes, and sulfur sticks that could be inserted under the fingernails and lit. The hangman walked very slowly, but finally he disappeared beyond the Lech Gate.

When Anna Maria Kuisl stopped to pick up Simon in front of the house a short time later, she found him staring into space. She poured him a goblet of wine, ran her hand over his hair, and then went to market with the twins to buy bread. Life went on, even if three little boys were dead and a presumably innocent woman was suffering unspeakable torture at this very moment.

Simon went into the hangman's spare chamber carrying the steaming brew and started to leaf aimlessly through some books. But he couldn't really concentrate and the letters danced before his eyes. Almost gratefully he looked around when the squeaking door behind him announced a visitor. Magdalena was standing there, her face tearstained, her hair tangled and unkempt.

"Never, never will I marry the Steingaden hangman," she sobbed. "I'd rather go and drown myself!"

Simon winced. With all the ghastly events of the last few hours he had completely forgotten Magdalena. He slammed the book shut and took her in his arms.

"Your father would never do such a thing, not without your consent," he said, trying to console her.

She pushed him away. "What do you really know about my father!" she cried. "He is the hangman. He tortures and kills, and when he isn't doing that, he sells love potions to old hags and poison to young sluts to kill the brats inside them. My father is a monster, a fiend! He'll marry me off for a few guilders and a bottle of brandy without batting an eye! To hell with my father!"

Simon held her tightly and looked into her eyes. "You mustn't speak like this about your father! You know that it's not true. Your father is the hangman, but God knows somebody must do it after all! He is a strong and a wise man. And he loves his daughter!"

Crying she clung to Simon's doublet, shaking her head again and again. "You don't know him. He is a monster, a monster . . . "

Simon was standing at the window looking vacantly into the herb garden, where the first green shoots were starting to appear in the brown earth. He felt so helpless. Why couldn't they simply be happy together? Why were there always people telling them how to live their lives? His father, Magdalena's father, the whole damn town . . .

"I just talked with him, with your father . . . about us," he began suddenly.

She stopped sobbing and looked up to him questioningly.

"And what did he say?"

Her eyes were so full of hope that he impulsively decided to lie.

"He . . . he said that he would think it over. That first he wanted to see if I was good for anything. Once the matter with Martha Stechlin was settled, he would make up his mind. He won't exclude the possibility, that's what he said."

"But . . . but that's wonderful!"

Magdalena wiped the tears from her face and smiled at him with puffy eyes.

"That means all you have to do is help him get Martha Stechlin out of the keep." With every word her voice became firmer. "Once he sees that you've got something inside your head he will also trust you with his daughter. That has always been what counted for my father. That a person should have something inside his head. And that's what you are going to prove to him now."

Simon nodded but avoided looking directly at her. In the meantime Magdalena had again gotten a hold of herself. She poured a goblet of wine and emptied it in one gulp.

"What did you find out this morning?" she asked, wiping the back of her hand across her mouth.

Simon told her about the death of the Strasser boy, and that the midwife had regained consciousness. He also told Magdalena of her father's hints and their planned meeting in the coming night. She listened attentively and only here and there interjected a short question.

"And you say Strasser had noticed that Johannes had often been covered with clay?"

Simon nodded. "That's what he said. And then your father gave him such a funny look."

"Did you get to look at the dead boy's fingernails?"

He shook his head. "No, but I believe your father did."

Magdalena smiled. Simon suddenly thought he was looking into her father's face.

"What are you grinning about? Do tell me!"

"I think I know what my father wants to do with you tonight."

"And what is that?"

"Well, he probably wants to have another look at the finger-nails of the other boys."

"But they were buried long ago in the cemetery at Saint Sebastian's!"

Magdalena gave him a wicked grin. "And now you know why you'll only get going at midnight tonight."

Simon's face turned white. He had to sit down.

"You . . . you think?"

Magdalena poured herself another goblet of wine. She took a deep gulp before continuing.

"Let's just hope the two boys are really dead. Who knows,

the devil might've really gotten into them. Best take a crucifix along. You never know ... "

Then she quickly kissed him on the mouth. She tasted of wine and earth. It was better than coffee.

CHAPTER
12

SLOWLY DUSK SETTLED OVER THE TOWN. ROADS
and fields still lay in the sunlight, but beneath the thick foliage of
oaks and beeches evening had already arrived. Shadows gradually spread into a clearing in the forest where four men sat round
a crackling fire. Above the fire, a spit with two rabbits was turning. Grease dropped onto the embers and gave off a smell that
made their mouths water. They had eaten nothing all day except
a few mouthfuls of bread and some wild plants and were accordingly in an irritable mood.

"How much longer must we sit on our backsides in this
damned place?" grumbled one of them, turning the spit. "Let's
go over to France. The war's still going on over there and they're
looking for people like us."

"And what about the money, eh?" asked a second man, who
was lolling about on the mossy forest ground. "Fifty guilders he
promised us for destroying the building site. And another fifty
once Braunschweiger got rid of those little bastards. Up to now

we've only seen about a quarter of the money. And that, even though *we* have fulfilled our part of the bargain."

He glanced over at a man who was leaning against a tree a short distance away, but the man didn't even look up. He was busy doing something with his hand. Something didn't seem to be right about it, for he squeezed, massaged, and kneaded it. On his head he wore a broad-brimmed hat with a few colorful rooster's feathers. His clothing consisted of a bloodred doublet, a black coat, and two worn, hip-high leather boots. In contrast to the others, he wore his beard carefully trimmed, so that a pale face with a hooked nose and a long scar was visible above it. He was short, wiry, and muscular.

At last he seemed to be contented with his hand. He smiled, then held it up so that it shone white in the light of the fire. His arm, from the elbow to the fingertips, was composed of pieces of bone held together by copper wires passed through holes drilled in the bone. It looked like the hand of a corpse. Not until now did the devil look over at his companions.

"What did you just say?" he asked quietly.

The soldier by the fire swallowed nervously but continued speaking. "I said that *we* have done our part. *You* insisted on killing the little brats yourself. Now they're still running around free, and we are still waiting for our money . . . " He looked cautiously at the man with the bony hand.

"Three are dead," whispered the devil. "The other two are somewhere around here. Don't worry, I'll find them."

"Yes, when the fall comes," laughed the third man by the fire as he carefully pulled the rabbits off the spit. "But I'm not going to hang around here that long. I'm leaving, and I'm leaving tomorrow. I've just about had enough of this, and I've had more than enough of you!" He spat toward the tree.

The devil ran over to the man and in a twinkling of an eye had snatched the iron spit from his hand. He held the iron to the soldier's throat, his face only inches from the other man's. When the soldier swallowed, the red-hot point of the spit touched his Adam's apple. He uttered a loud scream, and a thin trickle of blood ran down his neck.

"You stupid bastards!" hissed the devil, without withdrawing the spit as much as a hair's breadth. "Who got you this job anyway, hey? Who got you grub and booze up till now? Without me you would have starved to death long ago, or you'd be dangling from some tree. I'll get those little bastards yet, don't you worry, and until then we are staying here! It would be a pity to lose the money!"

"Let go of André, Braunschweiger!" The second man by the fire stood up slowly. He was tall and broad shouldered, and there was a scar across his face. He drew his saber and pointed it in the devil's direction. Only by looking closely could you see the fear in his eyes. His sword hand trembled slightly.

"We've stuck with you long enough," he hissed. "Your cruelties, your thirst for blood, your torturing, they make me sick! You shouldn't have killed the boy! Now we have the whole town looking for us!"

The devil whom they called Braunschweiger shrugged his shoulders. "He overheard us, just like the others. He would have betrayed us, and then that lovely money would have been lost. Anyway . . ." He grinned broadly. "They're not looking for us. They think a witch killed the children, and perhaps tomorrow they'll burn her. So then, Hans, put away your saber. Let's not quarrel."

"First you'll put down that spit you have pointed at André," whispered the man called Hans. Not for one second did the muscular soldier let the smaller man out of his sight. He knew how dangerous Braunschweiger could be, in spite of his rather diminutive size. He could probably slice all three of them to pieces right here in the clearing before they could strike a single blow at him.

With a smile, the devil lowered the spit. "Fine," he said. "Then I can tell you at last about my discovery."

"Discovery? What discovery?" asked the third man, who had been lying expectantly in the patch of moss up till then. His name was Christoph Holzapfel, and he was, like the other three men, a former soldier. They had been traveling about together for nearly two years, living on murder, robbery, and arson. They could not remember the last time they'd been paid. They were always on the run, no better than hunted animals. But deep inside them there still glowed a spark of decency, something left over from the bedtime stories their mothers had told them and the prayers that the village priest had drummed into their heads. And each of them felt instinctively that in the man they called Braunschweiger this spark of decency was missing. He was as cold as his bony hand that had been made for him after an amputation. Although it couldn't wield a weapon, it was a useful substitute for one. It instilled fear and horror, and that was what Braunschweiger liked best.

"What discovery are you talking about?" Christoph Holzapfel repeated his question.

The devil smiled. He knew that he had the upper hand again. He stretched out on the moss, tore a leg off the rabbit, and kept talking while nibbling on the leg. "I followed Moneybags. I wanted to know what he intended to do at the building site. He was there again last night, and I was, as well." He wiped the grease from his lips.

"And?" André asked impatiently.

"He was looking for something. Something that must be hidden there."

"A treasure?"

The devil shrugged. "Maybe. But you want to leave, so I'll just look for it myself."

Hans Hohenleitner grinned. "Braunschweiger, you're the biggest bloodsucker and swine I've ever met, but at least you're a clever swine."

A sudden noise made them turn round. The snapping of twigs, quiet but not quiet enough for four experienced soldiers. Braunschweiger signaled to them to keep silent, then he slipped into the bushes. A short time afterward they heard a cry, then groaning, panting, and branches crackling. The devil dragged a struggling form into the clearing. When he threw it down by the fire, the soldiers saw that it was the man they were supposed to be working for.

"I was coming to you," he groaned. "What's gotten into you to treat me like this?"

"Why did you creep up like that, Moneybags?" Christoph grumbled.

"I . . . I didn't creep up on you. I have to talk to you. I need your help. You must help me to look for something. This very night. I can't do it alone."

For a time there was silence.

"Will we share?" asked Braunschweiger at last.

"Half for you, word of honor."

Then he told them shortly what he intended to do.

The soldiers nodded. Their leader had been right once again. They would follow him. They could speak later about the sharing.

Martha Stechlin emerged from her swoon, and the pain hit her like a blow. They had crushed all her fingers and inserted splinters with burning sulfur under her fingernails. The midwife had smelled her own flesh burning. But she had remained silent. Again and again Lechner had questioned her and written all the questions word for word in his record of proceedings.

Whether she had murdered the boys Peter Grimmer, Anton Kratz, and Johannes Strasser? Whether she had scratched a devilish sign in the skin of the innocent children? Whether she had burned down the Stadel? Whether she had taken part in witches' dances and procured other women for the devil? Whether she had put a fatal spell on baker Berchtholdt's calf?

Her answer was always no. Even when Jakob Kuisl put the leg screws on her, she remained firm. At the end, when the witnesses had withdrawn with a carafe of wine for a short consultation, the hangman came quite close to her and whispered in her ear. "Stay strong, Martha! Say nothing. It'll soon be over."

The officials in fact decided not to continue the questioning until the following morning. Since then she had been lying in her cell, half awake and half asleep. Now and then she heard the church bells. Even Georg Riegg in the neighboring cell had stopped his nagging. It was shortly before midnight.

In spite of her pain and fear, Martha Stechlin tried to think. From what the hangman had said and from the questioning and accusations, she tried to form a picture of what had happened. Three children had died and two were missing. All had been with her on the night before the first murder. Jakob Kuisl told her of the strange sign they had found on the bodies. Her mandrake was missing too. Someone must have stolen it.

Who?

She drew the sign with a finger in the dust on the floor of the prison and immediately wiped it away, fearing that someone could discover her doing it. Then she drew it once again.

♀

It was indeed one of the witches' signs. Who had scratched it on the children? Who knew about it?

Who is the real witch in the town?

Suddenly she had a dreadful suspicion. She rubbed the sign

out and then drew it slowly for the third time. Could it possibly be true?

In spite of her pain she couldn't help laughing to herself. It was so simple. It had been right in front of her the whole time, and she had failed to see it.

The circle with the cross under it . . . a witches' sign . . .

A stone struck her in the middle of the forehead. For a moment everything went black before her eyes.

"Got you, witch!" Georg Riegg's voice rang through the prison. She could see him indistinctly in the darkness behind the bars on the other side of the chamber, his hand still raised. Near him the imprisoned watchman from the raft landing was snoring. "What the hell is there to laugh at? It's your fault that we're stuck in here. Admit it, you set fire to the Stadel and killed the children. Then we'll have peace in the town at last! You stubborn old sorceress! What are those signs you are drawing there?"

Another stone, big as a fist, struck her on the right ear. She sank to the ground, desperately trying to wipe away the sign again, but her hands would no longer obey her. She started to feel faint, then everything turned black.

The real witch . . . Must tell Kuisl . . . Let him know . . .

The clock in the church tower struck midnight as Martha Stechlin, bleeding, slumped down onto the prison floor. She no longer heard Georg Riegg, still scolding, calling for the watch.

The bell of the town parish church boomed over the roofs of Schongau. It struck twelve times, as two figures, wrapped in their coats, made their way through the mist on their way to the cemetery of Saint Sebastian. Jakob Kuisl had bribed the watchman at the Lech Gate with a bottle of brandy. To Alois, the old night watchman, it was a matter of indifference what the hangman and the young physician were doing out on the streets at this time. And the April nights were cold, so a swig or two of brandy would do him good. So he waved them in and shut the gate carefully behind them. He raised the bottle to his mouth, and immediately the brandy spread a comforting warmth in his stomach.

Once inside the town, the hangman and physician chose the narrow unfrequented way through the Hennengasse. No burgher was permitted out of doors at this time. It was rather unlikely they'd come across one of the two night watchmen, but nevertheless they avoided the market square and the broad Münzstrasse, where during the day and evening most people congregated.

They carried their lanterns under their coats so that there would be no light to attract attention and they would be completely enveloped in the darkness. A few times, Simon tripped against the curb or on piles of garbage left in the street and nearly fell. He cursed under his breath. When once again he stepped into the contents of a chamber pot and was about to let loose a whole string of curses, the hangman turned to him and gripped his shoulder hard.

"Be quiet, for God's sake! Or do you want the whole neighborhood to know we're grave robbers?"

Simon swallowed his anger and felt his way on through the darkness. In faraway Paris, he had heard, whole streets were illuminated with lanterns, and at night the whole city was a sea of light. He sighed. It would be many years before people could walk the streets of Schongau after dark without treading into a pile of excrement or banging into the wall of a house. He staggered on, swearing under his breath.

Neither he nor the hangman noticed that a figure was following them at a little distance. It paused at the corners of houses, ducked into niches, and did not creep on farther until the hangman and the physician had resumed their way.

At last Simon saw a flickering light in front of him. Candlelight shone through the windows of Saint Sebastian's Church, a votive candle left burning at this late hour. The light was just enough for them to see where they were. Next to the church was a heavy iron gate that led to the cemetery. Jakob Kuisl tried the rusty handle and swore. The verger had done his work well; the gate was locked.

"We'll have to climb over," he whispered. He threw the small spade, which he had carried with him under his coat, to the other side. Then he pulled himself up the six-foot wall and let himself down on the other side. Simon heard a soft thud. Taking a deep breath, he then pulled his own rather lanky body up onto the wall. Stones and masonry scraped against his expensive doublet, but at last he was sitting astride the wall and looking down into the cemetery below. Small candles were burning by the graves of rich burghers, but otherwise crosses and grave mounds could be seen only indistinctly. In a corner at the back, against the town wall, stood a small charnel house.

At this moment a light appeared in a house across the way in the Hennengasse. The shutters squeaked as they opened outward. Simon let himself down from the wall and with a stifled cry landed on a freshly made grave mound. He looked up cautiously. A housemaid appeared in the illuminated window opening and tossed out the contents of a chamber pot. She did not appear to have noticed him. A short time later the shutters were closed again. Simon shook the damp earth from his doublet. At least he had fallen softly.

The figure that had followed them hid in the archway and watched the two men in the cemetery from there.

The cemetery of Saint Sebastian was located directly by the town wall and had been laid out only a short time before. Plague and war had seen to it that the old graveyard near the town parish church was no longer sufficient for the town's needs. Grass and thorny shrubs grew in many places, and between them a muddy footpath led to the individual graves. It was only the rich who could afford a single grave with a carved stone. Their graves lay directly by the wall. Elsewhere crooked wooden crosses stuck up all over the broad field of the cemetery above shapeless mounds of earth. On most of these crosses several names were inscribed. Burials came cheaper if you shared the limited space in the ground with others.

A mound on the right near the charnel house still looked quite fresh. Yesterday morning, after being laid out for two days at their homes, Peter Grimmer and Anton Kratz had been buried. The ceremony was short—the town authorities did not want to risk further disturbances. A Latin prayer from the priest with only the family present, a bit of incense, and a few comforting words, and then the relatives were sent home. For Peter Grimmer and Anton Kratz a common grave was all the families could afford: neither had enough money for an individual burial.

Jakob Kuisl had trudged on ahead with his spade in hand. He stopped near the cross, looking thoughtfully at the names of the dead.

"Johannes will be lying here soon. Sophie and Clara, as well, if we don't hurry."

He took the spade and drove it deep into the soil. Simon crossed himself and looked anxiously across at the dark houses in the Hennengasse. "Is this really necessary?" he whispered. "That is desecration of the dead! If we're caught, you can reckon on having to torture yourself and light your own fire at the stake!"

"Stop talking and help me."

Jakob Kuisl pointed to the charnel house that had been dedicated only a few weeks before. A shovel was leaning near the door. Simon, shaking his head, took the tool and began to dig next to the hangman. To be safe he crossed himself once more. He was not particularly superstitious, but if God was going to punish anybody with a thunderbolt, then surely it would be someone who dug up the bodies of dead children.

"We won't have to go down very deep," whispered Jakob Kuisl. "The grave was almost full."

After only a few feet they did in fact find a layer of white lime. Under it appeared a small coffin and something wrapped in a bundle of linen, also small.

"I might have known it!" The hangman struck the spade against the stiff little bundle. "They didn't even get a coffin for Anton Kratz. And the family does have enough money. But the orphans, you can just shove them into a pit like dead animals!"

He shook his head, then lifted the bundle and the coffin with his strong arms and put them on the grass beside the grave. In his huge hands the child's coffin looked almost like a little tool chest.

"Here!" He held out a scrap of cloth to Simon. "Tie that around your head, they'll certainly stink pretty bad." Simon wrapped the cloth around his head and saw the hangman start to work with his hammer and chisel. One by one, he pried the nails out. A short time afterward the lid fell to the side.

Simon picked up his knife and slit the linen sack open length-wise. Immediately a sickly sweet odor spread out, causing the physician to retch. He had seen many dead bodies in his time and smelled them, too, but these two boys had been dead for more than three days. In spite of the cloth around his face, the stench was so strong that he had to turn aside. He raised the cloth a bit and vomited, then he wiped his mouth, coughing. When he turned around again, the hangman grinned at him.

"I thought as much!"

"What?" Simon inquired in a rasping voice. He looked down at the dead children, who were covered all over with black spots. A wood louse scampered over little Peter's face.

Contentedly Kuisl took out his pipe and lit it by the light of the lantern. After taking two deep puffs, he pointed to the fingers of the corpses. When Simon still did not react, he poked under Anton Kratz's fingernails with the point of his knife, then held the blade out for the physician to smell. Simon could make out nothing at first, but when he held the lantern very close to the knife he could see some fine red soil on the point.

He looked questioningly at the hangman.

"So?"

Jakob Kuisl held the knife so close to Simon's nose that he was frightened and retreated a step.

"Well, can't you see, you dunce?" hissed the hangman. "The soil is *red!* It's the same with Peter and Johannes. All three dead children had scraped about in red soil before they died. And what kind of soil is red? Well? Which soil is red?"

Simon swallowed before he spoke.

"Clay . . . clay is red," he whispered.

"And where around here is so much clay that you can bury yourself in it?"

The answer hit Simon like a blow. It was as if two broken parts had come together.

"The pit by the brick kiln just behind the tanners' quarter! Where all the clay tiles come from! Then . . . then is the children's hiding place there, perhaps?"

Jakob Kuisl puffed on his pipe and blew the smoke directly into Simon's face, so that Simon had to cough. But at least the smoke covered the smell of the corpses.

"Smart quack," said Kuisl and slapped the coughing Simon on the shoulder.

"And that is exactly where we're going now, to pay the kids a visit."

Hastily the hangman filled the grave in again. Then he seized the spade and the lantern and ran to the wall of the cemetery. He was just about to heave his heavy body up the stone wall, when a figure appeared on top of the wall. It stuck out its tongue at him.

"Ha, caught you at grave robbing! You look like the Grim Reaper in person, only a bit fatter."

"Magdalena, damn it, I—"

Jakob Kuisl snatched at his daughter's leg, intending to pull her down to him, but with a quick movement she jumped to one side and strutted along the wall. Disdainfully, she looked down on the two grave robbers.

"I figured you would go to the cemetery. Nobody puts one over on me! Well, Father? Did you find the same dirt under the boys' fingernails as with Johannes?"

The hangman looked angrily across to Simon. "Did you tell?"

The physician held up his hands trying to calm him down. "I never! I only told her about poor Johannes . . . and that you had examined the fingernails very closely."

"You idiot! You must not tell women anything, above all my daughter. She's too good at reading between the lines and figuring things out."

Jakob Kuisl tried once more to grab Magdalena's leg, but she was already a few steps farther on, balancing on the wall toward the church. The hangman hurried after her.

"Come down from there at once! You'll wake up the whole neighborhood, and then all hell will break loose!" he whispered hoarsely.

Magdalena grinned down at her father. "I'll come down, but only if you tell me what you've found out up to now. I'm not stupid, you know that, Father. I can help you."

"Yes, but come down first," growled Jakob Kuisl.

"Promise?"

"Yes, damn it."

"Do you swear by the Blessed Virgin?"

"By all the saints and devils, if I must!"

Magdalena jumped down from the wall and landed directly in front of Simon. The hangman raised his hand threateningly, but then let it drop with a sigh.

"And one more thing," Magdalena whispered. "The next time

you are standing in front of a locked gate, just look round a bit. Sometimes you can find things." She held a big shiny key in her hand.

"Where did you get that?" Simon asked.

"Out of a little hole in the archway. Mother always hides her key in the wall too."

Deftly, she put the key in the keyhole, turned it once, and with a little squeak the iron gate opened. Without speaking, the hangman pushed past his daughter and hurried in the direction of the Lech Gate.

"Come on!" he hissed. "There isn't much time!"

Simon had to grin. Then he took Magdalena's hand and hurried after him.

Sophie held her breath as once again steps passed quite close to her hiding place. She could hear the voices from where she was hiding with Clara, who in the meantime was sleeping peacefully. Since her last attack of fever at noon, Clara's breathing had steadily become more regular, and it seemed she was on the way to recovery. Sophie envied Clara for sleeping. She herself had hardly been able to close her eyes for four nights. She was tortured by the fear of discovery, and now once more she could hear footsteps and voices. Men were walking overhead and appeared to be looking for something. But they were not the same men as last time.

"There's no point in doing this, Braunschweiger! We can keep on digging until hell freezes over. The field is much too big!"

"Shut your mouth and keep on looking. There's a lot of money somewhere around here and I'm not going to let it rot."

The voices were now directly above her. Sophie held her breath, surprised. She *knew* one of them. Fear crept slowly from her stomach to her throat, and she was only barely able to keep from screaming.

Another man called out to the first two from a bit farther away. "Have you looked in the chapel? It must be here some-where! Look for some way in, a hole, a loose flagstone perhaps . . . "

"We'll do that in a minute!" said the voice above her. Then it suddenly became quieter. The man seemed to be speaking to the one standing near him. "That lazy dog Moneybags! Sits there under the linden tree and thinks he has to play the supervisor. But just wait. As soon as we've found the treasure, I'll cut his throat myself and sprinkle the blood all around the chapel!"

Sophie pressed her hands to her mouth. She had almost cried out loud. She also recognized the second, more distant voice, the man under the linden. She would never forget either of them.

She *remembered*.

"Little brat, why was he eavesdropping on us? Now the fish are drinking his blood. Let's look for the others . . . "

"Holy Mother of God, did you have to do that? Did you really have to do that? Look at the bloody mess! They'll be looking for the boy!"

"Oh, nonsense. The river'll wash that away. We'd better catch the others. They mustn't escape us."

"But . . . they're only children!"

"Children can tell stories. Do you want them to give you away? Is that what you want?"

"No . . . of course not."

"Then don't make such a fuss. Miserable Moneybags, earning your money with blood but unable to look at it. That's going to cost you something!"

Miserable Moneybags . . . Sophie breathed more rapidly. The devil was there, right above them. He had caught three of them, and only she and Clara were left. And now he would catch them. There was no escape. Surely he could smell them.

"Wait a minute—I have an idea where the treasure could be," called the voice. "How would it be if . . . "

At this moment there was a scream outside, and farther away someone groaned in pain.

A little later all hell broke loose. Sophie put her hands to her ears and hoped it was all just a bad dream.

Simon cursed as he slipped once more on the boggy ground of the clay pit and fell into the red mud. His hose was smeared all over with clay and his boots got stuck in it so firmly that he had trouble extricating himself. The hangman and his daughter stood at the edge of the pit and looked questioningly down at him.

"Well?" Jakob Kuisl called down into the pit. His face was lit by a torch so that it glowed as a point of light in the otherwise complete darkness. "Any hollows or niches?"

Simon managed to shake the largest clumps of dirt from his doublet. "Nothing! Not even a mouse hole." Once again he held up the torch and looked around the pit. The torch let him see just a few yards. All else was swallowed up in darkness. "Children, can you hear me?" he shouted once again. "If you are here anywhere, let us know! It's all right. We are on your side!"

Only the noise of a thin stream of water could be heard, otherwise there was silence.

"Damn it!" grumbled Simon. "What a stupid idea, to go looking for the children in the clay pit in the middle of the night! My boots are two slimy clods of dirt, and I might as well throw my doublet away!"

Jakob Kuisl grinned as he heard the young physician cursing.

"Don't make such a fuss. You know very well that time is short. Let's have a look in the tile kiln."

He held the ladder steady while Simon clambered up over the slippery rungs. When he reached the top, Magdalena's face appeared in front of him. She held the torch so that it shone right in his eyes.

"You do look rather . . . beaten up," she giggled. "Why did you keep falling over on your nose?"

With the corner of her apron she wiped the clay from Simon's forehead. It was useless. The colored soil stuck to his face like paint. Magdalena smiled.

"Perhaps I'll let you keep a bit of the dirt on your face. You're a bit too pale around the nose anyway."

"You be quiet. Otherwise I'll start asking myself why it was me who had to climb down into this damned pit."

"Because you are young, and a few tumbles in the mud won't hurt you," came the hangman's voice. "Anyway, you would hardly expect a young, delicate girl to climb down into such a filthy hole."

Jakob Kuisl had already strolled over to the kiln. The building stood at the edge of a clearing with the forest directly behind it. Kindling wood was piled up in six-foot stacks all over the clearing. The building itself was constructed of solid stone, and a tall chimney came out of the center of the roof. The kiln was situated between the forest and the river and was a good two furlongs from the tanners' quarter. To the west Simon could now and then see lights from lanterns or torches in the town. Otherwise the darkness around them was complete.

The tile kiln was one of Schongau's most important buildings. After a few devastating fires in the past, the burghers were now required by law to build their houses with stone and roof them with tile rather than straw. Also, the craftsmen of the stovemakers' guild fetched their raw materials from here for the manufacture of earthenware products and stoves. During the day, thick smoke almost continually covered the clearing. There was a constant coming and going, with oxcarts transporting the tiles to Altenstadt, Peiting, or Rottenbuch. But now, at night, there was not a soul about. The heavy door leading to the interior of the kiln was shut. Jakob Kuisl walked along the front of the building until he found a window whose shutters hung crooked on their hinges. With a determined tug he ripped off the right-hand shutter and held the torch in to illuminate the interior.

"Children, don't be afraid!" he called into the dark room. "It's me, Kuisl from the tanners' quarter. I know you had nothing to do with the murders."

"You really think they'll come out when the hangman calls them?" hissed Magdalena. "Let me in. They'll not be afraid of me."

She tucked up her skirt and climbed into the building over the low windowsill.

"A torch," she whispered.

Without a word Simon passed her his torch. Then she disappeared into the darkness. From listening to her steps the two men could hear how she tiptoed from room to room. At last they could hear the creaking of boards. Magdalena was walking up the stairs.

"The devil's in that girl," growled the hangman, sucking his cold pipe. "She's like her mother, just as stubborn and cheeky. Time she got married and had somebody to keep her mouth shut."

The physician wanted to reply, but at that moment a crash and a scream were heard above.

"Magdalena!" cried Simon and clambered into the interior, where he landed painfully on the stone floor.

He arose at once, took the torch in his hand, and ran in the direction of the stairs. The hangman followed him. They crossed the room with the kiln and rushed up the stairs to the attic. It smelled of smoke and ashes.

When they arrived upstairs, the air was full of red dust, so that in spite of the torch they could hardly see anything. From the corner on the right they could hear someone groaning quietly. As the dust was slowly settling, Simon could see broken tiles heaped and scattered all over the floor. Along the walls more tiles were piled up to the ceiling. In one place there was a gap. Several hundredweight of burnt clay must have fallen to the floor there. Under a particularly large heap something moved.

"Magdalena!" cried Simon. "Are you all right?"

Magdalena stood up, a red ghost, covered from tip to toe with fine tile dust.

"I think . . . I'm all right now," she coughed. "I wanted to push some tiles away. I thought there might be a hiding place behind here." She had to cough again. Simon and the hangman were now covered with the fine red dust too.

Jakob Kuisl shook his head. "Something's not right," he grumbled. "I've missed something. The red dirt . . . it was under their fingernails all right! But the children are not here. Where are they then?"

"Where do they take the tiles to?" asked Magdalena, who meanwhile had brushed herself off as well as she could and was sitting on a pile of broken tiles. "Perhaps the children are there?"

The hangman shook his head again. "That wasn't brick dust under their fingernails. That was red clay, damp clay. They must have dug in it. Where else is there so much clay?"

Suddenly a thought flashed through Simon's mind.

"The building site!" he cried. "At the building site!"

The hangman looked up, startled. "What did you say?"

"The leper house, the building site!" repeated Simon. "There were big heaps of clay there. They used it to plaster the walls!"

"Simon's right!" Magdalena cried and jumped up from the heap of tiles. "I myself have seen the workers with their carts taking clay there. The leper house is the only large building site in Schongau at the moment!"

The hangman kicked a tile against the wall, where it broke into small pieces.

"My God, you're right! How could I be so stupid as to forget the building site? We were there ourselves and saw the clay!"

He hurried down the stairs. "To the leper house, quickly!" he called as he was running. "Pray God that it isn't too late!"

From the kiln to the Hohenfurch Road it was a good half hour's brisk walk. The shortest way was through the forest. Jakob Kuisl chose a narrow path, which resembled a track for animals more than anything. The moonbeams broke only occasionally through the dense pine trees, otherwise an almost impenetrable blackness reigned. It was a mystery to Simon how the hangman managed to find the way. Together with Magdalena he stumbled along, guided by the hangman's torch. Again and again pine branches struck them in the face. Now and then Simon thought he could hear a cracking of branches in the underbrush nearby. But his own breathing was too loud for him to say definitely if it was his imagination or real footsteps. After just a short time he began to breathe heavily. It was like a few days ago, when he was fleeing from the devil, and he noticed how out of condition he was for such running through the forest. He was a physician, damn it— not a huntsman or a soldier! Magdalena ran on, light-footed, alongside him and because of her he tried not to let it show.

Suddenly they exited the forest and stood out in the open on a field of stubble. The hangman paused to get his bearings, then ran to the left along the edge of the field. "Head east, and then take a sharp right at the oaks!" he called to them. "We're almost there!" Soon indeed they passed a grove of oak trees and finally stood at the edge of a larger clearing. They could recognize shadowy outlines of buildings. They had arrived at the building site.

Simon halted, panting. Twigs, burrs, and pine needles clung to his coat. He had lost his hat somewhere in the pine thickets. "Next time you take a run through the forest, let me know ahead of time," he groaned, "so I put on something suitable. That hat cost half a florin, and my boots—"

"*Shhh.*" The hangman held his big hand over Simon's mouth. "Stop babbling. Look over there."

He pointed to the outlines of the building site. Small points of light were moving here and there, and they could hear bits of conversation that drifted over to them.

"We're not the only ones," whispered Jakob Kuisl. "I can count four or five torches. And I'll bet my backside that our friend is here also."

"You mean, the man you ran after last time?" whispered Magdalena.

The hangman nodded. "The same who almost slit Simon's throat. The one they call the devil. But this time we'll get him." He motioned to the physician to come over. "The torches are spread out all over the site," he said. "They seem to be looking for something."

"But what?" Simon asked.

The hangman grinned broadly. "We're soon going to find out." He picked a heavy oak branch up from the ground, broke off the twigs, and cradled it in his hand. "We'll take them singly, one by one."

"We?"

"Sure." The hangman nodded. "I can't do it alone. There are too many. Have you got your knife on you?"

Simon fumbled at his belt. Then, trembling, he pulled out his stiletto, which flashed in the moonlight.

"Good," growled Kuisl. "Magdalena, you run back to the town and wake Lechner at the castle. Tell him that the building site is being destroyed again. We need help, as quickly as possible."

"But—" The hangman's daughter was about to protest.

"No argument, or you'll marry the hangman from Steingaden tomorrow morning. And now, run!"

Magdalena pouted. But then she vanished into the shadows of the forest.

The hangman gave a signal to Simon and ran, bent over, along the edge of the wood. Simon hurried after him. After about two hundred paces they came across a pile of tree trunks that the workers had deposited near the forest's edge. The pile reached some distance into the clearing. Using the cover of the trunks, the hangman and the physician crept closer to the half-finished building. Now they could see that there were in fact five men, who appeared to be searching for something with lanterns and torches. One man sat on a boulder near the linden tree in the middle of the clearing, two were leaning by the well, and the other two were in other parts of the site.

"I'm getting tired of freezing my behind off here in the dark!" shouted one of the men, who was inside a big square of walls. "We've been searching here almost all night now. Let's come back again tomorrow, by daylight!"

"In the daytime the place is swarming with workers, you idiot," hissed one of the men by the well. "Why do you think we're doing all this at night? Why did we knock everything down after sunset? We'll go on looking, and if Moneybags has lied to us and there's nothing buried here, then I'll smash his skull on this well like a raw egg!"

Simon pricked his ears. *Something,* then, was buried there. But what?

The hangman nudged him on the shoulder.

"We can't wait any longer for the bailiffs," he whispered. "We don't know how much longer they'll stay here. I'm going to run over to that side wall and get one of them. You stay here. If you see anyone coming toward me, whistle like a jaybird. Can you do that?"

Simon shook his head.

"Damn it, then just whistle as best you can. They won't notice it."

Jakob Kuisl looked round for the last time, then hurried with long strides toward the wall and took cover behind it. The men had noticed nothing.

More shouting could be heard, now farther away, so that Simon found it increasingly difficult to understand them. He saw that the hangman, stooping, ran along the side of the wall, directly toward the man inside the square, who was trying to pry up the flagstones with a wooden stick. Jakob Kuisl was only a few strides away from him. Suddenly the man turned round. Something had aroused his attention. The hangman let himself fall to the ground. Simon blinked, and when he opened his eyes again, the darkness had swallowed Jakob.

He was just about to breathe a sigh of relief when he heard a sound in front of him. The second man, who had been walking around the site, was suddenly standing right before him. He looked just as surprised as Simon was. The man had evidently been looking for a hiding place on the far side of the pile of logs. Now he had turned the corner and stumbled right into Simon.

"What the devil?"

More he could not say, for Simon had seized a stick and had struck the man's legs from under him. The man fell over on his side. Before he could pick himself up, Simon was upon him pummeling him with his fists. The face of his adversary was bearded and scarred, and the blows seemed to bounce off him as if from a rock. With a sudden movement he grabbed the physician, held him up for a second, and flung him forward. At the same time he raised his right hand to strike a blow.

He hit Simon on the side of the head, and Simon fainted. When he came to, the man was sitting on his chest and throttling him with both hands, while his face was contorted into an ugly grin. Simon saw the rotten stumps of teeth and beard stubble, red, brown, and black like a mown field in October. Blood was dripping on him from the man's nose. Simon saw every detail with a clarity as never before. In vain he struggled for air, he felt that he was nearing his end. Scraps of thoughts and memories whirled wildly through his head.

Must pull . . . the knife . . . from the belt.

He fumbled for his knife even as he started to lose consciousness again. At last he found the hilt. Just before he lapsed into final unconsciousness he drew out the stiletto and lunged. He felt the blade slide into something soft.

A scream brought Simon back to the present. He rolled quickly to one side, gasping for air. The bearded man lay near him, rubbing his thigh. Blood was spreading over his hose. Simon had wounded him in the leg, but it was obvious the injury was not severe. The man was looking at him already and grinning. He drew himself up, ready to attack again. Out of the corner of his eye he saw a stone lying on the ground and bent over to pick it up. For one moment his face was turned away, and in this moment Simon threw himself on him with the knife. The man cried out in astonishment. He had expected the weedy-looking youth to just run away, and this sudden attack surprised him. Now Simon sat astride his opponent's broad chest, holding his knife in his raised right hand, poised to attack. Beneath him the man's eyes filled with terror. When he opened his mouth to scream again, Simon knew that he had to strike immediately. He could not risk the man being heard by the others. He felt the hilt in his hand, the hard wood, the sweat on his fingers. He felt the man writhing under him, looking certain death in the eyes.

Simon noticed his arm becoming as heavy as lead. He . . . could not strike. He had never killed. That was a threshold he couldn't cross.

"Ambush!" screamed the man under him. "Here I am, here behind the pile of logs . . . "

The oak cudgel whizzed right past Simon and struck the man in the middle of the forehead. The second blow crushed the skull and blood and white matter oozed out. The face changed to a bloody mush. A strong hand pulled Simon off the body.

"Damn! Why didn't you finish him off before he began to scream? Now they know where we are."

The hangman threw the bloodstained branch to one side and dragged Simon behind the woodpile. The physician could not answer. The face of the dead man had burned itself into his memory like a picture.

Soon afterward they heard voices coming closer.

"André, was that you? What's happened?"

"We must get away from here," whispered the hangman. "There are still four of them, and they're likely to be experienced soldiers. They understand about fighting." He grabbed the half-unconscious Simon and dragged him to the edge of the wood. Then they let themselves drop into a bush and watched what happened next.

It only took the men a short time to find the body. There were loud cries, someone screamed. Then they swarmed in all directions. Watching the torches, Simon could see that they always stayed in pairs. They went along the edge of the wood and poked their torches into dark places. Once they passed within a few steps of their bush. But it was too dark and they could not see anything. Finally they gathered together again by the corpse. As Simon was getting ready to breathe again, he saw that one of the points of light was approaching their hiding place. It was one man alone. From his gait he could see that the man had a limp.

At the edge of the forest, not far from their bush, he halted and raised his nose in the air. It looked as if he was sniffing. His voice reached them clearly.

"I know that was you, hangman," hissed the limping man. "And I know that you are somewhere out there. Believe me, I'll have my revenge. I'll cut off your nose, ears, and lips. The tortures you have inflicted on others are nothing to those you yourself will suffer. You'll beg me to smash your skull in, just as you have done to André."

The man turned abruptly around and was swallowed by darkness.

Not until some time had passed did Simon dare to breathe freely.

"Who . . . who was that?" he asked.

The hangman stood up and brushed the leaves from his coat. "That was the devil. And he's got away from us. All because you crapped your pants!"

Automatically, Simon turned away from him. He felt that he was not only afraid of the devil but also of the man next to him.

"I . . . I can't kill," he whispered. "I'm a physician. I've learned to heal people, not to kill them."

The hangman smiled sadly.

"There you are. But we are supposed to be able to do it. And when we do it, then you are horrified. Stupid lot, you're all the same."

He stomped off into the forest. Suddenly Simon was alone.

Magdalena knocked frantically at the little manhole down by the Lech Gate. The opening was just high and wide enough for one person to fit through it. In this way the watchmen didn't need to open the whole gate for latecomers, thus risking an attack.

"It's the middle of the night! Come back tomorrow; the gate opens when the bell strikes six," growled a voice from the other side.

"Alois, it's me! Magdalena Kuisl. Open, it's important!"

"What's next? First I let you in, then out again, and now you want to come in again. Forget about it, Magdalena, nobody comes into the town before the morning."

"Alois, down at the building site on the Hohenfurch Road there is more destruction in progress. Strangers are there! My father and Simon are watching them, but they can't hold out long! We need the bailiffs!"

The manhole creaked open. A weary watchman stared at her. He stank of brandy and sleep. "I can't help you there. You must go to Lechner."

Only a short time later Magdalena stood before the gate of the ducal castle. The guards let her in but would not allow her to wake the court clerk. She shouted and scolded, until at last a window opened on the second floor of the residence.

"What's all the racket down there, damn it?"

Lechner, in his nightgown, blinked sleepily down at her from his window. Magdalena seized her chance and told the clerk briefly what had happened. When she had finished her story, he nodded.

"I'm coming down right away. Wait there."

Some time later they were walking with the night watchmen and the guards along the Augsburg Road toward the Hohenfurch Road. The men were armed with pikes and two muskets. They looked tired and did not give the impression that it was their greatest desire to get up before dawn to hunt for a few marauding soldiers. Johann Lechner had hurriedly put on his doublet and cloak, and his hair was tousled under his official cap. He looked suspiciously at Magdalena.

"I only hope you are telling the truth. Otherwise both of you—you and your father—can look out for trouble. And anyway, what is the hangman doing outside on the Hohenfurch Road at this time? Respectable burghers stay at home! Lately, your father has had a bit too much to say for my taste. He should torment and hang, and otherwise keep his mouth shut, by God!"

Magdalena bowed her head humbly.

"We were gathering herbs in the woods. Haircap moss and mugwort. You know, they can only be picked by moonlight."

"Devilish stuff, that! And what was Fronwieser's son doing there? I don't believe one word of it, hangman's daughter!"

In the meantime dawn started to break. The watchmen extinguished their lanterns as they approached the misty clearing near the road. Further back on a pile of wood sat the hangman and the physician.

Johann Lechner stamped up to the two men. "Well? Where are your vandals? I can't see anything. And the building site looks exactly as it did yesterday!"

Jakob Kuisl rose. "They fled before they could destroy anything. I hit one of them in the face."

"Oh, yes. And where is he now?" probed the clerk.

"He . . . didn't look well. The others took him with them."

"Kuisl, give me one reason why I should believe this story."

"Tell me one reason why I should otherwise call you out here in the middle of the night."

The hangman now approached the clerk.

"There were five," said Kuisl emphatically. "Four of them were soldiers. The fifth was . . . somebody else. Their patron, I assume. And I believe he comes from the town."

The clerk smiled. "I don't suppose you recognized him, by any chance?"

"It was too dark," Simon now joined the discussion. "But the others talked about him. They called him Moneybags. He must be a rich burgher."

"And why should this rich burgher commission a couple of soldiers to vandalize the building site of the leper house?" Lechner interrupted.

"They didn't damage it. They were looking for something," said Simon.

"What now? Did they destroy the building site, or were they looking for something? First you said that they were going to destroy it."

"Damn it, Lechner," growled Jakob Kuisl. "Don't be so slow-witted! Someone hired these men to upset everything here, something that would hinder the workers, so that their patron could look for what is hidden here in peace!"

"But that's nonsense!" interrupted Johann Lechner. "They didn't gain anything by damaging things. The work is still proceeding in spite of everything."

"There were delays, though," added Simon.

Jakob Kuisl fell silent. The clerk was just about to turn away when the hangman suddenly spoke again.

"The foundations."

"What?"

"The patron must suppose that the treasure, or whatever it is, lies under the foundations. When the building work here is finished he won't be able to get at it anymore. Then buildings of stone will stand here, all mortared and walled up, so he has to interfere with the work and in the meantime turn over every bit of earth until he finds what he is looking for."

"That's right!" cried Simon. "When we were here the first time, parts of the foundation were dug out knee-deep. Someone had put the flagstones neatly aside. And tonight, too, one of the men was prying up the flagstones with a pole!"

Johann Lechner shook his head.

"Tales of treasure hunters and a mysterious search at midnight . . . Do you expect me to believe that?" He waved his hand over the clearing. "What thing of any value could be hidden here? The land belongs to the church, as you know. If there were anything to be found here, the parish priest would have discovered it in his documents. Every bit of church land is exactly recorded: the floor plan, position, previous history . . . "

"Not this one," Jakob Kuisl interrupted him. "This site was presented to the church by old Schreevogl, only a short time ago, to ease his entrance into paradise. The church knows nothing about this land, nothing at all."

The hangman let his eyes range over the clearing. The lower walls of the little chapel, the foundations for the hospital, the well, the linden tree, a frame of beams for a stable yet to be built, piles of wood . . .

Something is hidden here.

The court clerk gave him a benign smile. "Kuisl, Kuisl, stick to what you can do and leave all the rest to us members of the council. Do you understand? Otherwise I'll have to come and have a closer look at your house. People say you sell love potions and other witches' brews . . . "

Simon joined in. "But sir, he's right. The site . . . "

Johann Lechner turned around and looked at him angrily.

"As for you, Fronwieser, shut your insolent mouth, will you? Your little affair with this hangman's wench . . . " He looked across at Magdalena, who quickly turned her head away. "It's illegal and a disgrace, not only for your father. There are some aldermen who would like to see you both in the pillory. What a picture! The hangman putting the mask of shame on his own daughter! Up to now I have shown some restraint, out of consideration for your father, Fronwieser, and also for the executioner, whom I have respected up to now."

At the words "hangman's wench," Jakob Kuisl jumped up, but Magdalena held him back. "Leave him, Father," she whispered. "You'll only make things much worse for us."

Johann Lechner looked over the site once more and signaled to the watchmen to return.

"I'll tell you what I think," he said, without turning around.

"I think that there were in fact soldiers here. I'm even prepared to believe that some crazy Schongau patrician hired them to destroy the leper house. Because he was afraid that travelers would avoid the town. But what I do not believe is your tall tale about a buried treasure. And I do not wish to know who this patrician is. Quite enough dirt has been stirred up already. From now on a watch will be set here every night. The building work will continue as the council decided. As for you, Kuisl . . . " Not until now did he turn to the hangman. "You will come with me and do that for which God has ordained you. You will torture the Stechlin woman until she confesses to the murder of the children. That is the only thing of any importance. And not a few lousy soldiers on a ruined building site."

He was turning to go when one of the bailiffs plucked at his sleeve. It was Benedict Cost, who had been on duty in the keep this same night. "Sir, the Stechlin woman," he began.

Johann Lechner stopped. "Well, what about her?"

"She . . . she's unconscious and badly injured. At midnight she was drawing signs on the floor of her cell, and then Georg Riegg threw a stone at her, and now you can't get a peep out of her. We sent old Fronwieser to her to see if he could bring her around."

A red flush came over Johann Lechner's face. "And why haven't you told me this until now?" he hissed.

"We . . . we didn't want to wake you," stammered Benedict Cost. "We thought it could wait until the next day. I was going to tell you early this morning—"

"Wait until the morning?" Johann Lechner had difficulty keeping his voice calm. "In one or two days the Elector's secretary will be here with bag and baggage, and then all hell will break loose. If we can't produce a culprit, he'll undertake the search himself. And then God help us! It won't be just *one* witch that he'll find, you can be sure of that!"

Abruptly he turned away and hurried back to the road that led to Schongau. The watchmen followed him.

"Kuisl!" he called back when he reached the road. "You will come with me, and the others too! We're going to squeeze a confession out of the Stechlin woman. And if necessary I'll force speech out of a dead woman today!"

Slowly, the mists of the morning rose.

As the last of them left the site, a quiet sound of weeping was heard from somewhere.

Martha Stechlin was still unconscious and therefore not in a condition to be questioned. She had a high fever and was mumbling in her sleep as Bonifaz Fronwieser held his ear to her chest.

"The sign . . . the children . . . all deception . . . " She uttered scraps of words.

The old physician shook his head. He looked up submissively at Johann Lechner, who was leaning against the cell door and observing the medical examination with increasing impatience.

"Well?" inquired Lechner.

Bonifaz Fronwieser shrugged. "It doesn't look good. This woman has a high fever. She's probably going to die before she regains consciousness again. I'll bleed her, and—"

Johann Lechner gestured dismissively. "Oh, leave that rubbish. Then she'll die on us all the sooner. I know you quacks. Isn't there another way to bring her around for a short time, at least? After she's confessed she can die, as far as I'm concerned, but first we must have her confession!"

Bonifaz Fronwieser was thinking. "There are certain remedies, which I unfortunately don't have at my disposal."

Impatiently Johann Lechner drummed against the cell bars with his fingers. "And who has these certain remedies?"

"Well, the hangman, I suppose. But that is devil's stuff. Draw a large quantity of blood and the midwife—"

"Watchman!" Johann Lechner was already on the way out. "Bring the hangman to me. He must bring the Stechlin woman around, and quickly. That's an order!"

Hurried steps departed in the direction of the tanners' quarter.

Bonifaz Fronwieser approached the clerk apprehensively. "Can I be of assistance to you in any other way?"

Lechner only shook his head shortly. He was deep in thought. "Go. I'll call for you when I need you."

"Your pardon, sir, but my fee."

With a sigh, Johann Lechner pressed a few coins into the physician's hand. Then he turned back to the interior of the keep.

The midwife lay on the floor of her cell, breathing with difficulty. Near her, now almost illegible, the sign was still on the ground.

"Satan's whore," hissed Lechner. "Say what you know, and then go to hell." He kicked the midwife in the side, so that she rolled, groaning, onto her back. Then he wiped out the witches' sign and crossed himself.

Behind him someone rattled the iron bars. "I saw her draw that sign!" cried Georg Riegg. "And I threw a stone at her straight away, to stop her putting a spell on us. You can rely on old Riegg, can't you, sir?"

Johann Lechner spun round. "You miserable bungler! It'll be your fault if the whole town burns down! If you hadn't hurt her, she could sing her devil's song now, and we'd have peace at last! But, no, now the Elector's secretary is coming. And just when the town has no more money anyway. You stupid fool!"

"I . . . don't understand."

But Johann Lechner was not listening to him anymore. He had already walked out onto the street. If the hangman could not bring the Stechlin woman around by midday, he would have to call a council meeting. Things were getting out of his control.

CHAPTER
13

MAGDALENA WAS STRIDING UP THE STEEP ROAD from the Lech to the market square with a basket in hand. She could think of nothing but the events of the previous night. She hadn't slept a wink, and yet she was wide awake.

When Johann Lechner saw that the midwife was indeed unconscious and severely injured, he had dismissed the hangman and the physician, cursing violently. Now they were sitting in the hangman's house, tired, hungry, and at their wit's end. Magdalena had volunteered to go to the market to buy beer, bread, and smoked meat to help to revive them. After she had purchased a loaf of rye bread and a good cut of bacon in the market square, she turned to the inns behind the Ballenhaus. She avoided the Stern since Karl Semer, its landlord and the town's presiding burgomaster, was currently on bad terms with her father. Everyone knew that the hangman had taken the side of the witch. So she went over to the Sonnenbräu to get two mugs of beer.

When she stepped back into the street with the foaming tankards, she heard whispering and giggling behind her. She
looked around. A group of children clustered around the door
of the inn, eyeing her, partly out of fear, partly out of curiosity.
Magdalena was making her way through the throng of children
when she heard several voices strike up a little song behind her.
It was an insulting rhyme with her name in it.

"Magdalena, hangman's cow, bears the mark upon her brow!
Beckons all young men to play, 'cept for those who run away!"
Angrily, she turned around.

"Who was that? Speak, if you dare!"

Some of the children ran away. Most, however, remained
and looked at her, smirking.

"Who was that?" she asked again.

"You've put a spell on Simon Fronwieser, so that he follows
you everywhere like a puppy, and you're hand in glove with the
Stechlin woman, that witch."

A boy with a crooked nose, approximately twelve years old,
had spoken. Magdalena knew him. He was the son of Berchtholdt,
the baker. He looked her in the eye defiantly, but his hands were
shaking.

"Is that so. According to whom?" Magdalena asked calmly,
attempting a smile.

"According to my father," the Berchtholdt boy hissed. "And
he says you'll be next to end up burning at the stake."

Magdalena gave him a provocative stare. "Anybody else who
believes this sort of rubbish? If so, shove off now, or else you'll get
one behind the ears."

Suddenly she had an idea. She reached into her basket and
took out a handful of candied fruit. Actually, she had bought it at
the market for her siblings. She smiled as she spoke on.

"For everybody else, I might have some candy, if they want
to tell me a thing or two."

The children pushed closer to her.

"Don't take anything from the witch!" Berchtholdt's son yelled. "There's sure to be a spell on the fruit that'll make you sick!"

Some of the children looked frightened, but their appetite was stronger. With big eyes they followed all of her movements.

"Magdalena, hangman's cow, bears the mark upon her brow," the Berchtholdt boy repeated. But nobody sang along.

"Oh, shut up," another boy interrupted him. He was missing most of his front teeth. "Your father stinks of brandy every morning when I go to get bread. God knows all the crazy things he thinks up when he's drunk. Now shove off."

Crying and hollering, the baker's son ran off. Some followed him; the others crowded around Magdalena and stared at the candied fruit in her hand as if in a trance.

"Well, then," she began. "About the murdered boys, Clara, and that Sophie girl. Who knows what they did at the midwife's? Why didn't they play with you?"

"They were buggers, real pests," the boy in front of her said. "Nobody here misses them. Nobody wanted to have anything to do with them."

"Why would that be?" Magdalena asked.

"'Cause they were bastards, weren't they? Wards and orphans," a little blonde girl piped up, as if the hangman's daughter were a bit slow on the uptake. "And besides, they didn't want to have anything to do with us. They always hung around with that Sophie. And one time she beat my brother black-and-blue, that witch!"

"But Peter Grimmer wasn't a ward at all. He still had his father," Magdalena objected.

"He got bewitched by Sophie," the boy with the missing teeth whispered. "He was totally different since they met! They kissed and showed each other their bare arses. Once he told us that all the wards had entered a compact together and that they could cast a spell on other children to put warts on their faces and even smallpox, if they wanted to. And just a week later little Matthias died of smallpox!"

"And they learned their witchcraft from the Stechlin woman!" a little boy shouted from farther back in the group.

"They used to sit in her house, and now the devil has taken away his disciples," another one hissed.

"Amen," Magdalena murmured. Then she gave the children an enigmatic look.

"I know witchcraft as well," she murmured. "Do you believe me?" Frightened, her audience backed away a little.

Magdalena put on a conspiratorial face, waving her hands mysteriously. "I can make candied fruit rain from the sky."

She tossed the sweet candies high up in the air. As the children screamed and scrambled to get the fruit, she disappeared around the nearest corner.

She didn't notice that a figure was following her at a safe distance.

"I guess today I'll take a cup of your devil's brew." The hangman pointed at the small pouch dangling at Simon's side. The physician nodded and poured the coffee grounds into the pot of boiling water that was hanging above the fire. A strong, invigorating fragrance filled the air. Jakob Kuisl breathed it in and nodded appreciatively. "Doesn't smell bad at all. Considering it's supposed to be the devil's piss."

Simon smiled. "And it'll clear our minds, believe me."

He filled a pewter mug for the hangman. Then he sipped cautiously at his own mug. Every sip helped dispel the tired feeling in his head.

The two men were sitting across from each other at the large, worn table in the main room of the hangman's house, brooding over the previous night's events. Anna Maria, Kuisl's wife, had sensed that the two needed to be alone, so she went down to the

Lech to do her laundry and took the twins with her. Silence engulfed the room.

"I bet my behind that Clara and Sophie are still at that building site," the hangman growled after a while, drumming his fingers on the table. "There has to be a hideout there, and a good one at that. Otherwise we or the others would have found it long ago."

Simon winced. He'd scalded his lips with his hot mug.

"That's certainly possible, but there's no way of finding that out now," he said finally, running his tongue over his lips. "At daytime, the workmen are at the site, and at night there are the guards that Lechner dispatched. If they find out anything concerning those children, they're sure to inform Lechner . . . "

"And Sophie will end up at the stake together with Martha," the hangman concluded. "Jesus Christ, there's a jinx on all of this!"

"Don't say such a thing," Simon grinned. Then he turned serious again.

"Let's recapitulate," he said. "The children seem to be hiding somewhere at the building site. And there's something else hidden there as well. Something that a rich man would like to have. That's why he has hired a handful of soldiers. Resl from Semer's inn told me that these soldiers were meeting with somebody in the upstairs room last week."

"That would've been the mastermind, the patron."

The hangman lit his pipe on a chip of pinewood. Like a tent, the tobacco smoke billowed over the two men, mingling with the fragrance of the coffee. Simon had to cough briefly before he went on.

"The soldiers are vandalizing the building site for the leper house, so that they'll have more time for their search there. That makes sense to me. But why, in the name of God, does one of them slaughter the orphans? There's no sense in that!"

Thoughtfully, the hangman sucked on his pipe. His eyes were staring at a point in space. Finally, he spoke. "They must have seen something. Something that mustn't be brought to light under any circumstances."

Simon slapped his forehead, spilling the remainder of his coffee, which formed a brown puddle that spread across the table. But he didn't care about that.

"The patron!" he shouted. "They have seen the patron who is behind the destruction?"

Jakob Kuisl nodded.

"That would also explain why the Stadel had to be burned down. The devil had an easy time getting his hands on most of the eyewitnesses. He got Peter out there on the river. Anton and Johannes were unwanted orphans and therefore easy prey. But Clara Schreevogl was well protected as a patrician's child. The devil must somehow have found out that she was sick and in bed . . . "

"And then his cronies set fire to the Stadel to distract her family and the servants, so that he could get the child," Simon groaned. "There was a lot at stake for Schreevogl. He had his stock of merchandise down at the Stadel. Of course he'd rush down to the river."

The hangman relit his pipe. "Clara was home alone, sick in her bed. But she did get away from him somehow. And so did Sophie—"

Simon jumped to his feet. "We have to find the children at once, before the devil gets them. The building site . . . "

Jakob Kuisl pulled him back on his chair.

"Calm yourself. Take one thing at a time. We have to save not just the children, but Martha as well. And it is a fact that there was a witches' mark on each of the dead children. And that all of them had previously been at the midwife's. It's possible that the Elector's secretary will arrive as early as tomorrow, and Lechner wants to have the confession by then. I can actually understand why: if the secretary begins meddling in the matter, then one witch just won't do. That's exactly how it was with the last great witch hunt here in Schongau. In the end they burned more than sixty women in these parts."

The hangman looked deep into Simon's eyes.

"First we have to find out about these signs. And we have to do so very soon."

Simon groaned. "Damn these signs. There's nothing but one riddle after the other here."

There was a knock at the door.

"Who's there?" the hangman growled.

"It's me, Benedict Cost," came a frightened voice from the other side of the door. "Lechner's sent me to fetch you. You're supposed to be attending to the witch. She won't say a thing, and she's supposed to confess today. So now you've got to heal her again. You've got medicines and books that the old physician doesn't have, Lechner says."

Jakob Kuisl laughed.

"First I'm supposed to hurt her, then heal her again, and in the end burn her. You're completely crazy, you lot."

Benedict Cost cleared his throat.

"Lechner says it's an order."

Jakob Kuisl sighed.

"Wait there. I'm coming."

He went over to his spare chamber, grabbed a few bottles and jars, packed everything into a sack, and set out on his way.

"You come along," he said to Simon. "Time for you to learn something proper, not just those scribblings from university, from those buffoons who break up a man into four humors and think that's that."

He slammed the door behind them and stomped ahead. The bailiff and Simon followed.

Slowly, Magdalena walked past the Ballenhaus and across the market square. Around her, market women were loudly hawking the first vegetables of the spring: onions, cabbages, and tender little turnips. The fragrance of oven-warm bread and freshly caught fish was in the air, yet she heard and smelled nothing. Her thoughts were still focused on her conversation with the children. On a sudden impulse she turned around and headed westward to the Küh Gate. Soon she had left the shouting and the noise behind her, and only a few people were coming her way. A short time later she had reached her destination.

The midwife's house was in a terrible state. The windows were shattered and hung crooked on their hinges. Someone had forced the door open. In front of the entrance, pottery shards and splintered wood were lying about. It was obvious that the small home had been a repeated target of looters. Magdalena was certain that nothing of any value was left in there, let alone any hint at what had happened a week ago. Nonetheless, she stepped into the main room, looking around.

The room had been turned upside down. The kettle, the poker from the fireplace, the chest, and also the handsome pewter cups and plates that Magdalena had seen on previous visits were gone. Someone had pried open the chicken cage beneath the bench and made off with the chickens. Even the little house altar with its crucifix and statue of the Blessed Virgin had been stripped bare. All that was left off Martha Stechlin's possessions was a smashed table and countless pottery shards, which were scattered across the floor. Some were adorned with alchemistic signs. Magdalena remembered having seen those symbols on the jars that the midwife had kept on a shelf next to her stove.

Standing in the middle of the room, the hangman's daughter tried to imagine, despite the emptiness, how only a week ago the children had played with the midwife. Maybe Martha Stechlin had told them ghost stories, but maybe she had also shared her secret knowledge with them and shown them herbs and medicines. Sophie in particular seemed to be interested in those sorts of things.

Magdalena walked down the hallway and out into the yard. The midwife had been arrested only a few days before, but it seemed to Magdalena that the garden was already growing wild. The looters had yanked the tender shoots of early vegetables from the beds and had attacked the magnificent herbal garden. Magdalena shook her head. So much hatred and greed, so much senseless violence.

Suddenly she caught her breath and hurried back to the main room to look for something. It immediately met her eye.

She almost laughed at not having noticed earlier. She stooped down, picked it up, and rushed outside. In the street she actually did start to giggle, so that several burghers turned around and gave her a startled look.

They had long suspected that the hangman's daughter was hand in glove with the witch. Now here was the final proof!

Magdalena didn't let their looks intimidate her. Still laughing, she decided on a whim not to go home through the Lech Gate but rather through the Küh Gate. She knew a narrow, unfrequented path, little more than a trail, that followed along the base of the town wall and descended to the Lech. The April sun was warm on her face as she passed the gate. She greeted the sentry and ambled along between the beeches.

It was all so simple. Why hadn't they thought of it earlier? It had been there before their eyes the whole time, and they simply hadn't seen it. Magdalena pictured herself conveying the news to her father. Her fist was clutched around the object she was holding. The midwife might go free today. Well, not free, perhaps, but the torture would be suspended, and the trial would be reopened. Magdalena was convinced that now all would change for the better.

The branch hit her right on the back of her head, so that she fell forward into the mud.

She tried to push herself up, when suddenly she felt a fist grabbing her by the scruff of her neck and pushing her back into the mud. Her face lay in a puddle. When she tried to breathe, she tasted only dirt and muddy water. She struggled like a fish out of water, but her attacker kept pushing her head down. As she was losing consciousness, the hand suddenly yanked her up again. She heard a voice right in her ear.

"Let's see what I can do with you, hangman's wench. Once, in Magdeburg, I cut off a girl's breasts and made her eat them. Would you like that? But first I need your father, and you, you're going to help me with that, sweetheart."

A second blow made her skull explode. She could no longer feel how the devil pulled her out of the water and dragged her over the embankment down to the river.

The object slipped from her hand and sank to the bottom of the puddle, where mud slowly settled on it.

Jakob Kuisl was struggling for the life of the midwife he had previously tortured. He had cleaned her head wound and applied a bandage of oak bark. Her swollen fingers were covered with a thick yellow ointment. The hangman kept dripping some tincture from a small vial into her mouth, but Martha Stechlin had difficulty swallowing. The reddish-brownish liquid oozed over her lips and trickled to the ground.

"What is that?" Simon asked, pointing at the vial.

"It's an extract of Saint-John's-wort, nightshade, and several other herbs that you don't know. It'll calm her down, but that's all. Damn it, they should have cleaned the head wound right away. It's already getting inflamed. Your father is a confounded quack!"

Simon swallowed, but he couldn't argue with that.

"Where did you gather all that knowledge? I mean, you've never studied . . . "

The hangman laughed out loud as he examined the countless bruises on the midwife's legs.

"Studied! Nonsense! You silly physicians think you're finding the truth at your cold-blooded universities. But there's nothing there! Nothing but wise books written by wise men who copied from other wise men. But real life, real diseases, that's what you'll find out here. Learn from those, not from your books! That'll teach you more than the entire university library at Ingolstadt!"

"But you have books in your house as well," Simon protested.

"Yes, but what kind of books? Those books that you physicians have banned or chosen to ignore because they don't fit in with your dusty doctrines. Scultetus, Paré, or old Dioscorides! These are truly learned men! But, no. You prefer to bleed patients, look at piss, and believe in your stinking humors. Blood, phlegm, and bile, that's all that constitutes the human body in your eyes. If only I got to take a medical exam at one of your universities . . . "

He broke off, shaking his head. "But why should I get upset? I'm just supposed to heal the midwife and then kill her, and that's that."

At long last, Jakob Kuisl had finished his examination of the tortured woman. Finally, he tore some linen rags in strips, soaked them in the yellow ointment, and wrapped them around her legs, which looked like one large bruise. All the while he was shaking his head.

"I only hope I wasn't too rough with her. But the worst by far is the head injury. We'll see in the next few hours if her fever goes down or if it rises. If it does rise, then tonight will be Martha's last night on this earth, I'm afraid."

He rose to his feet.

"At any rate we have to tell Lechner that he won't get his confession tonight. That buys us time."

Jakob Kuisl stooped down to the midwife one more time to place her head on a fresh bale of straw. As he turned toward the door, Simon was still standing hesitantly at the sick woman's side, and Kuisl impatiently motioned to him to leave.

"There's nothing else we can do now. You may speak a prayer in church or say your rosary, if you wish. I for one will take my pipe, have a good smoke in my own backyard, and attempt to think things through. That will be of more help to Martha Stechlin."

Without so much as looking back he left the keep.

When Simon arrived home, his father was sitting in the main room with a goblet of wine, looking quite content. He even managed a smile as his son entered. Simon noticed he was a bit drunk.

"It's good you are back again. I'll need your help. Dengler's little Maria seems to have a skin disease, and Sepp Bichler—"

"You haven't been able to help her," Simon cut in abruptly.

Bonifaz Fronwieser looked at him in bewilderment.

"What's that you say?"

"You haven't been able to help her. You messed up, and as you were at your wit's end, you called for the hangman."

The old physician's eyes became narrow slits.

"I didn't call him, so help me God," he hissed. "Lechner wanted it. If I had my way, that quack would have been reined in a long time ago! It can't be tolerated that charlatans like that man are allowed to bring shame upon our trade. A man without university schooling. How ridiculous!"

"Quack? Charlatan?" Simon found it difficult to keep his voice from breaking. "This man has more knowledge and reason than your entire Ingolstadt crowd! If Martha Stechlin survives, it's due to him alone and not to you bleeding her, as you did, or sniffing her urine!"

Bonifaz Fronwieser shrugged and took a sip from his goblet.

"Anyhow, Lechner didn't let me have my way. Imagine him even paying attention to that charlatan. Who'd have guessed . . ." Then a smile spread across his face. It was meant to appear conciliatory.

"Anyway, I got paid for it. And believe me, if the midwife croaks now, it's best for her. She'll have to die at any rate. This way she can avoid more torture and the stake."

Simon raised his hand as if to deal him a blow and had difficulty restraining himself.

"You goddamned . . ."

Before he could continue there was a pounding at the door. Outside stood Anna Maria Kuisl. She was breathing hard, and her face was pale. She looked as if she had run the entire way from the Lech Gate quarter.

"Jakob . . . Jakob," she stammered. "He needs you. You have to come at once. When I returned from the river with the children, he was sitting on the bench like a stone statue. I've never seen him like that. Gracious God, I hope it's nothing serious . . ."

"What's happened?" Simon cried out, grabbing for his coat and hat as he rushed out the door.

"He won't tell me. But it's got to do with Magdalena."

Simon ran. He didn't see his father shake his head and carefully close the door. Bonifaz Fronwieser sat down again and continued drinking his pint of wine. You didn't really get the best quality for three pennies, but at least the stuff helped you forget.

Deep in thought Jakob Kuisl had walked homeward through the tanners' quarter down by the river. It was just a few hundred yards more along the main road to his house. Shortly before, he had informed Lechner that the midwife was unable to be questioned. The court clerk had stared at him blankly and then nodded. He wasn't accusatory, and Jakob Kuisl almost got the impression Lechner had expected as much.

At last, however, he gave the hangman a piercing glare.

"You know what comes next, Kuisl, don't you?"

"I don't understand, Your Excellency."

"When the Elector's secretary arrives, you'll have busy days. Keep yourself ready."

"Your Excellency, I trust that we are quite close to the solution . . . "

But the clerk had already turned away. He seemed to have lost all interest in the man facing him.

As the path took a turn around the last few blackberry bushes, Jakob Kuisl could see his backyard, which stretched from the lane all the way down to the pond. The meadow by the pond was heavy with pussy willows. Wolfsbane and daisies were sparkling in the damp meadows and the herbal garden, recently turned over, was steaming in the sun. For the first time this day, a smile played about the hangman's lips.

Suddenly his features froze.

A man was sitting on the bench in front of the hangman's house. His face was turned toward the sun, and his eyes were closed. When he heard Jakob Kuisl at the garden gate, he blinked as if waking up from a beautiful dream. He was wearing a hat with roosters' feathers and a bloodred doublet. The hand he used for keeping the sun from his face was bright white.

The devil looked at Jakob Kuisl and smiled.

"Ah, the hangman! What a wonderful garden you have here! I'm sure your wife takes good care of it, or little Magdalena, if I'm right."

Jakob Kuisl remained motionless at the garden gate. Casually, he picked up a rock from the wall, weighing and hiding it in his hand. One well-aimed throw . . .

"Ah, yes, little Magdalena," the devil continued. "A sprightly lass, ravishingly beautiful. Just like her mother. I wonder if her nipples get hard when one whispers cruel words in her ear. I'll have to try."

Jakob Kuisl clenched his fist around the rock so hard that the edges cut into his flesh.

"What do you want?" he murmured.

The devil rose and walked over to the windowsill, where a jug of water was standing. Slowly he put it to his lips and drank in deep gulps. Drops ran down his beard and dripped to the ground. Only when he had emptied the jug did he set it down, wiping his mouth with his hand.

"What do I want? The question is rather, what do you want? Do you want to see your daughter again, and in one piece? Or perhaps rather in two halves, like a carcass, after I've cut off her chattering lips?"

Jakob Kuisl raised his hand and hurled the rock directly at the devil's forehead. In a movement almost too quick to be seen, the devil ducked to the side, and the rock hit the door without doing him any harm.

For a brief moment the devil appeared startled. Then he smiled again.

"You're fast, hangman. I like that. And you're good at killing. Just like myself."

Suddenly his face contorted into a hideous grimace. For a moment Jakob Kuisl thought the man in front of him was going stark mad. But then the devil got a hold of himself again. His face became blank.

Kuisl took a long look at him. He . . . knew that man. He just didn't remember from where he knew him. He racked his brain, searching it for that face. Where had he seen the man before? In the war? On a battlefield?

The sound of the breaking ceramic jug startled him from his thoughts. The devil had casually thrown it behind himself.

"Enough small talk," he whispered. "This is my offer. You

show me where the treasure is, and I return your daughter. If not . . . " He slowly licked his lips.

Jakob Kuisl shook his head. "I don't know where the treasure is."

"Then find out," the devil hissed. "You're usually so smart. Think of something. We dug up the entire building site and didn't find anything. But the treasure *has* to be there."

Jakob Kuisl's mouth was dry. He tried to remain calm. He had to stall the devil. If only he could get closer . . .

"Don't even think of it, hangman," the devil whispered. "My friends are taking good care of the little hangman's daughter. If I'm not back within the next half hour, they're going to do to her precisely what I told them to do. There are two of them, and they will have great fun."

Jakob Kuisl raised his hands to calm him.

"What about the bailiffs?" he asked, trying to buy time. His throat was hoarse. "There are sentries at the building site both day and night."

"That's your problem." The devil turned to go. "Same time tomorrow I'll be back. By then you have the treasure or else . . . "

He shrugged, almost apologetically. Then he ambled off toward the pond.

"What about your patron?" the hangman shouted after him. "Who is behind all this?"

The devil turned around one more time. "You really want to know? There's enough trouble in your town as it is, don't you think? Maybe I'll tell you once you hand me the treasure. Maybe the man will be dead by then, however."

He strode off across the damp green meadows, leaped over a wall, and soon vanished in the thick forest by the river.

Jakob Kuisl fell onto the bench and stared into space. It took him some time to notice the blood that was dripping from his hand. He had clenched the rock so hard that its edges had dug into his flesh like knives.

Johann Lechner arranged the papers on his desk on the upper floor of the Ballenhaus. He was preparing for the upcoming meeting of the council, which he assumed was to be the last for quite a while. The clerk wasn't going to kid himself. The upcoming arrival of His Excellency, Count Sandizell, the Elector's secretary, would spell the end of Johann Lechner's influence. He was merely acting as a proxy here. Count Sandizell would start all over and certainly not content himself with one single witch. There was unrest in the streets already. Lechner had been told by a number of people that they would take sacred oaths that the Stechlin woman had jinxed their calves, brought hailstorms down upon their crops, and made their wives barren. Only this morning, Agnes from Steingaden had grabbed him by the sleeve in the street and whispered in his ear, her breath reeking of wine, that her neighbor Maria Kohlhaas was also a witch. She herself had seen her fly across the sky on a broomstick the night before. Johann Lechner sighed. If worse came to worse, the hangman would indeed have busy days.

The first aldermen were arriving in the well-heated council chamber. Richly dressed in their robes and fur caps they took their assigned seats. Karl Semer gave Lechner an inquisitive glance. He might have been the town's presiding burgomaster, but in official business he fully relied on the clerk. This time, however, it seemed that Lechner had failed. Semer pulled him by the sleeve.

"Any news of the Stechlin woman?" he asked. "Has she finally confessed?"

"Just a moment." Johann Lechner pretended he was signing an important document. The clerk hated these stuffed moneybags, these puppets, who only held their office by virtue of their birth. Lechner's father had been a court clerk as well and so had his great uncle, but no court clerk before him had ever been that powerful. The post of the district judge had long been vacant, and the Elector's secretary came to the town only occasionally. Johann Lechner was smart enough to let the patricians keep the illusion that it was *they* who ruled the town. Who really ruled was he, the clerk. Now, however, his power seemed to be wavering, and the aldermen sensed it.

Johann Lechner continued to arrange his papers. Then he looked up. The patricians looked at him expectantly. To his left and right were the seats of the four burgomasters and the superintendent of the almshouse, and farther on were those of the other members of the inner and outer council.

"Let me get right to the heart of the matter," Lechner began. "I have called this council meeting because our town is in a state of emergency. Unfortunately we have not so far been able to make the witch Martha Stechlin talk. Only this morning the witch fell back into a swoon. Georg Riegg hit her on the head with a rock and—"

"How is that possible?" old Augustin interrupted, turning toward Lechner, his blind eyes glistening. "Riegg was in jail himself on account of the fire at the Stadel. How can he throw a rock at the Stechlin woman?"

Johann Lechner sighed. "Well, it happened, so let's leave it at that. Anyway, she hasn't regained consciousness yet. It's possible the devil will take her before she can confess her crimes to us."

"Why can't we just tell the people that she's confessed?" burgomaster Semer murmured, mopping his sweaty pate with a silk kerchief. "She's dying, and so we burn her for the welfare of our town."

"Your honor," Johann Lechner hissed. "That would be a lie before God and His Serene Highness, the Elector himself. We have witnesses present at every interrogation. Shall they all swear false oaths?"

"No, no, not at all. I was only thinking . . . as I said, for the benefit of Schongau . . . " The first burgomaster's voice grew fainter and finally trailed off.

"When can we expect the Elector's secretary to arrive?" old Augustin queried.

"I have sent messengers," Lechner said. "The way things look, His Excellency Count Sandizell will give us the pleasure of his presence as early as tomorrow morning."

A groan passed through the council chamber. The patricians knew what was in store for them. The Elector's secretary complete with his entourage would settle in the town for many days, if not weeks. It would cost the town a fortune! Not to mention the endless interrogations of suspicious burghers concerning witchcraft, and until the true perpetrators had been found, anyone here could really be in league with the devil. Even the aldermen and their wives . . . During the last great witch hunt, a number of respected burghers' wives had been among the victims. The devil drew no distinction between a servant girl and a landlady or a midwife and a burgomaster's daughter.

"What about that Augsburg wagon driver we arrested on account of the fire at the Stadel?" the second burgomaster Johann Püchner asked, nervously drumming his fingers on the table. "Is he involved in the matter at all?"

Johann Lechner shook his head.

"I interrogated him myself. He's innocent. Therefore I released him this morning after giving him a severe warning. At least the Augsburgers won't give us trouble anytime soon. They got what was coming to them. But the Augsburg wagon driver did see that soldiers were fooling around at the Stadel . . . "

"Soldiers? What kind of soldiers?" old Augustin asked. "This story is getting more confusing by the minute. Please explain yourself, Lechner."

Johann Lechner briefly contemplated telling the aldermen about his discussion with the hangman down by the building site. Then he decided against it. Matters were complicated enough. He shrugged.

"Well, it seems as though a gang of marauding rogues have set fire to our storage shed. The same rogues also destroyed the building site for the leper house."

"And now they're roaming around killing little children and painting a witches' mark on their shoulders," old Augustin interrupted, impatiently rapping his stick on the expensive cherry-wood floor. "Is this what you're trying to tell us? Lechner, pull yourself together. We *have* the witch! All we need now is her confession!"

"You're misunderstanding me," the court clerk said, trying to calm the irate patrician. "These soldiers most likely caused the fires. But of course it's the devil and his helpmate who are responsible for the death of our children. The evidence is clear. We have found magic herbs in the Stechlin woman's house, the children frequently called on her, and there are burghers who will testify that she introduced the children to the art of sorcery . . . All we need is her confession. And you know as well as I that the *Constitutio Criminalis Carolina* stipulates that only someone who confesses may be sentenced."

"You need not lecture me on the Criminal Code of Emperor Charles. I know it sufficiently well," Matthias Augustin murmured, his blind eyes roaming in the distance and his nostrils dilating, as though he could perceive a distant stench. "I smell it again, the flesh of the burning women, just like it was seventy years ago. By the way, a district judge's wife died at the stake then . . . "

Hawklike, the blind man swung suddenly around toward the court clerk. Lechner turned to his documents again and replied quietly, "As you know, my wife died three years ago, and she is beyond all suspicion. If that's what you're alluding to."

"And what if we subject the witch to the water test?" suggested the superintendent of the almshouse, Wilhelm Hardenberg. "They did that in Augsburg a few years ago. The witch's thumbs are tied to her toes and then she's thrown into the water. If she floats to the surface, it's because the devil is helping her, and she's a witch. If she sinks, she's innocent, but you're rid of her anyway."

"Damn it, Hardenberg," old Augustin yelled. "Are you deaf? The Stechlin woman's unconscious! She'll sink like a stone! Who's going to believe in this water test? Certainly not the Elector's secretary!"

For the first time, young Jakob Schreevogl spoke now. "Why do you consider it such a bizarre idea, Augustin, that the soldiers might have murdered the children? Several witnesses observed a person leaping out of a window of my house at the time my Clara vanished. The man was wearing a bloodred doublet and a feathered hat, such as soldiers often wear. And he had a limp."

"The devil!" Berchtholdt the baker started up, crossing himself. So far, it seemed, he had been sleeping off last night's brandy. "Holy Virgin Mary, help us!"

Some other aldermen murmured quick prayers and crossed themselves.

"You're just taking the easy way out blaming it all on that devil of yours," said Jakob Schreevogl amid the general grumbling. "He's a solution for it all," he interjected. "But one thing I know for certain!" He rose to his feet and looked around angrily. "My Clara wasn't abducted by a monster with cloven feet but by a flesh-and-blood human being. The devil wouldn't be stopped by a locked door, nor does he jump out of windows. He doesn't wear a cheap soldier's hat, and he doesn't meet soldiers in Semer's inn for a mug of beer."

"Whatever gives you the idea that the devil frequents my house?" cried burgomaster Semer, jumping up. His face had turned bright red, and beads of sweat stood out on his forehead. "That is an insolent lie, and you're going to pay for it!"

"The young physician told me. He saw the man who abducted my Clara going up the stairs in your establishment and into one of the conference rooms." Jakob Schreevogl looked the burgomaster calmly in the eye. "He met someone there. Might that have been you?"

"I'll shut that Fronwieser up, and you at the same time!" shouted Semer, slamming his fist on the table. "I won't have my inn reviled in such cock-and-bull stories."

"Pull yourself together, Karl, and sit down again." Blind Augustin's voice was low and yet quite cutting. Stunned, Semer resumed his seat.

"And now tell us," Matthias Augustin continued. "Is there any truth in these . . . insinuations?"

Burgomaster Semer rolled his eyes and took a deep swig from his wineglass. He was obviously struggling for words.

"Well, is it true?" the second burgomaster Johann Püchner insisted. And Wilhelm Hardenberg, the superintendent of the almshouse, now turned to the respected landlord of the Stern Inn. "Karl, tell us the truth! Were there meetings of soldiers under your roof?"

There was a general murmuring at the council table. Some members of the outer council on the back benches began talking.

"This is a perfidious lie," burgomaster Semer finally snapped. Sweat was streaming down his face and into his lace collar. "It's possible that a few former soldiers were at the Stern. I have no way of checking that. But none of them went upstairs, and they certainly didn't meet anyone there."

"Well, that settles it," Matthias Augustin said. "Let's therefore turn to more important things again." His blind eyes turned toward the clerk. "What are you going to do now, Lechner?"

Johann Lechner looked at the undecided faces of the aldermen to his right and his left.

"To tell you the truth, I don't know. Count Sandizell will arrive here tomorrow morning. If the midwife hasn't talked by then, may God have mercy on us all. I fear . . . we should pray tonight."

He rose, packing away his quill and ink. The others rose, too, hesitantly.

"I'll go now and prepare everything for the count's arrival. Each of you will have to contribute. And as for the trial of the witch . . . we can only hope."

Lechner hurried out without a goodbye. The aldermen, talking animatedly, followed in groups of two and three. Only two patricians remained in the council chamber. They still had some urgent matters to clear up.

Slowly, the devil ran his bony hand over Magdalena's dress, brushing over her breasts and following the line of her neck up to her slender chin. As he reached her lips, she turned away, rolling her eyes. The devil smiled and pulled her head toward him again. The hangman's daughter was lying in front of him on the ground, tied up and gagged with a dirty rag. Her eyes flashed angrily at the man above her. The devil blew her a kiss.

"Very well. Very well. Just carry on being fresh, and we'll both have more fun later on."

A man appeared in the clearing behind them. He stood there for a moment, cautiously, then cleared his throat. It was the soldier Hans Hohenleitner.

"Braunschweiger, we should get out of here. Christoph was over in the town. People say the count's going to show up in person tomorrow on account of the witch. Then the place's going to be crawling with troops. Let's have some fun with the girl, and then off we go. It's enough that André is dead."

"And the treasure? What about the treasure?"

The devil whom they called Braunschweiger turned around. The corners of his mouth were twitching, as if he hadn't got full control of his face.

"You seem to have forgotten the treasure! Besides, Money-bags still owes us a whole lot of money!"

"To hell with the money. He gave us another twenty-five guilders yesterday for the destroyed building site and the Stadel fire. That's more than enough. There's nothing more to be gotten here."

Christoph Holzapfel, the third soldier, approached them. Long, shaggy black hair hung in his face. Furtively, he glanced at Magdalena, who was lying on the ground, struggling with her shackles. "Hans is right, Braunschweiger. Let's go. There is no treasure. We've searched the entire damned building site, we've turned over every single rock, and by tomorrow the count's men may be combing the forest here."

"Let's move on," Hans Hohenleitner said again. "My head's more important to me than a handful of guilders. They got André, and that's not a good sign, may his damned soul rest in peace. But beforehand, let's have a little fun . . . " He stooped down to Magdalena. When his pockmarked face appeared right above her mouth, she could smell brandy and beer on his breath. His lips were distorted into a sardonic grin.

"Well, sweetheart, do you feel a little twitching in the loins too?"

Magdalena's head shot forward. Her forehead hit Hans right on the nose, which exploded like a ripe fruit. Blood spurted forth.

"You damned filthy slut!" Whimpering, the soldier held his nose, then he kicked the girl in the stomach. Magdalena doubled up, trying to choke back the pain. They mustn't hear her scream. Not yet.

As Hans was about to kick her a second time, the devil restrained him.

"Cut it out. You're ruining her pretty face. And then we'll have only half as much fun with her later on, eh? I promise I'll show you things that are too dirty even for the Prince of Darkness."

"Braunschweiger, you're a sick man." Christoph Holzapfel shook his head in disgust. "All we want is some fun with the girl. I've had enough with the bloody mess you left behind in Landsberg." He turned away. "Just have your fun with her, and then let's clear out of here."

Magdalena doubled up, ready for the next blow.

"Not yet," the devil mumbled. "First let's get the treasure."

"Damn it, Braunschweiger!" Hans Hohenleitner said, holding his bleeding nose. "There is no treasure. Can't you get that inside your sick head?"

The corners of the devil's mouth started to twitch again, and his head moved in a wide circle, as if he was trying to release some internal tension.

"Don't you ever call me . . . sick again, Hohenleitner. Never again . . ." His eyes darted from one soldier to the next. "And now I'll tell you something. We'll stay here one more night, just one more. You take the girl to a safe place, and I'll get you the treasure by tomorrow morning. You'll have ducats coming out of your arse. And then we'll see to the girl, all of us."

"One more night?" Hans Hohenleitner asked. The devil nodded.

"And how are you going to find that treasure?"

"Leave that to me. You just take care of the girl."

Christoph Holzapfel stepped closer again.

"And where are we supposed to hide, huh? The place will be crawling with troops tomorrow."

The devil smiled.

"I know an absolutely safe place. They won't find you there. And you'll have a great view."

He told them the place. Then he set out for the town.

Magdalena bit her lips. Tears were streaming over her cheeks. She struggled to turn her face away from the soldiers. They mustn't see her cry.

The two men were standing near the building site watching the workmen. Some of the bricklayers and carpenters waved to them. Perhaps they were wondering what business the two men had here, but they didn't harbor the slightest suspicion. The two men there were respected burghers. Presumably they just wanted to see for themselves how the construction was proceeding.

There wasn't much left to see of the last day's damage. The walls of the leper house were being raised again, and there was a new roof truss on the walls of the chapel. Two bailiffs were sitting at the edge of the well in the middle of the clearing, killing time by playing dice. The court clerk had ordered the entire area to be guarded day and night, and his orders had been quite precise, as usual. They had nailed together a wooden shelter for the bailiffs, where they could get cover from the rain. There were lanterns hanging on the outer wall of the shelter, and two halberds were leaning next to them.

"And you have really searched the entire place?" the older man was now asking.

The younger man nodded. "Everything. And several times. I really don't know where else we could look. But it *has to be* here somewhere!"

The other man shrugged. "Maybe the old miser was lying. Maybe he was delirious on his deathbed. An old man's feverish ravings, and we fell for them . . . "

He groaned loudly and held his side. He had to bend over briefly for the pain to subside. Then he turned to walk away.

"One way or another, the matter is over and done with."

"Over and done with?" The younger man ran after him, grabbed him by the shoulder, and turned him around. "What do you mean, over and done with? We can still keep looking. I haven't paid the soldiers in full yet. For just a few more guilders they'll raze everything to the ground here and root about like hogs. The treasure is somewhere here. I . . . I can feel it!"

"Damn it, it's over and done with!" The older man pushed the younger man's hand off his shoulder almost in disgust. "The area is under surveillance. Besides, you've stirred up enough dirt as it is. Lechner knows about your soldiers, and the hangman and that Fronwieser fellow are on your heels. They stick their noses into everything. They even went to see the priest. It's too much of a risk for us. The matter is over and done with, once and for all!"

"But . . . " The younger man held him back another time.

Indignantly, the older man shook his head, holding his side once more. He gave a loud groan.

"I have plenty of other things to think about now. Thanks to your soldiers we'll have the count and his men in this town tomorrow. And presumably we'll have a big trial, people will be dragged off to the stakes again, and Schongau will go to the dogs. And all because of you, you damned idiot! I'm ashamed. For you and for our family. And now let go of me. I wish to go."

The older man stomped off, leaving the younger man behind at the building site in the mud. Mud was all over his shiny leather boots, but he wouldn't give up! He was going to show the others! A wave of anger came over him.

Some of the workmen waved at him, and he waved back, but they couldn't see his face, which hatred had turned to stone.

CHAPTER
14

SIMON RAN DOWN THE HENNENGASSE WITH ANNA Maria Kuisl to the Lech Gate and on through the tanners' quarter. The news that something might have happened to Magdalena spurred him on faster than he had ever run before. Soon he had left the hangman's wife far behind. His heart was racing, and a metallic taste filled his mouth. In spite of this he didn't stop until he arrived at the hangman's house. There it stood, in the most beautiful midday sunshine. Some finches were chirping in the apple trees in the garden, and from far off the calls of the raftsmen could be heard. Otherwise all was quiet. The bench in front of the house was empty, and the front door stood wide open. Under one of the apple trees an empty swing was moving slowly in the wind.

"My God, the children!" Anna Maria Kuisl had caught up with Simon in the meantime. "Not the children too—"

Without finishing her sentence she ran past Simon into the house, and he followed her inside. In the living room they

encountered two five-year-old angels of innocence sitting in a
pool of milk. Next to them lay a broken pitcher. They were eating honey with their fingers from an earthenware bowl and were
covered from head to toe in white dust. Only then did Simon see
that the flour barrel had also been toppled over.

"Georg and Barbara, just what are you . . . "

Anna Maria was about to begin an angry tirade, but the relief
at finding the twins unharmed was too great. She couldn't help
laughing out loud. However she quickly got a hold of herself
once more.

"Upstairs and into bed with you, you two! I don't want to see
either one of you down here for at least an hour. Just look at what
you've done!"

Contritely, the twins trotted upstairs. While Anna Maria
Kuisl wiped up the milk and swept up the shards and the flour,
she told Simon again briefly what had happened.

"I arrived here, and there he was sitting on the bench, as if he
had been turned to stone. When I asked him what had happened
he only said that Magdalena was gone. That the devil had taken
her. The devil, my God."

She threw the shards carelessly into a corner and pressed one
hand to her mouth. Tears ran from her eyes. She had to sit down.

"Simon, tell me, what does it all mean?"

The physician gave her a long look without answering.
Thoughts raced through his mind. He wanted to jump up and
do something, but he did not know what that might be. Where
was Magdalena? Where was the hangman? Did he follow her?
Could he perhaps know where the devil had taken his daughter?
And what did the man want with the girl?

"I . . . I can't tell you exactly," he murmured finally. "But I
think that the man responsible for kidnapping the children has
gone off with Magdalena."

"Oh God!" Anna Maria Kuisl buried her face in her hands.
"But why? Why? What does he want from my little girl?"

"I think he wants to blackmail your husband. He wants us to stop pursuing him and leave him alone."

The hangman's wife looked up with hope in her eyes. "And if you do what he wants, will he let Magdalena go?"

Simon would have loved to nod, to console her and to tell her that her daughter would come back soon, but he couldn't. Instead he stood up and walked to the door.

"Will he let her go?" Anna Kuisl's voice was pleading. She was almost shouting. Simon did not look back.

"I don't think so. This man is sick and evil. He will kill her unless we find her first."

He ran through the garden and back to town. Behind him he could hear the twins beginning to cry. They had been hiding on the stairs and listening. Although they could not have understood anything, they still could sense that something very bad must have happened.

At first Simon wandered aimlessly through the streets of the tanners' quarter and then down along the river. He had to get his thoughts together, and the Lech's lazy current helped him do that. There were two possibilities. He needed to either find the hiding place where the devil was holding Magdalena or discover who had given the devil his instructions. Once he knew who that was, he might be able to free Magdalena from her abductor's clutches—if she was still alive.

Simon shuddered. The possibility that his beloved could already be floating down the river with her throat cut open kept him from thinking of anything else. He could not allow this image to overwhelm him. Besides it made no sense. Magdalena was the devil's hostage, and he would not be quick to throw away this security.

Simon had no idea where the devil could have hidden Magdalena. But he had a suspicion as to where the children might be who could tell him who the devil's patron was. They had to be somewhere at the building site. But where exactly?

Damn it, where?

He decided to visit Jakob Schreevogl once more. After all, the property had once belonged to his father. Perhaps he knew about a possible hiding place that Simon and the hangman had not yet found.

A half an hour later he was once more up at the market square. The stalls were noticeably emptier in the early afternoon, as the burghers were done with their shopping. The market women were stowing away the leftover vegetables in baskets or looking after their whining children, who had to remain with them all day at the stand. Wilted lettuce leaves and rotting cabbage were lying on the ground amid horse droppings and oxen dung. Now people were hurrying home. Tomorrow would be the first of May, and for many this holiday was already starting. It was time to prepare for May Day. As in many other Bavarian villages and towns, Schongau would celebrate the beginning of summer tomorrow. This night belonged to lovers. Simon closed his eyes. Actually he had planned to spend May Day with Magdalena. He felt a lump in his throat. The more he thought about it, the more he felt fear creeping up on him.

Suddenly he remembered that tonight something entirely different would also be celebrated. How could he have forgotten. This was the night of April 30—Walpurgis Night! Witches danced in the forests and mated with the devil, and many people armed themselves against evil by means of magic: magic signs in their windows and salt before their doors. Did the terrible murders and strange symbols have anything to do with Walpurgis Night after all? Even though Simon doubted it, he still feared that this night could be a pretext for some burghers to kill the alleged witch in the jailhouse. His time was running short.

He walked past the castle into the Bauerngasse and was soon standing in front of the Schreevogls' house. A servant girl was standing on the balcony, warily looking down at Simon. Word had gotten around in the meantime that he was having an affair with the hangman's daughter. When Simon waved at her she disappeared into the house without a greeting to inform her young master.

A short time later Jakob Schreevogl opened the door and let Simon in.

"Simon, what a pleasure! I hope the suspicion against me has been dissipated. Do you have anything new about my Clara?"

Simon wondered for a moment to what extent he could confide in the patrician. As before, he was not sure of the role Jakob Schreevogl was playing in this drama. He therefore decided to be very brief.

"We believe that soldiers murdered the children because they had seen something they were not supposed to see. But we don't know what that could have been."

The patrician nodded.

"I suspect that as well. But the council does not want to believe you. Only this morning they met again. The bigwigs want to have everything sorted out. And so a witch and the devil fits their picture a lot better, especially now when time is running short. The Elector's secretary is arriving tomorrow."

Simon winced.

"Tomorrow already? Then we have less time than I hoped."

"Besides, Semer denies that the soldiers met with someone upstairs in his rooms," continued Jakob Schreevogl.

Simon uttered a dry laugh.

"A lie! Resl, Semer's maid, told me that it happened, and she was able to describe the soldiers exactly. And they did go upstairs!"

"And if Resl was mistaken?"

Simon shook his head.

"She was absolutely sure of herself. It's more likely that the burgomaster is lying." He sighed. "In the meantime I no longer have any idea who to trust . . . but I came for something else. We have an idea about Clara and Sophie's hiding place."

Jakob Schreevogl hurried over to him and grabbed him by the shoulders.

"Where? Tell me, where? I'll do everything I can to find them."

"Well, we believe they could be hiding at the building site for the leper house."

The patrician blinked in disbelief.

"At the building site?"

Simon nodded and started to walk up and down nervously in the antechamber.

"We found traces of clay under the fingernails of the dead children. Clay that could have come from the leper house building site. It is quite possible that the children saw something there from their hiding place and don't dare to come out now. However we did search all around and didn't find anything."

He turned again to the patrician.

"Do you have any idea where the children could have hidden? Did your late father tell you anything? About a cavern? A hole under the foundations? Was there some other building on the property, a building whose cellar could still exist? The priest was talking about an old altar from pagan times . . ."

Jakob Schreevogl settled into a chair next to the chimney and thought for a long time. Finally he shook his head.

"Not that I know of. The property has belonged to our family for several generations. I believe that even in my great-grandparents' time, they had cows and sheep grazing there. As far as I know, there was a chapel or church there long ago and quite possibly also some kind of sacrificial altar. But that was very long ago. We never did much with the property until I decided to have the kiln built there."

Suddenly his eyes shone.

"The town records . . . Something like this must be recorded there!"

"The town records?" asked Simon.

"Yes, there is a record in the town registers for every contract, every purchase, and even every donation made in town. Johann Lechner in particular takes great care as the court clerk to see that everything is in good order. When my father left the parcel to the church, an official certificate of donation was prepared. And as far as I can remember, an old map of the property still in my father's possession was attached to that document."

Simon felt his mouth go dry. He had the feeling of being close to a solution.

"And where are these . . . town records?"

The patrician shrugged.

"Well, where would they be? In the Ballenhaus, of course. In the clerk's office next to the council chamber. Lechner keeps everything in the closet there, everything that is of any importance for the town. You could ask him if you may have a look."

Simon nodded and turned to the door. There he turned around once more.

"You have helped me very much. Thank you."

Jakob Schreevogl smiled.

"You need not thank me. Bring me back my Clara—that would be thanks enough." The alderman ascended the wide stairs. "And now you'll excuse me. My wife is still sick. I shall go look after her now."

Suddenly he stopped once more. He seemed to remember something.

"There was something else . . ."

Simon looked up at him expectantly.

"Well," Jakob Schreevogl continued, "my father saved a good deal of money in his life. Very much money. As you know we had a falling out shortly before his death. I had always assumed that after the argument he had left his entire fortune to the church. But I spoke with the priest . . . "

"And?"

"Well, the only thing the church has is this piece of land. I've looked everywhere in our house, but I have not been able to find the money anywhere."

Simon barely heard him anymore. He was again outside, in the street.

In long strides the physician rushed to the Ballenhaus. He was quite certain that the court clerk would never let him look at the town records. At the building site that morning he had made it very clear to him and the hangman what he thought of their suspicions, which was pretty much nothing at all. Johann Lechner wanted peace in the town and not some physician snooping around in his records and possibly discovering a secret that could cost one of the patricians his head. But Simon knew that he simply *had* to see that contract. The only question was how.

In front of the Ballenhaus two bailiffs carrying halberds were hanging around and watched as the last of the market women cleaned up their stalls. Now, in the afternoon, the two guards were the only ones still on duty. Simon knew that there would also no longer be any aldermen in the building. The council meeting had been at noon today, the patricians had long gone home to their families, and the court clerk was over in the castle. The Ballenhaus stood empty. He only had to get past the two bailiffs.

Smiling, he approached the pair. One of them had been his patient at one time.

"Well, Georg, how is your cough?" he asked. "Did it get any better since I gave you the linden blossoms for your infusion?"

The bailiff shook his head. As proof he coughed a few times loudly.

"Unfortunately not, sir. It's gotten worse. And now my chest also hurts. I can barely do my service. I've already prayed three rosaries, but that didn't help either."

Simon looked at him thoughtfully. Suddenly his expression lightened up.

"Well, I may have something that could help you. A powder from the West Indies . . . " He pulled out a small bag and looked apprehensively up at the sky.

"Actually it should be taken as long as the noonday sun is straight overhead. It's almost too late now."

The bailiff Georg coughed a second time and reached for the little bag.

"I'll take it, sir. Right now. How much is it going to cost?"

Simon handed him the medicine.

"For you, only five pennies. However you must dissolve it in brandy, otherwise it has no effect. Do you have any brandy?"

Georg started to think. The physician thought that he would have to help him along, but then the bailiff's face lit up.

"I can get some brandy. Over at the inn."

Simon nodded and took the money.

"Good thinking, Georg. Run over there quickly. It won't take you long to get back."

Georg took off while the second guard stood undecidedly at his post. Simon looked at him pensively.

"Do you also have a cough?" he asked. "You look so pale. Any chest pains?"

The guard seemed to think it over, and then he looked over to where his colleague was just disappearing into the inn. Finally he nodded.

"Then go run after him, see to it that he gets more brandy," said Simon. "Each of you must dissolve it in a goblet, better even, two goblets full."

The bailiff's sense of duty was wrestling with the prospect of one or two goblets of brandy, and for medicinal purposes to boot. Finally he followed his friend.

Simon grinned. He had learned a few things from the hangman by now. Amazing what can be done with a little bag filled with clay!

The physician waited another moment until the two were out of sight. Then he looked around carefully. The market square was empty. He quickly opened the big door a crack and slipped inside.

A smell of spices and musty linen greeted him. Sunlight fell in narrow strips through the large, barred windows. It was already getting dark in the hall and shadows were creeping across the room. Bags and crates were stacked one on top of the other like sleeping giants against the wall. Alarmed, a rat scurried out from behind a crate and disappeared in the darkness.

Simon crept up the wide steps to the upper level and listened at the door to the council chamber. When he could not hear any sound he opened it carefully. The room was empty. Half-full wine pitchers and crystal glasses were standing on the big oaken table in the middle of the room, and the chairs around it were pushed back. A huge oven with green tiles, some of them painted, sat in the corner. Simon held his hand against it. It was still hot. It looked as if the aldermen had left the room for only a short recess and would return at any moment.

Simon crept through the room and tried as best he could to keep the floorboards from creaking. On the eastern wall hung a yellowed oil painting showing the Schongau aldermen assembled around the oaken table. He looked at it closer. At first glance he realized that it had to be quite old. The men were wearing the ruffled collars that were fashionable a few decades ago. The jackets were stiff, black, and buttoned all the way up. The faces with their carefully trimmed goatees were severe and expressionless. Still, he thought he could recognize one of the men. The alderman in the center, the one with the piercing eyes and the bare hint of a smile must be Ferdinand Schreevogl. Simon remembered that the old Schreevogl had once been presiding burgomaster of the town. The patrician held in his hand a document covered with writing. Simon thought he also knew the man next to him. But where had he seen him before? He thought about it, but much as he tried, he could not think of a name. He was certain that he had seen him lately, but of course now as a much older man.

Then he suddenly heard voices and laughter down on the market square. The two bailiffs had apparently followed his recipe. He grinned. It was quite possible, though, that the medicine was taken in a somewhat higher dose than prescribed.

Simon softly tiptoed through the council chamber. He crouched down as he passed the windows with the lead-lined panes so as not to be seen from the outside. Finally he reached the small door to the archive. He pushed the handle down. It was locked.

Cursing softly he reproached himself for his stupidity. How could he have been so naive as to think that the door would be unlocked? Of course the court clerk had locked it! After all, it led to his holy of holies.

Simon was about to turn back, but then he thought some more. Johann Lechner was a reliable man. He had to see to it that at least the four burgomasters had access to the archive, even if he happened to be absent. Did this mean that each of the burgomasters had a key? Hardly. It was much more likely that the court clerk would be keeping the key here for the others. But where?

Simon gazed around at the Swiss pine ceiling with its carved scrolls, the table, the chairs, the wine pitchers . . . There was no cabinet, no chest. The only large piece of furniture was the tiled oven; a monstrosity at least two paces wide and reaching almost to the ceiling. Simon walked over to it and gave it a closer look. In one row, about halfway up, scenes of country life were depicted on the painted tiles. A farmer with a plow, another farmer sowing, pigs and cows, a girl with geese . . . In the center of the row was a tile that looked different from the others. It showed a man with the typical wide hat and the ruffled collar of an alderman. He was sitting on a chamber pot brimming over with paper scrolls. Simon tapped on the tile.

It sounded hollow.

The physician took out his stiletto, inserted the blade into a crack and pried the tile out. It slid easily into his hand. Behind it was a tiny niche in which something was glittering. Simon smiled. As far as he knew, old Schreevogl had this oven built during his tenure as burgomaster. In the stovemakers' guild he had been considered a real artist. Here, one could also see something more—that he had also had a sense of humor. An alderman defecating scrolls? Would Johann Lechner's father, the court clerk at the time, have recognized himself in the drawing?

The physician removed the copper key, fitted the tile back into its place, and returned to the door that separated him from the archives. He inserted the key into the lock and turned it. With a slight squeak the door opened inward.

The room behind it smelled of dust and old parchment. Only a small barred window opened on the market square. There was no other door. The afternoon sun fell through the window; dust particles floated in the light. The space was almost empty. Along a rear wall stood a small, unadorned oaken table and a rickety chair. All along the left side there was a huge cabinet that reached almost to the ceiling. It contained innumerable little drawers stuffed with documents. Heavy leather-bound folios stood on the larger shelves. Several books and loose pages lay on the table, and next to them a half-full glass inkwell, a goose quill, and a half-consumed candle.

Simon groaned softly. This was the court clerk's domain. For him all of it had a certain order, but for the physician it was only a confusing collection of parchment rolls, documents, and tomes. The so-called town records were not books at all, but a huge box of loose slips of paper. How could anyone find the map of a parcel in here?

Simon approached the cabinet. Now he realized that letters were painted on the drawers. They were distributed apparently without rhyme or reason over the rows of shelves, abbreviations obviously familiar only to the court clerk and perhaps the members of the inner council. RE, MO, ST, CON, PA, DOC . . .

The last abbreviation gave Simon pause. The Latin word for a deed, a record, or any kind of instrument was *documentum.* Would deeds of donation also be kept in this drawer? He pulled the drawer out. It was filled to the top with sealed letters. Even a first glance showed him that he had been right. All the letters bore the seal of the town and were signed by high-ranking burghers. There were wills, sales agreements, and exactly what he was looking for—deeds, among them those of money, natural produce, and for parcels of land willed by burghers who had died without heirs. Further down were more recent documents, all of them indicating the parish church as the beneficiary. Simon sensed that he was reaching his goal. The Schongau church had recently received a number of gifts, especially for the construction of the new cemetery at Saint Sebastian's. Lately, anyone who felt his end nearing and wanted to secure an eternal resting place directly at the city wall willed at least part of his fortune to the church. Then there were donations of valuable crucifixes, holy images, pigs and cattle, and land. Simon kept looking and at last came to the bottom of the drawer. There was no contract regarding the piece of land on the Hohenfurch Road . . .

Simon cursed. He knew that somewhere here the solution of the secret had to be found. He could practically feel it. Furiously he returned the drawer to the closet to push it in and take out a new one. As he stood up he brushed against the pages that had already been lying on the table. They floated to the floor.

Hastily Simon picked them up, but then he stopped. A document in his hand was torn on one side, as if someone had quickly ripped off part of it. The seal had been broken in haste. He glanced down at it.

Donatio civis Ferdinand Schreevogl ad ecclesiam urbis Anno Domini MDCLVIII . . .

Simon froze. The deed of donation! However it was only the first page, the rest had been torn off very neatly. He quickly looked through the documents on the table and checked the floor. Nothing. Someone had taken the document from the closet, read it, and taken away the part that was important to him—probably a sketch of the property. He did not seem to have had much time however, in any case not enough to return the document to the drawer. The thief had quickly shoved the piece of paper under the stack of the other documents on the table . . . *and had returned to the council meeting.*

Simon shuddered. If someone stole this document, it could only be someone who knew about the key behind the tile. That meant Johann Lechner himself . . . or one of the four burgomasters.

Simon swallowed hard. He noticed that his hand, still holding the document, was trembling slightly. What had the patrician Jakob Schreevogl told him earlier about the meeting?

Burgomaster Semer denies that the soldiers had met someone upstairs in his rooms.

Could the first burgomaster himself be involved in this thing with the children? Simon's heart beat faster. He remembered how Semer had questioned him a few days ago in his own inn and had finally advised him not to continue investigating the case. And wasn't it also Semer who had always spoken against the construction of the leper house, purely in the interest of the town, as he said? Because after all, lepers before the gates of a trading town really didn't look good? But what if Semer wanted to delay the construction work only because he suspected that a treasure was hidden on that piece of land? A treasure he had heard about from his close friend, Ferdinand Schreevogl, a member of the inner circle of aldermen, just shortly before his death?

Simon's thoughts were racing. The devil, the dead children, the witches' marks, the abduction of Magdalena, the missing hangman, a burgomaster as the puppet master of a monstrous murder conspiracy . . . All these were racing through his mind. He tried to bring some order to the chaos raging in his mind. What was most important now was to free Magdalena, and to do that he had to find the children's hiding place. But someone had entered this room before him and had stolen the plan of that parcel! All he was left with was a first page on which the main facts of the donation had been inscribed. Desperately Simon looked down at the piece of paper with its Latin words. Quickly he translated them:

Parcel belonging to Ferdinand Schreevogl, bequeathed to the Schongau Church on September 4, 1658, parcel size: 200 by 300 paces; moreover, five acres of woods and a well (dried up).

Dried up?

Simon stared at the small words at the very bottom of the document: dried up.

The physician slapped his forehead. Then he put the piece of parchment under his shirt and ran out of the stuffy room. Hastily he locked the small door and returned the key to the niche behind the tile. A few seconds later he reached the entrance of the Ballenhaus downstairs. The two bailiffs had disappeared. Most likely they had gone back to the inn to fetch more medicine. Without paying any heed to whether anyone noticed him, Simon left the Ballenhaus and ran across the market square.

But from a window on the other side of the square, someone was indeed observing him. When the man had seen enough he pulled the curtain shut and returned to his desk. Next to a glass of wine and a piece of steaming meat pie was a torn-off piece of parchment. The man's hands trembled as he drank, and wine dripped onto the document. The red drops spread slowly across the document, leaving spots that looked like blood seeping out across it.

The hangman lay on a bed of moss, smoked his pipe, and blinked into the last rays of the afternoon sun. From a distance he could hear the voices of the guards at the building site. The workmen had already gone home at noon because of the May Day celebrations the next day. Now the two bailiffs assigned to guard duty were loafing around, sitting on the chapel wall, and throwing dice. Occasionally Jakob Kuisl could hear the sound of their laughter. The guards had pulled worse duty in their days.

Now a new sound was added to the others, a rustling of twigs coming from the left. Kuisl extinguished his pipe, jumped to his feet, and disappeared in a matter of seconds in the underbrush. When Simon tiptoed past him he reached for his ankle and pulled him down with a quick tug. Simon hit the ground with a soft cry and felt for his knife. The hangman's face appeared, grinning, between the branches.

"Boo!"

Simon dropped the knife.

"My God, Kuisl, did you ever frighten me! Where were you all this time? I was looking for you everywhere. Your wife is very worried, and besides . . . "

The hangman placed one finger to his lips and pointed toward the clearing. Between the branches, the watchmen could be vaguely made out as they sat on the wall throwing dice. Simon continued in a low voice.

"Besides I now know where the children's hiding place is. It is . . . "

"The well," Jakob Kuisl said, finishing the sentence for him and nodding.

For a moment Simon remained speechless.

"But . . . How did you know? I mean—"

The hangman cut him off with an impatient wave of his hand.

"Do you remember when we were at the building site that first time?" he asked. "A wagon was stuck in the ditch. And there were barrels of water loaded on the wagon. At the time I didn't think much of it. Only much too late did I wonder why someone would take the trouble of bringing water when there was a well there!"

He pointed over at the round stone well, which looked old and dilapidated. From the topmost row of stones, several were broken off and lay stacked up at the edge, as if to serve as small, natural stairs. No chain or bucket was attached to the weathered wooden framework above the circle of stones. Simon swallowed. How could they have been so blind! The solution had been before their eyes all this time.

He quickly told the hangman of his conversation with Jakob Schreevogl and about what he had discovered in the archives of the Ballenhaus. Jakob Kuisl nodded.

"In his fear, Ferdinand Schreevogl must have buried his money somewhere shortly before the Swedes arrived," he mused. "Perhaps he did hide it in the well. Then he had a fight with his son and bequeathed the parcel together with the treasure to the church."

Simon interrupted him.

"Now I also remember what the priest told me back then at confession," he cried. "Schreevogl supposedly talked about it on his deathbed, saying that the priest could still do much good with the parcel of land. At the time I thought he meant the leper house. Now I think it's clear that he was speaking of the treasure!"

"Someone among the moneybags in the council must have gotten wind of it," growled the hangman. "Probably old Schreevogl told someone when he was drunk or shortly before his death, and that somebody has done everything possible to stop the construction at the site and find that damn treasure."

"Obviously burgomaster Semer," said Simon. "He has the key to the archive, so he was able to get his hands on the map of that piece of land. It's quite possible that he also knows about the dried-up well by now."

"Quite possible indeed," said Jakob Kuisl. That makes it even more urgent that we take quick action now. The solution to the mystery lies at the bottom of that well. Maybe I'll also find some clue regarding my little Magdalena . . . "

The two men fell silent for a moment. Only the chirping of birds and the occasional laughter of the watchmen could be heard. Simon noticed that he had forgotten Magdalena for a brief moment over all the excitement of the past hour. He was ashamed of himself.

"Do you think they could have . . . " he started and noticed how his voice was breaking.

The hangman shook his head.

"The devil has abducted her, but he hasn't killed her. He needs her as a hostage, to make me show him the children's hiding place. Besides, that wouldn't be his way. He first wants to have his . . . fun, before he kills. He likes to play."

"It sounds as if you know the devil quite well," said Simon.

Jakob Kuisl nodded.

"I think I know him. Could be that I've seen him before."

Simon jumped up.

"Where? Around here? Do you know who he is? If so, why don't you tell the council so that they can have the scoundrel locked up?"

Jakob Kuisl dismissed Simon's questions with a movement of his hand, as if brushing away an annoying insect.

"Are you crazy? It wasn't around here! It was earlier. That is to say . . . a long time ago. But I could also be mistaken."

"Then tell me! Maybe it'll help us!"

The hangman shook his head with conviction.

"That won't do any good." He settled down on the moss and started sucking on his cold pipe. "Better to rest a little longer, until dusk. It's going to be a long night."

Saying this, the hangman closed his eyes and seemed to fall asleep immediately. Simon looked at him enviously. How could this man stay so calm! As for himself, sleep was out of the question. Nervously and with a trembling heart he waited for night to fall.

Sophie leaned her head against the wet stone and tried to breathe calmly and evenly. She knew that the two of them would not be able to stay down here much longer. The air was beginning to give out, and she noticed how she was growing more and more tired with every passing hour. Every breath of air tasted stuffy and stale. For days now, she had not been able to go outside. To answer the call of nature, she had had to go in a nearby niche. The air stank of fecal matter and spoiled food.

Sophie looked over at Clara, who was sleeping. Her breathing was getting weaker and weaker. She looked like a sick animal that had crawled into a cave to await its end. She was pale, her face was drawn, and she had rings under her eyes. Her bones stood out at the shoulders and rib cage. Sophie knew that her little friend needed help. The concoction she had succeeded in making her drink almost four days ago did put her to sleep, but the fever still had not broken. Besides, Clara's right ankle had swollen up to three times its normal size. Sophie could actually see the pumping and struggling that was going on beneath the skin. Her whole leg had become blue all the way up to the knee. The improvised compresses had not helped much.

Three times already, Sophie had crawled into the shaft to see if the coast was clear, but each time she checked, she heard men's voices. Laughter, murmurs, cries, footsteps . . . something was going on up there. The men no longer left her in peace, neither by day nor at night. But thank God, they had not yet discovered the hiding place. Sophie looked into the darkness. Half a tallow candle was still left. To save light she had not lit the stump since yesterday at noon. When she could no longer stand the blackness she crawled to the shaft and looked up into the sky. But soon the sunlight blinded her and she had to crawl back.

Clara did not mind the darkness. She was only half awake, and when she woke up for a moment and asked for water, Sophie squeezed her hand and stroked it until she sank back into sleep. At times Sophie sang songs for her that she had learned on the streets. Sometimes she still remembered verses that her parents had sung for her before they died. But they were only scraps, fragments from the past, linked to the hazy memory of a friendly face or laughter.

Eia beia Wiegele, auf dem Dach sind Ziegele, auf dem Dach sind Schindelein, behuet mir Gott mein Kindelein . . . Lullaby, my bonny love, our roof is safe above, our roof is finely tiled, God protect my little child.

Sophie felt her cheeks becoming wet. After all, Clara was better off. She had found a loving family. On the other hand, what good did it do her now? Here she was, breathing her last in a hole in the ground with her loved ones at home so near and yet so far away.

In time Sophie's eyes had become accustomed to the dark. Not that she could actually see anything, but she was able to distinguish lighter darkness from darker darkness. She no longer bumped her head when she stumbled through the tunnels, and she could see whether a tunnel branched off to the left or the right. Once, three days ago, she had made a wrong turn without a candle and after only a few steps had run into a wall. For an instant she was seized by an unspeakable fear that she would not be able to find her way back. Her heart beat wildly as she turned around in a circle with her hands reaching into emptiness. But then she heard Clara's whimpers. She followed the sounds and found her way back.

After that experience she had opened the seam of her dress and laid out the woolen thread all the way from her niche to the well. She was now always able to feel the rough thread beneath her bare feet when she groped her way to the shaft.

Thus days and nights passed. Sophie fed Clara, sang her to sleep, stared into the darkness, and became absorbed in thought. From time to time she crawled to the light also to catch a breath of air. She had briefly considered dragging Clara all the way to the shaft so that she, too, could get some fresh air and light. But first of all, the girl was still too heavy to carry, in spite of her frightening weight loss, and secondly Clara's constant whimpering could have revealed their hiding place to the men above. The loud scream yesterday had almost given them away. And so she had to stay in the niche, deep underground.

The children had found these tunnels when they were playing together in the woods, and Sophie had often wondered what they had once been used for. Hiding places? Meeting places? Or had they perhaps been built not by human beings, but by dwarves and gnomes? Sometimes she heard whispering, as if tiny, evil beings were mocking her. But then it always turned out to be the wind whistling through some distant crevice in the rock.

Now, again, there was a sound. It wasn't whispering this time, but stones falling down the shaft from the rim of the well and hitting the bottom . . .

Sophie stopped breathing. She could hear soft voices. Someone cursed. The voices did not come from above, as usual; they were very close, as if coming from the bottom of the well.

Instinctively Sophie pulled in the woolen thread until she felt the end of it in her hand. Perhaps they would not be able to find their way out. But right now it was more important that the men she heard not find them. She pulled her legs close to her body and squeezed Clara's hand. Then she waited.

When dusk came the hangman rose from his bed of moss and looked through the branches at the two watchmen.

"We shall have to tie them up. Anything else is too dangerous," he whispered. "The moon is bright, and the well is exactly in the middle of the clearing, easily visible from every direction. Like a bare ass in a cemetery."

"But . . . how are you going to take them down," stammered Simon. "After all, there are two of them."

The hangman grinned.

"There are two of us, aren't there?"

Simon groaned. "Kuisl, leave me out of this. I didn't cut such a good figure last time. I'm a physician, not a highwayman. It's quite possible that I'd mess everything up again."

"You could be right," said Jakob Kuisl as he continued to look toward the watchmen, who had started a small fire next to the church wall and were passing around a bottle of brandy. Finally he turned back to Simon. "All right, stay here and don't budge. I'll be right back."

He moved out of the bushes and crawled through the high meadow toward the building site.

"Kuisl!" Simon whispered as he left. "You won't hurt them, will you?"

The hangman turned back once more and gave Simon a grim smile. From under his coat he pulled out a little club made of polished larchwood.

"They'll have a pretty good headache. But they'll have one in any case if they continue to guzzle like that. So it amounts to the same thing."

He crawled on until he reached the stack of wood that Simon

had hidden behind the previous night. There he picked up a fist-size rock and threw it over the church walls. The stone hit the masonry and made a clanging noise.

Simon watched as the guards stopped drinking and whispered to each other. Then one of them stood up, took his sword, and walked around the foundation. Twenty steps later he was no longer visible to his colleague.

Like a black shadow, the hangman threw himself on him. Simon heard a dull blow, a brief moan, and then all was quiet.

In the darkness Simon could only distinguish the hangman's silhouette. Jakob Kuisl crouched down behind the little wall until the second watchman started to get nervous. After a while the bailiff began calling his missing friend—first softly, then louder and louder. When he got no reply he stood up, grabbed his pike and the lantern, and carefully walked around the church wall. As he walked past one particular bush, Simon saw the lantern flare up briefly and then go out. A short time later the hangman came out from behind the bush and beckoned to Simon.

"Quick, we have to tie them up and gag them before they come around again," he whispered when Simon arrived at his side. Jakob Kuisl grinned as if he were a young rascal who had just pulled off a successful prank. From a sack he had brought along he pulled out a ball of rope.

"I am sure they didn't recognize me," he said. "Tomorrow they will tell Lechner about whole hordes of soldiers and how heroically they fought them. Maybe I should hit them a few more times to provide them with proof?"

He threw Simon a piece of cord. Together they tied up the two unconscious bailiffs. The one whom the hangman had knocked down first was bleeding a little at the back of his head. The other one already had an impressive lump on his forehead. Simon checked their heartbeats and breathing. Both were alive. Relieved, the physician continued his task.

Finally they gagged the two watchmen with torn-off rags of linen and carried them behind the pile of wood.

"This way they can't see us, even if they should wake up," said Jakob Kuisl, walking right over to the well. Simon hesitated. He rushed back to the watchmen's post, fetched two warm blankets, and spread them out over the unconscious bailiffs. Then he followed the hangman. This had been necessary violence. If ever they should have to stand trial for it, his compassion would perhaps be counted as a mitigating factor, he hoped.

The moon had risen by then, throwing a bluish light over the building site. The watchmen's little fire still smoldered, but silence prevailed everywhere. Even the birds had stopped their chirping. Over the well stood a frail wooden framework from which a chain with a bucket must have hung at one time. A small pile of rocks served as stepping stones, making it easier to climb over the rim. Jakob Kuisl held his torch up to the beam extending across the shaft.

"Look, here! Fresh scratch marks," he muttered and ran his finger along the beam. "In some places you can see the light wood is showing underneath the weather-beaten surface."

He looked down into the well and nodded.

"The children threw a rope over the beam and climbed down."

"And why isn't any rope hanging there now, if they are down there?" Simon asked.

The hangman shrugged. "Sophie probably took the rope down so that nobody would become suspicious. To climb back out she has to throw it over the beam from below. Not exactly easy, but I believe Sophie is capable of it."

Simon nodded.

"That's probably the way she came out when she looked for me in the woods to tell me about Clara," he said and looked down. The hole was as black as the night surrounding them. He threw a few pebbles into the well and listened as they hit the bottom.

"Are you nuts?" cursed the hangman. "Now they know down there for sure that we're coming!"

Simon started to stutter: "I . . . I only wanted to see how deep the well is. The deeper it is, the longer it takes the stone to hit the bottom. And by seeing how long that takes . . . "

"You fool," interrupted the hangman. "The well cannot be more than twenty-five feet deep, or Sophie could never have tossed up the rope in order to come out and visit you in the woods."

Once more Simon was impressed by the hangman's simple and yet compelling logic. In the meantime Jakob Kuisl had fetched yet another rope from his sack and started tying it around the beam.

"I'll let myself down first," he said. "If I see anything down there, I'll wave the lantern and you follow me."

Simon nodded. The hangman checked the beam's strength by pulling hard on the rope. The beam groaned but held. Kuisl tied the lantern to his belt, grabbed the rope with both hands, and let himself down.

After a few yards, he was enveloped in darkness. Only a small point of light testified to the fact that a human being was dangling from the rope down there. The point of light descended farther and farther and suddenly stopped. Then the light swung back and forth. The hangman was waving with the lantern.

Simon took a few deep breaths. Then he too attached his lantern to his belt, grabbed the rope, and climbed down. There was a wet and musty smell down there. Just in front of him, muddy soil trickled to the ground. Like the clay they had found under the children's fingernails . . .

After descending a few more yards he saw that the hangman had been right. About twelve feet below he could see the bottom. A few puddles of water shone in the light of the lantern; otherwise the shaft was dry. When Simon reached the bottom he realized why. On one side of the shaft was a semi-oval hole at knee's height that reminded Simon of an arch at the entrance to a chapel. It looked as if it had been dug by human hands into the clay. Beyond, there was a low shaft. The hangman was standing next to the hole and grinning. With his lantern he pointed to the entrance. "A dwarf's hole," he whispered. "Who would have thought of that? I didn't know that there even were any in this area."

"A what?" asked Simon.

"A dwarf's hole. Sometimes people also call it a mandrake cave. I've seen many of these in my time during the war. The peasants used to hide in them when soldiers came, and sometimes they didn't come out for days." The hangman pushed his torch into the dark tunnel.

"These tunnels are made by humans," he continued in a soft voice. "They are ages old, and nobody knows what they were used for. Some people think that they were built as hiding places. But my grandfather told me that the souls of the dead found their last resting place in them. Others say that the dwarves themselves dug them out."

Simon had a closer look at the semi-oval. It really looked like the entrance to some dwarf's cave.

Or like the door to hell . . .

Simon cleared his throat. "The priest mentioned that witches and sorcerers were said to have met here in olden days. A heathen place for their unholy celebrations. Could that have anything to do with this . . . dwarf's hole?"

"Whatever the case," said Jakob Kuisl, sinking to his knees, "we must go inside. So let's go."

Simon closed his eyes briefly and sent a whispered prayer to the cloudy skies visible only twenty-five feet above them. Then he crawled behind the hangman into the narrow tunnel.

Up at the well's rim, the devil pointed his nose into the wind. He was smelling revenge and retaliation. He waited a few more moments before sliding down the rope into the depths.

———

As soon as Simon had crawled through the entrance, he noted that this would not be an easy job. After only a few feet the tunnel narrowed. To make any headway, they almost had to crawl sideways and push themselves forward with their shoulders. Simon felt sharp rocks scraping across his face and body. Then the tunnel widened slightly. Bent over, Simon stumbled forward, yard by yard, holding the lantern in one hand, leaning with the other against the wet clay wall next to him. He tried not to think of how his pants and doublet must look by now. But anyway, in the dark it didn't show.

His only point of orientation was the flickering hangman's lantern in front of him. He could see how Jakob Kuisl was having difficulty squeezing his broad, muscular body through this needle's eye. Earth kept trickling from the ceiling and fell into his collar. The roof was arched as in a miner's tunnel. At regular intervals sooty niches the size of a hand appeared in the walls. They looked as if candles or oil lamps had stood in them in the past. The niches enabled Simon to estimate the tunnel's length. Nevertheless he had lost all sense of time after only a few minutes.

Above their heads lay tons of rock and earth. The physician briefly thought about what would happen if the wet clay were to suddenly collapse over him. Would he even feel anything at all? Would the rock mercifully break his neck or would he slowly suffocate? When he realized that his heart was starting to race, he tried to direct his thoughts toward something beautiful. He thought of Magdalena, of her black hair, her dark, laughing eyes, her full lips . . . he could clearly see her face in front of him, almost close enough to touch. Now her expression was changing; it looked as if she wanted to cry out to him. Her mouth opened and closed soundlessly; her eyes shone with naked fear. When she turned around to look straight at him, the daydream burst like a soap bubble. The tunnel curved suddenly and opened into a chamber about six feet high.

In front of him, the hangman straightened up and shone his lantern all around the chamber. Simon tried without much success to knock the dirt from his trousers, then he looked around as well.

The chamber was almost square and about three paces wide and long. On the sides were small recesses and steps, almost like shelves. On the opposite side two more slightly sloping tunnels extended into the depths. They too had the oval shape Simon already had seen at the first entrance. A ladder was leaning in the chamber's left corner, leading to a hole in the ceiling. Jakob Kuisl inspected the ladder with his lantern. In the pale light Simon could make out its greenish, moldy rungs. Two of them had split completely. Simon wondered whether the ladder could still support anybody at all.

"It's surely been standing down here for ages," said Jakob Kuisl, tapping against the wood. "Perhaps one hundred, two hundred years? The devil knows where it leads. I believe all this is a goddamn labyrinth. We should call out for the children. If they're smart they'll answer us, and the hide-and-seek game will finally come to an end."

"And if . . . if someone else should hear us?" asked Simon nervously.

"Bah, who would that be? We are so deep down in the ground that I'd almost be glad if our shouts could penetrate all the way to the outside." The hangman grinned. "Maybe we'll be buried and need help. It doesn't look all that stable, especially that narrow tunnel at the entrance . . . "

"Please, Kuisl, don't joke about this."

Again Simon sensed the tons of dirt over their heads. In the meantime the hangman cast some light into the entrance on the opposite side. Then he called out into the darkness.

"Children! It's me, Jakob Kuisl! You have nothing to be afraid of! We now know who wants to harm you. With us you're safe. So be so kind and come out of there!"

His voice sounded strangely hollow and low, as if the clay all around them were sucking up his words like water. There was no answer. Kuisl tried it again.

"Children! Can you hear me? Everything will be all right! I promise you that I'll get you out of here all in one piece. And if anyone harms as much as one hair on your heads, I'll break every bone in his body."

There still came no reply. Only the soft trickle of a rivulet somewhere could be heard. Suddenly the hangman slapped his flat hand against the clay wall so that whole chunks came loose.

"Goddamn it, get a move on, you cursed bunch of creeps! Or else I'll spank your behinds so you won't be able to move for three days!"

"I don't think that this tone will convince them to come out," opined Simon. "Perhaps you should . . . "

"Shush." Jakob Kuisl laid his finger over his mouth and pointed toward the opposite entrance. A soft whimpering sound could be heard. It was very weak. Simon closed his eyes in order to make out the direction it was coming from. He couldn't. He couldn't tell with certainty whether it was coming from above or from the side. It was as if the voice was moving ghostlike through the earth.

The hangman seemed to have the same difficulty. Several times he looked up and then to the side. Then he shrugged.

"We shall have to split up. I'm going to climb up that ladder and you continue down into one of the tunnels. Whoever finds them shouts."

"And if we don't find them?" asked Simon, who almost felt ill at the thought of crawling once more through a narrow tunnel.

"Count to five hundred as you search. If you haven't found anything by then, turn back. Then we'll meet again here and we'll think of something else."

Simon nodded. Jakob Kuisl was already going up the ladder, which made ominous creaking noises under his weight. One more time he looked down at Simon.

"Oh, and Fronwieser . . . "

Simon looked up expectantly.

"Yes?"

"Don't get lost. Or else they'll only find you on Judgment Day."

Grinning, the hangman disappeared through the hole in the ceiling. For a brief moment Simon could hear him in the chamber over him, then there was silence.

The physician sighed. Then he walked over to the two holes. They were of identical size and equally dark. Which one should he enter? Should he just play eeny-meeny-miney-moe? On a pure whim he decided to pick the hole on the right side.

When he cast a light into the opening he could see that the waist-high tunnel was indeed sloping down. The clay underfoot was moist and slushy, and tiny rivulets were running down into the depths on either side. Simon fell to his knees and tapped his way forward. He quickly noticed that the ground beneath him had the consistency of slimy water plants. He tried to support himself with his hands on the sides, but since he was carrying the lantern in his right hand, he kept sliding against the left wall. Finally he could no longer steady himself. He had to decide whether to let go of the lantern and hold on or simply let himself slide down. He decided in favor of sliding.

Simon slithered down. The tunnel was getting steeper and steeper, and after a few yards he felt the ground beneath him disappear. He flew through the air, and before he could cry out, he had already landed. At the impact with the hard clay floor, the lantern flew from his hand and rolled into a corner. Briefly Simon was able to make out a rocky chamber similar to the previous one, then the lantern went out.

Darkness swallowed him.

The darkness was so deep that it seemed to him like a wall that he had been thrown against. After the first moment of terror he groped along on his hands and knees toward the place he suspected the lantern to be. His hand moved over stones and clumps of clay, dipped briefly into a cold puddle of water, then he felt the warm copper of the lantern.

Relieved, he reached for the tinderbox in the pocket of his trousers so he could light the lantern once more.

It was no longer there.

He began to search his pockets—first the left, the right. Finally he burrowed into the inside pocket of his doublet. Nothing. The tinderbox must have fallen out, either as he fell into the chamber or even earlier as he crawled through the tunnels. Desperately he held on to the useless lantern while he knelt and blindly tapped around with the other hand, trying to find the lost box. Soon he reached the opposite wall. He turned around and felt his way back again. After repeating this procedure three times he gave up. He would never find the tinderbox down there.

Simon tried to stay calm. Everything was still completely black all around him. He felt as if he had been buried alive; his breathing quickened. He leaned against the wet wall. Then he called for the hangman.

"Kuisl! I slipped! My lantern is out. You must help me!"

Silence.

"Kuisl, damn it, this isn't funny!"

He could hear nothing other than his own rapid breathing and an occasional trickling sound. Was it possible that the clay down here would swallow every sound?

Simon stood up and felt his way along the wall. After just a few feet his hand found emptiness. He had found the opening to the top! Feeling relieved, he felt around the spot. The approximately two-foot-wide hole started at chest level. This was where he had dropped down into the chamber. If he could manage to crawl up and back into the upper chamber he should actually meet up with the hangman. Though Simon had not counted to five hundred, his stay down here already seemed like an eternity. The hangman had certainly returned by now.

Then why didn't he give any sign of life?

Simon concentrated on what lay before him. He took the lantern in his teeth, swung his body up, and was about to push himself through the tunnel when he noticed something.

The tunnel was sloping down at a slight angle.

But how could this be? After all he had fallen down into this chamber. Therefore the tunnel must be rising! Or was it a different tunnel?

Horrified, Simon realized that he had gotten lost. He was just about to let himself slide back into the chamber to look for the right tunnel when he heard a noise.

Whimpering.

It was coming from the tunnel in front of him, the one going down, and it was very close.

The children! The children were down there!

"Sophie, Clara! Can you hear me? It's me, Simon!" he shouted down.

The crying stopped. Instead he could hear Sophie's voice.

"Is it really you, Simon?"

An immense feeling of relief came over him. At least he had found the children! Perhaps the hangman was already with them? Of course! He had not found anything in the upper chamber, so he had climbed down again and taken the second tunnel. And now he would be standing down there with the children, playing tricks on him.

"Is Kuisl down there with you?" he asked.

"No."

"Really? Children, you must tell me. This is no longer a game!"

"By the Holy Virgin Mary, no!" Sophie's voice came from below. "Oh God, I am so scared! I heard steps, but I can't get away because of Clara . . . "

Her voice changed into weeping.

"Sophie, you need not be afraid," Simon tried to calm her. "The steps you heard were certainly ours. We are coming to get you out of there. What's the matter with Clara?"

"She . . . she's sick. She has a fever and can't walk."

Great, thought Simon. *My lantern is out, I got lost, the hangman has disappeared, and now I also have to carry a child out of here!* For a brief moment he felt as if he could weep just like Sophie, but then he pulled himself together.

"We . . . we're going to make out all right, Sophie. For sure. I'm coming down now."

He took the lantern in his teeth and slid down the tunnel. This time he was prepared for the fall. He only fell a couple of feet and landed almost softly in a puddle of ice-cold muddy water.

"Simon?" Sophie's voice came from the left. He thought he could see her outline in the dark: a spot that looked a little darker and seemed to move slowly back and forth. Simon waved. Then it occurred to him how nonsensical that was in the dark.

"I'm here, Sophie. Where is Clara?" he whispered.

"She's lying next to me. Who are those men?"

"Which men?" While Simon spoke, he crawled toward the outline. He felt a stone step and on it moss and straw.

"Well, I mean the men I heard above. Are they still there?"

Simon tapped his way up the step. It was as long and as wide as a bed. He felt the body of a child stretched out on it. Cold skin, small toes. Rags covering her legs.

"No," he answered. "They . . . they're gone. It's safe. You can come out."

Now Sophie's outline was very close, right next to him. He reached for it. He felt a dress. A hand reached for him and held him tightly.

"Oh, God, Simon! I am so scared!"

Simon hugged the little body and stroked it.

"All will be well. Now all we have to do is . . . "

He could hear a scraping sound behind him. Something was slowly pushing through the opening into the chamber.

"Simon!" Sophie cried out. "Something is there! I can see it. Oh, God, I can see it!"

Simon turned around. At a spot not far from them, the blackness was darker than the rest. And this darkness was coming closer.

"Do you have any light down here?" screamed Simon. "A candle? Anything?"

"I have tinder and flint. It must be here somewhere . . . for heaven's sakes, Simon! What . . . what is it?"

"Sophie, where is the tinder? Answer me!"

Sophie started to scream. Simon slapped her face.

"Where is the tinder?" he cried once more into the blackness.

The slap helped. Sophie quieted down instantly. She felt around briefly, then handed him a fibrous piece of sponge and a cool piece of flint. Simon pulled the stiletto from his belt and struck the stone in wild blows against the cold steel. Sparks flew, the tinder started to glow, and a tiny flame flared up in his hand. But just as he was about to light the lantern with the glowing fibers, he felt a draft from behind. The shadow fell over them.

Before the lantern went out a second time, Simon saw a hand swoop down in the fading light. Then darkness overcame him.

In the meantime the hangman had gone through two more chambers without finding any trace of the children. The room he had reached with the ladder had been empty. Shards of an old pitcher and a few rotten barrel staves littered the floor. In the corner alcoves there were recessed stone seats. They were scrubbed smooth and looked as if hundreds of frightened people had squatted in them over the years. Two tunnels led from this chamber into the darkness as well.

Jakob Kuisl cursed. This dwarf's hole was indeed a damn maze! It quite possibly extended underground all the way to the church walls. Perhaps the priest had been right after all with his ghost stories. What secret rites could have taken place down here? How many hordes of barbarians and soldiers had already passed above, while deep down in the earth, men, women, and children listened fearfully to the conquerors' steps and voices? Nobody would ever know.

Above the entrance to the tunnel at the left were a few marks that Jakob Kuisl could not figure out. Scratches, arching lines, and crosses that could be of human or natural origin. Here, too, the passage was so narrow that one had to practically push one's self through. Could there be some truth to the stories that an old midwife had told him almost thirty years earlier? That the passages were built so narrow on purpose so that a body would surrender all that was bad, all sickness, all bad thoughts to Mother Earth?

He forced himself through the narrow hole and found himself in the next chamber. It was the largest so far, a good four paces to the other end, and the hangman was able to stand up straight in it. From there, a narrow passage went on in a straight line. There was another hole directly above Jakob Kuisl. Pale yellow roots, finger thick, were growing out of the narrow shaft, down to him, brushing over his face. Far above, the hangman thought he could see a tiny ray of light. Was it the moon? Or was it only an optical illusion, his eyes longing for the light? He tried to figure out how far he had moved away from the well in the meantime. It was quite possible he was standing directly beneath the linden tree, in the middle of the clearing. Since olden times, the linden tree had been considered a holy tree. The mighty specimen at the building site was certainly a few hundred years old. Had at one time a shaft led down from the trunk of the linden tree to this resting place of souls?

Jakob Kuisl tested the roots by pulling on them; they seemed to be tough and capable of supporting some weight. He briefly thought of pulling himself up on them to check whether they actually belonged to the linden tree. But then he decided after all to take the horizontal tunnel. If he found nothing on the other side he would turn back. Mentally he had continued to count. Soon he reached five hundred, the number he and Simon had agreed on.

He bent down and crawled into the narrow tunnel. This was the narrowest passage so far. Clay and stones scraped his shoulders. His mouth was dry, and he tasted dust and dirt. He had the impression that the tunnel was beginning to taper down like a funnel. A dead end? He was about to crawl back when he saw in the light of the lantern that the passage widened again after a few more feet. With difficulty he pushed forward through the last part of the tunnel. Like a cork being pulled from its bottle he finally landed in yet another chamber.

The space was so low that he had to stoop. It ended just two steps further on, at a moist clay wall. There was no other passage. This was clearly the end of the maze. He would have to turn back.

As he turned again toward the narrow hole he noticed something out of the corner of his eye.

On the left side of the chamber, something had been scratched into the clay at chest level. This time they weren't simple scratches or scribbles as before above the arch. This was an inscription, and it looked as if it had been made pretty recently.

F.S. hic erat XII. Octobris, MDCXLVI.

Jakob Kuisl caught his breath.

F.S. . . . that had to be the abbreviation for Ferdinand Schreevogl! He had been here on the twelfth of October, 1646, and he had obviously wished for posterity to know about it.

The hangman quickly calculated back: 1646, that was the year the Swedes had occupied Schongau. The burghers had been able to prevent the burning of their town only by paying a high ransom. In spite of this, all the outer boroughs of Schongau, that is to say Altenstadt, Niederhofen, Soyen, and even Hohenfurch, fell prey to the flames in the following two years. Kuisl tried to remember. Schongau, as far as he knew, had been surrendered to the Swedes in November of 1646. That meant that if the old Schreevogl was down here already in October of the same year, it could only have been for one reason.

He had hidden his fortune here in the maze.

Jakob Kuisl's thoughts were racing. The old man had probably always known of the tunnels, an old family secret that he had finally taken to the grave. When the Swedes came, he buried the major portion of his money down here. Jakob Schreevogl had told Simon that hardly any money was mentioned in his father's will. Now the hangman knew why.

The old man had left the treasure down here all that time, probably expecting hard times to come! And when he had a falling-out with his son he had decided to bequeath the land together with the treasure to the church—but without telling the church anything about it. There had been some hint, however. What was it that Schreevogl had once told the priest?

You would yet be able to do much good with that parcel of land . . .

Who knows—perhaps he wanted to tell the priest all about it and then died quite suddenly. Perhaps he wanted to take his secret to the grave. After all, Ferdinand Schreevogl had always been known to be an eccentric old bird. But someone must have known about the secret, and that someone had done everything to find it. The construction of a leper house had at first upset those plans. But then he had hired the soldiers to vandalize the building site so that he would have sufficient time to search without being observed.

Nor had that unknown person stopped at three murders. The murders of children . . .

Jakob Kuisl mulled it over. The children must have seen something, something that could have given the man away. Or did they actually know about the treasure, and had he tried to squeeze the secret out of them?

The hangman let the light from the lantern wander over the muddy ground. Rubble covered it, and a rusty shovel was leaning in a corner. Kuisl rummaged through the rubble with his hands. When he found nothing that way he took the shovel and started to dig. Briefly he thought he could hear a faint sound far away, like a voice calling softly. He stopped. When he heard nothing more, he dug deeper. The chamber was filled with the clanging of the shovel and his labored breathing. He dug and dug, and finally he hit hard rock. Nothing, no treasure. No shards, no empty box, nothing. Had the children been here earlier and taken the treasure?

Once more his gaze passed over the inscription on the wall.

F.S. hic erat XII. Octobris, MDCXLVI . . .

He stopped and moved closer to the wall. The area around the inscription looked lighter than the remainder of the wall. A rectangle, about three feet long, had been lightly covered with clay so as to obscure the difference with the rest of the wall.

The hangman seized the shovel and struck it with all of his strength against the inscription. The clay crumbled and behind it red bricks appeared. He struck one more time and the bricks split open. Behind them a hole appeared. It was only as large as a fist, but when the hangman struck three more blows, it widened and revealed an alcove behind it that had been walled up.

On the alcove's seat stood an earthenware jug whose opening had been sealed with wax. The hangman struck it with the shovel.

The jug burst open and a stream of gold and silver coins spilled all over the alcove. The coins shone in the lantern's light as if they had been polished only yesterday.

Ferdinand Schreevogl's treasure ... and Jakob Kuisl had found it.

As far as the hangman could see, these were silver pennies and golden guilders from the Rhineland, all in perfect condition and of impeccable weight. There were too many of them to count. Kuisl estimated that there were more than one hundred coins. With this kind of money one could build a new patrician home or buy a stable with the finest horses. Never before in his life had the hangman seen so much money at one time.

With trembling fingers he collected the coins and let them trickle into his bag. They jingled and the bag got markedly heavier. With the bag in his teeth, he finally struggled to push his way back into the adjoining chamber.

There he stood up, bathed in perspiration, knocked the clay dust from his garment, and started out for the first chamber. He grinned. Young Simon had probably long arrived there and was fearfully awaiting his return in the dark. Or he had already found the children. Didn't he hear someone calling softly a while ago? Either way, he would have a nice surprise to offer the young fellow ...

The hangman smiled a grim smile and walked past the roots dangling from the hole above him.

He stopped short.

Why were they moving?

Quite some time had gone by since he had last gone through this chamber and brushed against the roots. Yet they were still swaying softly back and forth. There was no wind down here. This meant that either someone had walked across the clearing directly above him, causing the roots to sway or else ...

Someone must have touched them from below.

Had someone else come this way? But who? And to go where?

The chamber had only two exits. He had come out of one of them just before and the other was a dead end.

Not counting the shaft above him, of course.

The hangman carefully approached the lower end of the hole and looked up. The pale yellow roots brushed like fingers across his face.

At that instant something huge and black, like an enormous bat, came flying down on him from the shaft. Instinctively Kuisl threw himself to one side and landed painfully on his shoulder in the wet clay. He nevertheless succeeded in holding on to the burning lantern. Frantically he fumbled at his belt for the larch-wood club. Out of the corner of his eye he saw a figure deftly rolling away on the floor and getting back on his legs. He was wearing a bloodred doublet, but his hat with the rooster's feathers had slipped off when he jumped. His right hand was holding a torch, and his bony hand was glimmering white in the light of the lantern. In his left hand he was clutching a saber.

The devil smiled.

"A good leap, hangman. But do you really believe you can escape me?"

He pointed at the club in Kuisl's hand. In the meantime the hangman had gotten on his feet and was balancing his massive torso back and forth in expectation of the assault. The club in his right hand really looked like a toy.

"For you I don't need more than that," he said. "When I'm through with you, not even your mother will recognize you. If indeed you ever had one."

He continued smiling, but inside Jakob Kuisl was cursing. What an ox he had been! He had shown the soldier the way to the children! Hadn't it been obvious that the devil would follow him? Like perfect fools, they had fallen into his trap!

From the corner of his eye, he tried to make out the tunnel behind him. The devil was right. He wouldn't have a chance against a man with a saber, if only because of the greater reach.

Besides, the man in front of him was an experienced fighter. From his movements alone and the manner in which he swung his saber in a circle, Jakob Kuisl could see that he was facing at least an equal adversary. The soldier's slight limp did not seem to affect him in any way. The disability probably only became a nuisance on longer marches. In any case the man in front of him was dangerous and itching for a fight.

Jakob Kuisl thought over all the possibilities left him. Retreat was out of the question. He could not flee through the narrow tunnel toward the well without being first cut to pieces by the devil. The only hope left was if Simon became aware of the fight soon enough and came to his aid. Until then he had to stall for time.

"Well, come on, or are you only brave against women and children?" Jakob Kuisl shouted, loud enough so that he could assume that Simon would hear him. Once more he glanced toward the way out.

The devil grimaced, feigning pity.

"Oh, you are hoping that help will come?" he asked. "Believe me, these passages branch out in so many directions and are so deep that your shouting only reaches as far as the nearest wall. I know burrows like these. I smoked out a number of them during the war. When the peasants came staggering out of them half choked to death, I was able to kill them off without any trouble. And as far as the physician is concerned . . . "

He pointed at the waist-high, narrow exit.

"It would be nice if he came. As soon as he sticks out his head I'll chop it off like that of a chicken."

"Devil, I swear to you, I'll break every one of your bones if you so much as harm one hair on Simon's or my Magdalena's head," whispered the hangman.

"Oh, yes, of course you can do that. After all it's your profession, isn't it?" said the soldier. "But don't worry, I'm saving your daughter for later. Although . . . I don't know what my friends are doing with her at this very moment. It's been a long time since they had a woman, you know? That renders them a bit . . . disorderly."

Anger was building in Jakob Kuisl's head. Rage was rising, immense rage.

I must pull myself together. He wants me to lose control.

He took a few deep breaths. The rage ebbed back to his innermost being, but it was not completely extinguished. Carefully the hangman took a few steps back, trying to cover the exit with his body while he continued to speak. If Simon crept out of the tunnel, the devil would have to get past him first. And then? A skinny student and an old man with a club against a well-trained, armed soldier. He needed time to think.

"I . . . I know you," he said. "We have met once before, that time in Magdeburg."

Brief hesitation flared up in the devil's eyes. His face seemed to become distorted, just as earlier in Jakob Kuisl's garden.

"In Magdeburg? What was your business in Magdeburg?" he finally asked.

The hangman swung his club in a circle.

"I was a soldier . . . just like you," he said. His voice was getting hoarse. "I'll never forget the day. It was on May 20, 1631, that we entered the city with Tilly. The old man had declared early that morning that everyone in Magdeburg was fair game . . ."

The devil nodded.

"That's right. So you were actually there too. Well, then, we indeed have something in common. How nice. Unfortunately I can't remember you at all."

Then recognition flashed across his face.

"You are . . . the man on the street! The house at the city wall . . . Now I remember!"

The hangman closed his eyes for the briefest instant. The memory was there again. That which had only been vague and fragmentary earlier in the garden in front of his home was taking on form now. The images rained down on him like hailstones in a summer thunderstorm.

Cannon fire . . . A breach in the wall. Screaming women and children running along the street. Some trip. The soldiers quickly grab them and cut everything to pieces with their sabers. Blood is running in streams down the street so that people shriek as they slip and fall. To the left is a patrician house from which crying and shrill screams are rising. The roof and the upper floor are already in flames. A man is standing in the open door, holding an infant head-down by its legs like a little lamb about to be slaughtered. The baby is screaming so loud that his cries rise above the cannon fire, the soldiers' laughter, the crackling of the fire. On the ground, a man lies in his blood. A woman crawls on her knees before the soldier and pulls on his doublet.

"Your money, where's your goddamn money, you heretic sow, speak up!"

The woman can only weep and shake her head. The baby screams and screams. And then the man lifts the writhing child higher and flings it against the doorjamb. Once, twice, three times. The screaming stops. A blow of the saber and the woman falls sideways. The soldier looks over to the other side of the street. Madness flickers in his eyes. A mocking light, his mouth twitching, convulsed. He raises his hand and waves. The hand is white, crooked bony fingers inviting others to share in the great blood frenzy. Then the man disappears inside the house.

From above, screams can be heard. You're running after him, jumping over man, woman, and infant, up the burning stairs, it's the room on the left. The soldier is standing before a young girl. She lies on a table among broken dishes and shattered wine carafes, her bloodied dress pulled up to her knees. The soldier smiles at you and makes an inviting gesture. The girl stares up with horror-widened eyes. You reach for your saber and you lunge at the man. But he ducks and runs out on the balcony. As you rush toward him he jumps down the ten

feet to the street. He lands the wrong way and rolls over. Then he
limps into a side street. Before disappearing he points at you with his
bony hand as if he wants to nail you down with his fingers.

A hissing sound.

Jakob Kuisl's remembrances were interrupted suddenly; the
devil swung his saber straight down toward the top of his head.
At the last moment the hangman was able to jump to one side,
but the blow grazed his left shoulder. He felt a dull pain. Jakob
Kuisl staggered back against the wall. The devil's face, distorted
by hate, glowed in the torch's light. The long scar going from his
ear to the corner of his mouth twitched nervously.

"That was you, hangman! You are the one who gave me that
crooked leg. It's because of you that I'm limping! I swear to you,
your death will be painful. At least as painful as your daughter's!"

The soldier had gone back to where he was at the beginning,
standing in the center of the chamber and waiting for his adversary's next opening. Cursing, Jakob Kuisl rubbed the wound on
his shoulder. His hand was smeared with blood. He quickly
wiped it on his coat and concentrated once more on the soldier.
In the light of the lantern he was hard to see. Only his foe's torch
gave Kuisl an indication as to where he should strike. He feigned
an attack to the right, then whirled to the left, throwing himself
against the devil. The soldier took a sudden step to one side and
let the hangman stumble past him, over to the wall. At the last
moment Kuisl lifted his club. The hard larchwood did not hit his
opponent at the back of the head as planned, but at least on the
shoulder blade. Crying out in pain, the devil jumped back until
he, too, was leaning against the wall. Panting, they were now facing each other, leaning against the wall, looking at each other
with icy stares.

"You're not bad, hangman," said the devil between two
breaths. "But I knew as much. Even back in Magdeburg I saw an
equal opponent in you. Your agony will amuse me. I have heard
that in the West Indies the savages eat the brains of their strongest

enemies in order to acquire their strength. I think I'll do that with you."

Without any forewarning he jumped directly toward Jakob Kuisl. The saber whirled through the air, aimed directly at his throat. Instinctively the hangman lifted his club, deflecting the blade to one side. The larchwood split, but it did not break.

Jakob Kuisl rammed his elbow into the devil's stomach, causing him to gasp with sudden alarm, then he ran over to the opposite wall. They had changed sides. Shadows were dancing across the walls, lantern and torch bathed the chamber in a reddish, flickering glow.

The soldier moved about, groaning in an almost lascivious way and holding his sword hand across his belly. Nevertheless he never for a second let the hangman out of his sight. Kuisl used the pause to look after his wound. There was a large gash in his doublet near his shoulder and blood was spurting out. Nevertheless the wound did not appear to be deep. Kuisl made a fist and moved his shoulder until he felt a stabbing pain. Pain was good; it meant that his arm was still working.

Only now did Jakob Kuisl have time to get a closer look at the bony hand of his opponent that had once caught his attention in Magdeburg. It actually seemed to consist of individual finger bones connected to one another with copper wire. On the inside was a metal ring. The devil had stuck the burning torch into this ring, where it was now swinging slowly from side to side. The hangman figured that other objects could also be attached to that ring. From the war he was familiar with different prostheses, most of them carved rather roughly out of wood. He had never seen a mechanical bone hand like this one.

The devil appeared to have noticed Kuisl's stare.

"You like my little hand, eh?" he asked swinging the hand and torch back and forth. "I like it too. These are my own bones, you know? A musket ball shattered my left arm. When the wound became gangrenous they had to cut off my hand. I had them make me this pretty souvenir from the bones. As you can see, it perfectly serves its purpose."

He held the hand up so that the light of the torch illuminated his pale face. The hangman remembered how the soldier had hidden earlier in the ceiling of the shaft. Only now did he realize that the man must have pulled himself up with nothing but his one healthy hand! What power lay in that body? Kuisl felt that he did not have the slightest chance. But damn it, where was Simon?

To gain time he continued his questioning.

"So you were told to mess up the building site, weren't you? But the children saw you doing it, and that's why they had to die."

The devil shook his head.

"Not quite, hangman. The children had bad luck. They had been hiding down here when we received our instructions and the first portion of our money. Moneybags was afraid they might have recognized him. He gave us the order to make sure they would never talk."

The hangman winced.

So the children had known the devil's employer, the patron! They knew who was behind all of it!

No wonder they didn't dare return to town. It must have been a very powerful man, someone they knew and someone they knew people would be more inclined to believe than themselves. Someone whose reputation was at stake.

Time. He needed more time.

"The fire at the Stadel, that was pure diversion wasn't it?" he said. "Your friends set the fire while you slipped into town to steal away Clara . . . "

The devil shrugged.

"How could I have gotten to her otherwise? I kept my ears

open. The boys were easy. After all the little rascals were hanging around outside. And sooner or later I would have caught that redheaded girl too. But little Clara was sick. She had caught a cold while snooping around, poor darling, and she had to stay inside . . . "

He shook his head compassionately before continuing.

"And so I had to figure out a way to make sure the dear Schreevogl family would leave their foster child alone at home. It was clear that this patrician had goods stored down in the Stadel. And when it burned, he and his servants came running immediately just as I expected. Unfortunately the little brat still got away from me, but now I'm going to get her. That is . . . as soon as I'm finished with you."

He feinted a move with his saber but remained standing where he was, as if trying to seek out his opponent's weak point.

"And the witches' marks? What are those all about?" asked Kuisl, speaking slowly and without leaving his post in front of the exit. He had to keep the other fellow entertained. Talk, continue to talk until Simon finally came to his aid.

A shadow of confusion passed over the devil's face.

"Witches' marks? What damn witches' marks? Don't talk nonsense, hangman."

The hangman was taken aback but did not let it show. Could it be that the soldiers had nothing to do with the marks? Had they been following the wrong track all this time? Did the Stechlin woman practice some witchcraft after all with these children?

Did the midwife lie to him?

Still, Jakob Kuisl continued to ask questions.

"The children had a mark on their shoulders. A mark just like the ones witches wear. Did you paint that on?"

There was a brief moment of silence. Then the devil burst out in shrill laughter.

"Now I understand!" he cried. "So that's why you locked up

the witch! That's why you all thought there was witchcraft involved! What a bunch of stupid moneybags you are in the end! Ha! The witch burns, and all is well once more. Amen. Three paternosters on top of it. Why, we couldn't have concocted anything better than that!"

The hangman thought frantically. Somewhere they had gone wrong. He had the feeling that the solution was very close. Just one more piece of the mosaic, and everything would fit together.

But which piece?

He had other problems for the moment. Where was Simon? Had something happened to him? Was he lost?

"If I am going to go to hell anyway," he continued, "why not tell me who employed you?"

The devil laughed again.

"Wouldn't you like to know, eh? Actually I could well tell you but . . . " He grinned viciously, as if he had suddenly thought of something very funny. "You know a lot about torture, don't you? Isn't it also a type of torture when someone is looking for a solution and cannot find it? When someone still hopes to know the truth even when dying and yet cannot find it? Well, that is my torture. And now, die."

Still laughing, the devil feinted once, then twice, and was suddenly directly in front of the hangman. At the very last moment, Kuisl held his club against the saber. The blade still kept moving closer and closer to his throat. Standing with his back against the wall he could do no more than return pressure for pressure. The man before him had immense strength. His face came closer to Kuisl's, and the blade with it. Inch by inch.

The hangman could smell the wine on the other man's breath. He looked into his eyes and behind them saw an empty shell. The war had sucked this soldier dry. Perhaps he had always been insane, but the war had done the rest. Jakob Kuisl saw hatred and death, nothing else.

The blade was now only a hairbreadth away from his throat. He had to do something.

He let his lantern fall to the floor and pressed the soldier's head backward with his left hand. Slowly the blade moved away from him.

I must . . . not . . . give . . . up . . . Magdalena . . .

Shouting, he gathered the last of his strength and threw the devil against the opposite wall, where he slid to the ground like a broken doll.

The soldier shook himself for a moment, then he was again up on his feet, saber and torch in hand, ready to strike again. The last of Jakob Kuisl's courage seemed to fade. This man was invincible. He would always keep getting up. Hatred was releasing energy in him that normal mortals simply did not possess.

Kuisl's lantern lay in a corner. Fortunately it had not gone out.

Fortunately?

An idea raced through the hangman's brain. Why hadn't he thought of it earlier? It was risky, but probably his only chance. Without taking his eyes off the devil, he reached for his lantern, still flickering on the floor. When he had it in his hands once more, he smiled at his opponent.

"Just a little unfair, isn't it? You with your saber, me with my club . . ."

The devil shrugged.

"All of life is unfair."

"I don't think it has to be that way," said Kuisl. "As long as we have to fight, then at least under the same conditions."

And with that he blew on the lantern's flame and extinguished it.

His face was swallowed in darkness. He was no longer visible to his opponent.

In the next instant he threw the lantern at the devil's bone hand. The soldier cried out. He had not counted on such an attack. Desperately he still tried to pull away his hand, but it was too late. The lantern landed on the white bones and ripped the torch from its anchor. It fell to the ground where it hissed and went out.

Blackness was so total that the hangman felt as if he had sunk to the bottom of a bog. He caught his breath and then threw himself with all of his strength on the devil.

CHAPTER
15

MONDAY
APRIL 30, A.D. 1659
ELEVEN O'CLOCK IN THE EVENING, WALPURGIS NIGHT

MAGDALENA, TOO, COULD SEE NOTHING BUT DARKNESS. Her mouth was filled with the musty taste of the gag, and the ropes were cutting into her wrists and ankles, so that all she could feel was a slight tingle. Her head wound still hurt but had apparently stopped bleeding. A dirty linen rag prevented her from seeing where the men were carrying her. She was slung over the shoulder of one of the soldiers like a dead animal. On top of all of this, the continuous swaying was making her quite nauseous.

The last thing she could remember was that this morning she'd left the town through the Küh Gate. Where had she been before that? She had been . . . looking for something. But for what?

The headache returned. She had the feeling that her memory of it was just beyond her reach, but every time she tried to grasp it, the headache struck her forehead like a hammer.

When she had awakened the last time, the man her father

called the devil was stooping over her. They were in some barn, and there was a smell of straw and hay. The man placed a piece of moss on her forehead to stem the bleeding, and with his left hand, which was strangely cold, he was caressing her dress. She pretended to be unconscious, but she could hear the soldier's words quite clearly. He had bent down and whispered into her ear: "Sleep well, little Magdalena. Once I return you'll be praying that all this may be no more than a dream . . . Sleep while you still can . . . "

She had almost screamed with fear but had successfully continued feigning unconsciousness. She kept her eyes firmly shut. Perhaps that would give her a chance to escape.

Her hope vanished when the devil bound and gagged and finally blindfolded her. Obviously he wanted to avoid at all costs her waking up and seeing where he was taking her. Slumped across his back, she had traveled through the forest for quite a while. She smelled the pines and the firs and heard the call of a screech owl. What time might it be? The cool air and the call of the screech owl made her assume that it must be night. Hadn't the morning sun been shining before she was captured? Had she been unconscious for a whole day?

Or longer, perhaps?

She was trying to stay calm and not tremble, but she was beginning to panic. The man carrying her mustn't notice that she was awake.

At last she was rudely dropped on the forest floor. After a while, she could hear the voices of men approaching.

"Here's the girl," said the devil. "Take her to the assigned meeting point and wait there for me."

Someone had brushed over her dress with a branch or something similar and pushed it up. She didn't move.

"*Mmm,* what a tasty morsel your girl is," a voice said right above her. "A hangman's wench, you say? And the playmate of that spindly quack . . . Oh, she'll be delighted to make the acquaintance of true men for a change!"

"You leave her alone, understood?" the devil thundered. "She belongs to me. She's my personal revenge on her father."

"Her father killed André," another deep voice said. "I've known André for five years. He was a good friend . . . I want to have fun with her as well."

"Right," the first one piped up again. "You're going to slit her open anyway. So why shouldn't we get to play a little before that? We're entitled to taking our revenge on that dirty cur of a hangman as well!"

The devil's voice took on a threatening undertone.

"I say leave her alone. When I come back we're all going to have fun. I promise. But until then, hands off her! She might know something, and I'm going to tickle it out of her. We'll meet no later than daybreak at the assigned place. And now shove off."

She could hear footsteps crunching across the forest soil, slowly becoming fainter. Then the devil was gone.

"Crazy idiot," one of the soldiers murmured. "I don't know why I keep standing for that sort of thing."

"'Cause you're scared, that's why," the other one said. "'Cause you're afraid he'll beat you up just like Sepp Stetthofer and Martin Landsberger! May God have mercy on their black souls . . . We're all of us afraid."

"Afraid! Nonsense," the first one said. "I'll tell you what we're going to do, Hans. We're going to take the girl and clear out of here. Let Braunschweiger dig for his goddamned treasure by himself."

"And what if he does find it, eh? Let's stay till dawn. What have we to lose? If he doesn't return, so what? And if he shows up with the money, we'll pocket it and leave. No matter what happens, I'm not going to travel with that chiseler anymore after tomorrow morning."

"Right you are," the second man growled.

Then he picked up Magdalena, who was still feigning unconsciousness, and flung her over his back. The swaying continued.

Now, dangling from the man's shoulders, Magdalena was racking her brains. What had happened before the devil knocked her out? She could recall having gone to market to buy food and drink for her father and Simon. There had been a talk with children in the street, but she couldn't exactly remember what it had been about. After that, all that was left were shreds of memory. Sunlight. People gossiping in the streets. A ransacked room.

Whose room?

The headache returned, and it was so severe that for a brief moment Magdalena thought she'd have to vomit. She swallowed the pungent taste and tried to concentrate on where they were going. Where were the men taking her? They were walking uphill, she could tell that much. She heard how the man beneath her was panting and cursing. The wind was stronger now, so they must have left the forest. Eventually she heard ravens cawing. Something was softly whistling in the wind. She was beginning to have an idea.

The men stopped, dropping her like a bundle of sticks. The ravens were cawing quite close by. Magdalena knew now where she was. She didn't need to see it at all.

She could smell it.

The black shadow flew toward Simon, putting his hand over his mouth. Simon struggled, trying to free himself. Where was his stiletto, damn it? Just a moment ago he'd struck it against his flint, but now it was lying somewhere out there in the dark and beyond his reach. The hand on his mouth was pressing harder, so that he could hardly breathe anymore. Alongside him, Sophie began to scream again.

Suddenly he heard a familiar voice right at his ear.

"Shut up, for Christ's sake! He's right nearby!"

Simon twisted and turned under the strong arm, which finally released him.

"It's you, Kuisl," he said. "Why didn't you tell me?"

"*Shh.*"

In spite of the darkness, Simon could now distinguish the hangman's massive form directly in front of him. It seemed oddly stooped over.

"I got him . . . the lunatic. Think he isn't . . . quite dead yet. Have to be . . . silent . . . "

Jakob Kuisl spoke haltingly and with difficulty. Simon felt something warm dripping onto his left upper arm. The hangman was injured. He was bleeding, and it wasn't just a small cut.

"You're wounded! Can I help you?" he asked, trying to feel for the wound. But the hangman gruffly brushed the physician's hand aside.

"There's no . . . time. The devil can . . . be here any moment. *Oohhhh* . . . " He was holding his side.

"What happened?" Simon asked.

"The devil followed us . . . stupid fools that we are. I . . . put out his light and fled. But I also whacked him a couple of times with my cudgel. Dirty bastard, damn him. May he go back to hell, where he came from . . . " The hangman's body shook. For a moment Simon thought he was trembling with pain, but then he realized that the huge man was laughing. Suddenly, the hangman fell silent again.

"Sophie?" Jakob Kuisl asked in the darkness.

The girl had been silent up to now. Now her voice came out of the darkness right next to Simon.

"Yes?"

"Tell me, girl, is there another exit?"

"There . . . there is a tunnel. It leads away from this chamber. But it's fallen in." Her voice sounded different, Simon thought.

More composed. She sounded like the orphan girl he had gotten to know on the streets of Schongau—a leader who was capable of mastering her fear, at least temporarily.

"We did start clearing away the rocks, because we wanted to know where the corridor went," she continued. "But we didn't finish it . . . "

"Then dig on," the hangman said. "And light a candle, in God's name. If this lousy rotten dog comes down we can always blow it out again."

Simon fumbled around on the ground till he found his stiletto, the flint, and the tinderbox. Soon, Sophie's tallow candle was burning. It was just a tiny stump, but its dim glow seemed to Simon like broad daylight bursting into the darkness. He looked around in the chamber.

The room wasn't much different from the others they had been in before. He could make out the hole he had fallen through. Along the walls there were niches that looked like stone chairs. There were also small recesses for holding candles and the like. Above these, all sorts of alchemistic signs had been scrawled into the rock in children's handwriting. Clara was lying in an oblong, alcovelike niche that looked something like a bench. The girl was breathing heavily and looked pale. When Simon laid his hand on her forehead he felt that she was burning hot.

Only now did he notice the hangman leaning against the stone bench next to the sleeping Clara and ripping strips out of a piece of his coat with his teeth to bandage his broad chest. There was a red, wet stain on his shoulder too. When he saw Simon's worried look, he only grinned.

"Save your tears, quack. Kuisl's not dead yet. Others have tried to do that before." He pointed behind himself. "Better help Sophie clear the corridor."

Simon looked behind him. Sophie was gone. He looked again and saw that a second corridor led away from one of the niches in the rear. After a few steps it ended in a heap of rubble. Sophie was struggling to drag the rocks out. At one point, there was already a hole in the pile the size of a fist, and he thought he could feel a current of air coming through it. Where did this corridor lead?

As he helped Sophie carry away the rocks, he asked, "The man who's lying in wait for us down here. He's the same as the man who chased you as well, right?"

Sophie nodded.

"He killed the others because we saw the men up there at the building site," she whispered. "And now he wants to kill us as well."

"What did you see?"

Sophie stopped in the middle of the corridor, facing him. The light of the candle was so dim that he couldn't see whether she was crying.

"This used to be our secret place," she began. "Nobody knew it. Here we used to meet every time the other children attacked us. Here we were safe. That night we climbed over the town wall to meet in the well."

"Why?" Simon asked.

Sophie paid no attention to the question.

"We agreed to meet down here. Suddenly we heard voices. When we climbed out, we saw a man handing money to four other men. It was a small bag. And we heard what he said."

"What did he say?"

"That the men were to destroy the building site. And if the Schongau workmen built it up again, they should destroy it again and again, until he told them it was enough. But then . . . "

Her voice faltered.

"What happened then?" Simon asked.

"Then Anton knocked over a pile of rocks, and they noticed us. And then we ran away, and I heard Peter screaming behind me. But I ran on and on until I reached the city wall. Oh, God, we should've helped him. We left him alone . . . " She began to cry again. Simon stroked her bedraggled hair until she calmed down.

His mouth was dry when he finally said, "Sophie, this is important now. Who was the man who handed the others money?"

Sophie was still crying silently. Simon felt the wet tears on her face. He asked again. "Who was the man?"

"I don't know."

At first Simon thought he hadn't heard correctly. Only gradually did he begin to understand what she was saying.

"You . . . you don't know?"

Sophie shrugged.

"It was dark. We heard voices. And I did recognize the devil with the men, as he was wearing a red doublet and we saw his bony hand. But the other one, the one who handed them the money—we didn't recognize him."

Simon almost had to laugh.

"But . . . but then it was all for nothing! All the murders, and your game of hide-and-seek . . . You didn't recognize the man! He only thought you did! All this didn't have to happen—all this blood, and all for nothing . . . "

Sophie nodded.

"I thought it was all a bad dream that would pass. But when I saw the devil in town, and then when Anton was dead, I knew he'd chase us, no matter what we'd seen. So I came here to hide. When I arrived Clara was here already. The devil had nearly gotten her."

She started to cry again. Simon tried to imagine what the twelve-year-old had gone through in the past few days. He couldn't. Helplessly he patted her cheek.

"It'll be over soon, Sophie. We'll get you out of here. And then everything will be straightened out. All we have to do is . . . "

He was about to continue when his nose caught a thin but pungent smell that made him stop.

It was the smell of smoke. And it was growing stronger.

Now they heard a voice somewhere above them. It was hoarse and shrill.

"Hey, hangman, can you hear me? I'm not dead yet! How about yourself? I've made a nice little fire up here. The oil from your lamp and a few damp beams make great smoke, don't you think?" The man above them faked a coughing fit. "All I have to do now is wait until you come crawling out of your hole like rats. Of course you can just choke down there as well. What's it going to be?"

Meanwhile Jakob Kuisl had followed them to the corridor. Dirty strips torn from his coat were wrapped around his torso. Simon couldn't see blood anymore. The hangman put his finger to his lips.

"You know what, little hangman?" the voice said again, somewhat closer. "I've changed my mind. I'm coming down. Smoke or no smoke, I'm not going to miss this chance . . . "

"Hurry up," Kuisl hissed. "I'll go to meet him. Simon, you've got to carry Clara. If you can't clear the corridor quickly enough, or if it's a dead end, come after me."

"But the devil?" Simon began.

The hangman was already hoisting himself into the hole that led out of the chamber.

"I'll push him down to hell. Once and for all."

Then he disappeared in the shaft.

Magdalena was lying on the ground, unable to move. She was still blindfolded, and the gag in her mouth barely allowed her to breathe. Her nose detected a faint smell of decaying flesh. Something was squeaking at regular intervals. She knew it was the chain that the hanged man was suspended from. Her father had usually seen to it that these chains were always well oiled, but after several months' exposure to wind, snow, and rain, even the best-oiled chain would eventually rust.

Georg Brandner, on whose remains the ravens were feeding up there, had been one of the many robber chiefs in the area. Toward the end of January, he and his gang had finally fallen into the trap set up for them by the bailiffs of the Elector's secretary. The robbers and their whole extended family, women and children, had dug themselves into a cave in the Ammer Valley. After a three-day siege they finally surrendered. They'd negotiated with the bailiffs safe conduct for their families, and they'd given up without resistance. The young robbers, children all of them, had their right hands chopped off and were banished from the country. The four main perpetrators were hanged on the gallows hill of Schongau. There wasn't much of an audience there. It was too cold for that. The snow was knee-deep. Therefore there was some dignity in the execution. No hurling of rotten fruit and not much abusive language. Magdalena's father made the men climb a ladder one by one, tied a rope around their necks, and pulled the ladder away. The robbers kicked their legs for a little while and wet their breeches, and that was that. The families of three of the men were permitted to cut them down and take them home. Brandner, however, was left hanging in chains as a warning. That was almost three months ago. At first, the cold had preserved him rather well. But by now his right leg had fallen off, and the rest didn't really look human anymore.

At least the robber chief had had a wonderful view at the hour of his death. The gallows hill was a mound north of the town from which one could see a good part of the Alps on clear days. It was in a solitary location between fields and forests, so that all travelers could see from afar what the town of Schongau had in store for highwaymen. The remains of the robber chief were an excellent deterrent for any other riffraff.

Magdalena felt the wind tugging at her clothes up there. She heard the men laughing not far from her. They seemed to be playing dice and drinking, but Magdalena couldn't hear what they were talking about. She cursed herself in her mind. This was indeed a well-chosen hiding place. Even if the Elector's secretary and his troops were to show up in a few hours, the soldiers had nothing to fear up here. The gallows hill was considered a cursed place. It had been the site of hangings since time immemorial. The souls of the hanged men haunted this place, and the earth was littered with their bones. Anyone who had no urgent business there avoided the mound.

And although it was clearly visible even from far off, it was a perfect hiding place. Anyone who wanted to conceal himself in the undergrowth a few yards down could be sure he wouldn't easily be found.

Magdalena rubbed her hands together, trying to loosen the ropes. How long had she been doing that now? One hour? Two hours? Already, some birds were twittering. Morning was approaching. But exactly what hour was it? She'd lost all sense of time.

By and by she noticed that the ropes weren't cutting into her flesh that deeply anymore. They were slackening. Carefully, she moved to the side a little until she felt a pointed rock under her. It was poking her ribs quite painfully. She shifted her body until the rock was directly beneath her wrists and began rubbing. After a while she felt the fibers of the rope coming apart. If she kept rubbing long and hard enough, she'd get her hands free.

And then?

Because she was blindfolded she hadn't yet seen the two soldiers, but as she was being carried she realized that at least one of them must be a powerful man. Besides, they were sure to be armed, and they were fast. How could she escape them?

When she had almost cut through the rope, the voices suddenly fell silent. There were footsteps approaching. Immediately she pretended she was unconscious again. The steps came to a halt next to her, and a gush of cold water splashed in her face. She snorted and gasped for air.

"I've won you, girl. At dice …" a deep voice said above her, and someone kicked her side. "Come, wake up, and we'll have some fun together. If you're nice to us, we might let you go before Braunschweiger shows up. But before you've got to be nice to Christoph here as well."

"Hurry up, Hans," the other voice mumbled from afar with a heavy tongue. "It'll be daylight soon, and the rotten bastard will be here any moment. Then we'll whack him over the head and clear out of here!"

"Exactly, girl," Hans said. He had stooped down to her and was whispering in her ear. His breath smelled of brandy and tobacco smoke. Magdalena noticed he was dead drunk. "It's your lucky day today. We're going to do that bloodsucker Braunschweiger in today. Then he won't be able to slice you up. And then we get away with the treasure. But first we're going to have it off with you properly. That'll be better than when your spindly physician slobbers over you . . . "

He pushed his hand under her skirts.

At the same moment Magdalena had finished loosening the final cords of the rope. Without any further thought, she flung her right knee upward, slamming it into the soldier's groin. With a muffled cry of pain he collapsed.

"You wicked hangman's wench . . . "

She ripped the gag and blindfold off her face. Dawn was breaking. It was still rather dark, but through the mists she could distinguish the soldier's outline as a gray lump on the ground in front of her. Magdalena rubbed her eyes. She had been blindfolded for such a long time that her eyes only gradually grew accustomed to the faint light. She looked in all directions like a hunted animal.

Above her rose the gallows hill. She saw the mortal remains of Georg Brandner swaying in the wind. About twenty paces from her she could see a small fire glimmering in the woods and a man getting to his feet and running toward her. The soldier was somewhat unsteady on his feet but approaching her at an alarming speed.

"Wait, Hans! I'll get the bitch!"

She was just going to run when she felt a blow to the back of her head. The man on the ground beside her must have gotten to his feet and hit her with a branch or the like. Pain darted like arrows through her head. For an instant she thought she'd go blind, then her sight came back, she stumbled forward, slipped, and felt herself roll down the hill. Twigs and brambles tugged at her hair, she tasted dirt and grass, then she scrambled to her feet again and stumbled into the undergrowth. Behind her she could hear shouting and fast steps approaching.

As she ran toward the mist-covered fields under the cover of the low shrubs, she felt memories of the previous day returning.

She could see everything quite clearly now.

In spite of her pain and fear she had to laugh. She was running for her life, the two soldiers in close pursuit. She was giggling and crying at the same time. The solution was so simple. It was a pity that she might not be able to share it with anyone.

The smoke grew denser and Simon had to cough repeatedly. Clouds of smoke were wafting into the corridor, enveloping Sophie, who was helping him lug one rock after the other from the entryway. They had wrapped wet rags around their mouths and noses, but those didn't help much. Simon's eyes were burning. Time and again he had to stop and mop his face. That cost him valuable time. Again and again he looked over at Clara, who was rolling about in feverish cramps in the alcove. For the sick girl the smoke must have been hell.

The hangman had disappeared a while ago. All they could hear now was their own panting and coughing. The hole, which had been no bigger than a fist, had grown considerably. Simon looked at it with increasing impatience. Sophie, who was twelve and rather slight, might be able to push herself through, but it wasn't big enough for him yet. As the physician moved a particularly big rock to the side, the opening they'd made with such effort collapsed, and they had to start again. At long last the gap was big enough for him to maneuver Clara through. A breeze of fresh air came in from the far side. Simon filled his lungs with it, then he hurried over to the chamber to pick up Clara.

The girl was as light as a bunch of dry sticks. Still, he found it difficult to push her through the gap.

"I'll go ahead and see if the corridor leads out," he said to Sophie breathlessly, when he realized he wouldn't get far like that. "Once I'm through I'll pull Clara after me, and you push from behind. We have to lift her up a little, so she isn't dragged along the rocky ground. Do you understand?"

Sophie nodded. Her eyes were sooty slits between her soiled hair and the rag that covered her mouth. Once more Simon admired how calm she was. But maybe it was a result of the trauma she had been through. This girl had seen too many dreadful things in the past few days.

The hole they had made was big enough for Simon to fit his shoulders through. At one time, the corridor must have collapsed here. The physician prayed that it wouldn't give in once more. He gritted his teeth. But what were his alternatives? Behind him were fire, smoke, and a raving mad soldier. Compared to that, a collapsed passageway seemed almost trivial.

He held the lantern out in front of him until he felt that the corridor was getting wider again. He moved his lantern around so he could see in all directions. The tunnel did indeed continue. It was tall enough for him to run through if he stooped. Again, small sooty niches lined the walls at regular intervals. A few paces ahead, there was a bend in the corridor, so he couldn't see any farther ahead, but a fresh breeze was coming toward him.

Quickly Simon turned around and looked back through the hole.

"You can push Clara through the opening now," he called to Sophie.

From the other side of the opening he heard groans and scraping noises. Then Clara's head peeked through. She was on her stomach, her pale face turned to the side. She was still unconscious and didn't seem to notice what was going on. Simon brushed over her sweaty hair.

It's most likely a blessing for the child. She'll think it's all just a bad dream.

At last he grabbed Clara's shoulders and carefully pulled her to his side of the opening. Although he was cautious, her dress trailed over the rocky ground and was torn open, so that her shoulders were bared.

On her right shoulder blade was the mark. For the first time, Simon looked at it from above.

☿

Simon's head was reeling. Smoke and fear were suddenly far from his mind. He saw only the sign. Before his mind's eye he could see all those alchemical symbols that he had gotten to know at the university.

Water, earth, air, fire, copper, lead, ammonia, ash, gold, silver, cobalt, tin, magnesium, mercury, salmiac, saltpeter, salt, sulfur, bezoar, vitriol, hematite . . .

Hematite. Could it be that easy? Had they simply focused on one single idea without taking into consideration other possibilities? Had the whole thing been one big misunderstanding?

There was no time for further thought. Above his head he heard an ominous crunching sound. Sand trickled down on him. Quickly, he grabbed Clara by her shoulders and pulled her all the way through to his side.

"Quick, Sophie!" he shouted through the hole. Clouds of smoke were billowing from the opening and getting thicker by the moment. "The corridor's falling in!"

A few seconds later Sophie's head appeared in the opening. Simon was tempted to glance at her shoulder, but he quickly changed his mind when a large rock crashed on the ground right alongside him. He helped Sophie through the hole. Then when the girl was able to scramble to her feet by herself, he flung the unconscious Clara over his shoulder and ran along the corridor, stooped over.

Looking back once more, he saw by the light of his lantern how thick smoke was filling the corridor. Then the roof fell in.

Jakob Kuisl pulled himself into the vertical shaft, fighting against the smoke, keeping his eyes closed. He couldn't see in the dark in any case, and when his eyes were closed they didn't sting as much from the smoke. From time to time he opened them just a bit and could see a faint glow at the end of the shaft above him. The smoke left him with hardly any air to breathe. He pushed himself up the steep passageway, struggling forward inch by inch with his powerful arms. Finally he felt the edge of the tunnel opening. Panting and groaning he hoisted himself into the chamber, rolled to the side, and opened his eyes.

When Jakob Kuisl squinted he recognized a knee-high hole to his right and another chest-high passageway leading upward. This was the shaft he had tumbled down after his struggle with the devil. The fire seemed to be coming from up there. But by now dense smoke was filling the chamber as well.

Jakob Kuisl's eyes filled with tears again. He wiped his face with sooty fingers. Just as he was about to examine the small passage to the right, he heard a sound from above.

A soft scraping.

Something was slowly sliding down the shaft. He thought he could hear hectic breathing.

The hangman positioned himself at the side of the shaft, raising his larchwood cudgel. The scraping sound came closer and closer, the sliding noise increased. By the flickering light of the fire he could see something slipping from the shaft and shooting past him. With a scream Jakob Kuisl assaulted it, swinging his cudgel.

Only too late did he realize that it was nothing more than a fragment of the decaying ladder.

At the same moment he heard a hissing sound behind him. He ducked to the side, but the blade went through his coat sleeve and sliced into his left forearm. He felt a dull, throbbing pain. He dropped to the ground, sensing something like a large bird sailing over him.

When the hangman got to his feet again and opened his eyes, he saw an enormous shadow on the wall across from him. The fire made the devil's frame appear twice its size, and his torso was spread across the ceiling. With his long fingers he seemed to be reaching for the hangman.

Jakob Kuisl blinked until he could make out the soldier at the center of the shadow. The smoke was so heavy now that he could only see the devil as though through a haze. That was all he could see until the devil raised his torch to his head.

His enemy's face was red with blood, which was streaming across his brow. His flashing eyes seemed to reflect the light from his torch and his white teeth glistened like those of a beast of prey.

"I'm . . . still here . . . hangman," he whispered. "This is it! You or me . . . "

Kuisl crouched, ready to pounce, clasping his cudgel. His left arm was in terrible pain, but he didn't show it.

"Where did you take my daughter?" he growled. "Out with it! Or I'll kill you like a rabid dog."

The devil laughed. As he raised his bony hand to a salute, Jakob Kuisl saw that two fingers were missing. Still, though, the torch was attached to the iron ring on the metacarpal bone.

"You'd ... like to know ... little hangman. A good place ... The best place for a hangman's wench ... By now the ravens may be pecking out her eyes ... "

The hangman raised the cudgel threateningly before he spoke.

"I'll crush you like a rat ... "

A smile played around the devil's lips.

"That's good," he purred. "You're like myself ... Killing, that's our business ... we're ... more alike than you'd think."

"Like hell we are," Jakob Kuisl whispered.

With these words he leaped into the smoke, right at the devil.

Without looking back again, Magdalena raced down the slope. Branches were hitting her face. Her legs kept getting caught in brambles, which tore at her dress. Behind her she could hear the soldiers' heavy breathing. First the men had called out her name from time to time, but now the race had turned into a wild but silent chase. Like hunting dogs they'd picked up her scent and wouldn't stop until they had the animal at bay.

Magdalena cast a glance over her shoulder. The men were within twenty paces of her. Here, a quarter of a mile beneath the gallows hill, there wasn't much vegetation. Instead of undergrowth, brown fields spread before her. There was no chance of hiding anywhere. Her only chance was in the trees on the steep banks of the Lech. If she could reach the firs and birches, there might be a chance of hiding in a grove of trees. But that was still a long way off, and the men seemed to be gaining on her.

As she ran, Magdalena frantically looked left and right to see if any peasants were already in the fields sowing. But at this early hour not a soul was to be seen. There were also no travelers yet on the Hohenfurch Road, which could be seen now and then between the hills on her left. No one to ask for help. And even if there were, so what? A single woman, pursued by two armed men—what peasant or merchant would risk his life for a hangman's wench? Most likely they would keep staring straight ahead, urging their oxen to move even faster.

Magdalena was used to running. Ever since her childhood she had walked long distances, often barefoot, to call upon the midwives in neighboring villages. Many times she had run along the muddy or dusty roads, just for the joy of it, until her lungs started aching. She had endurance and stamina, and by now she had found her own rhythm. But the men chasing her didn't seem to be willing to give up. Apparently, they had hunted down people before, and they seemed to enjoy it. Their pace was regular and determined.

Magdalena crossed the road and headed for the forest of firs on the high bank of the Lech. The forest was no more than a thin green line beyond the fields. Magdalena wasn't sure she'd make it that far. She had a taste of iron and blood in her mouth.

As she ran, thoughts swirled in her mind like so many ghosts. Her memory had come back. Now she knew where she had previously seen the witches' mark that was depicted on the dead children's shoulders. When she stepped into the midwife's house yesterday, she had noticed pottery shards on the floor. Those were the shards of clay jars that had been standing on one of Martha Stechlin's shelves—jars of those drugs that a midwife needed for her trade: mosses for staunching hemorrhages, herbal painkillers, but also powdered minerals, which she mixed into the infusions she prepared for pregnant and sick women. Engraved on some of the shards were alchemical symbols that the great Paracelsus had used and that midwifes liked to use as well.

On one shard Magdalena had seen the witches' mark.

At first she'd been stunned. What was this sign doing in the midwife's house? Was she a witch, after all? But as Magdalena turned the shard back and forth in her hands, she saw the symbol upside down.

And suddenly the witches' mark had become a harmless alchemical symbol.

Hematite. Bloodstone . . .

It was ground to a powder that was administered to staunch bleeding in childbirth. A harmless little drug, recognized as such also among learned doctors, although Magdalena had her doubts concerning its efficacy.

In spite of her fear she almost had to laugh. The witches' sign had been nothing but the symbol for hematite turned upside down!

Magdalena remembered how Simon had described to her the mark on the children's shoulders. Both the physician and her father had always looked at it in such a way that it resembled a witches' mark. But when looked at from above it turned into a quite harmless alchemical symbol . . .

Was it the children themselves who had scratched the marks on their shoulders with elderberry juice? They had been at Martha Stechlin's place a lot, so Sophie, Peter, and the others must have seen the symbol on the jar. But why would they do such a thing? Or had it been the midwife, after all? That made even less sense. Why should she draw the symbol of hematite on the children's shoulders? So it was the children after all . . .

As the thoughts swirled through Magdalena's head, she came closer and closer to the forest. What had at first been a narrow, dark green strip in the early morning light was now a broad band of birches, firs, and beeches not far ahead of her. Magdalena ran straight for it. The men had gained on her again. There were only ten paces between her and them now. She could hear their panting. Closer and closer. One of them burst in an insane laugh as he ran.

"Hangman's wench, I like how you run. I enjoy hunting for my deer before I eat it . . . "

The other one started to laugh too.

"We'll have you in a minute. No girl has gotten away from us yet!"

Magdalena had almost reached the forest on the high bank. A swampy meadow extended between her and the protective trees. Little puddles appeared between the beeches and willows where the last snow had melted and soon her feet sank ankle-deep in the soft mud. In the distance she could hear the Lech roar.

Jumping carefully, the hangman's daughter tried to hop from one tuft of grass to the other in the bog. She came to a place with a particularly wide gap between two of these little mounds, and she slipped and landed with both feet in the swamp. She struggled desperately to free her legs from the mud.

She was stuck!

The men were close behind. Seeing that their prey had been snared they howled with delight, circling the mudhole and leering, looking for a way to reach their prey without getting their feet wet. Magdalena pulled herself with her hands onto one of the grassy mounds. There was a sucking, slurping sound when the slush let go of her legs. One of the soldiers in front of her leaped at her head-on. At the last moment she ducked to the side and the man landed in the bog with a splash. Before he could scramble up, Magdalena slipped out between the two men and headed for the forest.

Entering the shadows of the trees, she realized at once that she had no chance. The trees were spaced much too far apart and there was almost no undergrowth to hide in. And yet she kept running, even if it was pointless, as the men had almost caught up with her. Before much more time had passed, the chase would be over. The roaring of the river grew louder. The steep embankment had to be dead ahead of her. The end of her escape . . .

Suddenly her left foot stepped into space. She leapt back, watching small pebbles tumbling downward. She pushed aside the branches of a willow and saw an almost vertical incline that led down to the riverbank.

Reeling on the edge of the chasm, Magdalena saw a movement out of the corner of her eye. One of the soldiers suddenly appeared behind the willow, reaching for her. Without further hesitation Magdalena plunged into the chasm. She tumbled over rocks and boulders, reached out for bare roots, and turned head over heels more than once. For a brief moment, she fainted. When she finally came to again, she was lying on her stomach in a hazel bush that had stopped her fall just a few yards above the riverbed. Directly beneath her lay a stretch of gravelly riverbank.

Doubled up with pain, she lay there a moment, then carefully turned her head and looked up. Far above, she could see the men. They were obviously looking for a way to get down to the river. One of the soldiers was already busy tying a rope to a tree trunk that jutted out over the chasm.

Magdalena clambered free from the hazel bush and crawled down the last few yards to the riverbank.

Here at this bend the Lech was rushing along at a dangerous speed. There were white eddies at the river's center, while along the banks the water was foaming, washing over small trees on the edge. At the end of April the water was still so high in the meadows along the river that some of the birches were underwater. More than a dozen felled tree trunks had gotten entangled and were now caught between the beeches. Angrily, the Lech was pushing against this obstruction. The trunks were shifting and moving, and it wouldn't be long before the flood of water would carry them off.

Between the trunks, a boat was bobbing.

Magdalena could hardly believe her luck. The old rowboat must have pulled loose farther upstream. Now it was trapped between the trunks, helplessly spinning between the whirling eddies. Looking closer, she could see a pair of oars lying in the hull.

She looked around. One of the soldiers was already letting himself down to the bank on his rope. It wouldn't be much longer before he reached her. The other one was probably still looking for another way down the slope. Magdalena looked at the trunks in front of her, then said a brief prayer, kicked off her shoes, and leaped onto the nearest trunk.

The log underneath swayed and rocked, but she kept her balance. Magdalena stepped delicately along the trunk and onto another gigantic log. It was spinning around rather dangerously, all the while drifting off to one side. She was agile enough to keep her balance despite the spinning. Looking back for a moment she noticed the soldier who'd let himself down on the rope standing at the riverbank, unsure what to do. When he caught sight of the boat, he, too, started walking cautiously from one log to the next.

Magdalena's backward glance had almost caused her to lose her balance. She slipped on the wet log and could only catch herself at the last moment before falling into the water. Now she was standing astride two logs, one foot on each of them. Beneath her, white water was foaming and gurgling. She knew if she fell in that she'd be crushed by the huge tree trunks like grain between two millstones.

She moved ahead cautiously. The soldier pursuing her had already covered some distance across the logs, and Magdalena saw the anxious, concentrated look on his face. It was Hans, the soldier who had first tried to rape her. The man was afraid, deathly afraid, there was no doubt about it, but it was too late for him to turn back now.

Deftly she leaped onto the last trunk that separated her from the boat. When she had almost reached the vessel, she heard a scream behind her. She turned around and saw the soldier hopping about on his log like a tightrope walker. For a brief moment he seemed to be suspended in midair. Then he toppled sideways and disappeared in the water. With a crunching noise, logs shifted over the spot where he had disappeared. Magdalena thought she caught a glimpse of a head bobbing up between the tree trunks. And then he was gone.

Above her, on the steep embankment, stood the second soldier, looking undecided at the raging waters down below. After a while he turned and disappeared between the trees.

With one last leap Magdalena reached the boat. She grabbed the side and pulled herself up. The inside was wet, with more than a half foot of water at the bottom, but luckily the boat didn't seem to be leaking. With a shiver, she collapsed and started to cry quietly.

When the morning sun had warmed her up a little, she sat up, grabbed the oars, and rowed downstream toward Kinsau.

When the corridor behind them collapsed, Simon threw himself over little Clara to protect her. Then he said a prayer. He heard a grinding sound and then a crash. Rocks thudded to the ground to his right and left. Huge clumps of clay fell on his back, then there was a final trickle of rock, and then silence.

Simon was surprised that the candle he had been clutching in his right hand hadn't gone out. Carefully, he knelt down to survey the corridor. The cloud of smoke and dust slowly settled, and he could see a few yards by the light of his candle.

Behind him Sophie lay huddled on the ground. She was covered by dirt and small lumps of clay as well as a brownish layer of dust, but beneath it Simon noticed a slight trembling. She seemed to be alive. Behind the girl was only darkness and rocks. Simon nodded grimly. There was no way back. But at least no more smoke could reach them now.

"Sophie? Good heavens, are you hurt?" he whispered to her.

The girl shook her head and sat up. Her face was deathly pale, but other than that she seemed to be all right.

"The corridor . . . it . . . collapsed," she mumbled.

The physician looked up cautiously. The roof directly above him seemed solid. There were no beams or joists, but smooth, stable clay. Its round shape that came to a point at the top lent further stability to the tunnel. Simon had seen things like that in a book on mining. The men who had built these corridors had been masters of their craft. How long did it take them to create this maze? Years? Decades? The collapse just now must have been due to the humidity that made the hard clay crumble. Water must have seeped in somewhere. Other than that, the tunnels were in perfect shape.

Simon was still amazed at the construction. Why on earth did these people spend so much energy creating a maze that had no obvious purpose? That it made no sense as an underground hiding place had just been convincingly demonstrated by the fire. Whoever built a fire in one of the upper chambers could be sure that people would come scampering like rats from the smoke-filled corridors to the surface. Or that they'd choke down there.

Unless this tunnel led to the outside somewhere . . .

Simon took Sophie by the hands.

"We've got to go on before the entire corridor comes down. It has to lead to the outside somewhere."

Sophie looked at him, her eyes wide with fear. She seemed to be frozen, rigid with shock.

"Sophie, can you hear me?"

No response.

"Sophie!"

He gave her a ringing slap in the face. The girl came to.

"What . . . what?"

"We've got to get out of here. Pull yourself together. You go ahead with the candle, and be careful it doesn't go out." He gave her an intense look before continuing. "I'll take Clara and stay right behind you. Understand?"

Sophie nodded, and they set out.

The corridor took a slight turn before it straightened out again. Then it began to rise, almost unnoticeably at first, then steeper and steeper. First they could only crawl on all fours, but then the corridor became wider and higher. Finally they could walk, stooped over. Simon carried Clara on his back, her arms dangling on both sides of his shoulders. She was so light that he barely noticed her weight.

Suddenly Simon felt a draft coming from up ahead. He took a deep breath. It smelled of fresh air, of forest, tree sap, and springtime. Never before had air seemed so precious to him.

A few moments later the tunnel ended.

Simon couldn't believe it. He took the candle from Sophie and looked around in a panic. No passageway. Not even a hole.

It took him a while to discover a narrow shaft that led vertically upward.

About fifteen feet above them, daylight was falling in through narrow cracks. Up above, well beyond their reach, was a flagstone. Even if Simon had taken Sophie on his shoulders she couldn't have reached the heavy slab of stone. And she certainly wouldn't have been able to lift it.

They were trapped.

Gently, Simon let the unconscious Clara slide to the ground and sat down beside her. This wasn't the first time today that he felt the urge to cry, or at least to shout at the top of his lungs.

"Sophie, I think we can't get out of here . . . "

Sophie snuggled up and put her head in his lap. Her hands clung to his legs. She was trembling.

Suddenly Simon remembered the mark. He tugged at Sophie's dress to reveal her shoulder.

On her right shoulder blade was the witches' mark.

He fell silent for a long time.

"You children painted these marks yourselves, didn't you?" he finally asked. "Hematite, a simple powder . . . You must have seen the symbol somewhere at Goodwife Stechlin's, and then you scratched it into your skin with elderberry juice. It was just a game . . ."

Sophie nodded, pressing her head into Simon's lap.

"Elderberry juice!" Simon continued. "How in the world could we have been so stupid! What kind of a devil would use a children's beverage to write his marks? But why, Sophie? Why?"

Sophie's body trembled. She was weeping into Simon's lap. After a while she spoke without raising her head.

"They beat us, they kicked us, they bit us . . . Wherever they saw us they spat on us and made fun of us."

"Who?" Simon asked, irritation in his voice.

"The other children! Because we're orphans, because we have no families! So anyone can walk all over us."

"But why the mark?"

For the first time Sophie looked up.

"We saw it on a shelf at Martha's place. On a jar. It looked a bit like . . . witchcraft. We thought if we had the mark on us it would protect us like magic. Nobody'd be able to hurt us then."

"Magic to protect you . . . a charm," Simon mumbled. "A silly children's prank, nothing more . . ."

"Martha told us about that kind of protective magic," Sophie continued. "She said there are spells to ward off death, illness, or hailstorms. But she didn't tell us about any of these. People would say she's a witch . . ."

"Oh my God," Simon whispered. "And that's exactly what happened."

"So we came down here to our hiding place, at the full moon, to make sure the magic would work. We scratched the mark into one another's skins and swore we'd stick together forever.

That we'd always help one another and spit on and detest the others . . . "

"And then you heard the men."

Sophie nodded.

"The magic didn't work. The men saw us, and we didn't help one another. We ran away, and they clubbed Peter to death like a dog . . . "

She began to cry again. Simon caressed her until she calmed down, and her crying became just an occasional sob.

At her side, Clara was groaning in her sleep. Simon felt her forehead. It was still burning hot. The physician wasn't sure if Clara would survive long down here. What the girl needed was a warm bed, cold compresses, and linden blossom tea to reduce the fever. Besides, her leg wound required attention.

Simon called for help, cautiously at first, but then louder and louder.

When nobody answered his repeated calls, he gave up, sitting down again on the rocky, damp ground. Where were the sentries? Still lying on the ground, bound and gagged? Had they been able to free themselves, and were they perhaps already on their way to the town to report the attack? But what if the devil had killed them? It was the first of May today. There was dancing and carousing up there in the town, and it was quite possible that it would be tomorrow or even the day after tomorrow before someone would come by. By then, Clara would have died of fever.

To drive away the dark thoughts the physician kept asking Sophie for more details. He kept thinking of new things that he or the hangman had discovered and that suddenly made sense now.

"The sulfur we found in Peter's pocket—that's part of your hocus-pocus as well?"

Sophie nodded.

"We got it from one of Martha's jars. We thought if witches used sulfur for casting their spells, it would probably work for us as well. Peter stuffed his pockets with it. He said it would make such a nice stink . . . "

"You stole the mandrake from the midwife, didn't you?" Simon continued. "Because you needed it for your magic games."

"I found it at Martha's," Sophie admitted. "She once told me about the miraculous power of the mandrake root, and I believed if I soaked it in milk for three days it would turn into a little man who'd protect us . . . But it just stank, nothing more. I used the rest to make a potion for Clara down here."

The physician glanced at the unconscious girl. It was almost a miracle that she had survived that drastic cure. But perhaps the mandrake root had done some good as well. After all, Clara had been asleep for days now, and that had given her body enough time to regenerate.

He turned back to Sophie.

"And that's why you didn't go to the court clerk or one of the aldermen to report what you saw," he observed. "Because you thought they'd suspect you of witchcraft on account of the mark."

Sophie nodded.

"When that thing with Peter happened, we were going to," she said. "So help me God, we wanted to go to Lechner right after the ten o'clock bell to confess the whole matter. But then you men found Peter down at the Lech and saw the witches' mark. And then there was all that turmoil and everybody talked of witchcraft . . . "

She looked at Simon in despair.

"We thought nobody was going to believe us then. They'd take us to be witches and put us to the stake along with Martha. We were so scared!"

Simon stroked her dirty hair.

"It's all right, Sophie. It's all right . . ."

He looked at the little tallow candle flickering by his side. In no more than half an hour it would burn down. Then the only light they'd have would be a tiny ray through the cracks of the flagstone. He considered making a cold compress for Clara's swollen ankle with a rag torn from his cloak but decided against it. The water that had gathered in little puddles down here was way too dirty. Presumably such a compress would make the girl even sicker. Unlike most physicians of his time, Simon was convinced that dirt caused infection. He had seen too many wounded men with soiled bandages perish miserably.

Suddenly something made him stop and listen. He could hear voices from far off. They came from above. Simon jumped to his feet. There had to be people at the building site! Sophie had stopped crying too. Together they tried to figure out whose voices they were. But they were too soft.

Briefly Simon considered the risk. It was quite possible that the people above them were soldiers or perhaps even the devil himself . . . That lunatic might have killed the hangman and climbed up through the well. On the other hand, Clara was certainly going to die if nobody got her out of there. He hesitated briefly, then he cupped his hands and shouted up the shaft in a hoarse voice.

"Help! We're down here! Can anyone hear us?"

The voices overhead fell silent. Had the men walked away? Simon kept shouting. Sophie was now helping him.

"Help! Can't anyone hear us?" both of them shouted.

Suddenly they heard muffled sounds and heavy footsteps. Several people were talking directly above them. Then there was a scraping sound as the flagstone was pushed to the side, and a beam of light fell on their faces. A head appeared in the opening. The sunlight was almost blinding after so many hours of darkness, and Simon had to blink. Finally he recognized the man.

It was the patrician Jakob Schreevogl.

When the alderman recognized his daughter down there he began to shout. His voice sounded broken.

"My God, Clara, you're alive! Praise the Blessed Virgin Mary!"

He turned around.

"Quick, a rope! We've got to get them out of there!"

A short time later, a rope appeared in the opening and was quickly let down the shaft. Simon tied it into a loop, put it around Clara's waist, and signaled the men to pull her up. Then it was Sophie's turn. He was hoisted up last.

Once he'd arrived aboveground, Simon looked around. It took him some time to get oriented. Around him he saw the walls of the new chapel. The shaft was underneath a weathered flagstone right at the center of the building. The masons seemed to have used an ancient foundation for the floor. The physician looked down once more. It was quite possible that at the spot there had already stood a church or another sacred building long ago that had been connected to the underworld by a tunnel. The workman presently employed at the current construction had obviously not noticed the flagstone.

The physician shuddered. An ancient tunnel straight down to hell . . . And below the devil himself was waiting for the poor sinners.

Further off Simon saw the two sentries of the previous night sitting on a half-finished wall. One of the two had his forehead in a bandage, rubbing his head and still looking dizzy. The other one looked relatively alert although his right eye was badly bruised. Simon had to grin in spite of himself. The hangman had done a good job without causing permanent damage. He was indeed a master of his craft.

In the meantime Jakob Schreevogl was attending to his foster daughter, dripping water into her mouth and mopping her forehead. When the young alderman noticed Simon's expression he began to talk without interrupting what he was doing.

"After you were at my house yesterday afternoon to ask for the old documents I couldn't put my mind to rest. I tossed and turned all night. In the morning I went to your place and then to the hangman's. I met nobody at either, so I came here to the building site."

He pointed at the two sentries, still sitting on the wall in a stupor.

"I found them behind the woodpile, gagged and tied. Simon, can you tell me what exactly happened here?"

Simon briefly related their discovery in the well, the dwarf's holes, the hangman's battle with the soldier, and their escape through the tunnel. He described what the children had seen in that moonlit night a week ago. However, he kept silent about his suspicion that old Schreevogl's treasure might be down there, and he also didn't mention that it was Jakob Kuisl who'd knocked out the sentries. The patrician had to assume that the devil had put the bailiffs out of action before he clambered down the well.

Jakob Schreevogl listened intently, his mouth agape. Occasionally, he interjected a brief question or stooped down to attend to Clara.

"So the children painted the witches' marks on each other to protect themselves against the other children," he finally said.

He stroked Clara's burning forehead. She was still asleep and breathing far more regularly now. "My God, Clara, why didn't you tell me? I could have helped you!"

He shot a glare at Sophie before he spoke again.

"Little Anton and Johannes Strasser might have been saved,

if only you hadn't been so pigheaded. What in the world were you thinking, you brats? There's a lunatic at large, and you just keep playing your games."

"We shouldn't scold the children," said Simon. "They're young, and they were scared. It's more important that we get the murderers. Two of them seem to have kidnapped Magdalena! And their chief's still down there in the tunnels with the hangman!"

He looked over at the well, where smoke was rising from below. What was going on down there? Was Jakob Kuisl dead? Simon suppressed the thought. Instead, he turned to the patrician again.

"I wonder who was the mastermind, the patron. Who is so intent on preventing the leper house from being built that he will even kill children for that?"

Jakob Schreevogl shrugged.

"Well, until a short while ago you even suspected me . . . Other than that I can only repeat what I told you. Most patricians in the town council, including the burgomasters, were opposed to the building because they were afraid of financial losses. That's ridiculous, if you remember that even Augsburg has a leper house like that."

He shook his head and then turned contemplative again.

"But would they destroy the building site and kill witnesses, let alone children? I can't imagine that in my wildest dreams . . . "

They were both startled by the sound of loud coughing and turned around.

A pitch-black form emerged from the well, pulling itself up on a rope. The bailiffs picked up their weapons and headed for the well, clutching their halberds in fear. The figure that pulled itself over the edge of the well looked like the devil himself. It was black with soot from head to toe, and only the eyes were shining white. His clothes were singed and bloodstained in many places, and between his teeth he was holding a larchwood cudgel, the tip of which was glowing red. Now he threw it out onto the ground.

"Jesus bloody Christ! Don't you know your own hangman? Quick, get me some water before I'm completely burned to a crisp."

The bailiffs withdrew, frightened, while Simon hurried to the well.

"Kuisl, you're alive! I thought the devil . . . God, I'm so happy!"

The hangman hoisted himself over the edge of the well.

"Don't waste your words. The damned swine is where he should've been long ago. But my Magdalena is still in the hands of those cutthroats."

He limped to a water trough to wash himself off. It took some time for the hangman's face to appear beneath thick layers of soot. He cast a glance at Jakob Schreevogl and the children, and nodded approvingly.

"You saved her. Well done," he growled. "Go back to Schongau now with them and the alderman, and we'll meet at my house. I'm going to look for my daughter."

He picked up his cudgel and headed for the Hohenfurch Road.

"You know where she is?" Simon called after him.

The hangman nodded, almost imperceptibly.

"He told me. Toward the end. Eventually you can get anyone to talk . . . "

Simon gulped.

"What about the bailiffs?" he called after Jakob Kuisl, who had already reached the road that led to Hohenfurch. "Won't you take them to . . . help you?"

The last words he said only to himself. The hangman had already disappeared around the corner. He was very, very angry.

———

Magdalena was stumbling along the road to Schongau. Her clothes were torn and wet, and she was shaking violently. Her head was still aching, too, and she was tormented by thirst and the fact that she hadn't slept all night. Again and again she kept looking around to see if the second soldier might be following her after all, but there was no one on the road—not even a peasant who could have given her a ride on his oxcart. Ahead of her, Schongau with its protecting walls sat proudly on its hill. To her right was the gallows hill, now deserted. Soon, very soon, she'd be home.

Suddenly she saw in front of her a small dot in the distance, a person with a limp hurrying toward her. The form grew larger, and when she blinked she realized that it was her father.

Jakob Kuisl ran the last few yards, even though it was difficult for him. He had a deep cut in the right side of his chest and one in his left upper arm. He had lost a good deal of blood, and he had twisted his right ankle during the struggle down in the tunnel. But considering all that, he was feeling remarkably well. The hangman had sustained graver injuries during the Great War.

He wrapped his arms around his daughter and patted her head. She almost disappeared within his broad chest.

"The things you do, Magdalena!" he whispered almost tenderly. "Getting yourself caught by a dumb soldier . . . "

"I won't do it again, Father," she answered. "Promise."

For a while they held each other in silence. Then she looked him in the eyes.

"Father?"

"Yes, Magdalena?"

"About me marrying Hans Kuisl, the Steingaden hangman, you know . . . Are you going to think that over again?"

For a moment Jakob Kuisl was silent, and then he smiled.

"Yes, I'm going to think that over. But now let's go home."

He wrapped his massive arm around his daughter again, and then side by side they walked toward the town, which was just awakening to a new day as the sun rose above it in the east.

CHAPTER
16

Tuesday
May 1, a.d. 1659
Six o'clock in the evening

From a window in the council chamber the court clerk Johann Lechner was looking down on the colorful scene in the market place below. He could hear the bells from the town parish church pealing the six o'clock hour. It was already dusk, and small fires were burning in braziers set up on tripods around the sides of the square. Children were dancing around them, and in front of the Ballenhaus the youngsters had erected a maypole, adorned with colored ribbons and a wreath of green boughs. A few minstrels were standing on a newly built pinewood stage still smelling of resin, tuning their fiddles and lutes. There was a whiff in the air of things boiling and frying.

Lechner's gaze wandered over the tables that had been put out for the May Day celebration. Burghers in their holiday attire were sitting around and enjoying the bock beer provided free by burgomaster Karl Semer. There was singing and laughter, but in spite of it all, the clerk could feel no holiday mood.

That damned witch was still unconscious, and the Landgrave

was expected this very evening. Johann Lechner was horrified at the thought of what would happen then. Investigations, torturing, spying, suspicions . . . If only the Stechlin woman had confessed, everything would have been all right. They could have had their trial and sent her to the stake. My God, she was as good as dead anyway! Death at the stake would have been a happy release for her and for the town as well!

Johann Lechner leafed through the old documents about the witch hunt of two generations ago. He had taken them down again from the archives near the council chamber. Eighty arrests, countless torturings . . . sixty-three women burned! The great wave of persecution had begun when the district judge had taken the matter into his hands and then finally the Duke himself had spoken. Then there was no more holding back. Lechner knew that witchcraft was a smoldering fire that would eat its way through society if not stopped in time. Now, presumably, it was too late.

The door squeaked on its hinges and he turned around. Jakob Schreevogl, his face red, was standing in the council chamber. He addressed the clerk with a trembling voice.

"Lechner, we must speak. My daughter has been found!"

The court clerk jumped up. "She's alive?"

Jakob Schreevogl nodded.

"I'm very happy for you. Where was she found?"

"Down at the building site for the leper house," the alderman said, still gasping for breath. "But that isn't all . . ."

Then he told the court clerk what Simon had told him. After hearing just a few words, Johann Lechner had to sit down. The young patrician's story was simply too unbelievable.

When Schreevogl had finished, Lechner shook his head.

"Even if it's true, nobody is going to believe us," he said. "Least of all the Landgrave, the Elector's representative."

"If we have the inner council behind us," the patrician broke in, "and we plead unanimously for the release of the Stechlin woman, then the Landgrave must also agree. He can't go above our heads. We are free burghers, established by the town laws. And the Landgrave signed the laws himself at the time."

"But the council will never vote for us," Johann Lechner reminded him. "Semer, Augustin, Holzhofer—they are all convinced that the midwife is guilty."

"Unless we present them with the name of the person who really did order the murder of the children."

The court clerk laughed.

"Forget that! If he really belongs to the inner council of the town, then he is powerful enough to keep his activities secret."

Jakob Schreevogl buried his face in his hands and rubbed his temples.

"Then I can see no hope any more for the Stechlin woman . . ."

"Or you sacrifice the children," the court clerk added, as if in passing. "Tell the Landgrave about the true origin of the witches' signs, and perhaps he'll let the midwife go. But the children? They've dabbled in witchcraft, and I don't think the Landgrave will let them off so easily."

There was silence for a short time.

"The midwife or your daughter. It's your choice," Johann Lechner said.

Then he went over to the window. From the north the call of a horn could suddenly be heard. The court clerk stuck his head out in order to hear exactly where it was coming from. He blinked.

"His Excellency, the Landgrave," he said, turning toward the patrician, who sat as if turned to stone at the council table. "It looks as if you'll have to make your decision quickly."

The boys playing down by the Hof Gate were the first to see the Landgrave. The Elector's deputy arrived by way of the Altenstadt Road traveling in a magnificent coach drawn by four horses. On each side rode six soldiers in full armor, with open helmets, pistols, and swords. The first soldier was carrying a horn, with which he announced the arrival of the Landgrave. Behind the coach came a second carriage, which was used for transporting the servants and the chests with the necessities that His Excellency required for the trip.

The gate had already been closed at this hour, but now it was quickly reopened. The horses' hooves clattered over the cobblestones, and most of the burghers who had gathered on the market square for the feast now ran down to the gate to see the arrival of the highborn man with a mixture of admiration and skepticism. Only rarely did such distinguished gentlemen come to visit little Schongau. Previously the Landgrave had visited the town more often, but that hadn't happened for a long time. Nowadays, any aristocrat who visited the town was a welcome spectacle and a change from the daily routine. At the same time the burghers were aware that the Landgrave and his soldiers would eat up their meager provisions. In the Great War, hordes of mercenaries had more than once descended on the town like locusts. But perhaps the Landgrave wouldn't stay all that long.

Crowds lined the streets, through which the procession advanced slowly toward the marketplace. The people chatted and whispered and pointed to the silver-bound chests in which the Landgrave, no doubt, carried his valuable household goods. The twelve soldiers looked straight ahead. The Landgrave himself was invisible behind a red damask curtain that covered the coach door.

Once they had arrived at the marketplace, the coach stopped directly in front of the Ballenhaus. Dusk had already fallen over the town, but the birch logs were still glowing in the braziers, so that bystanders could see a form in a green doublet descending from the coach. At the Landgrave's right dangled a dress sword. His beard was neatly trimmed, his long silky hair combed, and his high leather boots were brightly polished. He glanced briefly at the crowd, then strode toward the Ballenhaus, where the aldermen were already assembled at the entrance. Only a few of them had managed to don appropriate attire for the occasion on such short notice. Some had the corner of a shirt sticking out from under their doublet, and the coat buttons had been put in the wrong buttonholes. More than one passed his fingers through his untidy hair.

Burgomaster Karl Semer stepped forward to greet the Landgrave and offered his hand rather hesitantly.

"It is with—um—joyous anticipation that we have so long awaited your arrival, Your Excellency," he commenced, stuttering slightly. "How nice that your arrival coincides with the May Day festival. Schongau is proud to be permitted to celebrate the beginning of summer with you, and—"

The count interrupted him with a brusque gesture and surveyed, in a rather bored way, the coarsely made tables, the maypole, the little fires, and the wooden stage. It was obvious that he had experienced more splendid feasts than this.

"Well, I am also pleased to see my Schongau once more," he said finally. "Even if the occasion is a sad one . . . Anyway, has the witch confessed?"

"No, unfortunately she very cleverly fell into a swoon at the last questioning," the court clerk Johann Lechner replied. With Jakob Schreevogl he had just emerged from the door of the Ballenhaus to join the group. "But we are quite confident that she will come to before tomorrow. Then we can proceed with the questioning."

The count shook his head disapprovingly.

"You are no doubt aware that the use of torture in your questioning requires approval from Munich. You had no right to begin before you have it." He waved a threatening finger, half seriously, half playfully.

"Your Excellency, we thought we could speed up the proce-

dure by—" the court clerk began, but he was immediately interrupted by the Landgrave.

"No, you may not! First the approval. I'm not getting mixed
up in arguments with the Munich court council! I'll send a messenger as soon as I've seen for myself what the situation is. But
tomorrow . . . " He looked up at the clear, starry sky. "Tomorrow
I should first like to go hunting. The weather looks promising.
I'll see about the witch later."

The count chuckled.

"She's not going to fly away in the meantime, hey?"

Solicitously, burgomaster Semer shook his head. Johann
Lechner's face became pale. He rapidly calculated the expenses
that the town would incur if the count really intended to wait for
the approval from Munich. The soldiers would stay for a good
month, perhaps longer . . . That meant board and lodging for a
month, and also inquiries, suspicion, spying! And the matter
would not stop with one witch.

"Your Excellency," he began. But Count Sandizell had
already turned to his soldiers.

"Unsaddle!" he commanded. "And then enjoy yourselves!
We'll join in the feast. Let us greet the summer. I can see that
fires are already burning. Let us hope that here in a few weeks a
much larger fire will burn, and that the devilry in this town will
at last come to an end!"

He clapped his hands and looked up at the stage.

"Play up, musicians!"

The minstrels strummed nervously at a country dance. At
first hesitantly, but then more confidently, the first pairs stepped
out to dance. The celebrations began. Witches, witchcraft, and
murder were temporarily forgotten. But Johann Lechner knew
that all this would drive the town to its ruin before many days
had passed.

———

The hangman knelt down before Martha Stechlin and changed the bandage on her forehead. The swelling had gone down. Where Georg Riegg's stone had struck her, there was an ugly black-and-blue bruise. And the fever seemed to have gone down. Jakob Kuisl nodded, satisfied. The brew of linden flowers, juniper, and elderberries that he had given her that morning seemed to help.

"Martha, can you hear me?" he whispered and patted her cheek. She opened her eyes and looked at him vacantly. Her hands and feet were swollen like balloons from the torture. Everywhere dried blood covered her body, which was only barely concealed by a dirty woolen blanket.

"The children are . . . innocent," she croaked. "I know now how it was. They . . . "

"*Shhh,*" said the hangman, laying a finger on her dry lips. "You shouldn't talk so much, Martha. We know it too."

The midwife looked astonished.

"You know that they had looked at the sign at my house?"

Jakob Kuisl grunted in agreement. The midwife raised herself from her reclining position.

"Sophie and Peter were always interested in my herbs. Especially the magic ones. They wanted to know everything. I showed the mandrake to Sophie once, but that's as far as it went! I swear it to God! I know what can happen. How quickly the gossip spreads. But Sophie wouldn't leave me alone, and then she must have had a closer look at the signs on the jars . . . "

"The bloodstone. I know," the hangman interrupted her.

"But that is really quite harmless," the midwife began to sob. "I give the red powder to women when they bleed down there, infused in wine, nothing evil in it, by God . . . "

"I know, Martha, I know."

"The children drew the sign on their own bodies! And as to the murders, by the Holy Virgin Mary, I have nothing to do with them!"

Her body shook as she broke into a fit of sobbing.

"Martha," Jakob Kuisl said, trying to calm her down. "Just listen. We know who killed the children. We do not know who gave the murderer his orders, but I'm going to find him, and then I'll come and fetch you out of here."

"But the pain, the fear, I can't stand it anymore," she sobbed. "You'll have to hurt me again!"

The hangman shook his head.

"The Landgrave has just arrived," he said. "He wants to wait for approval from Munich before they question you any further. That'll take time. Till then you are safe."

"And then?" asked Martha Stechlin.

The hangman remained silent. Almost helplessly he patted her shoulder before going out. He knew that unless a miracle occurred, the death sentence was now only a formality. Even if the mastermind could be discovered, the fate of the midwife was sealed. Martha Stechlin would burn in a few weeks at the latest, and it was he, Jakob Kuisl, who would have to lead her to the stake.

When Simon arrived at the market square, the feast was already in full swing. He had been resting at home for a few hours, and now he wanted to see Magdalena again. He gazed over the square looking for her.

Couples were dancing arm in arm around the maypole. Wine and beer were flowing from well-filled jugs. Some drunken soldiers were already staggering around the edge of the fires or chasing screaming maidens. The Landgrave was sitting at the aldermen's table, obviously in high spirits. Johann Lechner must have just told him a funny story. The clerk knew how to keep the bigwigs in a good mood. They were all having a grand time. Even the parish priest, sitting a little to one side, sipped calmly on a half pint of red wine.

Simon looked over at the stage. The minstrels were playing a country dance that became faster and faster until the first dancers, laughing, fell to the ground. The squealing of women and the deep laughter of the men mixed with the music and the clinking of mugs to form one single sound ascending into the starry night sky.

That morning, when Simon, at the end of a long night, had climbed out of the tunnels, he had believed that nothing could ever be the same as it had been before. But he had been wrong. Life was going on, at least for a little while longer.

Jakob Schreevogl had taken Clara and also, for the time being, Sophie under his care. The council had decided not to interrogate the children until the following morning. By then Simon, in consultation with the young patrician, would have to consider what to tell the aldermen. The truth? But would that not deliver the children to a terrible fate? Children who played at witchcraft could end up at the stake as well as adults. Simon knew this from earlier trials he had heard of. Probably the Landgrave would question the children until they named the midwife as a witch. And then a lot of other witches would be added too . . .

"Hello, what's going on? Would you like to dance?"

Simon wheeled around, startled out of his gloomy thoughts. Before him stood Magdalena, laughing. She had a bandage around her head but otherwise looked well. The physician couldn't help smiling. It was only this morning that the hangman's daughter had fled from two soldiers. Two nights of horror and unconsciousness lay behind her, and nevertheless she was inviting him to dance. She seemed to be indestructible. *Just like her father,* thought Simon.

"Magdalena, you should go and rest," he began. "In any case, the people ..." He pointed to the tables, where the first maidservants were beginning to whisper and point at them.

"Oh, the people," Magdalena interrupted him. "What do I care about them?"

She took him by the arm and drew him onto the dance floor, which was built out in front of the stage. Closely embracing, they danced to the music of a slow folk dance. Simon felt the other pairs draw away from them, but he didn't care. He looked into Magdalena's dark eyes and felt himself sinking into them. Everything around merged into a sea of lights with them in the very middle. Worries and dark thoughts were far away. He could only see her smiling eyes, and slowly his lips approached hers.

Suddenly a shape appeared in the corner of his eye. It was his father hurrying toward him. Bonifaz Fronwieser gripped his son hard by the shoulder and turned him around to face him.

"How dare you?" he hissed. "Can't you see how the people are beginning to talk? The physician with the hangman's wench! What a joke!"

Simon tore himself free.

"Father, I must ask you . . . " he tried to calm him down.

"No!" snapped his father and pulled him a little away from the dance floor, without even casting a single glance at Magdalena. "I order you ..."

Suddenly Simon felt himself engulfed in a black cloud. The severe trials of the past few days, the deadly fear, the worry for Magdalena. He pushed his father violently away from him, causing the astonished man to gasp. At this very moment the music stopped, so that his words were clearly audible to all the bystanders.

"You've no right to give me orders! Not you!" he panted, still out of breath from dancing. "What are you anyway? A dubious little field surgeon, an opportunistic yes-man! Purging and piss smelling, that's all you can do!"

The slap hit him hard on his cheek. His father stood before him, white as a sheet, his hand still raised. Simon felt that he had gone too far. But before he could apologize, Bonifaz Fronwieser had turned away and disappeared into the darkness.

"Father!" he called after him. But the musicians struck up again, and the couples resumed their dancing. Simon looked at Magdalena, who shook her head.

"You shouldn't have done that," she said. "He's your father, after all. My father would have knocked your head off for that."

"Has everyone here something against me?" Simon mumbled. The brief moment of happiness between himself and Magdalena had evaporated. He turned away and left her standing on the dancing floor. He needed a mug of bock beer.

On his way across to where the beer barrel was set up on its trestles he passed the aldermen's table. There sat the patricians in cozy familiarity: Semer, Holzhofer, Augustin, and Püchner. The Landgrave had gone over to his soldiers to see if everything was all right. At last the patricians had the opportunity to talk about the coming days and weeks. They anxiously put their heads together and the clerk Johann Lechner sat firm as a rock between them lost in his own thoughts.

Simon stopped and from his position in the shadows observed the scene in front of him.

It reminded him of something.

The four patricians. The clerk. The table . . .

His head was hot from dancing. The efforts of the previous night still ached in his bones. He had already drunk two mugs of beer at home. He needed a moment before it came to him.

But then he felt as if the last stone of the mosaic had been put into its place.

They had simply not listened properly.

Hesitantly, Simon turned away. The parish priest was sitting alone at a table a little farther back and was observing the dancers. His expression alternated between disapproval and relaxation. As a representative of the church he could not of course approve of this wild, heathen activity. But he was obviously enjoying the

warm night, the flickering flames, and the rhythm of the music.
Simon went over and sat down beside him, not waiting for an invi-
tation. The priest looked at him in surprise.

"My son, you're not coming to confession now, are you?" he
asked. "Although . . . as I have just seen, you certainly seem to be
in dire need of it."

Simon shook his head.

"No, Father," he said. "I need some information. I think I
just didn't listen properly the last time."

After a short conversation Simon stood up again and returned
thoughtfully to the dancers. On the way there he had to pass the
aldermen's table once more. Abruptly he stopped.

One seat was now empty.

Without stopping to think, he hurried to a house at the edge
of the marketplace. Behind him the sounds of laughter and music
faded. He had heard enough.

Now he must act.

The man sat in a heavy armchair upholstered in velvet and
looked out the window. On the table in front of him was a bowl
full of walnuts and a jug of water. He could no longer tolerate
any other kind of food. It was difficult for him to breathe, and
stabs of pain went through his abdomen. He could hear the
sounds of the revelry outside, and there was a gap in the drawn
curtains through which he could have observed the activity
below. But his eyes were going bad, and the fires and dancers all
blurred into a misty picture without contours. His hearing,
however, was excellent, and so he was aware of footsteps behind
him, even when the intruder was endeavoring to enter the room
unnoticed.

"I've been expecting you, Simon Fronwieser," he said,
without turning around. "You are a nosy little know-it-all. I was
against you and your father obtaining burghers' rights back then,

and I have since been proved right. You bring nothing but unrest to our town."

"Unrest?" Simon no longer took the trouble to be quiet. With quick steps he hurried to the table, while he continued to speak. "Who has brought unrest to this town, then? Who ordered the soldiers to kill small children who had seen too much? Who caused the Stadel to be burned? Who saw to it that fear and hate returned to Schongau and that witches should burn at the stake again?"

He had worked himself up into a rage. With one more step he reached the chair and spun it round toward him. He looked into the blind eyes of the old man, who just shook his head as if he pitied him.

"Simon, Simon," said Matthias Augustin. "You still haven't understood. All this happened only because you and that wretched hangman interfered. Believe me, I don't wish to see any more witches burned. I saw too many people burned at the stake when I was a child. I only wanted the treasure. It belonged to me. Everything else that happened is the responsibility of you two."

"The treasure, that damned treasure," Simon muttered as he let himself fall into the chair next to the old man. He was tired, simply tired out. He spoke on, almost as if in a trance.

"The parish priest gave me the decisive clue in the church, but I didn't understand him correctly. He knew that you were the last one to speak to old Schreevogl before he died. And he told me that you and he were friends." Simon shook his head before he went on. "When I went to him for confession at that time, I asked him if anyone else had recently shown any interest in the site," he said. "Until today he had forgotten that you had indeed asked him about it shortly after old Schreevogl's death. It wasn't until today, at the May feast, that he suddenly remembered."

The gray-headed patrician bit his bloodless lip.

"The old fool. I had offered him a lot of money, but no, he

just had to build that damned leper house ... But the property should have been mine, mine alone! Ferdinand should have left the site to me. It was the least that I expected of the old miser! The very least!"

He took a walnut from the table and cracked it with a practiced hand. Fragments of shell scattered over the tabletop.

"Ferdinand and I had known each other since our childhood. We went to grammar school together, as little boys we played marbles together, and later we had the same girlfriends. He was like a brother ... "

"The painting in the council chamber shows you both in the middle of the patricians. A picture of trust and unity," Simon interrupted him. "I had forgotten about it until I saw you this evening at the table with the other aldermen. In the painting you are holding a paper in your hands. Today I asked myself, what was on it?"

Matthias Augustin's eyes turned to the light of the flames visible through the open window. He seemed to be looking into the far distance.

"Ferdinand and I were both burgomasters at that time. He needed money, desperately. His stovemaking business was nearly bankrupt. I lent him the money, a considerable sum. The paper in the painting is the receipt. The artist thought I should, as burgomaster, hold a paper in my hand. So I took the receipt, without the others noticing what it was. An eternal witness to Ferdinand's debt ... " The old man laughed.

"And where is the receipt now?" asked Simon.

Matthias Augustin shrugged.

"I burned it. At that time we were both in love with the same woman, Elisabeth, a redheaded angel of a girl. A bit simple perhaps, but of unsurpassable beauty. Ferdinand promised me that he would have nothing more to do with her, and in return I burned the receipt. Then I married this woman. A mistake ... "

He shook his head, regretfully. "She bore me a useless, stupid brat and then died during childbirth."

"Your son, Georg," Simon interjected.

Matthias Augustin nodded curtly. Then he went on, while his thin gouty fingers twitched.

"The treasure is mine by right! Ferdinand told me about it on his deathbed, and that he had hidden it somewhere on the building site. He told me I would never be able to find it. He wanted to have his revenge. Because of Elisabeth!"

Simon walked around the table. Thoughts rushed through his head in confusion, then came together again in a new pattern. Suddenly it all made sense. He remained standing and pointed to Matthias Augustin.

"You yourself stole the sketch of the deed of gift from the town archives," he cried. "Fool that I was! I thought that only Lechner or one of the four burgomasters would have known about the hiding place behind the tile. But you?"

The old man chuckled.

"Ferdinand had that hiding place made when he built the stove. He told me about it. A tile with a picture of a court clerk with documents coming out of his arse! He was always well-known for his coarse sense of humor."

"But if you had the sketch—" asked Simon.

"I couldn't make sense of it," Augustin interrupted him. "I turned it this way and that, but I couldn't see anything there about the damned hiding place!"

"So then you had the work on the building site disrupted so that you could have more time to look for it," reasoned Simon. "And then the children overheard you, and you simply had them killed because of the dangerous knowledge they had. Did you know that they hadn't recognized the instigator? All these murders were unnecessary."

Angrily, Matthias Augustin cracked another nut.

"That was Georg, the simpleton. He got his brains from his

mother, not from me. He was supposed to give the soldiers money only for the destruction of the building site. But even for that he was too stupid! He was careless and let himself be overheard, then gave the order to kill the children. He didn't seem to realize the trouble that sort of thing would cause!"

The patrician seemed to have forgotten Simon. He continued his rant, without paying any attention to the physician.

"I told him to stop! He was to tell that devil that it was enough. What great secrets could the children have revealed? And who would have believed them anyway? But the killing went on. And now the children are dead, the Landgrave is sniffing around looking for witches in the town, and in spite of all that we still haven't got the treasure! An absolute disaster! I should have left Georg in Munich. He has ruined everything!"

"But why do you worry about the treasure?" asked Simon incredulously. "You're rich enough. Why risk so much for a few coins?"

The old man suddenly pressed his hands to his stomach and bent forward. A wave of pain seemed to pass through him before he could speak further.

"You . . . don't understand," he panted. "My body is a lump of rotten flesh. I'm rotting away while I'm still alive. The worms will be eating me soon. But that . . . is . . . not important."

Once again he had to stop briefly and let the pain pass over him. Then the attack seemed to be over.

"What counts is the family, our reputation," he said. "The Augsburg wagoners have almost driven me to ruin. Damned pack of Swabians! Before long, our house will go to the dogs. We need this money! My name is still good enough to obtain credit, but soon even that will be of no use. I need . . . this treasure."

His voice turned into a soft rattle, while his fingers grasped the edge of the table convulsively. The colic pains returned. With increasing horror, Simon saw the old man twitch, jerk his head back and forth, and roll his blind eyes. Saliva drooled from the corner of his mouth. The pain must have been beyond imagining. Perhaps an obstruction in the gut, the physician thought, perhaps a growth that had spread over the whole abdomen. Matthias Augustin would not live much longer.

At this moment Simon noticed a movement out of the corner of his eye. As he started to turn around a mighty blow hit him on the side of the head. He sank to the floor, and as he fell he saw young Georg Augustin standing there, his hand grasping a heavy iron candlestick raised for a second blow.

"No, Georg!" his father gasped from behind. "You'll only make things much worse!" Then a black wave swept over Simon—he didn't know if the candlestick had hit him again or if he had lost consciousness from the first blow.

When he came to, he felt a tightness around his chest, hands, and feet. His head throbbed with pain, and he could not open his right eye. Presumably blood had run into it and clotted. He was sitting on the chair where he had been before, but he could no longer move. He looked down and saw that he was tied to it with a curtain cord from top to bottom. Simon wanted to call out, but only succeeded in uttering a choking sound. A gag had been stuffed into his mouth.

In front of him the grinning face of Georg Augustin appeared. With his sword he poked at the physician's doublet, and some of the copper buttons popped off. Simon cursed inwardly. When he saw that Matthias Augustin had disappeared from the May feast, he had not given a thought to this son of his but hurried directly to the Augustins' house. The young patrician must have secretly followed him, and now his perfumed and beautifully barbered head of hair was directly in front of Simon's face, looking him straight in the eye.

"That was a mistake," he hissed. "A damned bad mistake, you quack! You should have kept your big mouth shut and screwed your hangman's wench. It's such a lovely feast out there. But, no, you have to make trouble . . . "

He stroked Simon's chin with his sword. In the background the physician could hear old Augustin groaning. When he turned his head in that direction he saw the old man lying on the floor near the table. He dug his fingers into the cherrywood floorboards; his whole body twitched with cramps. Georg gave him only a brief glance before he turned again to Simon.

"My father will not disturb us any further," he said, casually. "I have gotten to know these fits. The pain increases until it is intolerable, but then it stops. And when it stops, he's just an empty carcass, much too exhausted to do anything. He'll fall asleep, and when he wakes up again, there'll be nothing left of you."

Once again the patrician moved his sword slowly over Simon's throat. Simon tried to cry out, but the gag only slipped down farther into his throat. He had a choking fit. Only with much trouble could he calm himself.

"You know," whispered young Augustin. He bent down to Simon again, so that the smell of his expensive perfume wafted over him. "At first I cursed when I saw you going to see my father. I thought that would be the end. But now, well . . . other possibilities have arisen."

He stepped to the fireplace, where a little fire was burning, and reached for the poker. Its tip was glowing red. He held it close to Simon's cheek so that the physician could feel the heat. Grinning smugly, he continued.

"When we were watching the hangman doing his torturing down there in the keep, I thought I might enjoy this sort of thing. The screams, the smoke rising from human flesh, the pleading looks . . . Well, the witch wasn't quite to my liking. You, on the other hand . . .

With a swift movement he lowered the poker and pressed it firmly to Simon's breeches. The heat ate its way through the fabric and hissed as it touched his thigh. Simon's eyes filled with tears. He gave a long howl but the gag wouldn't let out more than a muffled groan. Helplessly he tossed about on the chair. After a while Augustin removed the poker and looked in his eyes, smiling coldly.

"Your beautiful breeches . . . Or are these the latest fashion now, these—what do you call them—rhinegraves? It's a pity. You're a loudmouth, that's true, but at least you have a feeling for style. I can't imagine how a nobody like you, a vagrant field surgeon, would have breeches like these. But all joking aside . . . "

He took the other armchair and sat astride it, the back facing Simon.

"That just now was only a foretaste of the pain that you are going to feel. Unless . . . " He pointed the poker at Simon's breast. "Unless you tell me where the treasure is. Spit it out now. Sooner or later you're going to have to tell me."

Simon shook his head wildly. Even if he had wanted to, he didn't know. He had an idea that the hangman had found the treasure. In the course of the day Kuisl had given out one or two hints. But he wasn't sure about it.

Georg Augustin interpreted his shake of the head as a refusal. Disappointed, he stood up and went back to the fireplace.

"It's a pity," he said. Then we'll have to take it out on your fine doublet. Who is your tailor, quack? Not anyone from Schongau, surely."

The young patrician held the poker in the fire and waited until it was red-hot again. Meanwhile Simon heard music and laughter from outside. The festival was only a few steps away, but the only thing observant burghers might see from outside would be a brightly lit window and a man sitting on a chair with his back to it. It seemed certain that Georg Augustin would not be disturbed. The man- and maidservants were all down in the market place and had presumably been given permission to stay out until morning. It would probably be after midnight before anyone entered the patrician's house again.

Behind Simon, old Augustin squirmed on the floor, groaning

quietly. The pain seemed to be diminishing. But he was in no position to intervene. Simon prayed that the old man would not pass out. Matthias Augustin was the only hope he had. Perhaps he might succeed in bringing his crazy son to his senses. Simon had already established that Georg was not quite normal.

"My father has always considered me to be a ne'er-do-well," said the young patrician, turning the poker round in the fire. His eyes looked almost dreamily into the fire. "He's never believed in me. Sent me away to Munich . . . But that was my idea with the building site. I hired the soldiers in Semer's inn. I gave the burgomaster a lot of money to keep quiet about it. He let me in through the back door, the old fool. He thought I needed the soldiers to destroy the leper house because it was bad for business. As if I cared a damn about trade!"

He laughed aloud. Then he came toward Simon with the red-hot iron.

"And now my father will realize that I'm not as useless as he's always thought me to be. When I've finished with you, your little hangman's bitch won't recognize you anymore. Perhaps I'll have a go at her myself, the little tart."

"Georg . . . be careful . . . "

Old Augustin had managed to heave himself upright. He propped himself up, panting, on the table and appeared to be wanting to say something. But pain overcame him, and he collapsed again.

"You have nothing more to say to me, Father," whispered Georg Augustin as he moved nearer to Simon. "It'll all be over in a couple of weeks. Then I shall be sitting here and managing the business. You'll be rotting in your grave, but our house and our name will continue to exist. I shall buy a few new wagons with the money and some strong horses, and then we'll put those Augsburgers in their place!"

Desperately, the old man gesticulated toward the door behind his son.

"Georg, behind you . . . "

The young patrician, at first surprised and then obviously shocked, looked at his father, who was pointing his spindly fingers at the entrance. When he finally turned around, it was too late.

The hangman flew at him like an avenging fury, and with one single blow knocked Georg Augustin to the floor. The glowing poker flew into a corner of the chamber, landing with a clatter. Dazed, Georg Augustin looked up at the big man above him, who now bent down and pulled him up with both hands.

"You leave torture to me, you fop," said the hangman. Then he gave the patrician such a head butt with his hard skull that he sank lifeless into the chair. Blood ran from his nose. He keeled over forward, fell, and lay unconscious on the floor.

The hangman paid no further attention to Georg Augustin and hurried to Simon, who was rocking back and forth on his chair and quickly pulled the gag from his mouth.

"Kuisl!" panted the physician. "Heaven has sent you. How did you know?"

"I was at the feast to cool my Magdalena down a bit," the hangman interrupted him, growling. "Thought I'd catch the two of you flirting. Instead I heard you'd had a tiff. You're lucky she still likes you and saw you going into Augustin's place. She told me where you were. When you didn't come out, I went after you."

The hangman pointed to the tear in Simon's hose, under which burned skin, red-black, was showing.

"What's that all about?"

Simon looked down. When he saw the wound again the pain returned.

"The swine got me with the poker. He was going to burn me alive."

"Now at least you know what'll happen to the Stechlin woman," Kuisl growled. "What's the matter with him down there?" He pointed to old Augustin, who had meanwhile recovered and sat in his chair, his eyes full of hate.

"He's the mastermind we've been looking for so long," said Simon, while he bound up his wound with a strip of cloth as best he could. At the same time he told the hangman what had happened.

"The honorable Matthias Augustin," Jakob Kuisl finally growled when Simon had finished his story, looking at the old man. "You can't have enough of executions at the stake. Didn't my grandfather do enough of them for you? Haven't you heard enough women screaming?"

"As God is my witness, I wanted no such thing," said Matthias Augustin. "All I wanted was the money."

"Your damned money," said the hangman. "It's blood money. I want none of it. Take it—you can eat it as far as I'm concerned!"

He reached under his coat and drew out a small dirty linen bag. With disgust he threw it onto the table, where it burst open. Gold and silver coins poured over the tabletop and rolled jingling to the floor.

The old man looked on, his mouth wide open. Then he leaned over the table and grabbed the coins.

"My treasure! My money!" he panted. "I shall die with dignity. My house will live on!" He began to count the coins.

"A pity, really, all that money for a moneybags like you," grunted Jakob Kuisl. "I'm wondering if I should take it away from you again."

Fearfully Matthias Augustin looked across at him. He stopped counting, his fingers trembled.

"You wouldn't dare, hangman," he hissed.

"And why not?" said Kuisl. "Nobody would notice anything. Or are you going to tell the council that I took Ferdinand

Schreevogl's treasure away from you? Money that actually belongs to the church and you have unlawfully embezzled?"

Matthias Augustin looked at him with suspicion.

"What do you want, hangman?" he asked. "You're not interested in the money. What then?"

Jakob Kuisl lunged over the table with his massive body until his face was directly in front of the old man's toothless mouth.

"Can't you guess?" he mumbled. "I want you to persuade the council and the Landgrave that there is no witch. That it was all a children's game with elderberry juice and magic rhymes. So that the midwife will be freed and this persecution will be over. Help me do this, and you can have your goddamned money."

Matthias Augustin shook his head and laughed.

"Even if I wanted to do that, who would believe me? There were deaths, the Stadel burned down, the soldiers at the building site . . . "

"The destruction at the building site was an act of vandalism by some burghers who didn't want a leper house there. A trifle . . ." Simon interjected, when he had understood what the hangman was leading up to. "The Augsburgers started the Stadel fire," he hastened to add. "But so as not to upset neighborly relations, there will be no further consequences. And the dead children . . . "

"Peter Grimmer fell into the river, an accident, as the physician here can confirm," he continued in measured tones. "And the others? Well now, the war hasn't been over all that long. The region is swarming with robbers and highwaymen. In any case, who's going to bother with a couple of orphans when he can save the town with a lie?"

"Save . . . the town?" asked Matthias Augustin, astonished.

"Well," Simon added, "if you don't present the Landgrave with a good story, he'll hunt down more witches and keep on until half the women in Schongau are burned at the stake. Remember the witch trials in your childhood, when dozens of women were burned. The council will support you and swallow a few small lies if you see to it that the past does not repeat itself. You alone have enough influence to persuade the aldermen and the Landgrave. Use it! I'm sure you know all the mean little secrets that each of them has, which you can use to persuade them if necessary."

Matthias Augustin shook his head.

"Your plan won't work. Too much has happened . . . "

"Think of the money," the hangman interrupted him. "The money and your reputation. If we tell the people out there what kind of villains you and your son are, probably nobody will believe us. We ourselves know that we lack proof. But who knows? Somewhere something will stick . . . I know the people. They gossip, and even the fine people come to me from time to time for a love potion or a salve for warts, and so people start to talk . . . "

"Stop, just stop it!" Matthias Augustin cried. "You have persuaded me. I will do my utmost. But I can't promise you anything."

"We can't promise anything either," said the hangman, deftly sweeping up the money from the table into his big coat. The old man tried to protest, but a glance from the hangman made him fall silent.

"Come to my house in two days, after the big council meeting," said Jakob Kuisl. "I'm quite sure your son will be needing a jar of arnica." He looked down at Georg Augustin almost sympathetically as he lay huddled upon the floor, still unconscious. A small pool of dried blood surrounded his black locks. Then the hangman turned to the father again.

"Perhaps I can also find an elixir in my closet that will reduce your pain. Believe me, we shabby barbers and army surgeons know one or two mysteries that the university doctors still haven't heard of."

He went to the door and waved his goodbye with the bag. "If

the council gets it right, this bag will change its owner. If not, I'll throw it in the Lech. It's up to you."

Simon followed him out. Before he shut the door, he could hear the old man groaning once more. The cramps had started again.

The council meeting two days later was one of the strangest ever to take place in Schongau. Matthias Augustin had used the whole of the previous day to put the squeeze on individual members of the inner council. He had found something against every one of them. With threats, flattery, and persuasion he was able to bring every one of them over to his side. When he finally convinced the court clerk Johann Lechner, there was nothing more in the way of the final plan.

When the Landgrave appeared at the council meeting in the morning, he was confronted by a unanimous group of enlightened burghers who considered the slightest suspicion of witchcraft as belonging in the realm of legend. The investigations conducted by the council had determined without doubt that the witches' signs were nothing but a children's game, the fire at the Stadel was an act of revenge by the depraved Augsburg thugs, and the murdered children the victims of shady elements hiding in the forests around Schongau. All of it no doubt very sad, but no cause for mass hysteria.

In addition, by a stroke of luck, the former mercenary soldier and robber Christoph Holzapfel was arrested by the Landgrave's men on the morning of the third of May. Magdalena, the hangman's daughter, identified him immediately as her abductor, and by the evening the wicked soldier had confessed, in the keep, to having murdered three little children from Schongau out of pure malice.

Remarkably, no torture was necessary to obtain this confession. But the hangman must have shown him the instruments during the short time that he was alone with the abductor of his daughter. In any case, the murderer was afterward prepared to make a written confession, which he signed with his left hand. The right hand hung down like a damp red rag and seemed to be only held together by skin and sinew.

The Landgrave made a few lame attempts to have the Stechlin woman tried for witchcraft after all. But as she had not confessed up to then, he would have had to apply to Munich for permission to continue the torture. The four burgomasters and the court clerk made it clear to him that he could not rely on their support.

The final touch was supplied by old Matthias Augustin, who described in lively detail before the whole council the horrors of the last great witchcraft trial of 1589. Even the Landgrave did not want to do anything to bring that about again.

And so at noon on May 4, 1659, the entourage of the Landgrave Count Wolf Dietrich von Sandizell set out again for his estate at Thierhaupten, from there to direct the destinies of Schongau at a distance. As the soldiers in their shining breastplates rode through the town gates, the burghers waved a long farewell to their lord. Noisy children and barking dogs accompanied the carriage as far as Altenstadt. The burghers all agreed it had been nice to see such important people close up. It was even nicer to see them ride away.

The hangman went to the keep and had the door unlocked by the bailiffs. Martha Stechlin lay sleeping among damp straw and her own foul-smelling excrement. Her breathing was regular, and the swelling on her forehead had gone down. Jakob Kuisl bent down to her and patted her cheek. A smile came to his face. He remembered how this woman had stood by his side at the birth of his children—the blood, the screaming, and the tears. *Strange,* he thought. *People fight with tooth and nail when they come into the world, and when they have to go they fight too.*

Martha Stechlin opened her eyes. It took some time before she found her way out of her dreams back into the prison.

"What is it, Kuisl?" she asked, not yet fully conscious. "Will it go on? Have you come to hurt me again?"

The hangman smiled and shook his head.

"No, Martha. We're going home."

"Home?"

The midwife sat up. She blinked, as if she wanted to see if she wasn't still dreaming. Jakob Kuisl nodded.

"Home. Magdalena has been tidying up a bit at your house, and young Schreevogl has contributed heaps of money. For a new bed, pots and pans, whatever you need. It'll do for the beginning. Come, I'll help you up."

"But why?"

"Don't ask now. Go home. I'll tell you about it later."

He grasped her under the arms and pulled her to her feet, which were still swollen. Martha Stechlin limped along at his side toward the open door. Sunlight flowed in from outside. It was the morning of May fifth, a warm day. The birds were twittering, and from the town they could hear the cries of the maids and housewives haggling in the marketplace. From the fields the scents of summer and flowers wafted over to them, and if you closed your eyes you could even hear the murmuring of the Lech. The midwife stood in the doorway and let the sun shine on her face.

"Home," she whispered.

Jakob Kuisl wanted to support her by taking her under her arms, but she shook her head and pulled away. Alone she limped along the alley toward her little house. At the next bend in the road, she disappeared.

"The hangman, a friend of humanity—who would have thought it?"

The voice came from another direction. Jakob Kuisl looked around and saw the court clerk strolling toward him. He was wearing his dress coat, the brim of his hat was turned up jauntily, and in his right hand he held a walking stick. The hangman nodded a wordless greeting, then he turned to go on.

"Would you care to come for a little walk, Kuisl?" Johann Lechner asked. "The sun is smiling, and I think we should have a good talk. What's your yearly salary, actually? Ten gulden? Twelve? I find you are underpaid."

"Don't worry, I've earned a lot this year," the hangman growled without looking up. He filled his pipe calmly. The inside of the bowl seemed to him to be of more interest than the man standing in front of him. Johann Lechner remained standing and played with his stick. There was a long silence.

"You knew it, didn't you?" Jakob Kuisl asked at last. "You knew it all the time "

"I always had to think of the interests of the town," said Lechner. "Nothing else. That's all that counts. It seemed to me to be simpler that way."

"Simpler!"

The court clerk fiddled with his stick. It looked as if he was searching for notches in the handle.

"I knew that old Schreevogl owed a lot of money to Matthias Augustin. And it was clear to me that as a respected businessman he must have had more money than was mentioned in his will," he said, blinking in the sunlight. "And I knew about the old man's eccentric sense of humor. So when the sketch of the building site disappeared from the archives, it was clear that someone was very interested in the site. First I suspected young Schreevogl, but he had no access to the archives . . . Finally I realized that Ferdinand Schreevogl had certainly told his friend Augustin about the hiding place behind the oven tile. From then on it was all clear. Well, I'm pleased that everything has turned out for the best."

"You've covered up for Augustin," Jakob Kuisl grumbled as he drew on his pipe.

"As I said already, for the good of the town. I couldn't understand that business with the mark. Anyway . . . who would have believed me? The Augustins are a powerful family in Schongau. It seemed that the death of the midwife would resolve all the problems at once."

He smiled at Kuisl.

"Wouldn't you really like to come for a little walk?"

The hangman shook his head silently.

"Well, then," said the clerk. "A good day to you, and God's blessing."

Swinging his stick he disappeared in the direction of the Lech Gate. Burghers who saw him greeted him courteously, raising their hats. Before he disappeared into a narrow street, Jakob Kuisl thought he saw Lechner raise his stick once again as if he wanted to send him a distant greeting.

The hangman spat. Suddenly his pipe didn't taste good anymore.

EPILOGUE

ONE SUNDAY MORNING IN JULY 1659, THE HANGMAN and the physician were sitting together on the bench in front of the hangman's house. The smell of freshly baked bread drifted over to them from the house. Anna Maria Kuisl was preparing the midday meal. There would be hasenpfeffer with barley corn and turnips, her husband's favorite dish. Out in the garden, the twins Georg and Barbara were playing with Magdalena, their big sister. She had pulled a clean bedsheet over her head and, thus disguised as a frightening river spirit, ran through the flowering meadows. Screaming and laughing the children fled from her, seeking protection from their mother in the house.

Lost in thought, Jakob Kuisl puffed on his pipe and observed this scene. He was enjoying the summer and did only what was necessary. The trash in the streets had to be swept up every week, and now and then a dead horse had to be removed, or someone needed a salve for itching and stings . . . Over the past two months he had earned enough that he could afford to be a bit lazy. For the execution of the remaining soldier, Christoph Holzapfel, the town had paid him ten whole guilders! The condemned soldier, who had been arrested shortly after the arrival of the Landgrave, had been broken on the wheel to the applause of the watching crowd. Outside the town the hangman had broken his arms and legs with a heavy wagon wheel and braided him on the wheel next to the scaffold. Christoph Holzapfel lived, screaming, for another two days; finally Jakob Kuisl had pity on him and strangled him with a neck iron.

The body of André Pirkhofer, killed on the building site, was hung in chains next to his countryman, as was the corpse of Christian Braunschweiger, whom the townspeople, even after his death, referred to as "the devil" while crossing themselves three times. His charred corpse, shrunk to the size of a child, was removed from the tunnels before the entrance was sealed off once and for all. His lips were burned off and his scalp shriveled, so that the teeth stood out, grinning. The bony left hand shone out white among all the black flesh, and people said that even from the gallows it seemed to beckon. Two weeks later, the devil's entire body was just bone and mummified skin; nevertheless the council let it hang longer as a dreadful warning until the bones fell off one by one.

The fourth soldier, Hans Hohenleitner, was never found. Most likely the Lech had washed him down toward Augsburg, where the fish ate his corpse. But all this was of no more interest to Jakob Kuisl. Altogether the hangman of Schongau had earned more than twenty guilders in the past two months. That should be enough for some time.

Simon sipped his coffee, which Anna Maria Kuisl had kindly brewed for him. It tasted strong and bitter and drove the weariness out of his body. Last night had been strenuous. A feverish infection was going around in Schongau. It was nothing really serious, but people were demanding the new powder from the West Indies, which the young physician had been prescribing since last year. Even his father seemed to be persuaded of its efficacy.

Simon glanced over at the hangman. He had news that he did not wish to keep any longer from his friend and mentor.

"I was at the Augustins this morning," he said, as casually as possible.

"Well?" inquired Jakob Kuisl. "What's the young fool doing? I haven't heard anything from him since his father's death last month. Seems that he's devoting himself diligently to the business, so people say."

"He is . . . ill."

"A summer fever? May God see to it that he sweats and shivers for a long time."

Simon shook his head.

"It's more serious. I discovered red patches on his skin, which are gradually spreading. In many places he has no feeling anymore. I believe . . . he has an infection. He must have caught it during his last journey to Venice."

"Leprosy?"

The hangman was silent for a moment. Then he laughed loudly.

"Augustin a leper! Who would have thought that? Well, then, he'll be very pleased that the leper's house is nearly finished. First of all the half-wit sabotages the building and then he must move in himself. Say what you like: God is just, after all."

Simon had to chuckle. But immediately his conscience started to trouble him. Georg Augustin was a bad man, a lunatic, a child murderer who had, moreover, tortured him. The scar on Simon's thigh still hurt. But in spite of this, he would not have wished this disease on even his worst enemy. Georg Augustin's body would slowly rot away while he was still alive.

To turn their minds to other thoughts, Simon changed the subject.

"This betrothal of Magdalena with the Steingaden hangman," he began.

"What about it?" Kuisl grumbled.

"Are you really serious about it?"

The hangman took a puff on his pipe. It was some time before he answered.

"I turned him down. The wench is too stubborn. He doesn't deserve that."

A smile spread over Simon's face. It seemed that a heavy weight had been lifted from his mind.

"Kuisl, I'm really very—"

"You be quiet!" the hangman interrupted him. "Or I might change my mind."

Then he stood up and went to the door. Without a word he motioned to Simon to follow him.

They went through the living room, which smelled of fresh-baked bread, across to the little workroom. The hangman, as always, had to stoop to get through the low doorway. Behind him Simon entered the holy of holies. Once again he looked reverently at the massive cabinet, which reached up to the ceiling. *A treasure chest,* thought Simon. *Full of the medical knowledge of centuries . . .*

Immediately the young physician was overcome with the urge to open the cabinet so as to browse through the books and folios. As he moved toward it he almost stumbled over a small chest standing in the middle of the chamber. It was made of polished cherrywood, with silver fittings and a solid-looking lock, with the key still in it.

"Open it," said the hangman. "It belongs to you."

"But . . . " Simon interjected.

"Consider it as payment for all your trouble," he said. "You helped me to rescue my daughter and also save the woman who brought my children into the world."

Simon knelt and opened the chest. The lid sprang open with a little click.

Inside there were books. At least a dozen.

They were all new editions. Scultetus's *Wundarzneylisches*

Zeughaus, or *Surgical Armory,* the book of midwifery by the Swiss Jakob Ruf, the complete works of Ambroise Paré in a German translation, Georg Bartisch's *Augendienst*, Paracelsus's *Grosse Wundarzney*, bound in leather with illustrations in color . . .

Simon rummaged through them, turning pages. A treasure lay before him, much greater than the one they had found in the tunnels.

"Kuisl," he stammered. "How can I ever thank you? It's too much! That . . . it must have cost a fortune!"

The hangman shrugged.

"A few golden coins more or less. Old Augustin didn't notice it."

Simon sat up, shocked.

"You mean, you—?"

"I believe that Ferdinand Schreevogl would have wanted it like that," said Jakob Kuisl. "What use would so much money be to the church or the old moneybags on the council? It would have taken on dust just as it did down below in that hole. Now off you go and start reading, before I regret it."

Simon gathered the books together, shut the chest, and grinned.

"Now you can borrow a few books from me when you want to. If in return, Magdalena and I . . . "

"You rascal, be off with you!" The hangman gave him a gentle slap on the back of the head so that Simon almost tripped over the threshold with the chest. He ran outside and along the banks of the Lech through the tanners' quarter, into town, over the cobblestones of the Münzstrasse, and into the narrow stinking alleys, until he arrived panting at his house.

He would have a lot of reading to do today.

A KIND OF POSTSCRIPT

𝔍 DON'T KNOW WHEN I HEARD OF THE KUISLS FOR the first time. I must have been about five or six years old when, for the first time, my grandmother gave me a questioning look. It was the same thoughtful look she has to this day when she is busy classifying her entire family, by now consisting of more than twenty descendants, into Kuisls and non-Kuisls. At the time I wasn't quite sure whether or not Kuisl was something good or bad. It sounded like a quality, an unusual hair color, or an adjective that I did not yet understand.

Extrinsic characteristics such as an arched nose, strong dark eyebrows, an athletic body, or abundant growth of hair have been regarded for a long time as Kuisl-like in our family, as have our musical and artistic talents and a sensitive, almost nervous disposition. The latter includes an introverted nature, a tendency toward alcoholism, and a certain dark melancholy. In the Kuisl description left to us by my grandmother's cousin, a passionate amateur genealogist, we can read among other observations: "Bent fingernails (claws)" and "tear-jerking sentimentality and sometimes brutality." Altogether not exactly a sympathetic picture, but then you can't choose your family . . .

It was this same cousin who introduced me, much later, to the subject of what an executioner actually did. I was in my early twenties when one day I found a pile of yellowing papers on the table in our house—tattered pages, covered with typewritten text, in which Fritz Kuisl had collected everything about our ancestors. Along with them were black-and-white photos of instruments of torture and the Kuisl executioner's sword (stolen in the 1970s from the Schongau town museum and never recovered), a two-hundred-year-old master craftman's diploma belonging to my ancestor Johann Michael Kuisl, the last of Schongau's hangmen, typed copies of newspaper articles, and a handwritten family tree several feet long. I heard about Jörg Abriel, a remote ancestor, and his *grimoires,* or books of spells, which are still supposed to be kept in the Bavarian State Library, and learned that the Kuisl executioner dynasty had been one of the most famous of such dynasties in Bavaria. Supposedly more than sixty executions were carried out by my blood-stained ancestor during the Schongau witch trials of 1589 alone.

Since then the history of my family has never ceased to intrigue me. When Fritz Kuisl died some years ago, his wife, Rita, allowed me to enter his holy of holies, a small study filled to the ceiling with dusty files and old books about what an executioner is and does. In the tiny room were piles of chests full of family trees and copies of church registers, some from the sixteenth century. On the walls hung faded photographs and paintings of long-dead ancestors. Fritz Kuisl had recorded them on thousands of index cards—names, professions, dates of birth and death . . .

On one of those index cards my name was written, on another that of my son, who had been born just one year previously. Rita Kuisl had written in the name after the death of her husband.

The end of the line.

A shudder came over me at seeing these things, but also a

feeling of belonging, as if a large community had taken me under its wing. In the past few years, genealogical research has become increasingly popular. Perhaps one of the reasons for this is that we are trying, in a world of increasing complexity, to create a simpler and more understandable place for ourselves. No longer do we grow up in large families. We feel increasingly estranged, replaceable, and ephemeral. Genealogy gives us a feeling of immortality. The individual dies; the family lives on.

In the meantime I tell my seven-year-old son about his remarkable forefathers. I leave out the bloody details. (For him these people are like knights, which sounds better than hangmen or executioners.) In his bedroom hangs a collage made up of photos of long-dead family members—great-grandparents, great-great-grandparents, their aunts, their uncles, their nephews and nieces . . .

Sometimes at night he wants to hear stories about these people, and I tell him what I know about them. Happy stories, sad stories, frightening stories. For him the family is a safe refuge, a link binding him to many people whom he loves and who love him. I once heard that everyone on this earth is at least distantly related to everyone else. Somehow this is a comforting idea.

This book is a novel and not a scholarly thesis. I have attempted to stick to the facts as much as possible. Nevertheless for dramaturgical reasons I have often had to simplify. Even in those cruel times, torturing of a prisoner would have required a few more official documents, and the town of Schongau would probably not have tolerated such a dominating court clerk as Johann Lechner. In municipal matters it was the aldermen and the burgomaster who actually ruled, and not the Elector's representative.

So-called dwarf's holes or troll's tunnels (*Schrazellöcher* in German, like the ones where the children had their hiding place) are not found in the Schongau area, although there are many elsewhere in Bavaria. The purpose of such tunnels has not been established.

The figure of Johann Jakob Kuisl, unlike that of the physician Simon Fronwieser, is historical—as is that of Kuisl's wife, Anna Maria, and their children, Magdalena, Georg, and Barbara. Many Kuisls were considered to be well-read, and their reputation as healers extended beyond the borders of the town. It was probably for this reason that doctors with medical training always tried to interfere and reported them to the authorities. One of my ancestors complained bitterly in a letter that he was not allowed to take any medical examination. Otherwise he would soon show how much more progressive he was than those academic quacks!

Everything in this book about the work of a hangman is factual, according to the latest scholarly findings. I venture to express my doubts as to whether my ancestor actually came to the aid of a midwife whom he had tortured, but I can in any case imagine it to be possible. After all, he was my great-great-grandfather, and as we know, we never want to doubt our families.

Many people have contributed to the preparation of this book. I would like to especially thank the curator of the Schongau local historian's circle, Helmut Schmidbauer, who supplied me with necessary details; Franz Grundner of the Schongau Museum; Frau Professor Christa Habrich of the German Museum of Medical History; Rita Kuisl, who graciously allowed me access to her husband's archives; my brother Marian as initial editor, friend, and supporter; my father as adviser for medical matters and Latin; and last but not least my wife, Katrin, who bravely struggled through the pages in the evening—and earned the money we needed so that I could during this time fulfill the dream of my youth.

OLIVER PÖTZSCH, MAY 2007

ABOUT THE AUTHOR

Oliver Pötzsch, born in 1970, has worked for years as a scriptwriter for Bavarian Public Television. He is himself a descendant of the Kuisls, one of Bavaria's leading dynasties of executioners. Oliver Pötzsch and his family live in Munich.

ABOUT THE TRANSLATOR

Lee Chadeayne is a former classical musician, college professor, and owner of a language translation company in Massachusetts. He was one of the charter members of the American Literary Translators Association and has been an active member of the American Translators Association since 1970.

His translated works to date are primarily in the areas of music, art, language, history, and general literature. Most recently this includes *The Settlers of Catan* by Rebecca Gablé, a historical novel about the Vikings and their search for a new world (2005), and *The Copper Sign* by Katja Fox, a medieval adventure in twelfth-century England and France (2009), as well as numerous short stories. He presently serves as an editor for the American Arthritis Association newsletter and editor-in-chief of the *ALTA News* of the American Literary Translators Association.

As a scholar and student of both history and languages, especially Middle High German, he was especially drawn to the work of Oliver Pötzsch, author of the best-selling novel *die Henkerstochter* (*The Hangman's Daughter*), a compelling and colorful description of seventeenth-century customs and life—including love, murder, superstitions, witchery, and political intrigue—in a small Bavarian city.